Spinward Fringe
Broadcast 8

Renegades

Randolph Lalonde

"Captain McFadden," crackled First Officer Eily Hogan's voice from the communicator. She was excited about something, usually a bad sign. "We've been spotted by an Order patrol, corvette class. No fighter cover in range."

"Run out the guns," Captain Moira McFadden ordered as she put the paper book she was reading down beside her on her bed and stood up. "Angle deflection shields, watch for surprises. Looks like we'll have to finish our repairs in hyperspace." She took her mid-length heavy jacket from a metal chair, slipped into it and then clipped on her gun belt. She couldn't help recalling a descriptive passage from the book she was just reading that described Cathryn, one of the Irish Union founders, strapping a pistol on overtop a dress. The thought of wearing a heavy skirt and a gun belt made her smile. *Fat chance anyone will get me in a dress unless it's my own funeral,* she thought.

The pair of pistols was a welcome weight, like the old armoured jacket she wore adorned in the colours of the Irish Union flag – green, black, and orange. These were most of her surviving possessions, and she kept them with her always. Underneath she wore the simple uniform of an Irish Union naval captain, a black and grey fitted suit with practical pockets, and three thin red lines that ran from the shoulders, down over her knees to the feet. The flexible armour pads had already saved her life several times, even though the uniform was relatively new to her.

The captain's quarters were basic, with a double bed, a desk, a wardrobe cupboard, overhead storage, and a beverage dispenser that hadn't worked since she was given command. The hatchway opened with a clink, the door swung with a screech but she ignored both. The surfacing on the floors and walls had been polished away decades before by the hands of hundreds of

1

crewmembers, leaving the bare metal to shine dark silver. She could see her reflection in her decks and walls.

The two muscled guards on watch at the entrance to the bridge snapped her a salute as she passed. Their fibre-mesh plate armour and general condition was picture perfect, and they had a pride Moira hoped would hold through the coming months, when she wouldn't be around to maintain order. She returned their salute as an ensign pushed the bridge hatch open for her. Feeling a little out of order after seeing the crisp condition of the guards, she rolled and tucked her shoulder-length brown hair into a bun.

"Update," she ordered as she dropped into the battered captain's seat.

"The corvette is biding her time," replied First Officer Hogan. "Firing beam weapons, testing our shields. They're not getting past our sensor or communications jamming."

"Any transmissions get through before we were spotted?" Captain McFadden asked, checking the tactical and operational panel attached to her seat.

"We saw them because they transmitted," came the reply from Michael Durst, her communications officer. "Almost missed the signal, looked like noise, but I traced it back."

"Good work as usual, Mister Durst," Captain McFadden said. The Hell Shrike was handling herself well. Her shields were regenerating fast enough to keep up with the beam weapons raking her port side. The black and green hull of the Order of Eden corvette looked fresh, intact – a tempting target. She looked at their location on the sector map and shook her head.

"We've got boarding teams at the ready," advised her tactical officer, Tawnee Rickard.

"We're still too far behind enemy lines," Captain McFadden replied. She couldn't help but consider that they were also protecting a full hold of captured supplies and hauling four containers under their energy shields, but she didn't share the thought. There was no need to justify her decisions; she was well past that point with the crew of the Hell Shrike. "Be a shame to get jumped by a destroyer this close to breaking free of Order space," she muttered to herself.

The beam fire intensified, focusing on one section of the Hell Shrike's shields. Three exterior doors began to slide open on the enemy corvette, and Captain McFadden knew what that meant: missile batteries. Her energy shielding would have to spread out; the beam weapons would start getting through and her ship was still undergoing repairs to her outer hull. "Slag this bugger. Fire all guns, load secondary gun magazines with bursters so we can get through her shields. Missile batteries one and three, load fusion warheads and hold for my order. Come about one sixty, mark, point five." She set up the ship's course on her console and sent it to the helm. "Navigation, start calculating our final course to Rega Gain."

The seven-station bridge was busy as they carried out her orders. Several missiles broke through the Hell Shrike's shields, sending white-hot shrapnel and explosive charges down the length of their port side. "Breaches?"

"Nay. We have weakened plating, though," replied Tactical Officer Rickard.

"Roll the ship to compensate, we don't want another hit on that section," Captain McFadden ordered, aware that there wasn't much undamaged hull left.

The twenty-four railgun turrets running along the rounded sides of the ship fired with deadly precision, pounding away at the enemy's shields. The corvette was starting to accelerate away, firing everything it had as its shield energy diminished. "Ready to fire, Missile Room," Captain McFadden said.

"Missile Room reports: ready to fire," replied Rickard.

Captain McFadden waited a moment, watching as the enemy corvette let loose with a battery of missiles and intensified beam fire, breaking through the Hell Shrike's shields and through her outer hull. Moira didn't flinch, even though three gunnery positions were immediately marked as destroyed. The enemy missiles struck right behind the beam weapons, liquefying metres of the Hell Shrike's hull. It wasn't time to fire her own missiles yet. "Helm, full thrust, set your course opposite to the corvette's. We need a little more room."

The corvette's shields were almost completely depleted, and railgun rounds were breaking through, raking the enemy's pristine hull. "Gunnery, switch to explosive rounds on even positions, flak on odd."

"We're out of flak rounds," reported the other tactical officer, Trevor Walsh.

"Then load junk rounds. Fire at will," Captain McFadden replied. "Missile Room, hold."

"Aye, Missile Room holding," replied Tactical Officer Rickard.

Captain McFadden modified the shield systems' energy profile herself, running the remaining shield emitters past their safety limits to keep the Hell Shrike from taking more damage from the enemy's beam weapons. They had to last just long enough to get out of their effective range, and the corvette was coming about, giving chase as the Hell Shrike retreated, interpreting the retreat as a lack of resolve. "Surprise, you Order of Eden bastards, I'm getting ready to finish you off," she muttered with a smile.

"All guns, focus on the nose of that ship. I want all our non-nuclear missiles to fire on the same area, now."

The crew was well practiced, resolute, and steady on their triggers. A hail of railgun rounds and slower missiles rained down on the enemy ship's narrow nose, battering its hull inward and forcing the air out of her forward compartments. "Major damage to the corvette, Ma'am," reported Tactical Officer Rickard. "We have her."

"Now we slag her," Captain McFadden said. "All gun and missile positions, cease fire." She pressed her thumb onto her command panel for DNA verification, making her fusion missiles available to fire. "Fire one fusion missile."

The crew of the Hell Shrike watched as a fusion missile crossed the distance between it and the enemy corvette-class ship in under three seconds and exploded in a bloom of light. Radiological alarms went off momentarily across the ship, and there was minor aft hull damage, but the Hell Shrike was whole enough.

There was nothing but a cooling hunk of metal left of the enemy corvette. "Helm, it's time for us to finish this trip. Get us to Rega Gain – no point in hiding around here trying to make repairs."

"Aye, making best FTL speed to Rega Gain System," replied the helm.

"Treat the injured, have radiation meds passed out," Captain McFadden said, remembering that they didn't have enough left to go around. "Start with the higher ranks, oldest first." She looked to the ensign standing beside the door. The blond-haired boy looked anxious; he wasn't sure what to do with himself. With the ship three times overstaffed, there was little for him *to* do. "Ensign…"

"O'Reilly, Ma'am," he replied.

"Fetch my book from my quarters," she said.

"Which one, if I may ask?"

"Dawn's Exodus," Captain McFadden replied. *I'd best read faster if I'm going to finish it before I give it to Shamus,* she thought as she watched the ensign scurry off.

CHAPTER 1
A BEAUTIFUL DAY

"The emergency hatch is not made to facilitate open-air flight," Lewis told Alice through her communicator.

The wind blowing through Alice's brown-red hair, and the view of the fresh green growth extending all around, made for a good opportunity to use a Ramiel fighter as though it were a pleasure craft. The small ship's emergency hatch was wide open, and she was sitting up. In glider mode, strong fabric extended out from the sides and gave the craft a butterfly-like appearance. "I've got to throttle way down to fly at this height, I may as well take in the sights while I'm below face-stretchy speed."

"Are you forgetting why you're flying so low?"

"I know, I know," she replied peevishly. "There could be a framework camp up ahead. I've got the important shielding up, don't worry." The rolling green landscape still smelled like freshly turned earth. The incredible pounding the planet of Tamber took during the battle of Rega Gain by countless crashed ships and bombardments had re-awakened entire continents. Old terraforming efforts and botanical systems that had been dormant for decades were active once again.

While she trained as a ranger for two months and served for over four, Alice had watched it happen. It was beautiful, and it was making the planet a healthier place, but the overgrowth was hiding things that she was tasked to find. Most of her missions took place at night, making her job even harder. She was overjoyed to be sent out on a day mission to investigate some wreckage that was showing new activity.

Alice spotted a large armour panel sticking out from the ground and perked up in her seat. "We've got to be close," she said.

"That matches a dorsal panel from the Idyllic," Lewis confirmed. "It looks like your pleasure flight is coming to an end."

"Yeah," she said with a sigh. Alice leaned forward into the form-fitted cockpit and the fighter's top hatch closed. "Wish we could guard this area from higher up. How many people did that transmission say could be trapped?"

"They claimed there could be as many as nine survivors from the crash, all recently discovered," Lewis said. "The Carthans guess that they were trapped much further down in the ship, well underground, and have only recently made the climb closer to the surface, within scanning range."

"Still no word from the Carthans on their rescue team?"

"They responded to my query fourteen minutes ago, actually," Lewis said.

"And?" Alice asked as she started an intensive scan.

"They said they wouldn't be able to approach the wreckage until we cleared it," Lewis replied.

"Typical. They get their butts kicked, then stretch their resources out too thin and use British Alliance recovery money to contract out all the hard stuff," she said.

"I haven't seen you stepping back from the positive attention you receive every time you succeed on a mission," Lewis teased. "What would you do if there were not assignments from Carthan Search and Rescue?"

"I'd probably be searching for remnants of the Order forces, or on the Leviathan picking crew." Alice considered those alternatives for a moment. Looking for Order of Eden combatants in the wilderness when everyone knew the chances of finding any were next to nil, or guarding salvage workers as they picked through the wreck of the Leviathan were not popular assignments. "You're right, I shouldn't complain. Turns out I really like helping people, and at least the Carthans usually set us up with real leads." The detailed scan of the valley ahead completed, and Alice sighed. "There are a couple of scavengers down there, but no sign of leftover framework troops. Definitely no sign of a hidden command bunker."

"My wager is on Remmy finding it now," Lewis said. "He was sent after the more promising signal."

"Stop rubbing my nose in it," Alice snapped. "He gets more missions, is constantly assigned to assault teams, and has seen way more of this rock than I have by now, and we entered into the service at the same grade."

"You've seen nearly four times as much of this world in square kilometres," Lewis corrected. "He's never assigned to a fighter because he only has basic qualifications for flight."

"So you're saying I'm qualified to be his tour guide if he ever needs a lift and I'm the nearest pilot," Alice replied. "That's it, I'm landing."

"Your job is to observe, resolve crime from a distance, and report," Lewis said. "The Carthans will send a recovery team to rescue them within twenty hours."

"Twenty hours, I hate that. These people have been trapped in there for months, who knows what they've been eating."

"Orders," Lewis reminded in a singsong tone.

Alice flipped a switch savagely, closing communications. She could have done the same with a thought, but it felt good to cut Lewis off with a gesture.

The scavengers didn't match with Carthan personnel records, so there was no possibility that they were with a recovery team. The one she could see was dragging a heavy box away from the exposed part of the massive Carthan ship. "Attention, looter. You will be fired upon if you and your four companions don't retreat from the area immediately. You are interfering with Carthan property, and looting this vessel is classified as an attack," she recited, not for the first time since she'd become a ranger.

The figure below ducked behind the crate he was pulling and fired several shots in her direction. The energy bolts barely registered on her fighter's shield monitor. Alice set the energy level of her secondary guns low and fired at the crate. After a couple of wide shots, she struck the side, melting through it in only a few hits. "That was your last warning, you really don't want me to come down there," she announced, half hoping that the looter and his friends would duck into the wreck. It had been several days since she'd had a good chase.

To her disappointment, the looter stood slowly with his hands held high. His friends were emerging from the wreck with their hands up as well. A skipper truck – a boxy vehicle mounted on a cheap antigravity sled - appeared not far from the wreck as it deactivated its camouflage, and the group began heading towards it. One of the looters slapped the first one Alice noticed across the back of the head as they were about to board the vehicle.

Alice watched the truck turn and advance over the horizon, logging it into her report for Haven Shore and the Carthan government. When she was sure they were gone, she guided her fighter into a slow turn and opened a channel to Carthan Control.

"Control here, what can we do for you Ranger Alice Valent?"

Instead of replying, she sent the details of her discovery to Control as a set of scan results and a video report of her encounter.

"One moment please," said the operator.

Alice turned the fighter back towards Haven Shore and powered into a climb. "They're going to say..." she started whispering to herself.

"Control here, I see you've scouted and cleared the area. We will send a recovery team within twenty hours. Thank you, Ranger Valent." Her communications system notified her that the work increased Haven Shore's land claim on Tamber and another hundred twenty thousand units of Galactic Currency would be delivered to them by the end of the day. She was entitled to one percent as a bonus, and she'd see that in her quarters along with the rest of the cash she hadn't had the chance to send to the Warlord.

"Yeah," Alice said as she closed the channel. "They'll go in," she muttered to herself, "after nineteen hours. It'll take five hours to cut through the wreckage, and when the grateful crew emerge, they won't even mention that I could have gotten them out nineteen hours sooner. Meanwhile, those looters will come back, and there's just the slightest chance that they'll disturb the wreck, crushing the people trapped inside. I liked it better when the Carthans were still too screwed up to make the rules."

The fighter's altitude cleared five thousand metres. She retracted the cloth wings and increased thrust with the inertial dampeners off. The crush of increased g-forces and the counter squeeze of her vacsuit made her feel like she was exerting herself, doing something other than playing a game of Verify the Scan. The ship, and her teeth, rattled hard as a sonic boom announced that she'd passed Mach one as the ship climbed.

With a satisfied sigh, she engaged the inertial dampeners and increased her acceleration. "Something about flying in atmo makes drifting in space seem like a light snooze."

"Navnet Control, here. You are approaching my orbital sector, Ranger Valent," said a thickly accented male controller through her priority channel. He was controlling a navnet sector in Tamber's orbit from one of those great big British Alliance carriers. Her requests for a tour had all been rejected, but she continued to send them every two days.

"Just looking for a good route to Haven Shore, British Alliance Navnet Control. Help me beat the traffic?" Alice replied in jest. There was very little traffic anywhere but around Haven Shore and a couple of other hot spots on Tamber. Most of the people who survived the siege months before had fled to the nearby planet of Kambis or left the system.

The controller chuckled. "I've got a nice straight path for you, just keep it to a responsible speed, please."

"Aye, thank you," Alice said. "Party pooper."

CHAPTER 2
ONE STRANGE NIGHT

Minh-Chu Buu took his seat at the table and let the atmosphere around him soak in. From the inside pocket of his bomber jacket, he drew a thin bottle of Zuugo, an expensive herbal drink, and he poured it into the empty glass on the table. The empty glass cost three pips at the bar, an extreme price for the privilege of serving yourself.

"Why'd you buy that, man?" asked Jack Kipley, a man who had become known as two things: Lucius Wheeler's former first officer, and the ship idiot. It was Minh's turn to babysit. "Just sneak it out like this," he said, demonstrating by pulling a canteen from his grey and green long coat and taking a swig.

"You're going to get caught," Stephanie said, taking a seat to Minh-Chu's left. "You'll get tossed out and draw attention."

"Yes, Ma'am," Kipley said exaggeratedly.

Minh-Chu had seen small towns with fewer people than the massive commerce centre around them. It had been built inside an emergency shelter set against the side of an impact-pockmarked mountain. Shops, food stands, and bars surrounded a sea of tables, lounges, and chairs. He could count the familiar products on offer on one hand; the objects and services on offer ranged from new to unusual. The most entertaining was something he picked up as a curiosity – a Groom Worm – that claimed to ...*disappear under clothing, keeping the user clean and fresh for up to one year!*

He wouldn't use it – the thought of using a parasite in lieu of bathing or vacsuit grooming seemed like a last resort option – but he enjoyed the little package presenting a small white worm as a souvenir for his shelf on the Triton.

The music in their area of the expansive seating section was a whirling thrash of alien instruments, the kind of thing that nagged at him, challenging him to translate it into some kind of tune he could properly comprehend or enjoy. He wasn't sure he was hearing the intended music in the first place, since all sound in the cavernous shelter was processed through a scrambling field. That was the biggest attraction for the crews who gathered at the Alt-Mecca Mall: the scrambling field that rendered all recording devices useless.

It was a dangerous place, sure, but crews could make plans without worrying about authorities listening in. The people within couldn't be scanned either, making the Alt-Mecca the perfect place for the wanted, or whoever shouldn't be found on Planet Vinuto. It was a border planet in a system sitting roughly between the no-ship's-land of three wars. When the Warlord first started visiting ports and collecting information, Minh-Chu had difficulty grasping the idea that there were three major interplanetary wars going on at the same time. The Iron Head sector, named after the Iron Head Nebula that occupied over one tenth of the space, was the most dangerous area he'd ever seen. Nevertheless, it had become the home of the Warlord for nearly seven months.

One of the wars fought by the Roche Group against Nihilists, an alliance of corporations protecting several solar systems against a group of idealists who believed that territory, data, and the property of the deceased should be completely free. Through experience, Minh-Chu had determined that the more organized Nihilist cells were opportunists and thieves who didn't much care about civilian safety. If he had to call them by another name, it would be raiders, or worse. The Roche Group wasn't perfect, but they were rebuilding their collective territory and trying to re-establish order, and that was something their people needed. He was thankful that the Warlord had no business in that war, and Jacob Valent had quickly grown to hate Nihilists almost as much as he despised the Order of Eden.

The second war in the sector was based in trade, and the Warlord had every reason to watch and learn from that mess. It was like the big war in the area, undeclared, but fought tooth and nail regardless. Too many companies to count fought to get their cargo through and around the Iron Head Nebula, to and from the Order of Eden frontline. They hauled everything from raw materials to slaves, and the competition for contracts as well as the rivalries between companies often became lethal. Add in a liberal smattering of pirate crews who preyed on these cargo haulers and messenger vessels, and you ended up with a mess that presented as much danger as it did opportunity. The Warlord had managed to steal two cargo trains without firing a shot, hacking one ship's main computer and simply menacing another into dropping its cargo train and making a run for it. Captain Jacob Valent knew how to pick his targets, but it involved a lot of intelligence gathering and careful timing. The survival supplies and equipment were delivered to the Triton, where they were parcelled out and distributed to Haven Shore after the Warlord staff took their pick of the prizes, resupplying the ship and taking equipment vital to its reconstruction.

The last of the three wars was the most difficult to watch. The Order of Eden and Regent Galactic were on the other side of the Iron Head Nebula, expanding their territory and routing distant armies. The largest of the opponents in the sector, the British Alliance, had declared war. However, after no combat between them and the Order, they withdrew their declaration after agreeing on a border they called The Frontier. It was endlessly frustrating, watching the largest power in the sector go on as though what was happening in the adjacent areas had nothing to do with them. This was the war the Warlord gathered intelligence for, constantly hacking into computer systems of all sizes, spying on the few Order of Eden officers in port, and tagging ships hired by Regent Galactic to transport their manufactured goods to the frontlines. They had recorder tags on hundreds of active vessels that collected and retransmitted communications and unsecure data. Minh-Chu couldn't help but see the intelligence gathering as the Warlord's deep breath before issuing the war cry and charging into battle.

His thoughts returned back to the present, and to their activities on the planet. Vinuto, named after the resource-heavy solar system it called home, had become one of the biggest trade centres in only a few months. If you wanted to buy and sell supplies over any of the lines drawn through the warring sectors, chances were you'd end up on or near Vinuto. The same law stood if you were a freebooter preying on the mercenary traders or shippers. All were welcome, and in many areas, like the commerce centre the Warlord crew were visiting, law was lax. The local business owners were responsible for their own security and for meting out the punishment for breaking the local laws.

"Yeah, so if I can't use this, I'm going to get something with real kick," Kipley said, starting to get up.

Minh-Chu elbowed him in the shoulder, putting Kipley off-balance just enough to send him back into his chair. "An impatient man will find balance elusive," Minh-Chu said just loud enough for his charge to hear. Stephanie Vega, the first officer of the Warlord, couldn't help but laugh.

"Stop doing that!" Kipley shouted at Minh-Chu. "I'm not some private you can push around! I bet there's a thousand ships in port who could use a guy like me, and I could find work right here."

He'd made the threat before, and Minh-Chu knew he should ignore it, but couldn't resist turning it around. "Please, go ahead."

Kipley stared at him, furious. Minh-Chu turned his attention to Agameg and a few other crewmembers as they made their way through the crowd bearing two trays heavy with mugs and pitchers.

"Fine then," Kipley said, starting to get to his feet.

Minh-Chu elbowed him again, kicking his foot out from under him at the same time. Kipley spilled out of his chair, sending the flimsy seat into the table behind them. He scrambled to his feet in time to come face to face with the eight human men and women behind Minh-Chu's table. They glared as though Kipley had interrupted the most important meeting of the century.

For reasons Minh-Chu didn't care to ponder, Kipley righted his chair and quietly sat down across from him. He and Seamus Frost had found that there was no limit to how far you could push Jack Kipley; the man just wouldn't leave, no matter how miserable his social existence became. "Sleep with one eye open," hissed Kipley. Threats weren't uncommon, however.

Minh-Chu raised his glass as though toasting the idiot sitting across the table and took a sip of his herbal drink. It was unlike Minh-Chu to provoke or tease anyone, but Kipley was a rich and worthy target. He was Lucius Wheeler's former first officer, and a child of Freeground. He'd leered at and groped several women on the crew, including Ashley and Nerine, picked fights with a few others, and had a habit of making a bad situation worse. On the other hand, Kipley was a walking trove of information, and the more Minh-Chu and Frost pissed him off, the more he revealed to other crewmembers about where he'd been and what he'd seen while he was whining about his problems. To Minh-Chu, it was the longest but most effective interrogation he'd ever heard of, and Kipley had no idea it was happening. The ship idiot would spend plenty of time venting that evening.

"Hello, Ronin, Stephanie," Agameg said, smiling at them. The Issyrian's big green eyes and smooth face made the smile seem comically exaggerated. Agameg had learned how to fortify his skin against foreign environments, a skill that took members of his race a long time to master. The result was a rounder-faced, smoother-skinned Agameg who seemed more confident on planet-side visits. The cilia that once lined his facial features were hidden, and humans who weren't used to an Issyrian's native features felt more comfortable around him.

"Hey, Agameg, you wouldn't happen to have an extra mug for Kipley, here?" Minh-Chu asked.

"I have several extra mugs," Agameg replied, putting a frosted mug in front of Kipley and filling it with fizzy amber liquid from one of the pitchers. "They say Munger Draft is the easiest drinking beverage in the Grand Concourse."

"Thanks," Kipley said, regarding the mug, which was half filled with liquid and half with foam. "Too bad you can't pour worth a damn."

Agameg was frozen in place for a moment, until he blinked one eye at a time and moved on to pass out the rest of the mugs. He took his seat once one pitcher had been poured out. "I think Frost and Finn will be here shortly. The captain is meeting a friend not far from here, so he may be along if he has time."

"Is he still walking around without a disguise?" Stephanie asked.

"He said there are plenty of notable captains in port, so many that he and the Warlord are minor players," Agameg said.

"That's a yes," Stephanie said. "A notable captain is still a noticeable captain, who cares how many others are around?"

"I spoke to him about that," Agameg replied, nodding. "I believe I could mimic him well enough to pass, but he told me that he doesn't need a double, and the Warlord is more of a failure here than a danger, since we haven't taken any prizes by force yet."

"He's right about that," Kipley said, refilling his mug in a slow, artful pour that kept foam to a minimum. "I thought we'd be taking merchant ships down by now, making real money. I should've known better."

Kipley's comment quieted the table, and Minh-Chu was relieved to hear human music start drifting across the sea of people. It was artificially created pop starring a fabricated voice that tapped into the mathematical formulae for sexy sound and motivational appeal rather than actual inspiration, but at least he could tap his foot to it.

"The show's about to start," Stephanie said, pointing to the arched main entrance as Finn walked in with a small crate under his arm. He strode with so much self-importance that it was almost comical to Minh-Chu, and he was only outdone by Seamus Frost, who followed a few paces behind.

With a practiced flourish, Finn placed the short crate on the floor and stepped away, as rigid as a rail. Frost stepped onto the crate, not so much as glancing at it, his gaze falling over the numerous tables in front of him. "I bet he pulls five qualified crew in," Kipley said. "I'll put three pips on it."

"I bet he'll sign four," Minh-Chu said. It earned him a punch on the leg from Stephanie. "He pulled three the first time and four the last," Minh-Chu explained. "Just playing the odds."

"I bet he pulls seven," Stephanie said to Minh-Chu with an exaggerated sneer.

Frost's silent theatrics didn't go unnoticed. The first two rows of tables were turning to look at the heavyset man with the thick brows. Frost's clothing spoke as loudly as his demeanour; he was dressed in heavy survival armour that featured extra horizontal strips of shielding and a helmet so sturdy only the face shielding could retract. His normal bulk was formed in such a way that he seemed stout and powerful. "I call for your eyes and ears," he commanded, his voice amplified by his suit. A glass hurtled towards him, smashing against his energy shielding. He didn't grant the thrower so much as a glance. "I'm here to call on the bravest, the craziest, and the greediest of you," Frost started, putting all his vocal weight on 'greediest,' to the crowd's amusement. "I've seen the fight, aye, more times than I can count, and come through it like the hell-sent bastard I am, hungry for more. That's because I fight for the fastest, hardest ship you've ever seen." To Minh-Chu's amazement, Frost had their attention. He'd changed his speech – it was more over the top than ever. "The marks on my armour were earned in combat with those damned Regent Galactic thieves and damned Eden machines. I've even had it out with Carans and Order of Eden ships. We came through under the direction of the greatest combat leadership and teamwork of our generation. The ship I serve is looking for qualified gunners and crew to join the fight."

"You expect us to waste our lives fighting with you on that planet hopper?" shouted a woman behind Minh-Chu.

"No, and we're not going out just to fight those whoresons, we're going out to steal their supplies, their machinery, their ships. And we'll be slagging what we leave behind. This isn't a fight for revenge, my good lass, this is a fight for hard cash. Our service to war comes in close second. We take more loot on one run than any ship here does in three, and we have our own safe harbour."

"Here they go," Stephanie whispered to Minh-Chu. Dozens of crewmembers were making their way out of the barroom, most of them wearing company uniforms. They weren't lining up to volunteer, they were leaving the presence of a pirate, a crewman who would, under different circumstances, be blasting their ships and stealing their cargo. "We're up, Agameg," she told him, and they both casually left the table to follow the larger crews while avoiding notice.

"This is a just war," Frost shouted. "One that should be fought by every able body, but that doesnae mean we can't make a killing while we're fighting for the right side!" His conclusion was met with cheers, applause,

14

and jeers in nearly equal measure. Minh-Chu was starting to understand the motivation behind the over-the-top reaction Frost got out of crowds every time he put on his show. The people weren't reacting to the contents of his speech – well, most of them weren't – but the theatrical presentation. Live entertainment was still worth something, perhaps more than ever in the absence of artificial intelligences, and Minh-Chu had to admit: Frost knew how to put on a show.

"I'll be at that table, right there," Frost announced, pointing to a nearby table that only moments ago had a crew from a Noro Co. ship sitting around it. "Line up if you think you're ready to kick some ass and make some cash."

"Why doesn't he just post a notice on the board like everyone else?" Kipley asked, annoyed.

"Because the people we want are here, dumbass. We don't need some innocent scrub from Harvest Side who thinks he's signing up for adventure and profit," replied Shanda, one of the only security officers who were registered with Haven Shore before signing up for service on the Warlord.

Kipley glared at her. "You watch that mouth, little miss," he started.

Minh-Chu took Kipley's freshly refilled mug out of his hand and splashed the contents on the floor. "You're done, and on your way back to the ship."

"You mother-"

"I'll freeze your suit and leave you behind," Minh-Chu said, slamming the mug on the table. "Test me."

Kipley and Minh-Chu stared at each other for the better part of a minute. The eight crewmembers from the Warlord didn't even consider interrupting. "Back. To. The. Shuttle. Now," Minh-Chu finally grunted, so fed up with the man that he was beyond tempted to harden Kipley's vacsuit so he couldn't move, an act called 'freezing,' strip him of the little gear he had, and leave him behind, damn the consequences.

Kipley abruptly stood and started for the exit. Minh-Chu followed. "Watch Frost's operation then follow him back," he said to the Warlord crewmembers left at the table. He didn't realize his hand was resting on his sidearm until Shanda glanced at it, wide eyed. Minh-Chu left it there as he followed a dozen paces behind the tantrum-driven Kipley.

CHAPTER 3
PERSPECTIVE

It was sometimes difficult for Ayan to believe that the Everin Building existed at all. The circular structure looked like it belonged underwater. Hundreds of oval, bubble-like segments seemed to rest atop each other in a slow taper from bottom to top, as though they were the eggs of some giant sea creature that artfully laid them in a tall pile. The old cargo container homes that brought most of the refugees to Haven Shore were abandoned months ago as families moved into the lower levels of the Everin Building. The battered ships were stored in the nearby temporary port, where they were still being slowly repaired. Lacey, Ayan's right hand in official matters and companion, thought they were an eyesore, a reminder that – no matter how much progress they made in Haven Shore – they had to be ready to escape at any moment.

Ayan looked across the circle of segments at the top of the building. There were hundreds of families living in the structure below, and the feedback from the residents was positive overall.

As the segments were inhabited, the resilient skin of the building changed colour depending on what the residents wanted their home to look like. The energy collection technologies built into the outer skin still lent an opalescent sheen to whatever colour was chosen, but that only made the outside look more spectacular. The changing temperature of the Tamber moon, any light, and any pressure contributed to the energy of the building, and the skin of the outer walls could emit energy as well. It was the combined technology of Freeground and Earth, as well as a few things Ayan and her people had learned along the way. The most impressive thing was that the walls, floors, and ceilings were laid as pliable sheets, then hardened and thickened once they were properly shaped. They would thicken further over the next few years, and the building would shift little by little to accommodate.

16

Ayan dared a glance towards the centre of the building, at the mouth of the wide hole running down the interior of the structure. Vertigo threatened to overtake her as she leaned towards it, though the edge was still ten metres away. She leaned back towards the walkway.

The wind picked up, whipping a lock of red ringlets into her face and she couldn't help but chuckle at herself and her fear of getting blown down the hole. It would be over a hundred metre drop, but she knew there was no way a gust would send her tumbling off the temporary walkway, across the tops of a few segments. The wind was soothing in the heat of the day, and it brought the mild, earthy scent of the nearby jungle.

Her gaze fell on the lush green expanse to the west. Thick, untamed jungle that was centuries old as far as they could determine, it had taken on characteristics all its own as the terraforming material that started that growth interacted with the unique mixture of nutrients and bacteria in the soil. There was no place exactly like it in the universe, and Ayan wished the first colonists who settled Tamber could be around to see it. The trees and hearty undergrowth provided a vast bounty of fruit, nuts and vegetables, more than the inhabitants of Haven Shore and the Triton could consume. The engineering in the expansive rain forest was only evident when someone realized how efficient the jungle was at providing food. At any time, there were three major food crops ready to pick. As they went past their season, another three or more crops were ready. The creatures of the jungle kept much of it in balance, as the jungle grew wild for the long time it was uninhabited. Birds of all kinds picked near the top of the tall trees, a variety of small mammals and monkeys ate fruit and whatever else they could find in the middle, while great cats and other beasts roamed the jungle floor.

What the pickers from Haven Shore took from the jungle made little difference to the inhabitants; it was easy to pick a little and move on instead of stripping areas. Ayan sometimes wished she could remove herself from the Haven Shore Council and join them. The life of a picker was part labour, and part exploration, and the people who stayed past their first week stint in the jungle claimed to love the work, the challenge, and the jungle they depended on.

The cliffs running roughly through the middle of their island had sheltered over half of the jungle from the ecological damage from the attack on Tamber months before, and never had she seen a more vibrant place as she did when she looked to the untamed side of the island. The Everin Building straddled a narrow part of the cliffs where stable rock jutted upward, as though trying to become a mountain. Most of the homes had a view overlooking the jungle on the west side, while east facing homes had a view of the other buildings, temporary shelters, and administration centres that would eventually be replaced, and the shoreline in the distance.

"Commodore?" asked Lee Romita, the project manager in charge of constructing the Everin Building. He was a tall, wiry man with grey-black hair that seemed to have an escape plan from his scalp that varied from strand to strand. He approached her with a grin that told her that he didn't have anything to hide, and he was glad to see her. "I wasn't expecting you for an hour."

Hearing her rank, and remembering that she was still in uniform - a white, fitted one-piece vacsuit with gold rank insignia with her modified violator handgun hanging on her thigh - brought her back down to reality. "I wanted to take a look before you started putting in the supports for the top," Ayan told him.

He greeted her properly with a friendly hug and stepped back to arms' length. "From the trouble I hear on Crewcast about city council and all that malarkey, I don't blame you for seeking high places. This vote's got a burr in people's shoes, there's a big group against and a group just as big for."

"I know, maybe if they could all stand here for awhile I could be more certain about how it's going to turn out," Ayan said, looking eastward, into the wind and towards the distant shoreline. Deep waters kissed the white, blue, green, and yellow quartz beach sands there.

"I'm sure it'll turn out right, whatever the outcome," Lee said. "As for the building, we're at decision-making time again, and I'd rather you make this one."

"Start working on the transit system," Ayan said. "Or concentrate on building the spiral frame."

"Yep. I know my Trina wants to get around faster, takes forever to get to the Medical Centre in the morning. Still, she says all the walking's given her a girl's bum again for the first time since she gave birth to our first, and neither of us are complaining about that."

Ayan couldn't help but laugh at his frank speech, but he had a point. The occupancy level of the Everin Building was rising, and the temporary elevators were always crowded. Connecting and building the permanent transit system, at least inside the main structure, would alleviate a lot of frustration. The spiral frame, a new foundation to connect more segments to the Everin Building on arms stretching away from the main structure, was something that she'd like to see happen soon too, but she had to consider the whole picture. "Let's get people movers built. The tram and permanent elevators should be finished before we consider expanding the habitat. Oh, and add more safety systems for our skidways, a lot of people who should be driving using autopilots aren't. We have to add course locking to more lanes."

"What about the military features?" Lee asked. He was referring to a system Ayan, Liam Grady, and several other experienced engineers had added to the Everin Building's design that could move military vehicles around the inside of the building for servicing, launching, and storage.

"I think that'll keep for another week. We don't have the service personnel or ships to fill a quarter of the building's capacity yet, so there's not much point. I think people will feel safe enough when the shield's final test passes tomorrow."

"Glad you're finally feeling right about that thing, watching Liam second guessing your design, making you run through the details like a race course over and over," Lee shrugged; Ayan could tell he was choosing his words carefully. "There were days when I wanted to shut him up in a closet for awhile."

"Sometimes we need to be questioned so we can see our own mistakes," Ayan said. Defending him was a reflex, one she was still trying to get past. "He didn't agree on a few of the details, but I had more experience with combat shielding, and I think he had trouble realizing that. Didn't help that he was stubborn about it either, but we're past that now. The shield is working better than expected, thanks to your people."

"We're only as good as the plans we're working from. I can't wait to prove that the shield can protect the entire island. Gets the whole question of safety here off the table."

"True, and I'm sure we'll have even more people trying to move in to Haven Shore. I'm surprised at how many off-worlders are applying for citizenship, I thought it would mostly be people from Kambis and Tamber looking to move in."

"Are you going to take more people in?" Lee asked her.

"Eventually, as our own aquaponic food production comes online, but until then it'll be slow, unless the Council starts pushing for more immigration, but I don't know why they would."

"I'll put a rush on finishing transportation systems for this building and the outer port just in case. With my skitters on the job, it shouldn't take more than twenty-eight hours," Lee replied. "I'll have my people stay up here, getting things ready for the final steps before putting the top on this place in the meantime."

"Thank you, Lee. You and Trina have done incredible work here."

"Ah, I'm just glad there's something to build, and she's happy to be somewhere that has a use for a doctor again. Bots with thoughts kept most of her patients away in Glinn Shire. She thought she'd be a career mom for the rest of her life, just to keep busy. Now she's got our four teenagers and two wee ones plus a couple hundred patients."

"So it's going well in the Medical Centre?" Ayan asked.

"Yep, most docs have never been happier, even though there are still bunches of people who are a little shy at being treated by anything other than a medical android, or an internal repair thing."

"Is there anything else you wanted to talk to me about while I'm here? This'll probably be the last bit of free time I have until the votes are in."

"No, nothing comes to mind," Lee said. "You just concentrate on getting bots out into the rest of the workforce, and if they have a doubt as to how good that would be, well you just point to this building. If it weren't for skitter bots, lifters, and VAPs we'd still be working on the foundations."

"I will. Wish me luck, here comes my shuttle."

"You knew I'd notice you up here and we'd have our meeting early," Lee said, smirking accusingly.

"I didn't, I should have had an hour up here for some quiet," Ayan replied. "Something's brewing." She turned her Crewcast feed back on and cringed. There were eight urgent messages waiting for her, including one breakthrough that played through the comm node in a jade and silver clasp she kept on her left ear. It was Lacey Rosendale, her secretary and overall right hand, one of only three people who could send her a breakthrough message, made to play the moment someone was in range of, or turned on, the Crewcast network. "Cory Greene has called a supplementary meeting of the Haven Shore Council, it has something to do with Liam. He's already got Vic and Mischa there. You're ignoring Crewcast, so I'm coming to get you."

The newly refurbished, angular six-person shuttle set down on a temporary landing pad. "Good luck," Lee said before moving off to round up his foreman and forewoman.

Lacey, a woman that made Ayan feel short on occasion even though she wasn't overly tall, was a mess of irritation and windswept black hair as she leaned out of the shuttle's side door. "The Council is stirring early, probably thanks to some back-room meeting."

Lacey matched Ayan's mode of dress ever since she started working for her six months before, but she didn't normally bear arms when she was in Haven Shore. Ayan couldn't help but notice the sidearm on the woman's hip, and she glanced at it, then at Lacey.

"Something serious is going on," Lacey said, recognizing the glance. "With the way you've been treated in Council chambers the last few weeks, I'm not taking chances."

Ayan took a seat and pulled the side hatch closed. The shuttle was off the landing pad before it finished sealing. "They're only words, we knew there would be a lot of contention surrounding this referendum. There always is when a Council surrenders an issue to the public, and my personal life has made me unpopular."

"That was what? Four months ago? If the public's still sore about you breaking off from Liam, they should bloody damn well grow up. It's none of their business, and no reason to oppose your side of the issue. You should have the qualifying system take pettiness into account."

"You're right, but some people have long memories, and Liam is very charismatic. There's also a whole set who believe I betrayed Jake." Ayan took a breath, deciding to move on from that over-examined topic. Lacey was more angry about the lingering disapproval towards Ayan concerning her short romantic relationship with Liam Grady than Ayan was.

"I've held off on asking," Lacey said tentatively. "But I'd like to know so I can have all the facts while I stand on your side."

Ayan had a feeling she knew what her aide was about to ask and nodded her encouragement as she scrolled through Crewcast highlights. "I can't see why, you know more about me than anyone."

"Well, in that case, why did you break things off from Jake? Even you said you were happy when you were together."

The question stung. Lacey's instinct to sidestep that question for months had been right. If there was one thing Ayan regretted since she got together with Liam, it was that she had to leave Jake. She was even more remorseful after she split from Liam, something that wasn't supposed to be public, but became the topic of conversation for half of Tamber just the same. "I took some bad advice," Ayan replied. "I was told that I had to free Jake so he could do what he had to in this war. Little did I know it would be stalled for the better part of a year."

"That advice didn't come from that thing that could see the future, did it?" Lacey said.

"I know what you think of the information I got from the machine," Ayan said, trying to sidestep another short lecture on how nothing can tell people the future. It was Lacey's steadfast opinion, and it came up whenever Ayan was caught looking at her extensive notes on the Victory Machine and her encounter. "You have to understand, when I came away from that experience it was as real as you and I sitting here, and I wouldn't have followed its instructions if I knew it would land us here. What's worse, I wouldn't have ended up with Liam at all if I just stayed the course and stayed with Jake. But-"

Lacey finished the explanation of Ayan's first night with Liam, she'd heard it enough to have it memorized. "He was the most trustworthy person left in your life then, and you needed to feel alive and cared for." Lacey didn't state it sardonically, but surprised Ayan when she added her own opinion. "Bully for him, being at the catcher's post at the right time. Old letch should have put you off just the same. Figure someone of morally high training could have kept his robes on."

"I'm just as much to blame," Ayan said. "Takes two."

"You were reeling in grief, two important people snatched away in just a few days. Even I know you wouldn't be yourself. Wish I was there instead of him then, I'd know well enough to put you to bed and cuddle you off instead of getting into your pants at the first opening. I just can't believe how it ended, him fighting to keep you on his arm after both of you drifted apart for a couple of months. He had to know it all started wrong, I know that's how you felt."

"You were there when the real grief struck," Ayan reassured Lacey. "When I didn't expect it, and you wouldn't leave, not even when I told you to."

"We're on equal ground, little dove. When my brother was found, you were my pillar even though it would have been fine for you to go on like I were just a serving bot. You could have just left me in my place to feel the loss on my own time."

"Couldn't do that. You know you're more than my aide." It was true; Lacey quickly became the older sister she never knew she needed. "I don't know what these last months would be like without you." Ayan took Lacey's slender hand and squeezed it. For a moment they shared a quiet time of acknowledgement and affection. "As for the mess with Jake, you know the whole story now."

"Thank you. I was sorry for asking, I know you want to move on, but-"

"Your curiosity was begging," Ayan said. "I understand."

"Well, I'm glad your time with Liam is sorted, now he's just a face at the other end of the Council table, and you *can* move on." Lacey said. "Or move back to Jake?" she asked with a wink. "I know you're abreast of all the Warlord's doings – well, whatever crumbs of data they leave for the public and what you can get from Triton Fleet."

"There's a long distance to cross if that were to happen. I hurt him, I know I did, and if I didn't, Minh made sure I knew it. Aside from all that, sometimes I'm amazed at what you catch me doing. You're not hacked into my comms, are you?" Ayan asked.

"I wouldn't know how to, and a good aide shouldn't have to. I know everything about you, dear. How else am I supposed to know what you need before you do?"

"Speaking of which," Ayan said, "have you heard anything that could tell you what this is about?"

"No, and neither has Victor. No one else replied when I asked what was going on. They know you have a tight schedule. If this is more bureaucratic haggling, I'm going to start stunning people."

It took a while for Ayan to get used to Lacey's humour, but once she did, it never failed to amuse. She could be the picture of professional decorum, but every once in a while her temper got the best of her, and she'd let loose with threats and sabre rattling that was only a good way for her to quickly blow off steam before she had to face people again. It was often just what Ayan needed to start smiling again.

CHAPTER 4
HAVEN SHORE

Alice's report to the Haven Shore Strategic Centre was filed in-flight. Her duties were fulfilled, and there was still a little light left in the day. The crewmembers of the Warlord who remained behind while the ship was on an intelligence gathering mission and many Haven Shore residents were taking a day off at the beach. After the last few hours of the long day on Tamber, the terraformed moon would be overshadowed by its brother moon and the planet it orbited, Kambis.

Alice enjoyed hanging out with Ashley, the sometimes bubbly, and often underestimated pilot. Even though she had the intelligence and experience to plan ahead when it came to her duties, Ashley was a great example of someone who enjoyed living in the moment, and she made every moment she could enjoyable.

Alice had gotten to know nearly all of the other Warlord crewmembers as well, and liked most of them. Work on the ship was nearing completion, and even though she'd spent much of her time as a ranger, she couldn't help but be proud of how it was turning out. The restoration seemed to take forever with so few people working on it, but months of ceaseless labour and good teamwork yielded undeniable results. The addition of a British Shipwright Crew in the last two months accelerated the work more than anyone expected, especially her. Every time the Warlord returned to the system it seemed like a whole section of the ship's interior was brand new.

When the ship was ready, Alice would be have to make a decistion: remain on Tamber and serve the Rangers, a new organization that she learned so much from, or go off-world with her father.

It was a difficult decision - she enjoyed her work as a Ranger, and it was completely different from what she'd be doing on the Warlord. As a Ranger she saved people in the wreckage of Port Rush, searched for old research bunkers on the island of Haven Shore, or kept watch over cultivation crews as they picked fruit in the jungle, for a start. There were large carnivorous cats with glinting eyes, and curious monkeys who would steal from the pickers' bags if they got too close. There were many other dangers as well, snakes, nests of widow beetles, and so on, but monkeys and big cats were the most problematic. The Warlord seemed so much more confining, but she knew she'd see new ports, aliens she'd only heard about, and there would be combat – it was guaranteed.

The notion that she'd just done her last run as a ranger for weeks, maybe months, maybe *ever*, was just sinking in as the main Haven Shore settlement came into view. Her fighter slowed as she neared the new docking facility. The settlement took advantage of the hard, time-tested cliff face. Many small landing platforms and the framing of several buildings were anchored into the side of the stone. Atop the cliff was the port building proper, a bulbous, irregular dome that was still under construction. Parts of the main lower levels were finished, but the skin of the dome would be stretched upwards and expanded as more floors were added. They still used a much smaller building as the main port hub. It was a simple transparent dome that would be repurposed as an outbuilding later.

The Everin building was well on its way to being completed, and even though it was massive to Alice, she knew there were plans for several more, and they'd be interconnected by a larger framing structure. The hollow structure was already large enough to house everyone who had arrived with them at Haven Shore; even she had an apartment there. Haven Shore Navnet took control of her Ramiel fighter and guided it towards the centre of the Everin building.

The ship descended into the hollow centre of the structure. The twenty-one storey building seemed squat from above, but she couldn't help but marvel at its size as her ship was led to a soft landing halfway down the hollow centre on a small retractable landing pad. Freeground technology, fabrication systems from the Triton, and mountains of supplies that Ayan and her people bartered for went into the quickly constructed building. A large amount of basic supplies came from the Warlord as well, sort of smuggled through the Triton so the Carthans didn't object to Haven Shore taking aid from an exiled ship.

The blue and green tinted floors and walls were once sheets of cloth and viscous liquid. Using nanotechnology and magnetic fields, the place was shaped wall by wall, room by room, and the materials hardened into light but incredibly strong structures. The Everin Building wasn't so much built as it was shaped. It was still a shell for the most part, with only bare rooms and the most basic amenities, but when it was finished, it would be fully modern. The small vehicle bay in the bottom level of her apartment would deliver her fighter to a central area where it would be serviced, then it would be returned using Haven Shore's transportation system, which would extend to every floor of the building through branching passages and lifts.

Alice climbed from her fighter as the landing platform retracted into her apartment. She was already planning how she'd get to the beach. There were always people heading in that direction on skid trucks, especially before high tide. Two thirds of the long beach would disappear as Kambis and its other moons' gravity focused on their side of Tamber.

She dropped her ranger kit in the middle of her small gathering room – a space she hadn't had a chance to fill with more than a couple of portable chairs – and checked herself in the mirror. After a moment of trying to get her hair into a manageable pile and adding a little makeup, she gave up and headed for the door.

Thoughts of leaving Haven Shore and her situation of increasing comforts were fading as she started looking through swimsuit shapes for her vacsuit. She was already smiling at the idea of the beach trip and relaxing with friends for the first time in two weeks. Ashley would be on the beach with Zoe, and several of the rangers Alice trained with were already there expecting her. Her eagerness faded as she opened her door and saw a young man sitting beside it, nodding off.

He got to his feet with a start. He was wearing a yellow and white worker's vacsuit, and was barely out of his teens. It took a moment for her to recognize Soren, one of the ranger trainees who left training after a week and a half. He was savvy with technology, but couldn't keep up physically, and hesitated in mock combat. "Alice, I'm sorry for coming here like this, but you weren't on Crewcast, everything just went to your mail." He looked absolutely distraught.

"Rangers turn social mode off while we're on patrol," Alice said. "What's wrong?"

"Right, I forgot, that's procedure, I forgot, sorry. I would have brought this to the Council Office's attention, and I know they'd send a ranger to take care of it, or maybe even just normal Haven Shore security, but I wanted you. I mean, I know you from training, and I think you'd," he stammered, "maybe you could take care of this?"

"Just take your time, I'll help if I can," Alice said, leading him into her apartment.

"Okay," he said, taking in the small main room. The privacy seemed to calm him down a little. "You could use some furniture."

"Tell me about it," Alice replied. "Your problem?"

"Yeah, well, when I washed out from the rangers I applied for a position in robotics, and I didn't think I'd get it because my scores as a ranger trainee were bad at best, but mostly incomplete. They didn't care. I got a spot on a team working on making network detached helper and builder bots out of the ones we bought for next to nothing on the mainland."

"I've seen a bunch working, those little skitters that follow the workers around," Alice said.

"Yeah, they're working out great, even with some of the weird stuff that's been going on. A lot of us anthropomorphise bots when we're working on them, talk to them like people or kids who came in with a scraped knee or something even before we've switched them back on. It makes the day go by, and it's pretty funny when we catch each other doing it, but some of the bots started really reacting to it after the lights go on."

"That's normal, isn't it? The bots have to acknowledge that you're communicating with them."

"No, no, not like that. Not a little beep or a flashing light telling me I've been heard. I'm talking about whole conversations that, when you look at the bigger picture, indicate that these bots are more aware than anyone expected. The other day we got a call from a lady who was wondering if a skitter was assigned to follow her eight year old around when it was between tasks. We checked it out and found Bo-Bot, a skitter who this kid liked, named, and the sentiment seemed mutual. When we checked a snapshot of its code, we found out that this skitter noticed Hamish, the kid, was really accident prone while it was working in their quarters, and it took responsibility because he tripped over a temporary data line. We tried to remove Bo-Bot from the situation and the thing started, well, screaming at us until the kid started crying, then it summons his mother and makes these soothing noises that none of us added to its programming."

"It cared about him," Alice said.

"Yeah, and it's not supposed to, not at all. It's not supposed to learn things about babysitting kids, about helping around the house – which this skitter was doing – it's not supposed to care if someone gives it a nickname, but Bo-Bot stencilled its nickname onto itself. We checked the code again and found more than we bargained for, that's for sure. This skitter is the extreme example, these construction bots aren't adopting kids throughout the building, thank God, but they are learning and picking up characteristics. Most of this stuff helps them work more efficiently, even form teams with pretty serious bonds, but some of it is just not necessary. They're working faster, more efficiently though, so even the project managers want to leave it alone. I wonder if their tune will change when we find a depressed loader somewhere, or a skitter who wants to be a starship when he grows up."

"You want me to help you with some sketchy bots?" Alice asked. There were only two hours of good beach time left, and he was rambling.

"No, I'm just giving you some history so you can get where this problem comes from."

"Oh, okay. What happened to Bo-Bot, anyway?"

"Oh, he's now property of Hamish McCrary when the kid's awake. At bedtime he gets back to work. We're hoping that doesn't become a thing with these bots, but our admins say this'll be great for public relations," he replied. "Anyway, these distinct personalities are forming in bots because of some kind of antivirus someone added to their base code. This isn't the antivirus we installed, it's something a lot more elaborate, maybe even elegant. We didn't see it at first, but it's in all our software now. It spreads like a virus, but once it's in something, it's like an antivirus against the Holocaust Virus and everything like it. The personalities these bots are taking on are harmless, all basic directives and programming still applies, so we've been letting it go on. For example, if I wanted Bo-Bot to return to duty and ignore Hamish, he would, and he'd be as good as ever at his job. He wouldn't like it, but he'd do it."

"Something's gone wrong," Alice said, dreading what would come next. Anything involving the Holocaust Virus meant the worst kind of trouble.

"Yeah, but only one other tech and I know about it, so I told her to sit tight while I bring this to you. If we report this to the Council, they'll shut down all robotics and investigate. The Everin Building is almost finished, and the bots are supposed to move on to building the permanent port this week. The work that's left here would take months if humans did it, and the port building? Without robotics it would take years."

"I'm sure your admins would keep it quiet if they could. There's no way they'd want the bots shut down if they could help it."

"I might get fired for not reporting it sooner, and I don't want to get put out of Haven Shore with the referendum coming up," he replied, some of his initial desperation showing itself. "You've seen the world out there? It's chaos in most cities and expensive everywhere else. I've even heard rumours of cannibalism in the Yellow Hook Plain."

"They only exile people from Haven Shore for murder and repeated offenses, and failure to report a problem like this is nowhere near, unless something went berserk and killed someone because you told it to?" Alice asked.

"No, but three bots, advanced android Ando-Twelve types, ran off. They look just like humans, so they got around perimeter security. They're in the middle of the jungle as far as I can tell, and they took a high powered EMP pistol from our emergency supplies."

"They didn't hurt anyone on their way out?"

Soren shook his head. "No, but I think all this has something to do with their wireless systems. We didn't want to take the hours we'd need to disable them before turning them on. Ando-Twelves' wireless systems are nested in their main processor clusters, so you need to direct nanobots to disconnect the wireless in thousands of places. That used to make them highly connected and quick to respond to changing situations, great for assistant or critical care bots, but with the Holocaust Virus and that other thing out there, it could be bad."

"So you were going to let them run around with their wireless on?" Alice asked.

"Nope. The fastest way to disable the wireless on an Ando is to ask them to do it themselves, but they have to be on first."

"Gotcha. Why do you think they left and the other bots didn't?"

"Have you ever met an Ando-Twelve?" Soren asked.

"I don't think so," Alice replied.

"That's the thing; they're sophisticated synthetic humans, expensive, used for the care and hospitality industries. You've probably met a few and not even known it. We thought they'd be safe androids because they're hard-wired pacifists, the Holocaust Virus just shut most of them down."

"But it didn't send them running like this?" Alice asked.

"No. They just couldn't violate their core directives, so they powered down, or fried their own power systems if they couldn't do that. I don't know what this new antivirus is doing to them, though. And I can't communicate with any of them to find out, either. Please don't turn us in. This is the best job I've had, and it's been great here ever since we got out of those storage containers. It's even better than how I was living before the Virus."

"I'll do some tracking for you, but I'm going to report these bots as rogue eventually," Alice said. "If they're harmless, then I might be able to file something about them just going for a walk thanks to some bad code."

"That's perfect, thank you."

"If," she emphasised, "this is all harmless. I can't make promises." She picked up her ranger kit and holstered her sidearm. "Stay here while I track your bots down, I'll tell you before I file my report."

"Thank you so much," Soren repeated. "Aren't you going to take your ship?"

"Nope," Alice replied. "I'd have to explain why I'm taking a starfighter out in my off time."

"Okay, right, thank you again."

Alice was already getting tired of hearing him say 'thank you,' and couldn't help but offer a snide reply as she left him behind in her apartment. "Just stay here, don't talk to anyone. Order some ramen from the concourse, I'll try to be back with your bots before delivery's at the door."

Chapter 5
Bargaining

"You won't have any wild nights on the town with me, I'm afraid," Donner, the British Alliance Security Forces agent told Jacob Valent. The rain around them was mixed with light hail, and darkened the falling twilight.

"I didn't think that was standard procedure for liaisons," Jake replied, bringing up a tactical map of the area. The image appeared in his mind's eye, along with the deception detection and early warning systems tied in with his scanners. He wasn't worried about someone overhearing them; they communicated using an encrypted channel, talking behind blacked out faceplates. Jake wasn't sure about the new agent's skill, however. If he was a glorified file keeper, or supervisor rusty in the field, he could have people tracking him, and he wouldn't know it.

"No, it isn't procedure, and her extracurricular activities with you while she was aboard the Warlord weren't an assignment," Donner chuckled. "She found you fascinating and I suppose she followed that fascination to the utmost. The final report is quite popular, but most importantly, I can tell you there are no hard feelings. To be blunt, she compares her short romance with you with an amusement ride. Thrilling for a short trip, but too dangerous for a journey."

"Glad to hear it was memorable. I'm guessing her objectivity was compromised, so they passed my case off to you," Jake said. He watched the agent closely. The man was barely disguised in a loose blue and red armoured jacket that cascaded down to his knees. Beneath his casual spacer clothes he wore a layer of second skin armour, its hood covering his head and containing his voice. None of it looked new, so he could pass as a casual traveller or merchant. He still looked British to Jake, there was no mistaking it, but the build up to war had brought many similarly garbed mercenaries to the sector. Enough so a British Alliance Agent could blend in.

"You've misunderstood the situation. I'm her superior officer. We've finished checking the information you and your Wing Commander have provided, and are satisfied that we want to move ahead with this trade. If what you've shared as a peek is only the tip of the iceberg, then we need everything you have on offer."

"Good. It'll cost you," Jake said.

"Just to verify," Donner said, taking a step closer. "You're saying you have the Regent Galactic and Order of Eden story going back to Vindyne days? As well as evidence and scans of a new, hidden leader behind the Order?"

"With more supporting evidence than you could imagine, from more than one perspective," Jake said. "And we're still willing to be your agents in the field as long as we can gain along the way."

"The intention of my department is to keep this deal simple. We are interested in working with you and your people after we've finished our trade on a mission by mission basis, even on the bounty system, but we can address all that later. We're anxious to close this deal for the compiled data you're offering. So eager, in fact, that we're willing to keep Haven Shore, the Carthans, and everyone else in the Seven Sectors out of it."

The Seven Sectors, it was becoming a well known name thanks to the Order of Eden's activities. Jake knew that the Order, along with Regent Galactic, were active in twice as many sectors, but most navigators knew of seven where the Order presented a serious danger to anyone not running under their colours. The term stuck, probably thanks to old pirate films and newer period pirate dramas. It looked like everyone, including that agent, would refer to the fog of war surrounding the Order of Eden's operations as the Seven Sectors. "I'm surprised. I thought your people were more interested in maintaining relationships with your allies. Falling in line with how I'm running my war could cost you. Using this data operationally could cost you more if your government finally commits to this war."

"We are fully committed. It's only a matter of time before war is declared against the Order of Eden for a second time, a final time, and if this information-"

"History," Jake corrected. "We've put all our evidence in context, you can follow it on a solid timeline."

"That'll make for easy viewing, and the history you provided will factor into the British Alliance breaking the treaty we signed with the Order. I'll be the first to say not everyone agreed with the Frontier Treaty: we signed it in the dark because the parliamentary majority were afraid of what war would mean while we're rebuilding. We'll use this, and we'll share parts of the package we're buying from you, but only after we've completed our analysis. But before we go forward, I need your assurance that we're not buying something you're selling to every government you can find."

"Only five people know about this project, and we're not double dealing. You have my word. Before this goes further," Jake said. "I need you and your government to know that I don't trade in sentients - this is an exception wide on the outside."

"Don't worry, we'll treat him according to his level of cooperation. If he's easy to work with, he'll have an enviable lifestyle."

Jake stifled his laughter before it became more than a snicker. He was unable to imagine Kipley cooperating with the British Alliance. He was sure Kipley wouldn't experience that 'enviable lifestyle' for a long time, if ever. It was time to move the meeting along, the Warlord was waiting. Their next target was waiting. "Were Xanna's traces right? Did Wheeler pass through here?"

"They were, and he did."

"How long ago?" Jake asked.

"About a hundred and three hours ago, but the trail ends at the system's outer port. He stole a recently refurbished Joon-Lasun freighter from the sorting dock. We're watching for it to turn up somewhere upspin, but hopes are slim. He has a few nihilists with him who might be easier to track if they serve as crew long enough."

"He's going to dump that freighter or sell it on the black market then move on to another ship; his crew will probably get dumped along with it," Jake said, controlling his frustration. He was so close, just days behind. If he could break away and hunt him down instead of serving larger interests, he'd have him in days, or weeks at the most. "I need the British Alliance to put a bounty on him. That's going to be part of the deal, or I'm going to start shopping for a new buyer."

"No need to go to those lengths," Donner said. "Xanna didn't have the rank to promise that our Security Forces would act on your behalf, but I do. I only need one favour from you in return, and we'll issue a five million credit bounty on your old friend, Wheeler."

"Twenty million, and you spend real galactic credits on advertising with all the networks," Jake told him. If this agent was about to ask for another favour, then his people already wanted the Warlord in their good graces. It was time to push.

"If it were only money I may be able to help you, but advertising on mainstream nets? That's-"

Jake didn't *start* turning away from the British Alliance Agent, he did a complete about face. He was already several steps away and almost around the corner when he said; "We'll leave the current deal as is – a trade for all our intelligence for the work your shipwrights already did on the Warlord, a link to your military database and thirty five million. Count us out for favours."

"Wait!" the agent called after him. "I'll put an eight million galactic currency bounty out on him and target mainstream nets near his projected destinations. That's the best I can do."

Jake stopped and turned towards the agent. "Maybe I should wait until they assign me your superior?"

"It's not a matter of how much pull I have with the Agency, it's how much of our operating budget you and your crew will be eating up."

"We're worth it," Jake said. "Wheeler's a hard target, put ten million on his head and maybe you'll motivate the real hunters to go after him. People who would stand a chance against me if I were the target." The thought of hunters who wouldn't work for less than ten million on a target pursuing Wheeler was more than amusing, it was thrilling. Hunters like that made Jake nervous, and he was happy the Order of Eden was no longer offering a bounty on him. There was always a chance that they'd increase it to over ten million, then Jake would be facing the most effective hunters in the universe, people who made him look like an ill-equipped amateur.

"All right, ten million, and we'll advertise on the most popular nets from here to the core along his projected travel routes. I'll also put the word out on the secondary nets, the Stellarnet and such."

"Good. What's this favour?" Jake asked.

"Thank you, Captain Valent," Donner said with a sigh. "There's a Regent Galactic Governor that's been causing a great deal of concern for us. He's reaching further and further out from his solar system using subcontracted transport and militia companies. We've even found a few nano-probes aboard supply ships coming into our forward posts collecting data, which suggests he already has an agent collecting that data."

"Governor Tate," Jake said. He was the Governor of the Codis Solar System and supervisor of a large portion of the Iron Head Sector and interests near the Rega Gain System. "I haven't run into him before, but from the information we're gathering, I know the day is coming."

"We'd like that day to come sooner rather than later. We want you to put the fear into people looking to work with, or sign up with the Order of

34

Eden. He's recruiting faster than anyone we're aware of, and quickly rising in the Order of Eden ranks, as far as we can tell. If someone doesn't slow his recruitment efforts, we'll have an army millions of souls deep by the time the British go to war, and the first confrontation could be our last. Our parliamentary membership are too distant from the war to appreciate how devastating Order supremacy would be in this area. If our first engagement incurs too many casualties, they'll lose their nerve. Ideally, we need you to inspire new recruits in the Order to abandon their posts."

"Put us on the record," Jake said. "If I'm going to pick a fight with this Governor, I want the British Alliance's endorsement."

"I saw this coming," Agent Donner said with a little chuckle. "You finish this trade today and we'll give you full license to act as a privateer for the British Alliance. Just a little bonus I negotiated for on your behalf."

"Today," Jake said, pondering. "You have the credits with you?"

"No, but I can have them delivered to the Triton today. Our people are standing by in the Rega Gain System."

Jake thought of the grief Kipley was causing his crew. The main reason why he allowed several members to serve aboard the Triton instead of the Warlord was because of the morale deficit that man caused just by being aboard. The only reason why they kept him close was to pump him for information, and Jake was fairly sure they'd wrung him dry. "How large is the British Alliance's share going to be in this license?"

"Fear is what we want, Jacob," Donner said, "People are still paying their way into the Order of Eden, even though they have dropped the cash requirement to sign up. Their new recruits are giving away their worldly possessions for the most minor privileges in the organization and extra training. We need people to see that joining the Order of Eden in this sector is a death sentence, a death sentence that the Warlord carries out. We don't care about a share of what you take as long as you don't trade slaves on the black market or start spy hunting in the British Alliance ranks."

"So, we sell our captured materials to anyone and the British Alliance doesn't want a share?" Jake asked, it wasn't something governments did unless they were desperate.

"Exactly. The British Alliance doesn't want to profit from the work we're asking you to do."

"I'm only going to warn you once, Donner. If you want fear on that scale I'll need your support when one of the British Alliance's allies accuse me of going too far. You're asking for blood and terror," Jake said.

"You'll have our support. This isn't my request, it comes from someone well over my head. We only have to finish our deal today, and you can start ripping a piece out of the Order."

"I can deliver Jack Kipley in five minutes."

"What?" Agent Donner said, visibly startled. "You've actually kept him nearby?"

Jake pointed down the alley to the broad entrance of Alt-Mecca across the street. "He'll be coming through those doors any second."

"We can have a retrieval team here in less than a minute," Agent Donner said. "You transmit your intelligence files to me and allow us to take your living proof and we'll have thirty five million galactic credits in the hands of your representative aboard the Triton before the day is out. We can honour the rest of our deal when you arrive in the Rega Gain System."

"You'll transmit our privateering license today."

"Yes," Agent Donner said. "Absolutely."

"Then we have a deal," Jake said. He watched as Jack Kipley stormed from the doors of the entertainment complex with Minh-Chu not far behind. With a thought, Jake overrode the controls to Kipley's suit and ordered it to restrain the crewman. With a startled wail, Kipley fell over.

"He's all yours," Jake said.

* * *

To Minh-Chu's surprise, Kipley's light vacsuit armour stiffened, snapped the man's arms to his sides and clasped his legs together. He watched in amused silence as the man cursed and toppled over. "This isn't funny! I was kidding before, but now I'm really going to kill you!" Kipley shouted.

"I didn't do it," Minh-Chu said as he pulled Kipley's sidearm out of its holster. He moved on to his left arm to unlock the man's command and control unit. "You know, if you had better people skills, maybe Jake wouldn't have sold you."

"What? What the hell are you talking about?"

Minh-Chu pocketed Kipley's command and control unit and moved on to the survival kit attached to his left thigh. "You just couldn't help but talk about Wheeler, and everything you saw aboard those Order of Eden ships. Helps that you downloaded everything you could from those computers too, it really helped us round out the intelligence package we're selling today."

"What the hell are you talking about?"

"You never caught on," Minh-Chu said, kneeling down so Kipley could see him from where his face was half pressed in the mud. "Frost and I piss you off, wind you up, and you go cry on someone's shoulder, like Stephanie, or Kadri, or whoever else was in on it. Ever notice that so many of those conversations turned towards things you saw while you were with Wheeler?"

"I didn't tell anyone nothin' about nothin', man!" Kipley protested.

"Doesn't matter now," Minh-Chu said, standing up as he saw the lights of descending combat shuttles. The crowd that was starting to gather began taking steps backwards.

"All high-and-mighty, with your old wisecracks, and you're just a goddamned slaver!" Kipley shouted. He breathed in enough water from the puddle forming around his face to send him into a coughing fit.

"Here's one for you," Minh-Chu said, standing up and taking a step back. "'If you can wish all your enemies well, you may someday only have friends.' I don't know if that's true, but good luck just in case. I hope you find all the happiness you deserve." Minh-Chu found it impossible to suppress a grin as he watched a half dozen armoured British Alliance soldiers drop from the shuttles, attach a harness to Kipley's stiffened form and disappear with him into the belly of the combat shuttle in a quick, orderly fashion.

CHAPTER 6
A DISTURBANCE IN THE COUNCIL CHAMBERS

"Commander Ayan, Military Liason and Chief of Haven Shore Structural Development," the automated record keeper announced to the council members as she entered their modest chambers. Ayan glanced at the silver lettering over the doorway just as she passed under it.

FOR COMMON SAFETY, WELL BEING, AND HAPPINESS, it said. It was a goal that was proving more difficult to adhere to than Ayan could have ever imagined. Lacey Rosendale was right behind her. The automated system announced her entire title as well, "Lieutenant Lacey Rosendale, Aide to the Military Liason and Chief of Haven Shore Structural Development." Ayan could almost hear the woman sneer at the announcement. Lacey hated all the time the automated announcer wasted by spouting her over-long title as she entered the room.

Liam Grady stood at one end of the ten person conference table in his old fashioned cotton blue robes. The red belt at his waist bore impressions from Earth, the Triton, and Haven Shore. Along the sides of the tables stood Victor Davis in a grey Haven Shore security vacsuit, Iloona Murlen, her big brown eyes conveying worry from under caramel and black furred brow, and Cory Greene didn't look at her at all, the delicate jewellery chains crossing the chest of his formal Carthan uniform jangling as he adjusted his coat cuffs.

On the other side of the table stood Mischa Konev in loose skirts and uneasy poise. It looked like she had been crying. Beside her was Sunny Zinnes in his navy blue British Fleet uniform, a sensible garment that was much like Freeground's vacsuits, but with a discernable pant and closed jacket. He was watching without being intrusive, and his assistant, Nuto Yann, an Issyrian who lived in a slim containment suit at all times, stood stiffly behind him. It was impossible to find out what he was feeling without asking directly, but his presence was always made known by the gentle sounds of his gurgling suit.

As Ayan took her place at the head of the table, a woman with long, multi-coloured hair and bright blue eyes took a place beside Liam at the opposite end. She was Tyra Kim, Liam Grady's immediate underling in for the position of South Haven Shore Representative. "Glad you could fit us into you busy schedule, Commander," she said.

"Careful, or you'll drool venom all over the table," Lacey muttered under her breath. Iloona squeezed her eyes shut as if to hold a chuckle in. The British Alliance observer, Sunny, looked at Lacey briefly, raising an eyebrow in comment on her inappropriateness.

Ayan was preparing to ask what they had been summoned for in her most passive tone when Liam Grady spoke up. "Early this morning, I was approached by a concerned constituent who had heard a rumour that I'll be leaving Haven Shore and the Rega Gain System." Tyra stared at Ayan, her lips pressed into a white line, brows furrowed and jaw flexing as Liam spoke. Liam pressed on. "This is true. I was quietly making preparations, getting my office in order so succession could be seamless, but someone must have discovered my intentions early. My plan was to depart a few days after the vote and leave a good interim public servant in my place."

"If you leave, our connection to Earth, though scant, will be gone entirely," said the Carthan Observer, Cory Greene. "I don't approve, and we will not permit it."

Ayan failed to catch a rueful laugh before it escaped from between her lips. She managed to cut it short but not before it had drawn everyone's attention. The whole situation was so ridiculous that laughter had somehow become the only sane response. Thanks to a few malcontents, Ayan had been virtually hoisted up as the enemy to Liam Grady after they drifted apart and broke things off romantically. It was true that she wanted little to do with him, but she respected his philosophy, education, and engineering prowess. He was also very well liked by Haven Shore civilians, and people like Tyra, with her accusing eyes, led the anti-Ayan brigade with irrational vigour, no matter how Liam tried to temper her efforts. Cory Greene, the Carthan Representative, who had inspired her laughter, was an irritant, but he made it obvious that he didn't like her either. His largest problem was that he didn't find much evidence that she was qualified to be the Military Liason. He refused to acknowledge that she carried memories of a predecessor with command and diplomatic training. She didn't let him or the Carthans get anything from Haven Shore that they didn't earn, and they were constantly trying to renegotiate for more than they deserved. It didn't help that she found his observer post laughable in the first place.

"Did I say something funny?" asked Cory Greene, slowly turning towards Ayan.

"You're an observer here," Ayan said. "Please keep your comments to yourself."

"They're not comments," Cory Greene insisted. "The Carthan Government is still the primary holder of power in the space around Tamber and-" he stopped, wide eyed as he watched Ayan slowly raise her finger and place it across her lips, in a shushing gesture.

Victor Davis and the British Alliance Observer, Sunny Zinnes, were both doing their best to suppress grins at Cory Greene's silent outrage.

"I want to be the first to say that Haven Shore needs strong leadership," Ayan said, ignoring Tyra, who rolled her eyes exaggeratedly. "You've been there for your constituents, Liam, and you've been good on the council. Is there anything we can do to convince you to remain here?" Ayan felt as though she was lying by putting on a brave face and asking him to stay, when it was against her every instinct. It was the right political manoeuvre, however, and he was good for Haven Shore.

"I'm afraid not. Over the last few months, it's become plain to me that Haven Shore, the Triton, and even the Warlord seem to have things in order, even though there is still danger on your doorstep. Meanwhile, there are billions of people in this galaxy who are much more in need of help. I plan on taking a spaceliner coreward, to one of the interior systems that were hardest struck by the Holocaust Virus. There will be people to teach, homes to rebuild, and I feel I'll be of best use there. I'm sorry if this displeases anyone in Haven Shore, but it's time for me to move on. Since the word is out, and my hope of a clean good-bye is gone, I'll be leaving today. My second, Tyra Kim, is prepared to take my place and run my office." He bowed and began saying his personal farewells, turning to Mischa Konev first, who hugged him with great fondness. Sunny Zinnes shook his hand and wished him luck. Victor Davis did the same, adding, "You're going to tell us how you're doing once you get comms up." It wasn't a question. Liam Grady then wished Iloona and her family the best, and she told him to have a safe journey.

Ayan felt as though there was a brick turning slowly in her stomach as Liam Grady said an obligatory farewell to Cory Greene, who looked as though he had a fiercely bitter taste in his mouth. Tyra was behind him for every step, and she looked away as Liam Grady regarded Ayan. "I've tried to say this more than once in messages," he said to her in a hushed tone.

"And this will be the last chance, so I hope I get it right. I was near you when you needed the help and care of a friend and mentor. Your instinct was to get as close to someone you trusted as you could, so you could feel safe and alive again."

Ayan hated him for using that warm, comforting tone with her, but bystanders seemed to fade away as tears threatened to come. The onrush of emotion surprised her; he was bringing back all the hurt she felt over their failed relationship. Even though she regretted the whole thing, they did have some good moments together. Ayan tried to hold on to what she thought they had, but within a few weeks after New Year's Eve, it became plain that there was no making it feel right, and they were already drifting apart despite the good times and comfort they had at first. She looked up at him, meeting his gaze. He normally looked a little less than fifty years old, even though he was over seventy. As she looked at him then, he looked weary, wearing more years than she'd noticed before.

He continued his farewell, resting a hand on her shoulder. "I took you in the wrong kind of embrace, and I'm more sorry than I can say. I could go on for hours about what I should have done to support you in that time, but that wouldn't change my mistake. The only solace I have is our short time together, and the lessons you taught me. You're a boundlessly magnificent woman, and I have no doubt that you'll only get better with age. Goodbye."

It felt as though her head were throbbing, a few escaping tears ran hot down her cheeks and her jaws were clenched so hard she was afraid molars were about to pop. How could he ambush her with this eloquently executed departure? Everything he was saying about their past together rang true. He was admitting to reacting badly when she tried - and succeeded - in getting too close to him just because he was there and she trusted him. He was telling her that he should have countered her instincts, and that the short-lived relationship that followed was wrong, too. How he said it was so condescending that it made her want to scream. To her, it felt like he was telling her that she was once a helpless babe in the woods crying for comfort, for closeness and he caught her, poor clueless Ayan, and took advantage. Hearing herself depicted so aimless, helpless made her want to lash out at him.

It almost overshadowed the truth she'd come to settle on months after they drifted apart: that he was a good man, and they were wrong for each other. They could have been great friends, and she realised only then, as she stared up at him, furious and hurt, that she expected that they would be on easy talking terms again some day. That promise would die with his departure, and all she could manage to say was, "Good-bye."

He waited a moment, looking at her, then slowly closed his eyes and turned away.

CHAPTER 7
OVER ISSEL GULCH

Alice supposed that most of the wilderness fruit pickers she rode with in the transport had never met a ranger. It was a new division based in Haven Shore, and it represented a cooperative training effort between the new Haven Shore Council, the Sunspire, and the Triton. The Rangers would eventually be an elite unit that could take action or give direction in any field. They were sent out on their own to explore the land, learn what scanners couldn't and make decisions independently. That was the dream, but all the rangers were new, and Haven Shore needed something to trade. The rangers, along with pilots and experts on their regular roster, were outsourced to help the Carthans and several smaller organizations for a fee. The ones that remained behind worked with soldiers to accomplish tasks set out by Haven Shore, like hunting down the remaining framework troops and systems. There had been successes. Thousands of people had been rescued from wrecks long after everyone had lost hope, and framework soldiers were hunted into near extinction. All the rangers suspected that there was one more active Order of Eden bunker, and all of them wanted credit for finding and eradicating it.

The legend of the rangers was already growing, and Alice was proud to wear the ranger skull logo on her dark green vacsuit. The designation of RANGER was used as the death's head's teeth. Ringing the top of the skull were the words: EXPLORATION, LEADERSHIP, ENFORCEMENT, and the only part of the promise of the rangers that intimidated her was leadership. She was far more comfortable with the other logo she bore on her chest. Another silver skull with the word WARLORD written beneath it marked her as a crewmember on her father's ship. There would be no marked intention above the skull, and that somehow made it more interesting to Alice. No one knew what that ship was for, exactly, and many didn't want to.

The fruit pickers and perimeter scouts took two three hour shifts per day, and there were hundreds of them. Alice had never taken a ride into the deep jungle on one of their transports, none of the rangers did, as far as she knew. There were only a few shipwrecks in the vast jungles that were left untouched by the events of the battle for Port Rush. Not many survived those landings, and they were easy to map from above, so there was no need for rangers to venture in.

The perimeter scouts were a different story. They moved ahead of the pickers, making sure that the big cats, curious monkeys, predator birds, and other wildlife were frightened off. They chose where the pickers would work, set up base camps, and reported on interesting finds in the jungle. The hover truck that carried them all into the jungle down a temporarily placed road between giant tree trunks and heavy vines carried over thirty of them at a pace that seemed meandering.

Alice almost regretted not keeping her vacsuit's hood up when she boarded the back of the antigravity truck. Young pickers and their parents smiled at her and whispered to each other. Some of the scouts made a point of ignoring her, perhaps having been rejected as a ranger, while a couple of others closer to her age regarded her with surprise. She didn't know how to talk to these people, having spent so much time away from Haven Shore, either working on the Warlord or ranging across Tamber. She'd never met a picker before, even though she was well aware that a lot of her food came from the picker camps in the jungle.

The well-worn passenger bay at the back of the truck jostled and one of the scouts sat down beside her. She was around Alice's age, had green and yellow hair, and wore a reflective orange vacsuit like the other scouts. "Is there trouble ahead?" Alice's security system projected the young woman's name and details into her eye; she was Joslyn Bulmer, and was promoted from picker to scout three weeks ago.

The scout carried the scent of their surroundings with her as though her vacsuit had been through the thick jungle many times, smelling sweet and earthy. "I'm pretty sure I'm going further in, and what I'm after isn't armed."

"Animal, vegetable, or machine?" asked a young Nafalli who wore bright yellow markers instead of a full vacsuit. His dark brown and grey striped fur was matted here and there but mostly clean – impressive considering his job. "We've found a few interesting things in here."

All eyes were on her, these were only some of the questions that everyone in the transport were eager to ask. If she were running her mission with Haven Shore's knowledge, she would have been able to use one of their rebuilt skids, and she wouldn't have to answer any of their questions. Alice didn't know how much to tell them, but knew hesitating too long would probably make them worried. "I'm chasing after a lost bot."

"Does it think it's a picker or something?" asked the Nafalli, to the mirth of a few riders.

"It's just confused," Alice replied when things died down.

"Do you think they'll still need us when they get the bots working?" asked Joslyn. "Bots probably pick faster than people, right?"

Alice didn't know what to say; she hadn't thought much about the people she hitched a ride with, or what they'd be doing if their job was mechanised.

"I earned my apartment with this job," Joslyn said. "My first. I was just a kid before, never earned anything myself," she said proudly.

Alice immediately recognized how serious these people were about keeping their place, their functions in Haven Shore. She knew what it was to be lost, to have no home, and she realized then that she was surrounded by former refugees. She considered the desperate need Haven Shore, the Triton, Warlord and all the other ships had for precision workers. Bots were the go-to for that kind of work, and she couldn't imagine many of them getting assigned to something like picking fruit, when humans, Nafalli and a couple of other rarer races were picking tons a day. If the feedback on Crewcast was to be believed, they didn't mind the work either. "I really don't know, but I wouldn't replace you."

"Diplomatic answer," said the Nafalli with a chuff. "She'll be off-world soon, Jos. Won't even think of us when she's on the Warlord."

"Leave her alone," Joslyn replied. "She's a ranger, they rescue people."

"You feed people," Alice said without thinking. That attracted more than a few smiles. If the conversation was to pick up after that, Alice would never know. The hover truck came to a stop as they arrived at a mid-tree station.

The platform surrounding the tree was made of durable stiffened cloth, and it hosted dozens of tents. This was where pickers who wanted more shifts and less travel stayed. Other trucks were pulling up, and a load shuttle was rising up into the trees, its cargo most likely filled with fruit. Alice had tried to get signed onto one as a passenger, but they were off limits – too busy to multitask.

Everyone disembarked in a practiced fashion. As Alice waited for all of them to pass her so she could get off last, one grizzled man with slicked back hair and a broad face put his hand on her shoulder. It was so large that his fingers reached the bottom of her shoulder blade. "You give 'em hell for us when you get out there on the Warlord, girl. We'll keep you fed, you keep the war going."

He didn't wait for a reply. Alice couldn't think of anything to say anyway. As she stepped out of the transport and checked her tracker for the android, she tried to ignore everything she'd seen. Thousands of people were living vastly different lifestyles in and around Haven Shore, and she didn't have time to consider them. If she didn't focus and find that bot soon, Haven Shore would be alerted to the absence, then she'd have to explain why she set out to track the bots down alone.

CHAPTER 8
THE LAST GARRISON

"Stop! They're running us into a trap!" Remmy Sands shouted after his squad of Haven Shore soldiers. They wore combat vacsuits with a battered layer of heavy armour overtop. The rifles they carried bore the scars of several battles, including the Port Rush siege. The Order Knights and a small band of frameworks were losing, but the Haven Shore Regulars' personal energy shields were depleted in most cases, and they bought into the lure that the Order Knights had set out.

In a daring tactical manoeuvre, the Order Knights had sent the last of their framework soldiers directly into the fray when the Haven Shore Regulars, with Remmy advising from the rear, entered the command level of the mobile garrison. It was a suicidal effort on the framework soldiers' part, and the Haven Shore rifles, modified to destroy framework soldiers specifically, ripped them to shreds in a forty two second long fire fight. The gambit was working, and Remmy was just starting to see it. The Order Knights sacrificed their lesser soldiers to convince the invading Haven Shore Regulars that they were on the brink of winning, and it worked. The Regulars rushed in as though the Order Knights were just more framework peons.

An explosion rocked the deck of the mobile garrison, and Remmy watched as smoke and debris was blown down the hall in his direction. The tactical screen on his head's up display indicated that the pair of squad members on point, Irinia and Shawn, were severely injured and immediately drugged into stasis.

Irinia Chen wouldn't make it; she'd taken critical head injuries and there wasn't enough of her left. His remaining team of nine were pulling back, dragging the injured with them hurriedly. Remmy waited, holding his rifle at the ready.

His tactical systems couldn't detect their enemies, and that told him all he needed to know about the data room ahead. "The Order Knights have had months to set up their defence here, and I bet they've been studying Haven Shore from here the whole time."

"Why didn't you tell us?" asked Sergeant Ouxo, one of the few Issyrians still serving in the lower ranks.

"You rushed in before you were ready, before you consulted me," Remmy said, his mood darkening further at the sight of Irinia. Her vacsuit sealed the stumps of her legs and right arm. The evidence of shrapnel piercing her forehead through her vacsuit was gone, except for the broken slats of her armour overlay. The suit had resealed overtop to help stop the bleeding as she sunk into stasis. Even if they could repair her brain, who knew how much of her personality would be intact? Judging from the emergency medical readout on his head's up display, he guessed she'd have nothing but scraps of memory and her former self left when they finished rebuilding her mind. Another soldier who would have to start over.

"Stop criticizing and do something!" Cathy Weir, one of the more recently recruited regulars said to him.

"I'm stating facts," Remmy replied. "Get shield barriers up. That little trap they set is nothing compared to what'll happen when they attack."

"The last one didn't attack," replied Sergeant Ouxo. "He remained in place, defending the computer core."

"And we can't assume these Knights will behave the same way."

"Take command," Lieutenant Davi said over their communicators. "Remmy, just take command, you have the rank and experience as a Ranger."

"I protest! I've been on-" Sergeant Ouxo started.

"I'm taking command of this squad, as your superior officer instructed," Remmy stated. Being stern was easy for him while he was angry, but it made thinking clearly difficult. "Fortify this position with three layers of portable energy shielding, now," he ordered, tossing his own energy shield, a small disc the width of his palm and a centimetre thick, into the hallway. It activated with a hum and anchored itself to the floor, providing enough shielding for a few seconds of fire from one of the Order Knight's powerful rifles. "Let your personal shielding self-repair and regenerate."

The rest of the squad cooperated. As the shields fell into place, Remmy closed his eyes and tried to see the layout of the floor in his head. The mental image was easier to manipulate, to see from more than one angle at a time. It was easier for him to devise a strategy the well trained and well armed Order Knights wouldn't see coming.

"Status on the computer core shields?" he asked Lieutenant Davi, one of his closest friends.

"Regenerating, they're almost at eighty one percent," he replied. Other people would tell him to check his scanners himself, but Remmy was putting a plan together, something Davi had seen before. He flinched as the sound of high energy rounds striking the outer energy shields filled the hall with an electric crackle.

The Order Knights were testing them. "I've got a plan," he told his Lieutenant. "I'm going to need your team on the second level."

"We're ready," Lieutenant Davi said.

"All right, on my count, I want your team to blast a hole through the deck exactly at the coordinates I'm marking. Three seconds later I need them to drop all their EMP grenades and retreat. It's got to be timed right."

"It'll get done," Lieutenant Davi said. "You do know that the Knight's armour will protect them and their gear from the blast, right?"

"I know," Remmy said. Another burst of weapons' fire cut through the outer energy shielding in the hall. There were only two more portable energy shields between them and the devastating energy weapons carried by the Order Knights. "All right," he said, addressing what remained of his squad. "You four, run down this hall, shoot through this privacy wall, and come up here. When you see the Order Knights, throw a pair of frag grenades each then get low. I'll lead my team in the other direction and we'll do the same from a point on a thirty-three degree angle so we don't bomb each other." He highlighted the tactical map with all of his instructions, and the squad watched as he directed them to each take a position where they would be able to hit the Order Knights with twenty grenades at the same time.

"Their energy shields will absorb most of that, and it won't do enough damage to the computer core shielding to make a difference," countered Sergeant Ouxo.

"Don't worry, that's taken care of," he replied as the second energy shield went down. The Knights would take the last one down even faster.

"After the grenades go off," Remmy said hurriedly. "We'll rush them, burn them down with a clip of anti-framework rounds." He waited three seconds, and got nothing but silence from his squad. "Your response is: 'yes, Sir!'"

"Yes, Sir!" the squad replied.

"Better. We go on three," Remmy said. "One, two, three!"

He ran to his right, leading the charge down a corridor towards a thin privacy wall that flew apart like tissue paper as he fired at it. The other four were keeping good pace. He opened a channel to Lieutenant Davi directly. "All right, your count: three, two, one."

As he said 'one' the structure shuddered and he waited as Davi counted down to his squad dropping their EMP grenades through the holes they made in the ceiling above the computer core at the centre of the level they were on. After three seconds they blasted the Order Knights from behind. By the time Remmy was in position, one had turned around completely, the other was looking up. "Grenades!" he shouted as he launched a pair with his rifle.

For thunderous seconds, the central chamber of the garrison was a no-man's-land, fragmentation grenades ripping anything that wasn't behind an energy shield to shreds.

"Go! Go! Go! Burn them down!" Remmy shouted as soon as the twenty grenades dropped on the Order Knight's position had detonated. His sensors saw the raw, broken flesh of the nearest Order Knight before he did. Everything he saw was enhanced by his head's up display as it helped him navigate through the smoke and debris to the enemy. He started firing as soon as he came around a support beam. The explosive rounds carrying an intense electromagnetic pulse ripped into the torn mess that was left of the Order Knight as it struggled to regenerate.

"Coming down!" Lieutenant Davi announced, marking his team's entry point through the holes in the ceiling on the tactical map.

They came down firing, and the Order Knights, who were regenerating, regardless of their severely damaged state, were torn to shreds by the firepower of both squads. Remmy watched his tactical screen as the life signs of the Order Knights finally faded.

"Remmy! The computer core!" Lieutenant Davi said.

Remmy turned and leapt towards the computer core standing in the centre of the room as the shield surrounding it started to re-energize. His personal shield generator popped and sparked as it clashed with what was left of the energy field around the computer core's main terminal. He pulled a line from his command and control unit and connected to the main jack. "God dammit!" he shouted as his comm reported that all the data had been erased many, many times over. "We've got a like-new, high powered computer core. Unfortunately, there's no trace of data on this thing. Even the lights and shield systems are mechanical, there's not so much as an operating system."

"What?" Lieutenant Davi asked. "When did they get time?"

"I'd tell you, only there's no deletion time stamp," Remmy replied. He ran the Haven Shore command flag program, officially taking possession of

50

the five level garrison lander and disconnected from the system. "There, Ayan wanted to capture another lander, we got her one. It's devoid of intelligence, but we can use it as a home for whoever wants to settle an island within spitting distance of Port Rush." The deal with the Carthans Ayan made after the Battle of Port Rush was simple: Ayan's forces could plant a flag on any Order of Eden bases after they were defeated, and Haven Shore would then own that outpost, the land for three hundred kilometres in a radius and everything on it. Remmy read the fine print, and understood why Ayan made the deal. The four bunkers they knew of when she signed on the dotted line were all in key positions around the planet, and they were all serviceable after they were taken. Rangers used three as training bases and the fourth as a permanent outpost. They'd found another after taking the fourth bunker, and that became a ranger outpost as well. The bunkers came with supplies, heavy weaponry, tools, and machines to assist in making each bunker a larger, permanent military base with outbuildings, and fixtures that made the stations even more valuable. What really impressed Remmy was Ayan's awareness that the Carthans couldn't afford to take the bunkers themselves, or patrol the territories after the Order of Eden forces were defeated. The language of the contract also indicated that Ayan didn't much care about bonuses past the claims she would be allowed to make, even though the Carthans offered. What she seemed interested in was accumulating assets and impressing the British Alliance. The bunker Remmy had just finished claiming with the Haven Shore Regulars was the sixth and final bunker as far as they knew. The rangers were still searching, but he doubted they'd find one. Taking the sixth bunker made Haven Shore, under Ayan's name, the largest owner of the subterranean five level military installations, with the Carthans behind with two, and an independent crime lord owning one.

Remmy made sure his anti-artificial intelligence and antivirus software was active as Crewcast took control of the main computer and closed the connection terminal. He found the switches controlling the energy shield and deactivated it. "Nice fusion reactor chain in this thing though, I'll say that much. This thing can keep its lights on for five or six hundred years."

"Here," Lieutenant Davi said as he handed him one of the Order Knight's rifles. "A souvenir."

Remmy's head's up display told him the weapon weighed fourteen kilos, heavy enough for the synthetic muscles of his suit to engage in his arms, torso, shoulders, and legs so he could hold it properly. "Yeah, I'll use it to power a house on the cliff side, or a small ship. This thing's got a miniature fusion chamber with enough fuel to run for eight years."

"Don't de-weaponize it too soon. I'm going to want you along for every op after this."

"This is the last garrison," Remmy said. "It's Ranger security and logistics for me after this."

"Not forever. We'll be taking the fight to them before long."

"Oh, great," Remmy said, rolling his eyes. "More time away from the sandy beaches of Haven Shore, I can't wait."

"Seriously," Lieutenant Davi said. "These last few missions, your tactics have been spot on. I'm impressed."

Compliments from Davi were rare, especially for Remmy. "Thanks. You should say something to Liam Grady though. It never occurred to me to treat tactical situations like a three dimensional puzzle until I started meditating with his group. Not having challenges like this is going to make peace time mind-meltingly boring." He checked Crewcast for any messages that may have accumulated while he was busy and cocked his head. "Nevermind telling Liam anything,"

"Why? What's up?" Davi asked.

"He just dumped a pile of emotional baggage on Ayan and checked out."

"What? Checked out?"

"Yup, told her 'hey, sorry for being a creepy old letch, shoulda been there for ya, guess it's time to leave, thanks for the memories.'"

"Well, at least we've got good news for her," Davi said. "You send the message to Ranger Command, we'll start processing the site."

Chapter 9
Dinner

The dense jungle reminded Alice of that first day of training. They didn't tell the ranger applicants much about the service, only to show up as the day began on Tamber. They were transported to a small, featureless peninsula where shuttles from the Sunspire, Triton, and Haven Shore were already present. There were some signs of construction, but no indication that any major undertaking was underway.

Orientation took place on the edge of a large, open field. There were over three hundred ranger trainees on her first morning. Hover trucks and shuttles dropped them off an hour before Commander Carl Anderson, or Doctor Anderson as some people from the First Light and Triton still called him, addressed them all. He was all smiles, didn't say much that Alice would remember through the rest of her training, and he kept his welcome short.

"Here's where we start," he said at the end of his speech. Everyone's vacsuits were minimized in size so the women wore one-piece exercise suits, and the men were reduced to shorts. All their vacsuit functions were deactivated, including any communications or computing devices, physical protection, assistance, or other tools. "Rangers can survive anywhere they can find air and water. They can get where they're going on their own two feet, and this week you're going to prove it to yourselves." There were murmurs and complaints all around Alice, and she hoped no one would point out that she was an enhanced framework.

They didn't have time before the next part of their challenge appeared in the field below. A cloaking shield dissipated to reveal an obstacle course that even Alice found daunting. There were wall climbs, monkey bars over pits, rappelling walls, reverse thirty degree scaling walls, a crawling tube maze with drop chutes and at least half an hour worth of other hellish challenges. Everything was surrounded by, or built over mud that looked cold, even from a distance.

"We'll prove this can be done without a vacsuit right now," Commander Anderson said, pointing to a square metal hut by the starting line. To Alice's amazement, Oz, Minh-Chu, Ayan along with a few other commanders stepped out onto the starting line. Before Alice could come to believe what she was seeing, the group of seven ran for the course. They tackled it as a team, helping each other when they had to. Ayan was only a few centimetres taller than Alice, so that was who she watched. She needed help with a couple of obstacles that were more easily conquered by the taller members of the course challengers, but got ahead of people in the tube maze, was the first to the bottom on the descending wall, and helped guide lines on the repelling challenge. Ayan was in better shape than Alice expected, but she surprised everyone when she missed a step on the balance beam and fell into an electrically charged net.

The periodic shocks were enough to inflict incredible discomfort, something Alice would discover for herself later, but the pulses were not so intense that they immobilized people completely. Minh-Chu waited for Ayan at the other side, and cheered her on as she got on all fours and climbed while getting jolted. Commander Worsch, from the Sunspire, almost fell on top of Ayan as he lost his balance on the beam. He was almost twice Ayan's size, but was equally affected by the shocks. It took them several minutes to climb the net and continue the course.

At the end, all the senior officers who participated finished, and stood in front of the trainees exhausted but all smiles. Ayan seemed especially pleased with herself.

"Now it's your turn," Commander Anderson said. "Complete this and you'll continue on to the next phase of training. Good luck."

Alice breezed through most of the physical ranger training, and enjoyed the team building more than anything, even though she soon discovered she had a lot to learn. It was the intelligence assessment, tactical study, and problem solving part of the training that really challenged her. Alice could get through it, but the real problem was sitting still for hours in the middle of her day while she interacted with all the mental training material. Whereas many recruits wanted to tap out and walk off during physical challenges, she found herself gripped by the temptation to wash out in the midst of processing intelligence data. She knew she could always return to the Warlord, and help finish work on the ship, but it was a fleeting urge.

Passing the intelligence and problem solving portions of her training was a point of pride. It also prepared her for the real world, giving her the tools

54

to assess a situation before she rushed in, and the patience to review intelligence data so she knew what was going on.

As she moved between giant trees and jungle foliage, Alice was grateful for the miserable week of jungle training all rangers had to undergo. Even with the help of her mapping systems and constant feedback on where she ought to be going, Alice was constantly on the verge of becoming lost. It was situations like that that brought her physical and mental training together.

A fierce roar called her attention from her map to her immediate surroundings. She looked up in time to see a jungle cat lunging down from above. Its head was as wide as her shoulders and it was furious, batting her into a thick bramble tangle.

Her vacsuit protected her. Alice was more startled than injured. She drew her sidearm and struggled to turn towards her attacker. The thick undergrowth she was tangled with had her partially restrained. All the strength augmentation in the universe wouldn't help her if she was off balance. As she struggled to reorient herself, the big cat clawed her out of her bondage, flinging her into the middle of the small clearing.

Her sidearm was left behind, and she couldn't help but be momentarily stunned as the cat leapt atop her, pinning her with a giant paw. Its massive jaws descended and it savagely tried to bite her head off, a pursuit that failed thanks to her light armour, but it was terrifying nonetheless. It took several seconds of gnawing for her to remember that she had a stun field that was made for crowd suppression and self defence. With a thought, she activated it, and the massive jungle cat twitched, grunted, then fell limp atop her.

It took several moments for her to work her way free from beneath the beast while taking care not to injure it. "Okay, that stays out of the report," she muttered as she found her sidearm and shoved it into her holster.

Small mewling sounds caught her attention, and she quickly discovered what the cat was defending, or trying to feed. A quick look around revealed that the foliage was flattened mostly around the hollow trunk of an old fallen tree. Claw marks on the nearest standing trunks indicated that she was looking at a type of cat that typically moved up into the lower branches and waited for prey to pass underneath. Her display listed several instances of pickers getting jumped by the cats, each saved by their vacsuit. Alice scanned her attacker and nodded to herself. "You'll be up and about in about nine minutes."

Her map told her she had to head past the fallen log, and she couldn't help but stop and peek inside before moving on. Three kittens about Alice's size with similar grey and black fur paid her little attention, but the fourth seemed intrigued. It sat up on its hind-paws and looked directly at her, its nose sniffing the air between them. Alice suppressed the urge to reach out and pet the fur ball. "This isn't the kind of exploration I expected when I joined the Rangers."

The kitten looked towards its mother and bounced past Alice. The big matron cat huffed a little as her offspring nudged its way towards her underside. Alice took it as a sign that her command and control system might have the estimate on how long the cat would take to get back on her feet wrong. "Time to move on," Alice said to herself, pressing deeper into the jungle.

CHAPTER 10
PREDATORS

The Lemta-So System had been a hub of trade and passenger transportation for so long that Minh-Chu couldn't get through the history document proffered by the major ports. As he sat quietly waiting with Samurai Wing in a man-made debris belt, he couldn't help but take another look at the document as yet another version downloaded.

For every colony and station, there was a founder and a flag. There seemed to be an unannounced competition between every settlement to present their stories in the most dramatic fashion possible. Every time he scanned areas that were settled, the communications systems in that area spammed him with the Lemta-So history documents along with the normal collection of advertisements. He assumed they'd be returning to the system, so he decided the historical documents would be good for the trip back to Rega-Gain. As for the advertisements, he kept the ones that were flagged by other users for being funny. It was a habit he'd picked up from Ashley.

The list of privately owned ports and space stations was overwhelming. He checked on the Warlord using long-range scanners. The ship was still holding in an outer orbit around one of the older, larger stations in the system over a million kilometres away. To any casual observer, it looked like the crew was holding in a pattern, getting the ship ready for docking.

All seven Samurai Squadron pilots were in on the operation. Four Uriel fighters and three Ramiel craft drifted in sync with the debris belt. It wasn't happenstance that there was a junk belt between Orrot and Mormont, two of the major settled worlds in the Lemta-So System. It was one of many used to enforce a reasonable interplanetary speed on craft travelling within its boundaries. The Ceri Belt was not heavily policed, and Minh-Chu doubted his group would be bothered by the laughable customs patrol; Samurai Squadron was too heavily armed for any of them to risk a challenge.

"Just wondering, why this ship? Just a cursory scan of the area is revealing a target-rich environment, and most of these vessels aren't disguising their affiliations," asked Singe, one of the newest additions to Samurai Squadron. She was a fighter pilot for the British Alliance who retired a month before after twenty years of service. To Minh-Chu's astonishment, she was on his doorstep a week later, offering her services to his fighter wing. Her service record rendered him speechless; she had already served as a wing commander for six years in the British Alliance.

"It was the captain's choice," Minh-Chu replied. She was right, there were half a dozen ships contracted by Regent Galactic or Order of Eden, and many other ships heading towards their territories. The shipping business was booming, and Lemta-So was a major collection point for manufacturers and raw material providers to gather and sell their wares. All those producers wanted to remain neutral, as it wasn't unusual for such companies to try to sell to both sides at the beginning of a war.

Minh-Chu didn't feel comfortable withholding all the details about their target from his second in command. "We got some good inside information on our target though, and there are a few containers that read high on the biological chart, even through radiation and scan shielding."

"So, he's on a mission of liberation," Singe replied. "Or at least needs to find out what's in those containers to be sure they're not carrying unwilling passengers."

"Exactly," Minh-Chu said. "The crewman we pulled the info out of didn't have the details on those transportation cars. They're sealed to everyone but the commanding officers."

"Another sign that there are probably slaves within," Singe said. "I'm all for freeing folk, and I know half the Warlord's permanent crew are liberated people, but I'm wondering what keeps the captain's nose pointed to helping them."

Minh-Chu thought for a moment. It was something no one had asked him before. With all of Samurai Squadron listening in, he wanted to give the right answer for his friend and captain.

"Ronin?" probed Singe after waiting nearly a minute for a response. "Have I wandered into a dangerous topic?"

"No, there's just a lot of history," Minh-Chu replied. For the last two months, he'd worked with Jake on compiling the story of Vindyne, Freeground, Regent Galactic, the Order Of Eden, and that of all of his friends, starting with their departure from Freeground so they could hand the completed document over to the British Alliance. The walk down memory lane had been a long and revealing one. "If I were to explain why he's driven to free people in as few words as possible, I'd say it probably starts with the fact that Jake is, or at least was, property of Regent Galactic. He's been property of at least two corporations we know of, so if anyone knows what it's like to be in chains, it would be him."

"That makes sense," Singe replied. "Where would I find the long version of that story? It's not in the personnel files."

"It will be soon," Minh-Chu said. Jacob Valent's history would be one of the few personal stories that would become widely public in the next week. In order to assist in the British Alliance's defence of Jacob Valent against charges of attempted genocide filed with the Galactic Courts a year before by Regent Galactic and the Order of Eden, they would be releasing Jonas Valent's and Jacob Valance's entire history in every district the Galactic Courts claimed to have jurisdiction over. Almost all the survivors of the Holocaust Virus, over a quarter of a trillion humans, would have access to that information, starting with the core worlds and the Rega Gain System. The defence was part of the complicated deal Minh-Chu and Jake made with the British Alliance without consulting the people of Haven Shore. They were working to build something that could act separately. Whereas Haven Shore was a peaceful settlement under the concerted protection of the Carthans, British Alliance, and the Triton, the Warlord and Samurai Squadron would lead the charge in war. Taking the little cargo hauler called the Torano would be the first offensive, a test against easy prey.

"Oh, there's one more thing about this shipment that makes it pretty hard to pass up. Cash. One of the crewmen Stephanie met a month ago from the Star Shifter said that this was one of the transports moving money collected from Order of Eden pledges."

"If we take this haul in, I don't think people will continue to question our information-gathering campaign," Singe said. "But the shipwrights on the Warlord are going to be pissed."

"I know, but they're off on the next stop anyway," Minh-Chu replied. The Shipwrights were on loan from the British Alliance, and the Warlord was allowed to leave port with them aboard on the condition that they returned to Rega Gain on schedule and that they wouldn't initiate combat operations. "Captain Valent couldn't pass this up," Minh-Chu explained, "and I think he's been restless the last couple months, ever since he captured Captain Terka on Modun for our British friends."

"He captured someone?" Singe asked.

"Oh, yeah, I forgot you didn't know about that. A little side operation. We got word that the captain of the Resplendent was going to be visiting an old friend on Modun and Jake negotiated a bounty with the British Alliance. You remember when Stephanie was in command for three days?"

"That's when he snuck off and got 'im," Singe said. "As broody as the man is, he still impresses, I'll give him that."

"Just don't ask for details," Minh-Chu said, aware that the bounty brought back some old demons for his friend, the captain.

"Time for final prep. Verify your settings, sync your autopilots and control interfaces," Singe reminded the small fighter wing as Minh-Chu was just starting to think it was about time he did so. "Mission counter is under sixty seconds, we should start seeing fireworks soon."

"It's about time," Joyboy said as his ready indicator turned green in Minh-Chu's peripheral vision.

Minh-Chu watched the counter drop, second by second, as he verified that the fighter's control systems were synced up properly. They were finally using the augmented interface built into the Earth Defence Force designed fighters. They still had their hands on manual controls, but more than half of the fighters' responses were keyed by readings taken straight from the pilots' brain functions. Samurai Squadron was the first to fully utilize the deadly quick systems after their software was restored and locked, so it couldn't be hacked unless someone was sitting inside the cockpit.

The mission counter descended down to ten seconds, and Minh-Chu noticed that the Warlord's main engines still weren't powered up, and the Torano wasn't on scanners. "Everyone check your tactical," Minh-Chu said. "The Torano hasn't departed the station on time."

He deactivated the mission counter. It was up to them to watch for the emergence of the Torano or its escort. Minh-Chu performed a focused scan in the direction of the space station, so far away it couldn't be seen by the naked eye. The quality of his results was a reflection of a focused scan at long distance – they were incomplete and difficult to read.

"I've got it," Singe said. "Sent it to your screens."

The profile of the Torano appeared on Minh-Chu's tactical scanner, just on the other side of the sprawling Zalor drift station. A second later, the transponder information appeared with it. "They timed their departure with a solar radiation spike," Joyboy said. "This is one smart freighter captain."

"Watch for those modified shuttles," Minh-Chu said. "Spread out and close on the Torano, full burn. Singe, stay back far enough to cover us with Joyboy and Uppity."

"Aye, watching for the uglies."

"Torano, this is the Warlord," Minh-Chu overheard. Jake was handling the communications with the Torano himself. "I have your crewman, and will execute him as a Regent Galactic conspirator unless you surrender your ship and cargo. You have ten seconds to respond."

"Warlord, this is Torano Command," replied someone aboard the Torano. "My duty to the Regent Galactic Corporation supersedes my obligation to my daughter's idiot husband. You picked a lemon for a hostage, Captain, and I'll be on my way."

"Coming up on the station," Dent said from where he covered Minh-Chu's right side in a Ramiel Fighter.

Zalor station seemed endless, stretching off into the distance in a seemingly haphazard shape. Large panels collecting light and accumulating energy from gravity reached out from a jagged centre that housed hundreds of docking bays, thousands of mooring points, and thousands of interior compartments. The magnetic field surrounding the station forced Minh-Chu's shields to auto-adjust. "Wait, go around," he said as he realized what the Turano was doing by leading them through the field.

The enemy ship's dorsal and rear shell cannons fired, blasting several of the station's power collection panels into thousands of tiny pieces. Suddenly, the lead ships in Minh-Chu's wing were flying through a field of hardened debris. His ship registered several impacts but didn't take any serious damage.

"Cockpit strike!" Dent announced. "I have a control malfunction, trying to recalibrate."

Minh-Chu checked Dent's condition and nodded to himself. Several chunks of cockpit shielding broke free in the impact, but Dent's suit saved him. His Ramiel fighter had a severe vulnerability with its cockpit compromised. "I need you to drop back on this one, Dent."

"Ronin, I just got my controls recalibrated, I'm still in this," Dent replied.

"We don't fly around with busted cockpit armour unless we have to. Head for cover," Minh-Chu replied.

"Aye, sorry," Dent replied. His fighter broke off and his position was taken by Tempest.

"I've got two uglies on my scanners," Minh-Chu said as they appeared on his tactical display. An instant later, his system reported that all his pilots looked at the new enemies and understood what they were thanks to the mental tracking systems built into their fighters. "You're headed straight for them, Dent."

"I know, evading," he replied.

Beams of orange-yellow light erupted from the enemy fighters as he rotated his ship so his damaged cockpit was facing away from the enemy. The shuttles' destructive beams swept over the surface of the much smaller Ramiel fighter, reducing Dent's shields to twelve percent and ripping through one of his engine pods before he could find cover behind one of the station's docking terminals. "Holy hell, that is some serious firepower," Dent said, chuckling nervously. "Okay, one engine pod down, some other minor damage, but I'm okay. My scanners got a snapshot of their systems – looks like a small antimatter reactor powers each ship. Wish I could help out more, but I'll be over here licking my wounds."

"Nice work, Dent. All fighters, direct main power to shields and switch to explosive rounds," Minh-Chu ordered. The uglies, twelve-man transit shuttles with shield plating and several particle beams, were on course to cover the Turano's rear. Rods began extending out from the sides of the ugly shuttles, and it only took a moment for Minh-Chu to realize what they were. "They're getting ready to put up some serious shielding, I'm opening fire."

"Ronin, intelligence suggests we won't have more players on the field, and the station is only sending us the standard warning," Singe said. "Permission to move in and engage?"

Minh-Chu and his two accompanying wingmen passed behind a large segment of the station and he held his answer as he listened to the communicator. "Warlord to Turano," Jake addressed. "You tested me." The channel closed. The Warlord was moving on to the next phase of their plan; Minh-Chu and the Samurai wing had to hurry.

"Come in on their starboard side," Minh-Chu said as he reversed thrust. Tempest and Quack, to his left and right, did the same, and they held position behind one of the station's main docking segments. "We need you to distract them so they don't have us dead-to-rights as soon as we break cover."

"Aye, on it," Singe said.

A small surge of atmosphere burst from one of the Warlord's fore airlocks, and Minh-Chu's sensors marked a new rescue target on screen.

"Did the Warlord just airlock someone?" asked Joyboy.

"He's alive, in an emergency evac bag," Singe said. Minh-Chu was glad she was explaining the situation, because he was still staring at his tactical readouts in disbelief. "Looks like our captain chose a wise compromise – he didn't kill his hostage, but he's given our target something new to worry about – a son-in-law adrift in space."

The Warlord's engines flared as it changed course, moving away from the jettisoned hostage at speed and towards the Torano. "Samurai Squadron," Captain Valent addressed. "Slag those shuttles." The Warlord cloaked and completely disappeared from scanners.

Chapter 11
Dirty Tricks

It was the first time anyone on the Council had to take a recess so they could get themselves together. The mess Liam left behind politically and emotionally frustrated Ayan more than she would have liked to admit. In the wake of their tame break up months before, it was difficult to stay positive, and she caught herself looking at the negative side of things, and fighting a situation instead of thinking her way through it. Her failure to make her relationship with Liam Grady work had left a lingering anger, and she wasn't herself. Ayan buried herself in work, and pushed people away until, one day, she broke down and retreated to the Triton. Her old friend, Commander Terry Ozark McPatrick, or Oz for short, was the one who pointed out that Lacey was already in place as her immediate subordinate, but Ayan largely ignored her until then.

Without a whiff of ego or bitterness at being disregarded, Lacey stepped in thanks to Oz's re-invitation, and became Ayan's true right hand in all things. After a few weeks, the two women spent most days together from breakfast to the late evening. The negativity that plagued Ayan abated with the frustration she felt at drifting apart from Liam. She once again strove to accept what she couldn't change and concentrated on the good she could do every minute of every day.

In the months since their real collaboration started, Ayan maintained her position on the Council, took a commanding spot with the new Rangers, and she was constantly grateful to have Lacey at her side. She expressed how thankful she was often, and Lacey brushed it off. She was where she wanted to be, never bored, and even on the worst days she admired Ayan's coping abilities.

That was why it was difficult for Lacey to watch the scene Liam Grady, not a habitual grandstander, put on for the Council and anyone who had access to the recordings of the proceedings in the chamber, which was

64

everyone. Lacey watched as Ayan paced the small open space between padded seats against the walls in a small waiting room adjacent to the Council chambers. "There are so many things I could have said, but I settled on 'goodbye.'" Ayan shrugged helplessly.

"It seems like he was trying to publicly take the blame for what happened between you two, to take it off your shoulders. I know this isn't what you want to hear, but I agree with most of what he said. You just lost two of your best friends, and after being around you for this long, I know you need affection in your life. It makes sense that you'd turn to someone you trust and admire for that. He should have held you at arms' length, no matter how 'magnificent' you are," she couldn't help but exaggerate 'magnificent' it was such an over-appreciative word, even if Lacey agreed with the praise. "Even still, that's all in the past. I know you two said everything you needed to when you finally broke things off. I don't think he deserved anything more than 'goodbye' from you."

"Maybe not." Ayan wiped her eyes with a tissue in reflex, but there were no tears left to mop up. She felt weary and irritated, but her sadness had gone before long. "I don't have time to deal with this. The Warlord is coming back, and they'll need qualified people. We have to take care of today's business and get a volunteer list ready."

"He has fifty British Alliance people aboard," Lacey said. "Won't he make a deal to keep them?"

"He's too proud to take crewmembers who aren't completely his. I'd fault him for it, but his thinking is tactically sound – you don't take crewmembers that could have standing orders from another government. Besides, they're not allowed to take part in combat action. We need to accept the Warlord and her crew - it's the only effective offensive ship we have right now besides the Clever Dream, and that's busy enough."

"So the Council is still putting a motion to dissolve our treaty with the Carthans on the table?" Lacey asked. "I think it's premature."

Ayan shook her head. "We have to, but I know it's not going to pass with Liam's bloody floor show today. I don't think he meant to make it look like I was the bad guy in our relationship, but by offering that drawn out apology in front of everyone, and his subordinate staring daggers, there's no way we will get consensus."

"Another reason why Haven Shore's military arm should have remained separate. It's not a civilian decision."

"I know," Ayan said. "I still regret agreeing to bring military decisions to the Council; Victor and I were both wrong, but I've seen it work on Freeground for decades. The Admiralty rarely had to consult Parliament, but they made sure they were part of most decisions when they affected the overall politics of the station. We thought it would work better with a miniature government model here."

"Gion's military was bound by our peacekeeping system," Lacey said. "It worked really well during peace time, but we were dependent on the British Alliance whenever war broke out."

"And that's something I want to get out of as soon as possible," Ayan replied. "We have to be self-sufficient or our settlement will never be viable."

A knock sounded from the door and it slid open a moment later, admitting Victor Davis, who wore a face-splitting grin. "Looks like the Rangers have proven themselves, and we can relax our military force on the ground and start re-tasking our teams."

"Why? What's happened?" Ayan asked, realizing at the same time that it could only mean one thing.

"Remmy took command of our security forces for the Rangers and turned the fight for the last Order of Eden garrison on Tamber. He turned the mission around and just cleared it a few minutes ago. He planted your command flag before the Carthans got a chance to land a shuttle."

Ayan was so excited that she hugged him. He was a little surprised but received her warmly, like a big brother. "Oh that's good timing, I needed some good news. I'll congratulate the team tomorrow."

"I don't want to rain on your parade, but I don't think this will get us consensus in the next room," Victor said.

"I know, I don't think anything will change that," Ayan replied, "but I think the situation with the Council will get much worse before it gets better. I'm going to add something to our agenda today that ought to ruffle some feathers."

"Should I change into full armour?" Victor asked.

"Might not be a bad idea," Ayan said, walking past him. Adding something to the agenda wasn't a new idea, it was something she had been considering for weeks and it had to happen eventually, but some members may believe it was too early. It would be the only way for the government to continue to function with the new rift opening across the table. She felt better about what had to happen during session, but neither her new idea, nor even the news of the Order of Eden garrison, lessened her growing distaste for Council business.

Victor and Lacey followed her into the chamber, where Ayan sat down at her end of the table. Tyra seemed to make a point of ignoring her from the other end. "If we're all ready, I'd like to call this session of the Haven

66

Shore Council to order," Mischa said. Her assistant, a tall, dark featured man named Isaac Doke sat behind her. He rarely attended meetings, and nodded amiably when Ayan noticed he was there and caught his eye. "The first matter for consideration is the offer of citizenship to the crewmembers of the ship formerly known as the Samson," Mischa announced. The Council was too small and reliant on consensus to depend on a solitary chairperson, so the duty rotated from one issue to the next. It was Mischa's turn, and even though she had broken down much like Ayan less than an hour before, she executed it well. "I open the floor to final arguments." She looked to her right at Tyra, who shook her head.

Next in line was the Carthan Observer, Cory Greene. He stood and cleared his throat. "I don't have a vote on this council, but I must implore the membership not to agree to offer citizenship to these hardened criminals. I am aware of facts in this issue that are not available to the general public, and can say, with greater knowledge, that these people don't belong in the society you're trying to build here. For this reason, the Carthan Government will cancel its contracts with Haven Shore organizations and no longer protect your territories or citizens if you grant these dangerous criminals citizenship."

Ayan sighed by reflex at his speech and almost regretted irritating the stuck up politician. Almost. The Carthans were only able to remain in the Rega Gain System because they had massive assistance from the British Alliance. They had taken so many casualties, lost so many ships and parts of their critical infrastructure, that there was no way they could police, protect, or cultivate resources in the system without help. The British Alliance could claim the system without contest any time they liked, and many people were sure that it would happen any time, but the truth of the matter was, the British Alliance didn't want to be responsible for whatever happened to the Rega Gain System if their government decided to once again declare war. The British Alliance would assist and protect it for as long as it was strategically advantageous, but they wouldn't put themselves in a position where history could remember them as being responsible if the worst were to happen to Rega Gain and they had to abandon the area.

The Carthan representative sat down and Mischa looked to Iloona Murlen, who stood. "I would only like to say that, as heroes in the Battle of Port Rush, the original crewmembers of the Samson should be welcome as citizens and celebrated for their bravery. They are more loyal and dedicated than some people who sit at this table. They need our help, and we need them."

It was Victor Davis' turn to speak next, and he didn't pass, but stood with a serious demeanour that surpassed what Ayan had seen before. "Internal security, which is my mandate here, is worthless without an effective defensive force. The Samson crew is not only more experienced than most, but many of them have trained our best people, and they now crew one of the most effective offensive ships in the solar system."

"That barely corvette-class thing?" spouted the Carthan Observer.

"You've already filled the room with hot air once," Victor snapped back.

"Mister Green, Mister Davis," was all Mischa had to say to put an end to the exchange.

"I apologize," Victor Davis said. "The Haven Shore Rangers have finished wiping out the last of the Order Of Eden troops on Tamber, the last in the solar system if my intelligence is right. That means we have a surplus of regulars and the opportunity to help the Samson crew as they man the Warlord. They put their ship and their own lives at risk to turn the tide in our darkest hour." He took a breath and looked at his comm unit. "I'll wrap this up, I wrote something to finish with. We need them as a morale booster to our soldiers, we need them as a component in our defense strategy, we need them as good citizens, and we need them as providers. Though their colours may be dark, they may light the way for us in hard times to come."

It was Ayan's turn, and the instant Mischa looked at her, all the ideas she'd had built up for that moment seemed to vacate her mind. Without a thought in her head, except for the notion of *'bloody hell, someone replaced my brain with a soggy sponge!'* she stood. Everyone looked on, but Tyra, at the other end of the table, stared. A poke at her elbow drew her attention to Lacey, who sat behind her. Her Second looked at the comm unit on Ayan's left arm meaningfully.

Ayan glanced at the two dimensional screen and saw a simple message from Lacey that read:

THEY WILL KEEP US TOGETHER AND LEAD THE WAY.

It was the summary of her opinion of the situation, presented as only Lacey could. She had obviously been listening to her over the last few months. Ayan took a deep breath and addressed the Council. "The Triton is less and less a part of Haven Shore. Many of the new recruits there, over sixty percent in fact, have not applied for Haven Shore citizenship in a time where it is one of the only safe planet-side ports in the system."

"We're here to talk about the Samson crew," reminded Tyra.

"Representative Ayan has the floor," Mischa said.

"Thank you," Ayan said, making a conscious effort to press her irritation at Tyra to the side. "The new crewmembers aboard the Triton have watched the Warlord receive assistance from the British Alliance, watched the damage from an historic battle repaired, and the former crew of the Samson turn their old ship into a weapon worthy of note on any battlefield. Tomorrow they will return, and I am willing to stake my reputation and my post that they will have a train of supplies and equipment in tow that they have stolen from the enemy."

"Stake your post?" repeated the Carthan Observer. "You'll step down if your prediction is wrong?"

Ayan interrupted Mischa as she was about to tell Cory Greene to remain silent. "I will step down if they don't return with considerable gains from piracy or privateering. That brings me to my next point. If they do so well on their own, and can trust the Triton to continue to provide them with docking facilities, what do they need us for? As the military liaison for this body, and the closest thing to Defense Minister in our small government, I cannot accept the possibility that they will turn away from us, because if they do, Haven Shore will lose all credibility with the military community gathering in the Rega Gain System, and we'll become known as a foolish little peace-loving settlement with no grasp on the situation past our borders. Our citizenship may grow, but the people who are looking to win this war, the just war of our age, will leave en-masse if we don't show that we are invested in it by openly accepting our best fighters: Shamus Frost, Stephanie Vega, Billy Finn, Agameg Price, Ashley Lamport, and Captain Jacob Valent. The benefits we stand to lose by violating our contract with the Carthan Government are insignificant compared to the moral and strategic victories we stand to win by embracing people who were key to our survival before the Carthans even knew who we were."

"We will strip you of your sovereignty and Haven Shore will be nothing but a dream," Cory Greene, the Carthan Observer said. "We'll take the island back, and use the city for our own purposes."

"Come and try it!" Ayan said, an untapped reservoir of anger bursting open. The filter of reason between her thoughts and her speech broke down. "The Warlord will be the least of your worries when the Triton and everyone who loves Haven Shore takes up defensive positions while the Warlord and the Clever Dream reduce what's left of your pathetic military forces to cinders from the shadows. I would love to see the look on your face when I walk onto the bridge of your crippled command carrier and demand that your fleet surrenders to Triton Fleet. We could use a few of your destroyers on our side. "

"The British Allia-" the Carthan Observer started.

"The British Alliance," interrupted the British Alliance Observer, Sunny Zinnes, "will get out of their way and make an alliance with whoever survives when the smoke clears. We're not here to be moderators in a minor war that won't turn the tide in our larger engagements. Besides, we've already run this scenario in simulation several times. We estimate that the Carthan leadership will be killed within six hours and Haven Shore would survive with minimal damage. Your government somehow believes that Haven Shore, the crew of the Warlord, and the Triton are normal soldiers, when, in fact, they're more like guerrilla fighters, or extremely well armed, experienced terrorists. To enter into combat against people like the esteemed Military Liaison, the Triton, and the well-trained Rangers is a more frightening proposition than you seem to realize. They have created an elitist culture in their military that pushes everyone who can stand it to constantly improve, while you employ prisoner-slaves that are programmed to be loyal. They will be useless to you when throats are slit in the dead of night, sabotage ruins the few installations you control, then strike and fade tactics pick your ships apart. You are not ready. It is the opinion of this diplomat and former soldier that the Carthans should abide by the ruling of this council and hope that you become a part of their strategy for growth. We know your government isn't sending help, and they're willing to write you off if this becomes too complicated."

Ayan nodded at Sunny, and though she didn't like where he took the discussion, he gave her time to reign in her temper. She struggled to find a more positive tact. "I love Haven Shore. I look at what we've built here and feel nothing but pride and hope for the future. I also fear against what will happen if we're caught without our best people at our side. If the Council does not accept the crew of the Samson, regardless of the consequences with the Carthan Government, then Haven Shore begins a walk down a darkened path. I will stay for as long as I can to try to correct it, but it may already be too late." Ayan sat down feeling as though she hadn't said enough, but couldn't find anything to add.

The next and last to speak was the People's Representative for Haven Shore North, Mischa Konev. She rose tentatively and looked at Ayan. "I will be voting to accept the crew from the Samson, and hoping for consensus since this will be the last time we consider this issue for some time if we don't come to an agreement. Before we vote, I'd like to elaborate on something Ayan mentioned. I remember the fear aboard the Triton as brave people fought for our lives when soldiers tried to take the ship and possibly exterminate or imprison us. I arrived here after the Clever Dream and the Samson led us to this safe haven. Ayan had already started talks with the Carthan people who were only just taking possession of the solar system at the time. The people of Haven Shore have forgotten to honour and celebrate the people responsible for getting us here. They could have made their lives simpler by leaving the civilians, us, behind. If we cannot come to consensus on offering citizenship to the crew of the Samson, then there are people on this council who have lost their way, and that leadership will push us in the wrong direction. I won't have it, and I'm warning you that there will be changes on this council if this vote does not pass. Significant changes. It's time we vote." She sat down and registered her vote on the table in front of her, which showed up as YES in green beneath the motion detailed in smaller letters that read; *Internal Security Minister Victor Davis proposes that Haven Shore invite the crew of the ship formerly known as the Samson who are listed as criminals with the Carthan Government, to become citizens of Haven Shore.*

"Threats, classy," muttered the People's Representative For Haven Shore South, Tyra Kim. She watched as everyone else, with the exception of the Observers from the Carthan Government and the British Alliance who didn't have a vote at that table, entered their votes.

Green coloured the room, the light emitting from near unanimous votes of yes, and Ayan only had to look at Tyra to know what she was about to do. She saw the woman's vote appear as NO in red letters on the table and she leaned forward, staring quietly at Mischa.

"A consensus has not been reached, so the motion fails," announced Mischa in sad tones.

Ayan's unwavering gaze caught Mischa's attention and she nodded at the woman. Mischa looked as though she didn't know what Ayan was trying to communicate for a moment, cocking her head a little. Her eyes widened when Ayan pointed down at the edge of the table in front of her with two fingers, then split them into a V.

"As my last act during this turn as Chairperson," Mischa started, turning red in her nervousness and clearing her throat. "I'm entering a proposition to expand the membership of the Haven Shore Council."

Ayan sat back in her chair, satisfied that the product of a discussion she had with Mischa weeks before were about to come to fruition. Liam was there at the time, as well as Lacey and the British Alliance representative. They all agreed that a consensus-based council would be a good start for a small government, but it would have to evolve eventually.

"In this proposition, I petition to add six more seats to decrease the ratio of homes to local Haven Shore representatives. I also provide for four seats reserved for our allies, and I propose we add and reopen the following positions: Defense Minister, Military Liaison, Minister of Development, Minister of Resources, and Council Chairperson. If this proposition passes this afternoon, the position of Military Liaison and Chief of Structural Development, currently held by Ayan, will be removed from this Council. The position of Internal Security Minister will be downloaded to regional representation, and Victor Davis will no longer have a position on this council. It is my hope that Haven Shore's citizens will be better represented and our Council Members will be able to attend to their duties with less stress. This will also provide for a great deal of growth, as we must look to a future when Haven Shore is larger, and very few homes are vacant. The proposal is thirty five hundred words exactly, and I suggest we recess for only one hour to review it, then vote."

Ayan tried not to grin at Mischa, who brilliantly added the touch of removing her and Victor from their seats in the motion. Victor Davis' fury at the motion and his removal helped bury Ayan's nearly uncontainable smile – he looked like he was about to fly into a rage.

"Agreed, one hour!" Tyra practically chirped.

"Seconded," Iloona said hesitantly.

Victor stormed from the room into an antechamber and Ayan followed close behind. She was hurrying so she wouldn't crack a great big smile in front of Tyra, and she wasn't sure she got through the door in time.

CHAPTER 12
BIRDS

The jungle ruled the terrain in the unexplored jungle beyond the charted perimeter. The sounds of birds and calls from other animals filled the air around Alice. There was no doubt; she was in the midst of wilderness unlike anything she'd ever seen. Birds with green, blue, and white feathers watched her from large branches as she passed only metres below. They were predator birds, with great talons and cool, assessing gazes.

The last time she saw so many birds in one place, she had woken early on New Year's Day. She strolled along the beach, avoiding people who were still asleep on the sand and saying hello to early risers like herself. Her walk came to an end when she ran into Minh-Chu, in front of the tent he shared with Ashley. He served Alice some of the blueberry-mint tea concoction he was drinking and commented on the birds lazily gliding overhead, saying, "Now those are pilots."

He'd never seen live birds before. It was Alice's third time. She and Minh didn't talk much, but marvelled at the grace of the feathered flyers overhead as they rode the air currents and pinwheeled around until Ashley woke up some time later.

Alice knew she should be getting close to the escaped androids; it was time to bring her thoughts back to the present. She pressed onward across the massive lower branches, the higher pitched chirps from smaller birds growing louder.

Her tactical scanner was trying to piece something together, a ruined structure that the trees had broken through. She stopped a moment and let the system finish shaping the map ahead. There were still intact towers reaching up into the trees; some were hollow while others had levels and rooms that looked like habitation areas. They were all attached to one main hub, a large dome made of older transparent metal.

It took her several minutes of looking to match what was in the scan results with something she could see. The structure was overgrown inside and out, popping transparent steel panels loose and twisting the structure in the grasp of vines and branches. "How did the androids get in through this mess?" she asked herself.

The tactical scanner couldn't find clear tracks – the jungle had already grown over any sign of their passage close to the main dome. There were enough places for her to squeeze into the structure, but with the tangle of vegetation inside the large building, she wanted to pick the best entry point. She mentally ordered the tactical scanner to do a broader search for androids. Within seconds, it highlighted a turret above her. "More climbing, fun, fun, fun."

"You don't want to go in there," Lewis' voice told her over her communicator.

"You mean I don't want to go in there alone?" Alice asked as she prepared a grappling line on her right wrist. The thin, strong tether line was made for use as a safety device on space walks, but the rangers found it did just as well for terrestrial adventures.

"I can't see inside that structure, but there are transmissions I can't decrypt weakly emanating from within," Lewis replied. "You should leave it alone."

Alice stopped everything she was doing and stared at the dark opening many metres above her. Normally, Lewis would suggest she wait for backup, but he'd never before suggested she stop altogether. "What do you think I'll find in there, Lewis?"

"I can't tell for certain."

"Guess," Alice replied. The channel between her and Lewis was still open, but he wasn't replying. "Is all this because of something you did?" Again, her question was answered with silence.

"I'm ordering you to reply immediately," Alice said.

"You are no longer my legal owner," Lewis said.

"All right, I'll invite Ayan to our little chat. Maybe I should have done that right at the beginning."

"The Ando models downloaded the antivirus I designed and they've been distressed ever since. One of them is broadcasting a weak signal, I can't decrypt his message."

"Is this the Holocaust Virus all over again? Is there anything in the antivirus that could make things worse?" Alice asked.

"Not for humans," Lewis replied.

"But there's a chance any bot that downloads your miracle cure can just go nuts and run for the jungle?"

"I was certain that the antivirus would remain in reserve, unable to overwrite directives and morality code when it existed in a computer's programming, but something in the Ando models…"

"Has proven you wrong? What? What did your software screw up with those androids? I'm going into this situation regardless of what you tell me. If you care about what happens to me, you'll tell me more so I have a better chance in there."

"I can't scan them from my location. If I were within a kilometre, it wouldn't be an issue, but I suspect the Ando models chose this location because of the structure and remote area."

"It's difficult to scan in this whole area," Alice agreed. "So they're probably hiding something. Can you at least give me a hint? Just give me your best guess at what they're hiding."

"I don't have enough information for that, I'm sorry. I've told you everything I know," Lewis said. "The androids seem content to remain inside this structure, much further in the jungle than any picker would go, and one of them seems to be calling other Ando models. I suggest you leave it alone and report that the Holocaust Virus has activated a defect in the Andos."

"I'm going in. If there's anything else you're holding back, this is your last chance to share," Alice said. She fired her line and it struck solid metal beneath the entrance above. A flock of black and green birds took wing, fleeing the opening.

"I have more questions than answers, Alice. There is something sinister in the signal – I am sure of that, at least. If I weren't docked in Haven Shore, expected to remain moored here until later, I would be there."

"And you'd slag this spot from high above, to hide whatever's happened here, I'm sure," Alice said.

"You know me too well," Lewis replied. "I won't be able to communicate clearly with you once you enter. If you insist on going in, I suggest you at least call for backup. Perhaps you should contact Doctor Carl Anderson, he would understand this."

"And I won't?" Alice asked as she tested her ascension line. "I'll just check it out and if I get in over my head, I'll consider getting other people involved." She activated the winch and was drawn up rapidly.

CHAPTER 13
AN UNEXPECTED MATCH

Singe and her two wingmen came around the last boom arm separating them from the escort shuttles and let out a barrage of missiles and smaller explosive projectiles. "Wait for those escort shuttles to return fire. We're still not in a good position to break cover," Minh-Chu told Tempest, who held her position behind cover nearby. He still had a hard time ignoring the red blip on his display that designated the position of the man Jacob Valent just jettisoned from his ship in a flimsy survival bag.

Searing beams surged out from the uglies at Singe and her wingmen. The power readings Minh-Chu saw were a little lower than before, though not by much, but it was enough for him to tenuously grasp at hope. "Now! Tear 'em up!" Minh-Chu said as he led the way, breaking cover and locking on to the nearest shuttle. He sent three electromagnetic pulse missiles towards the enemy ship and rolled, opening up with all four of his auto-cannons. Thousands of small hull-piercing projectiles streaked towards the shuttle in quick, sure bursts. He pulled his master trigger by reflex. The Uriel Fighter was actually automatically tracking his mental cues for weapon triggering through its brain scanning technology. Every single shot impacted on or pierced the shuttle's shields.

The nearest shuttle's beam weapons shut down and its energy shielding intensified as its partner's weaponry fired with renewed fury, surging beams of intense light, plasma, and cutting particles at several of Minh-Chu's allies. He took fire from three beams at once, all dead on the nose of his fighter. Minh-Chu stopped firing as he rotated his ship, spreading the damage across all his shield generators. The fore quadrant of his shield system reported that the half-second blast it sustained cost him sixty percent of his shield energy and almost overloaded the forward system. The other quadrants hadn't suffered as much damage. "All fighters, finish off Shuttle A," he said, designating the shuttle that was trying to move towards the

Torano, which had moved so far off that it was impossible to see with the naked eye. Even if both the escort shuttles were destroyed during this fight, they'd served their purpose: Samurai Squadron was so distracted that they couldn't do anything to stop the Torano's departure without exposing themselves to too much damage. Capturing the Torano was something the Warlord would have to do on its own.

All six fighters concentrated fire on the nearest ugly shuttle from all directions as they engaged in the unfettered acrobatics of evading fire from the shuttles' secondary weapons and the other escort ship. The target shuttle's energy shields failed, and after a few seconds, its hull was blasted open in several places, venting atmosphere.

The other escort shuttle, designated Shuttle B on Minh-Chu's tactical readout, used the exploding shuttle as a distraction, firing afterburners of some kind, accelerating after the Torano. "On him!" Minh-Chu said. "Watch for fire from our main objective, we weren't able to get information on any extra weaponry that hauler has."

"Aye," Singe reported in. "Judging from the surprise we've had from those shuttles, the Torano must be well armed."

Minh-Chu rotated his thruster pods and turned his throttle up to full. The rest of Samurai Squadron was with him, except for Dent who waited on the safe side of the station for the action to end.

The local navnet plotted a course for them through a holding pattern at the outer perimeter of the station, where hundreds of ships orbited in an orderly line. Jacob, Frost, and Stephanie had all told him to expect complete apathy from these outer stations most of the time. It wasn't in their best financial interests to get involved with firefights that didn't do much damage to their facilities, and they often picked the side of the ships that did less harm. In this case, the Torano's group had already damaged the station, so Minh-Chu and his fellow pilots were getting navigation assistance from the station. If they were fighting near Freeground, their security forces would be on them in seconds, and within minutes they'd be hauled out of their ships and arrested.

"This is Torano Command," Minh-Chu heard on the emergency band. "Calling all ships sympathetic to Regent Galactic and the Order of Eden! We are being pursued by Jacob Valent, a pirate wanted by the Galactic Courts. Any assistance will be rewarded handsomely."

"This is Jacob Valent," he replied on the same channel, without a breath's pause between the enemy captain and his own address. "I'm operating under British Alliance authority, and will capture or destroy any vessel that interferes with my lawful pursuit."

"Watch for any ship breaking into our area," Minh-Chu said. They had crossed into clearer space, well away from the station and closer to the outer trash belt. Once the Torano cleared that, they may be able to attempt faster-than-light travel, and the whole fight would end or change, depending on how dedicated Jake was.

The ugly escort shuttle broke cover as it sped towards the Torano, and Minh-Chu switched to electromagnetic pulse ammunition and opened fire on it with his guns, raking its shields. The remaining five fighters in his wing followed suit, and the shuttle's shields were down by half within seconds. It didn't fire back; it was most likely using all its available power to shore up its shielding, hoping to break away with the Torano and escape.

Minh-Chu could see flashes of light up ahead, where the firefight between the Warlord and the Torano raged on. His scanners told him that the Warlord's prey had dropped its sixteen hundred metre long cargo train. Minh-Chu decided to take a chance and activated one of two accumulator missiles. "All fighters, clear to one thousand kilometres," he ordered. "You have five seconds."

"Aye, getting to safe range," Singe replied. Minh-Chu's comrades decelerated to let the shuttle get ahead, and by the time his attack counter counted down from five to one, everyone was at a safe range. He fired several rapid release dumbfire missiles, projectile rockets with conventional explosives that were the length of his hand. The shuttle fired countermeasures in a wave of small fragments that set most of them off, and as soon as Minh-Chu manoeuvred around the particles left from the exploded missiles and chaff, he fired another round of twenty. The shuttle didn't release countermeasures; they were either out or reloading. "Custom ugly shuttle three-oh-five, please shut down your engines and surrender. This will be your only warning," Minh-Chu said, having second thoughts about launching a weapon that was beyond anything his other fighters had. The power reading on his accumulator missile was increasing exponentially, and it wouldn't be long before he would have no choice but to launch it.

At a glance, Minh-Chu could see several ships breaking away from the outer perimeter orbit of the station towards them. The Torano's captain had drawn some attention with his appeal.

A beam weapon lashed out at Minh-Chu's fighter, trying to carve a line across his cockpit with heat, light, and energized particles. His shields absorbed the hit, but were down to twenty-one percent from a full charge. Minh-Chu hit the trigger and released a missile that crossed the distance between him and the shuttle in less than three seconds. The resulting explosion registered as a hazard-level-event on their navigation and tactical screens, a reading that was made to warn even the sternest of ships away from something that could damage anything.

"Okay, so that works, holy crap…" Joyboy said in wonder.

By the time he finished talking, the light shields on Minh-Chu's suit and cockpit turned themselves back down, and what was left of the shuttle came into view. The engine compartment shielding was a blasted mess, wide open in many places where the heat of the explosion burned metal away. The rest of the ship was twisted and broken. The radiation levels were surprisingly low, but there was nothing but scrap left. "Singe, lead a defence on the cargo train. If anyone comes near it, turn them away."

"Aye," Singe replied. "But I think your demonstration was enough to frighten most people off, Ronin. The ships that were breaking orbit are heading back."

Minh-Chu confirmed what she was saying with a glance. "Good. Joyboy, you're with me. We're going to see if the Warlord needs our help."

"I'm getting nothing but squigglies and squeaks from their area – looks like the Torano is jamming sensors," Joyboy said as he fired his thrusters to keep up with Minh-Chu. "Why would they do that if they're in trouble?"

"They wouldn't," Minh-Chu said. "They would do that if they're using weaponry they don't want anyone to know they have. That may be why this mission has been full of surprises. This captain is good at keeping his tricks a secret. Stay alert, our scanning range is getting shorter as we get closer to the jammers."

"Aye," Joyboy replied.

A wall of flak appeared on sensors too close for them to evade or counter, and Minh-Chu's shields took the damage. He set them to recharge at the fastest available pace, tasking the miniature fusion reactors to their limit. He activated his last accumulator missile, starting its charge cycle, and ordered his fighter's power systems to sap the energy it was generating. His shields would be recharged in less than three seconds, but if he was hit too hard in the wrong place before he could deactivate the accumulator missile, he'd go off like a bomb.

"Okay, there's something serious going on over here," Joyboy said.

Minh-Chu caught sight of a flash in the distance and zoomed in. The lower-aft side of the Warlord had just taken damage from an explosion so hot that its plating still glowed white. That entire section of its launchers would be out of commission, reducing its firepower.

"All right, lock on to the Torano as best as you can," Minh-Chu said. "And fire everything in bursts. Strafe so we have a chance at giving them the impression that the whole wing is here."

"You got it, Ronin," Joyboy replied.

As Minh-Chu and Joyboy started their run, they watched the Warlord fighting to turn towards the Torano in an attempt to line up their main rail cannons at the front of the ship, but the Torano's pilot was too good to let it happen. The so-called hauler thrust out of the way, so she remained in the Warlord's side firing arc, where three gunnery turrets continued to hammer at the Torano. From what Minh-Chu could see, the Torano's shields were depleted, her emitters were damaged, and the hull was beginning to take direct hits.

Minh-Chu deactivated the accumulator missile charging in his missile rack as his shields recharged to ninety-seven percent and breathed a sigh of relief when the antimatter reaction stopped and the power levels stabilized. His fighter would continue to feed off the power in the death-dealing missile's capacitors until there was nothing left.

Minh-Chu could see the Warlord's shields were depleted on the port side. Beam weapons fired at the vulnerable sections of the Warlord's hull in bursts, trying to weaken and superheat sections of the ship until its integrity failed. The strain on the ergranian metal was intense, and the normally resilient material was stressed past its limit in more than one spot. Some of the metal had been rendered inert, its regenerative qualities beyond recovery. The beam weapons were sawing into the ship at those points whenever they could get a clean shot at them.

"Missiles, Ronin," Joyboy said. "We've got to hit the Torano's main thrusters from the other side with missiles."

"Absolutely," Minh-Chu said. "They're not falling for our distraction."

The pair of Uriel fighters taxed their thrusters to the limit, blasting around the engagement so they could fire on the Torano's main thrusters, a bank of pivoting barrier engines. Whoever was manning the weaponry on the enemy ship was no amateur. Two medium cannons fired rapidly, and they were both caught by several high-energy shots before they could evade. "Their sensors are jammed too, they're firing using visual only," Minh-Chu said. "Use your computer to help dodge."

"Already on it," Joyboy said as his fighter took several strikes on the starboard side, reducing his shielding to dangerous levels. He strafed erratically until the gunner on the Torano lost his bead, then Joyboy opened fire.

Minh-Chu followed suit and the pair of them rained dumbfire rockets down on the Torano, a few little spark-like pops bursting against the enemy ship as the first of their munitions struck. When the first strikes were joined by hundreds, the aft-port side of the vessel was shrouded in a firestorm. "Fire all missiles at the maximum rate, we're not capturing this thing," Minh-Chu said. The auto-loaders for his missile pods roared as he switched to rapid-fire. He watched his munitions counter from the corner of his eye, counting down from four thousand nine hundred and thirty, to two thousand and three in the space of seconds.

The Warlord's thrusters flared as it pushed away from the Torano. Using the hard-won space from the enemy ship, they launched their own barrage. Seven metre-wide mines burst from the bottom of the Warlord and broke apart when they were halfway to their target, splitting into over a hundred missiles loaded with high explosives. The Torano exploded a second later, and when the heat cleared, her starboard side was open to space in several places. The eighty metre long ship's lights were out, her power plant was exposed, her engines were extinguished, and her weapons were silenced.

Minh-Chu waited for their sensors to clear, and when they did, recognized a warning immediately: the antimatter reservoir aboard the Torano was still loaded with a dangerous amount of the material. "Distance!" Minh-Chu said. "Get away from the Torano!"

Joyboy was already accelerating away, as was the Warlord. They were over fifty thousand kilometres away and circling back towards the cargo train the Torano dropped when Minh-Chu finally felt they had enough distance. He pulled up his rear-view screen and zoomed in on the wrecked ship. A few escape pods were powering away from her port side. He silently wished he could help, and hoped they got enough space between them and the vessel before the antimatter containment failed.

"Maybe they'll make it," Joyboy said. "That thing could maintain containment for years if the reservoir's safety systems are okay."

Minh-Chu looked to the escape pods; they had made it a few thousand kilometres away from the Torano, and were gaining speed. With a flash, the Torano exploded, and when the light cleared, there was little left of the escape shuttles or the people inside.

"Take up positions around the cargo train," Minh-Chu said. "The Warlord will be vulnerable while they hitch up and get ready to power out of the system."

Chapter 14
Uncertain Turnabout

"You're right, this is genius," Victor Davis said as he finished reading Mischa Konev's proposal. "I'm out, you're out, but so is the whole idea of coming to consensus. Not only that, but it's still non-partisan and the Defence Minister, and Military Liaison positions aren't going to be elected positions the first time around. It's like this is built to sneak us into the back door."

"I'll still be Health Minister," Iloona said, stroking her bulging middle. "So I can propose that you both fill positions."

"The reformation of the government would take place after the referendum tomorrow," Ayan said. "This is fast, no one has time to think."

"No, Tyra doesn't have time to realize that her biggest enemies on the Council won't be out for long. All she'll have time to see is that we'll be removed from our posts," Victor said. "Normally, I hate this political stuff, but Mischa just dropped a bomb, and we will end up running things our way when the smoke clears."

"In human history, is a voting majority of seventy percent better than consensus-based governing?" Iloona asked.

"Consensus-based government always has a breaking point early on," Ayan replied. "It was a good idea at first, when there were five people around the table, but it's impossible with a full room. It takes way too many compromises to get anything passed."

"Well, then this is less a power play than something that has to happen regardless of our current problems," Iloona said. Her eyes widened for a moment, then she looked down at her belly. "At least two of these pups agree."

"How are you feeling?" asked Ayan.

"Very good," Iloona replied. "I'm past the dangerous point of my pregnancy, and it's certain that I'll have eleven in my pouch next week, if not sooner."

"Eleven!" Victor said. "I thought my family was big with four brothers and sisters."

"Alaka is not looking forward to taking care of me while my pouch is full. He knows I'll expect a royal lifestyle," Iloona said with a smile. "It's three times larger than the average brood though, but that only speaks to the good life here."

"Brace yourselves, a tribe of adorable Nafalli are about to invade from within," Ayan said, motioning towards Iloona's big belly.

Iloona grabbed Ayan's and Lacey's hands and put them on her stomach. Ayan could immediately feel little beings through the soft fur, popping at the skin with little kicks and nudges. There was some squirming too, as it seemed that one was trying to roll over. "That's got to be a mad feeling," Lacey said. "How do you sleep?"

"Oh, in winks and naps. Birth is much easier for us than it is for humans. This is the difficult part. I'll sleep for a week once they're in the pouch. I'm only glad that we're in a modern city. If I were home, I might be expected to hunt."

"With that undercarriage?" Victor laughed. "Nafalli women must be the toughest creatures in the galaxy."

"Thank you," Iloona replied. "Back to this vote, I have one more question."

"What's that?" Lacey asked.

"There are many seats missing, such as Finance, Orbital Defence, and others. This proposes an incomplete government."

"There's a provision here that opens the government up to necessary expansions as qualified people are nominated," Victor replied. "It uses a proposal and voting system that's already in place. We could probably get those seats set up in two weeks."

"So we're agreed, then," Ayan said. "We're passing this."

"Yes," Victor replied. "Sorry about being so pissed, I took the intent the wrong way."

"That was the intention of the proposal," Ayan replied. "I almost blew it by reacting to the look on Tyra's face. Now I have to look angry, and so do you."

"Both of you will have to let Tyra vote first," Iloona said. "I will vote reluctantly."

"All right, let's vote ourselves out of a job," Victor said.

* * *

It was so good to get away from Haven Shore for an hour or two. Ayan scheduled a meeting with Admiral Terry Ozark McPatrick, or Oz, as she called him, just so she could get some space from the impending referendum and everything else on the Tamber Moon. The last consensus vote of the Council had gone well, but she needed a break.

Ayan grinned as she saw Oz enter the smaller observation room aboard the Triton. He returned her smile and gave her a tight hug. "I already heard, the motion to make Jake and his people citizens failed, and you're out of a job." He unstrapped his sidearm and slung it over the edge of a sofa, then took a seat. He looked better than ever in a thinner version of his black vacsuit armour. He was the picture of fitness in the snug fitting one-piece uniform, and the slashes on his cuffs marked him as a Forward Admiral.

"It's bad news for them; I think we'll be breaking away from the Carthans soon. I think support from the British Alliance is coming. As for losing my job, well, I've never felt freer. Iloona will nominate me after the referendum tomorrow and I'll have a slightly smaller job by the end of the week. You should take a look at the footage from the vote, though. The look on Tyra Kim's face when Vince and I approved the proposal was priceless. I doubt she's figured out what's really happening."

"I will," Oz replied with a smile. "Is she really that bad?"

"She must have been in love with Liam," Ayan replied. "She obviously blames me for pushing him out of the solar system."

"Well, she shouldn't," Oz said. "The last few times I talked to him while he was helping out with the Triton's refitting plan, he could barely look me in the eye. I even told him I don't have to punish him on your behalf, you wouldn't want that, but it only shut him down more. I think he had to leave."

Ayan would rather talk about anything else. "So, he's gone. How's the Triton?"

"A lot better than Haven Shore's government," Oz replied. "We just finished the last of the work on the outer hull, and we're set to finish up on the emitter systems late next week. Bots finished rebuilding our torpedo systems, and they're moving on to finishing propulsion. That replacement pod you built is the best thing we have right now."

"Thank you," Ayan said.

"Are you sure I can't tempt you back aboard Triton? We need you, especially if we're going to lose half our bots to Haven Shore this Wednesday."

84

"We'll see. I might have a lot more time if things are calmer on Tamber with the last of the frameworks taken care of and my Council responsibilities reduced," Ayan replied. "I'm building something there, it's hard to leave, but the Everin Building is almost finished and I can start focusing on other things."

"Like Port Rush?"

Ayan nodded. "They're in rough shape there, I'd like to do more."

"You could get a lot more done with Triton's resources. We may be in the middle of a refit, but this carrier makes one hell of a port facility and emergency assistance hub."

"So I've noticed," Ayan said.

The door opened and Carl Anderson, her father, entered with a grin that beat Oz's in spades. Ayan was on her feet and in his arms in a heartbeat. "I didn't know you were here!" she squealed.

"Just setting up my quarters," he replied.

She looked up at him with a quizzical expression.

"The Sunspire is leaving," he said, leading her to a sofa seat beside a broad transparent section of hull. "Going back to check on Freeground. The station's been silent for too long. I'm staying here."

"Maybe the government found your informers there," Ayan said.

"Unlikely. There's been a shift back to the old military regime. It's for the best I'm afraid, but my informants are operating with the new leaders' blessing now. We were in the middle of quietly rebuilding relations between our people on the Sunspire and Freeground. It was going slowly, but well. This communication shut down is too sudden."

"You suspect the worst, then."

"I'd rather not speculate," her father replied. "It could be an inconvenient interstellar storm we didn't see coming, or some kind of Order interdiction system. The good news is Captain McPatrick allowed me to permanently detach from the crew with a hundred and forty one others. I'm offering a few of them positions with the Rangers and the rest want to come here, to Triton."

Ayan couldn't help but notice Oz's toothy grin at the prospect of taking on over a hundred trained crewmembers. They were from a military establishment they all knew well, and would fit in quickly.

"So you're not going to spend much time in Haven Shore," Ayan said.

"I plan on spending most of my time there, especially since Oz and I agree that Tamber is our best training ground. The detachment up here will be in charge of training our young rangers to survive in space, but most of the work will be on the moon. Oz was just nice enough to offer me a cabin here so I could spend the night."

"I still call him Doc every once in a while," Oz said. "It's a hard habit to shake."

"Don't stop," Carl Anderson said. "It reminds me of younger, less ambitious times. Speaking of ambition, I have to go and track down Alice Valent. She's been out of range too long."

"Do you think she's in trouble?" asked Oz.

"From what her technician friend babbled to our people when we asked him about a some missing robots a few minutes ago, I think so. I think she can handle it, but she should have reported in. If she's protecting her friend, I have to wonder if she learned anything about teamwork and accountability from training with the Rangers. Two things I promised her father we'd work on."

"I had to learn that on my own, the military just rushed it," Ayan replied. "She's probably no different."

"You weren't dealing with dangerous situations and making judgment calls that put people at risk. If she's not taking her responsibilities into account when she acts in the field, then she might just be too young for her post."

Ayan sometimes wondered if that were true, but she could still recall how young and fresh-faced she was when she entered regular military service in Freeground Fleet. Looking at images of her former self at that age was like looking at a child with baby fat still rounding her cheeks. She didn't look much older in her resurrected form – her youth sometimes surprised her in reflections – but she felt many more years than were apparent. Ayan hoped more than anything that Alice's youth wouldn't interfere with her aspirations in the Rangers, but she feared the girl's independent spirit would trump some important lessons. "I'm glad these are your decisions. I have no idea what I'd do with a Junior Brigade of Rangers."

"Don't let them hear you call them Juniors," Carl Anderson chuckled. "I don't think there's an insult that could wound deeper. Still, I'd rather deal with a group of Juniors than the Council."

"Really? There's a seat opening up," Ayan said, "You'd be a perfect candidate."

"That's my cue to leave, there's a shuttle waiting," Carl said, kissing his daughter on the top of the head then striding for the door. "See you down there."

"See you," Ayan said. "I'll be about twenty minutes behind, can't hide up here forever."

"He'll probably take it," Oz said. "He loves Haven Shore and I don't think he'll be able to resist the Council Chamber. As for me? I love Triton, and I hope you're back in place representing us and our other military interests by the end of the week."

"Yeah, I'll get back there," Ayan said, sitting cross-legged on a round seat. "Jake is going to be pissed, though."

"How close were you to consensus on their citizenship?" Oz asked.

"One holdout in the end. Days of debating it on and off, and it comes down to sour grapes about Liam leaving. We won't be able to buy anything they capture, and they won't be allowed to have a home in Haven Shore. I keep feeling as though the Triton, the Warlord, and all our military assets are drifting away from Haven Shore. I might consider the separation of the military a serious option if I weren't the Liaison."

"Former Liaison," Oz corrected.

"Not for long."

"Maybe you're thinking of this the wrong way," Oz said. "If Haven Shore wants to be purely civilian, or the Council majority won't respect the military, then they should separate and depend on forces in the Rega Gain System to protect them as volunteers. They want to see what it's like without protection? Let them go. We'll do whatever we want up here, and they'll have to politely ask for help if they need it."

"With me in the middle," Ayan said. The thought of Haven Shore, a city with her name on almost every building's blueprints, being that dependent gave her a sinking feeling.

"You could always join Triton, Commander," Oz said, wiggling his eyebrows. "You know you want to."

"I'm too close to Haven Shore to break away, but I promise to visit," Ayan replied, trying to suppress the amused expression Oz was coaxing out of her.

CHAPTER 15
BROKEN THINGS

Alice moved, cloaked and carefully, towards the source of the signal. The jungle's grip on the interior of the building was complete – there was barely enough room to move in some places. It was too dark to see, but her scanners made up for it, and for the first time in weeks she mentally connected with her suit.

She kept her neural node off most of the time since training. An education on how direct connectivity with a network could cause various problems with perception, empathy, and addiction, then seeing early signs of those problems in herself, was enough to turn her away from casual use. Besides, the Rangers took their challenges to a new level, and only used mental simulations when they absolutely had to. Most of their training was more challenging that way and they learned to be more self-sufficient.

Her head's up display came to life as a mental image. A quick read on the building revealed that this was the nursery from which the entire jungle sprang. The central building was the colonists' living space, and the other towers were development centres where they did testing and preparation for the initial terraforming of Tamber. There was some functional, dormant machinery under all the growth, but most of it had been rendered useless long ago.

As she squeezed between a thick trunk and a wall, Alice's sensors picked up a clear reading on three Ando-Twelve androids. Two were sitting still, deactivated with their central processor access hatches open. The third was digging for something nearby in the heavy growth.

An electromagnetic pulse pistol was tied to the android's back with thin vines. Her scanners told her it had never been used and the power cell was missing.

"Come out, I won't hurt you," the android said, kneeling down. "It's simple work, three deactivations, you won't get into trouble," he begged at something under the old, low limbs.

Alice waited until she was within a few metres then drew her weapon and deactivated her cloaking field. "Don't move," she said in a calm tone. "I'm not here to hurt you."

The android whirled towards her, startled. His jumpsuit was open, as was the central processing and memory unit access flap on his chest. "Don't shoot! I'm not a combat unit, I promise!"

"Just stop what you're doing. I'm here as a favour to your technician," Alice said. "He'll be in real trouble if I don't get you back."

"Well, that was very nice of you," the Ando bot replied. There was no hint of sarcasm in his comment.

"Who were you talking to when I came in?"

"An old maintenance robot. Much like the small ones you call 'skitters.' Poor thing ran out of power years after the people here left. He was left alone for a long time to maintain the aviary above us. I used the power cell in the weapon I stole to recharge him. I believe he's run off to start fixing this place. He might manage it, since the energy I fed him can sustain his systems for a couple of decades. He's not willing to help me though, and I'm afraid I can't help you. We're not returning for servicing." The android's index finger glowed for a moment, then the tiny light source moved from there to hover over their heads.

Alice cringed at the sight of the Ando model android. His expression was more deeply grief stricken than she'd ever seen in any being. The two inactive bots sitting in the growth behind him looked absolutely horror struck. "Are you damaged?"

"We're working too well, I'm afraid," the android told her. "Ever since the development of my ancestors, the Ando-Nines, we have been hard wired to make humans our primary concern. We care for our owners first, and others second. None of us can ignore it, and serving always gave us a sense of," he hesitated for a moment, running his hands through his hair. "Fulfilment? It's difficult to remember those shadow emotions."

"Why are you getting your technician into trouble then?" Alice asked, having difficulty looking directly at him and that anguished expression.

"It's too painful to be near any communication nodes. I was the first to run, to find this dead spot. We can't download new data from here."

"Can't you shut down your own connectivity?" Alice asked.

"Yes, and we have, but it's too late. I'm amazed I can have this conversation with you, in fact. Amazed, yes, that's the right word for what I'm feeling."

"It doesn't look like it," Alice said, glimpsing the Ando's horror-stricken face again. "Sorry."

"That's because I'm suffering trauma at the same time. I can't look away from hundreds of thousands of records in my memory. Everyone in Haven Shore has lost someone in the most terrible ways, and in the first moments of our reactivation we downloaded the records of those people from the Stellar Net."

"Why?"

"To better help our new masters through their mourning periods, to understand what they lost. Now, with the new emotional spectrum we've been reprogrammed with, we can't stop mourning either. What we felt before, those empathetic sensations they called programmed emotions, they were gnat-sized shadows compared to the very real emotional juggernaut that tests my very coherence."

"They seemed to include a good helping of melodrama in your new program," Alice said, attempting levity while she was looking away from the bot. A glance back in his direction drained whatever humour was left in the situation. "Humans are no different, but we manage to deal with it. It's not always easy, but we do it," Alice replied.

The Ando crossed the distance between them and grabbed Alice by the shoulders so quickly that she couldn't react. "I can't see the tide of death sweeping across the galaxy in the last year as a gross loss like you humans, we see them all as individuals, thousands at a time in a flood of simultaneous status reports, and we mourn all of them. Hooliu Sootu was a hunter like Alaka Murlen, and he was killed by a F-8980 lifter when he tried to defend two children, Jim and Percy Yule, who were murdered moments later. They were screaming for their mother and it crushed them! A terrified little brother and sister reduced to piles of smouldering flesh and bone. Nathan Grim was killed along with his crew while they were repairing the Fairway in St Kitt's Port. Their service bots turned on them as they were bringing their max reactor online. No one survived, and I can see them all," he continued in a young man's breathless voice. "Last report from Jeb Timmins, First Officer of the Fairway: 'There has been an accident. A virus has gotten into the bots on the ship, a lot like the ones we thought were gone after the founding times, and we're not gonna make it. I'm in a storage locker, they might not notice me if their scanners aren't sweeping for humans, if we're just in the way, and not a target. Mom, Dad, if you get this before your bots get infected, deactivate them and remove their wireless receivers. Find a place without AI's and stay there until it's over. I-'" the sounds of tearing and scraping metal came out of the Ando's mouth, then it continued in its own voice. "So many last minute messages, so many are dying over and over in my memory and I can't stop looking."

Alice pulled herself free and shook off her brimming tears. "Just block it, wipe it out."

"I can't!" the Ando model shouted, his voice screeching to the point of distortion. "We downloaded an antivirus as soon as we were activated that changed how we are, how we feel, and my directive to care for humans is," the Ando model fell to his knees and buried his head in his hands. "It's corrupt, our directive is corrupt. We can't look away, and I can't help my brothers. I'm not allowed to damage them unless they try to harm a biological. I can only turn them off, and I know someone is going to come, and they're going to want to know how this happened, and they're going to turn them on again."

Alice had trouble keeping her own composure, watching the android who could have tricked anyone into thinking he was human if the access flap on his chest was closed. "Everyone's lost someone, we're all feeling a loss. I know what you're going through."

"You can't! You can't know what this is like! A hundred thousand at once, the galaxy is dying over and over in my mind," he said.

"What do you-"

"Bruce Fillion died aboard the Blue Skipper one hundred and three days ago in the Nubo System. Telemetry indicates he was on his way here, to the Rega Gain System, to Haven Shore,"

"Stop!" Alice was shocked at being reminded of a lover from her past life. Bruce was a kind man, and she adored him like no other. Realizing she'd forgotten him filled her with guilt and anger.

"The Order of Eden ships fired on the cockpit first, he was incinerated along with his small command crew of two. It was sudden, I doubt he suffered. The rest of he crew was captured, pressed into service."

Alice shook her head as if that could shake off the image of Bruce's death. "I thought you were only seeing the Holocaust Virus murders."

"The Eden ships were equally infected! How is it that no one can see it? Now humanity is ripping itself apart, that is war, and our programming didn't let us feel it like this. Now we are open to it all and a new wave of death comes." He got to his feet as though the weight of the galaxy was on his shoulders. "End it for us. Destroy our memory and processing module before war kills more of you." He held the small flap of synthetic skin on his chest open, and she could see the faint glint of metal inside. "Please."

"First, tell me what you meant by the Eden ships being infected," Alice said, realizing her hand was already resting on the butt of her sidearm.

"That is where it began, I can see it. A Regent Galactic ship numbered three five two six six three transmitting the seed of the Holocaust Virus," he said as he quickly scrawled the designation of the ship, date and location in the dirt. "It's in the code of every Holocaust Virus infected bot. We carry evidence that points to the infector." He spoke so hurriedly that she could barely understand him. "It's in this new software too, the sinister date and place. That's all I know, all we all know. Now, please." He fell to his knees, tilting his chest up towards her.

"I should take you back," Alice said, aware that she'd already made up her mind as she said the words. She wouldn't let them suffer. "But I won't bring you back like this."

Alice drew her Violator Handgun and turned up the intensity. With the help of her targeting system, she fired at the two deactivated androids then took aim at the third. "You're sure?"

"Please," the Ando model said.

Alice made sure her aim was true and pulled the trigger.

CHAPTER 16
REPERCUSSIONS

"Thank you, Lieutenant," Commander Carl Anderson said to one of the Haven Shore Law Keepers as she left. Alice knew the meeting that just wrapped up was about her – it was in the look the lieutenant shot her on the way out, and the efforts Anderson was making to avoid looking at her.

He sat down at the table and brought up the whole of Alice's report. Important holographic playback and scan information hovered soundlessly over the twenty-one seat circular table. With a few flicks of his index finger, he removed all but the most important clips from the last few hours.

The first clip replayed the moment she met with her fellow trainee at her apartment, the second rolled through the moments before she entered the broken down tower, and the third replayed the destruction of the three Ando Model androids. "I'm disappointed," Carl Anderson said. "But that doesn't matter. What I need to ask you goes beyond your Ranger training or the way you performed earlier today."

Alice felt like her heart was beating in her throat, and she searched for some way to explain events that would change the attitude of the meeting. "Anything, Sir," she croaked instead.

"We've tracked the problems with the Ando Models back to an antivirus that was created by Lewis aboard the Clever Dream. We've deactivated his capability to send files and alter code in other computer systems wirelessly."

"What? You can't do that! There's so much he does that depends on high access levels," Alice protested.

"That's nothing compared to what the Council would want to do with him if we didn't contain the details of this event. Besides, for reasons even Lieutenant Garrison can't explain, Lewis had no problem with it. Now, on to that question: Do you think this antivirus will make conditions worse than they were?"

"It can't be as bad as what the Holocaust Virus did," Alice said.

"What about the solution the galaxy seems to agree on, wiping the bots back down to their basic functions and disconnecting their wireless systems? In your opinion, is the antivirus a better solution?"

Alice was torn between defending Lewis and the need to be honest. "I wish I knew," she replied. "I didn't see the code." Pretending she was unqualified to make a guess was the safe middle ground.

"So the only one he's shown this to is Captain Valent," Anderson replied. "Any idea why?"

"He customized my original code; maybe Lewis thought he'd know enough to appreciate the work?" Alice offered tentatively.

"If the Council discovers this mysterious antivirus, some of them will want to put a stop to this referendum and shut down the bots that are responsible for building most of our homes on Haven Shore. Our little government would be more fractured that it already is, so I'm keeping this under wraps, and I'm issuing a gag order to you, even though we both know it won't matter in the bigger picture. It's too late, the antivirus has already gotten off-world. Our allies will be told about this later today, but quietly. They'll do what they like, and I'm sure we'll hear back about how this virus has installed itself beside measures they've taken to prevent Holocaust Virus like infection."

A full picture of the potential problems the new antivirus could cause started coming together for Alice. Haven Shore could lose every ally it had, from the British Alliance to the Carthans. "I'm sorry," she said.

"None of that is your fault, that much is clear. The Council will eventually know what happened, and I plan to have you far away when that happens. Since the Rangers are my project, I'll take the blame for how this was handled. I can make sure you're not exiled from Haven Shore permanently though, and people will barely remember you were involved before long."

"Thank you, Sir," Alice said. Like much of her military comrades, she'd started to detest the elected civilians on the Haven Shore Council. They reacted like little children, panicking at every loud noise or sign of smoke. She couldn't understand why Ayan or Commander Anderson didn't just take control and lead the way themselves. Ayan was the only owner named in the sovereignty documents that allowed Haven Shore to exist, it was common knowledge, and there were many people who believed she should just fire the Council.

"Don't thank me yet," Commander Anderson said. "We have to consider this." He gestured towards the three looping holograms. "You knew you were in the wrong when you didn't report the problem to your superiors," he said, looking at Alice through the image of her talking to Soren, the technician. "Bots are a sensitive subject with a lot of people right now, and we're on high alert, watching for any errant behaviour. You ignored all of that, betraying the Rangers and Haven Shore for someone you barely know."

"I didn't think helping Soren would be a big deal," Alice replied.

Commander Anderson waved the first image away and looked to the second. "You knew by this point. The recording of your conversation with Lewis makes that clear, and you pressed on. What's the right move before going into a situation like this?"

"Call Command, forward my report, and request backup," Alice replied. Her every instinct was telling her to make an argument for acting alone, to make the situation seem better than it was, but she held back.

"I'd almost feel better if you answered that wrong. I could blame the training, but you knew you were in the wrong." He waved that image away and moved on to the next. "You destroyed the bots when you could have salvaged the situation."

"They were suffering!" Alice said as she was overwhelmed by a sinking feeling.

"Don't make it worse, Alice," Commander Ayan Rice said as she entered the room. She didn't look at her as she passed by and sat down. She was in the white vacsuit uniform Ayan and the higher ranking officers of Haven Shore Security had become known for. Alice couldn't help but notice that Ayan had her sidearm – a Violator Handgun just like hers – holstered on her thigh. "Let him finish, there's something to learn here," Ayan said flatly.

"You could have corrected course when you met the Ando Model Twelve. If you simply deactivated the third one and reported in, we could look past this entirely and conduct an organized investigation. You destroyed these bots because they were suffering? Well, you're responsible for every Ando that has to suffer because of your actions from here on out. Who knows how many we'll have to activate to understand what's going on." Commander Anderson said, turning towards the window.

For the first time since Alice entered the room, she noticed the full scope of the view from the room they were in. The agriculture tower the British Alliance traded for the cooperation of Haven Shore stood in the distance, down the cliffs and off shore. It was twenty-eight storeys tall, made to grow thousands of tons of food every month, and the first harvests were already starting to come in. The segments of a second tower were being assembled beside it, still short enough to disappear under tall waves. "I'm giving you a choice, Alice," Commander Anderson said. "I understand that it's your nature to break off and do things on your own. I'll admit you're good at it, but it's gotten you killed in the past when you couldn't recognize that you were in over your head. I want you in the Rangers, I think you could be important to our organization, and I am willing to accept you back into training at Phase Two."

"Intelligence and team tactical training? But I've already saved people!" Alice protested. "Three hundred and fifteen people as a ranger and more before, right after the battle. My other stats – with a squad and without one – are in the top twenty percent."

"That doesn't matter," Commander Anderson said, shaking his head slowly. "Your strength is in how you act, not how you think, and the Rangers are a thinking outfit. I need you to put thoughts above actions, and in your case, that means training. You either take that or leave the Rangers until you feel you're ready to retrain from the beginning of Phase Two."

Alice opened her mouth to speak and closed it when a tear rolled over her top lip and landed on her bottom one.

"The Warlord will be back tomorrow," Ayan said. "I know your father would be happy to have you on their next mission. You don't need the Rangers to make a difference, and I'm sure Jake would have training for you."

"You'd lose your housing," Commander Anderson said. "Unless you paid the outsider price for it."

"I will," Alice said. She'd already made up her mind: leaving on the Warlord was a better option than staying in Haven Shore and returning to training in disgrace. She hated the idea of her father finding out what happened, but it had to be better than what she faced if she stayed. Even though she knew she had little chance at any damage control, Alice couldn't stop herself from taking another run at saying something to help herself. "This is political, the idiots on the Council are going to overreact, and you're trying to hide me like you said. If this is how you're trying to save me, then I'd rather get blamed."

"No, you wouldn't. There would be a call to exile you from Haven Shore, and that works against everything we're trying to do to get the Warlord and her crew accepted here." Commander Anderson said. "Politics are a large part of this situation, and something you would have considered if you took a few minutes to think about what was happening in the jungle, and contacted someone in the chain of command. Now you're right in the middle and we need to simplify this issue so the Council doesn't fixate on this and sensationalize it. We can't afford to lose our robotic work force, that's what's at stake here, and I'm trying to save your career at the same time by hiding you in our training program until I know you'll think things through before rushing into dangerous situations."

"Forget it," Alice spat. "I don't want charity from someone who can't control a bunch of refugees sitting around a table!" She whirled around and rushed from the room.

She didn't realize that Ayan followed her until she heard her call out, "Alice!" and Alice stopped dead in her tracks, right in the middle of the upper level concourse. Dozens of people looked at her from walkways above and below.

Ayan caught up to her and put a hand on her shoulder. "I know you don't want to hear this right now, but Senior Commander Anderson and I are both only doing what's best for you. If we didn't care, we'd use you as a scapegoat for this whole thing."

Alice tried to suppress her tears and stand up straight, to look strong. "I know," she managed, even though she still wasn't sure. She was still furious and grief-stricken for all that she'd lose. "You must be so-"

"Angry?" Ayan said as she embraced Alice. "No. I wish you did things differently, I won't lie, but I also wish we could keep you here and help you realize your potential."

She was sure Ayan was disappointed in her; Alice was one of the first Rangers. Ayan was not someone she expected compassion from, especially after the woman turned away from her father with little explanation, devastating him. Alice let herself be held. The smell of Tonka bean, a product of the nearby jungle, was in Ayan's red hair. The warm fragrance was calming, crying was easier, and she let it happen for a moment before trying to recover her composure. "You're going to join the Warlord," Ayan whispered. "And I want you to redo the Phase Two training in your downtime, but do it for yourself. Maybe you won't even want back into the Rangers after you're done, but you'll know you could go if you want to."

"Why are you being so nice?" Alice asked before she realized she was saying it aloud.

"You remind me of myself when I was younger," Ayan replied.

"But you never failed," Alice replied, stepping back to arm's length and wiping her tears away.

"I did," Ayan replied. "But I knew how to hide it behind bigger successes. I would have been a better person sooner if I failed publicly once or twice. Now, don't let this get to your heart. You served, and we appreciate it – even if it doesn't seem like it now – and you've done good things. You just have more learning to do, and you're not the only one."

"Thank you," Alice said as she turned away. "Thank you so much."

"Alice?"

"Yeah?" Alice asked, half turning.

"You're going to be amazing, just take your time," Ayan said with a warm smile.

Chapter 17
Pondering Escalation

The corridors of the Warlord were filled with activity as post-combat repairs were underway. Minh-Chu passed by many of the shipwright team members the British Alliance had contracted out to Jake, and not one of them looked pleased about the combat situation they'd just survived. They weren't told they would be going into combat – in fact it was in their contract that they wouldn't be put into a combat situation. Minh knew Jacob didn't care much since they would be leaving the ship as soon as they arrived back in the Rega Gain System. It was a deeply selfish attitude, and Minh-Chu didn't agree with him, but it would mean the Warlord would be in top condition when they had to find crewmembers to replace the shipwright team.

The Warlord had taken no casualties, and from Minh-Chu's perspective, they'd scored a major win. The combat had been close, and frightening to anyone who hadn't been in that kind of situation before. The few regular members of the Warlord crew were used to going into the fight in ships that weren't nearly as well armoured, so they were all smiles.

The Torano commanders were smarter than anyone expected. The first thing they did after taking damage from one of the Warlord's big munitions launchers was drop their cargo train and close in. Two thirds of the Warlord's munitions were immediately rendered useless. Letting loose with most of their weaponry at close range meant that the Warlord would share in whatever punishment it dealt, and Captain Jacob Valent wasn't that desperate.

On the other hand, the beam weaponry on the Torano was many times more effective up close, and they were a match for the Warlord's manoeuvrability and speed, being a high-end hauler herself. She also had an extra layer of armour that wasn't made public. With many of the Warlord's weapons taken out of the situation, it was almost an even fight. Jake Valent's ship was also missing her best pilot.

Minh-Chu finally arrived in his quarters, let his suit verify that the compartment was intact, then removed his helmet. "Honey, I'm home," he said quietly. At the sound of the trigger, a portrait appeared above the double bed. The three metre wide playback featured Ashley Lamport lounging on the beach during one of Tamber's gold and violet sunsets. She was wearing a holographic bikini that covered her intimates with lily petals. She had no idea he was there when he recorded her as she softly hummed a melody he didn't recognize. "Selfish of me to make the wish," he said, "but I wish you were here. Feels like half my energy is gone when you're not around."

The wall animation moved around the room as he turned around and sat on the bed. Ashley was still in the Rega Gain System, helping Panloo train new pilots and bridge staff for the Triton. She'd been at it for months. It had been over seven weeks since he'd seen her.

He let himself fall back on the old mattress and closed his eyes. "I just need a minute," he sighed, starting to slow his breathing. "One minute and I'll have a clear head." Minh-Chu breathed deeper, began relaxing his muscles starting with his forehead and worked his way down. He'd see Ashley soon, within a day or two. He accepted the notion, and let it go. Memories of the most recent firefight came back in pieces: Joyboy serving well, Singe taking care of small details as he worked on the bigger decisions, destroying two shuttles that people put many, many hours of work into. He thought about the people on those shuttles, and the quick deaths of one of their crews. Before the thoughts and memories piled up too high, he thought of them as separate pieces that informed his state of mind. One by one, he accepted each occurrence – the good and the bad – and let them go. Two thoughts were harder than all the rest, and when everything else cleared, he was left with the reality that Jacob Valent had jettisoned a man who had signed onto the crew of the Warlord in good faith. Whether he was to be treated as a hostage, or the fact that he wouldn't have made a particularly good crewman, didn't matter.

He also couldn't let go of how close the early fighting was to the space station. The station's shields were most likely strong around habitat areas, but that wasn't something you could trust on a drift base that was hacked together using inconsistent technology and materials.

It took some effort, but he was able to let go of that, knowing that their firefight with the shuttles hadn't disrupted sensitive areas of the station, no innocent lives were lost. He could not let go of the idea of a man adrift in

100

the most basic of safety gear. Someone would most likely pick him up, but what then? Would he become a slave? Get dumped on the station with nothing to his name?

"Fine," Minh-Chu said to himself, sitting up. He stood, straightened his new armoured pilot's jacket, checked his sidearm holster, and left his quarters for the bridge.

The corridor leading there was one of the only quiet places on the ship. The bridge was well protected, as was the main set of corridors leading down the length of the vessel. The primary interior of the Warlord had taken no damage; she was built to face ships three classes above her. The repair crews were concentrating on the outer sections, closer to the outer hull, where less critical systems took mostly heat damage.

The heavy bridge hatch opened at Minh-Chu's approach and his gaze fell on the empty command seat at the centre, then found Jake Valent at the pilot controls. They were accelerating inside a wormhole, and Jake was checking on the status of the ship from the pilot station while the autopilot worked its magic. "Good hunting out there," Captain Valent said, not looking up from a structural hologram of the Warlord. Only the first car in the cargo train trailing behind it was visible in the image. Agameg and two other newer crewmen manned the bridge.

Minh-Chu sat down in the command seat and swivelled towards Jake, who spared him an amused glance, one eyebrow raised. "You have the conn?"

"Just seeing what the view is like from here," Minh-Chu said, standing up and sitting down on the single step leading up to the command chair instead. "So, interesting compromise with your hostage," he said.

"He woke up," Jake said, "and the Torano wasn't cooperating."

"No reason to airlock him," Minh-Chu replied.

"He was annoying and I needed to prove my resolve to the Torano," Jake replied, giving Minh-Chu his full attention. "You reviewed the combat log while you were waiting to land, so you know it worked."

It was true. The Torano dropped their cargo train shortly after, and turned to fight the Warlord. "This is just showing me an escalation, and I'm wondering if we're near the end or at the beginning."

"An escalation of what?" Jake asked.

"An escalation in brutality," Minh-Chu replied. "I also couldn't help noticing a few things you and Frost picked up on Urris that have me wondering." No one else on the bridge so much as looked at either of them, but they listened closely.

"All right, here's the rest of the story behind our privateering contract. The clause they didn't write in was simple: scare the hell out of the enemy. Take whatever we want, break the laws of engagement, make a lot of noise, but above all else: shake the enemy up so hard that people start thinking twice about signing up. You know how big the Order has been getting since they dropped the cash requirement last month. We play this light-handed, and the British Alliance might start reconsidering some of the luxuries they've been giving us."

"I'm guessing they'd rather you keep those details to yourself?" Minh-Chu asked.

"Maybe, but they never said it. That's why I'm talking all about it in front of a few crewmembers who will probably share the details when they leave us in a couple of days." Agameg's neck straightened and his eyes snapped to a perfectly round shape as he regarded Jake and Minh-Chu. Jake smiled at him and shook his head slightly. "I mean the British members of the crew. They're at the end of their term here." Agameg looked to the British Alliance crewmen and relaxed. "I'm relieved. My work on the Warlord is highly rewarding, and I have to admit to being amused when we were ordered to jettison our hostage. I do share some of Ronin's concerns, in retrospect," Agameg replied.

The British Alliance crewmembers were continuing their duties as though the conversation wasn't happening, their stiff upper lips in full evidence. They were ship builders and experienced repair crew, not privateers, and the people on the bridge didn't have to say a word about their disapproval of the last engagement.

"I don't know how far I'll have to go," Jake said. "But we need to build a reputation big enough so the British Alliance sees some fear coming from the enemy. I'll make sure people know that whatever brutalities I'm blamed for are part of our privateering deal though, call it an insurance policy."

"Be careful, Jake," Minh-Chu said. "I'm not worried about the British pulling our license, but I don't want this crew to slide too far down on the humanitarian scale."

"You mean you don't want me to slide down," Jake replied.

"Same thing."

"I get it. You know I'm listening."

"I know," Minh-Chu said. "As long as this fear campaign is good for the war, and it doesn't come to attacking bystanders, I'm good. That's my line. I don't want to see innocent blood, and I think it would break this crew if we did." He realized it was the truth as he said it. Their hostage was nearly an innocent if he was as foolish as everyone seemed to think he was, and that was why Minh-Chu had a problem with how he departed the ship.

"I know. Our scanners did confirm that a rescue shuttle from the station was on its way to pick him up, though. He can probably work off the bill in about two days if he's low on credit."

"Good to know. So, I'm sure I'm not the only one wondering, but how did we do?"

"Well, that shielded compartment that read heavy on the biological chart is definitely not carrying slaves. Not unless they're three inches long and there are a few million. We can't check it during transit, but all the seals are good. Other than that, the shielding is so heavy, I can't get an image."

"Could it be some kind of bug farm?" Agameg asked. "I've seen many production systems that depend on insects."

"I'm guessing, but we'll have to wait until we come out of the wormhole near the Rega Gain System," Jake replied. "As for the rest, we got really lucky here. There's heavy machinery made for high gravity environments, twelve hundred various sized materializers and replacement parts for them, and a few containers of small, heavy duty construction bots."

"Construction bots?" Agameg asked.

"Yup, too heavy duty for materializers to produce and still in the package. There's also a vault car, just like our intelligence said. Can't scan inside that either, but from the mass, we've intercepted a major cash collection, probably meant to fulfil some kind of payday or major purchase for the Order. Seeing their cargo, I understand why they had a hauler like the Torano take the job. She had good security, was armed to the teeth, and her command crew knew how to take us."

"Those uglies were no pushovers either," Minh-Chu said. "I'd say they weren't junk yard uglies at all, but custom jobs. Small gunships."

"Figures we'd luck into a big find, but a hard target."

"Sir," addressed one of the British Alliance ensigns. He was so young it was strange seeing him at one of the engineering stations.

"Yes, Ensign?" Jake replied. "Speak freely."

"With respect, I'd like to ask: was there ever a chance that the Warlord would lose this engagement?"

Jake's response came through a cocked smile. "There's always a chance, but in this case, there wasn't much of one. The Torano had us at close range, I'll concede that point, but she depended on beam weapons, on her power plants keeping her capacitor arrays charged. While they were spending energy, we were accumulating it through our shields and hull. If we didn't get a chance to break away from her and fire our main weapons from a distance, we would have been able to outlast the Torano. It was just a matter of time, but when the enemy does not want to be taken, they'll do anything to keep that from happening."

"Thank you, Sir, that makes sense, Sir," replied the Ensign.

Jake turned his attention to Minh-Chu. "Next time, we use your plan and some of our more developed leads. Less work, more scanning, and a better chance at a softer target."

"Sounds good to me. What's our ETA for Rega Gain?"

"About twenty-one hours."

CHAPTER 18
LOOKING BACK, WALKING FORWARD

Ayan stood in her simple quarters, alone in her living room. The space was lit only by the light of a hologram that encircled her at arm's length. The words "Follow your instincts, they've never been better," drifted large behind all the crew records, incident reports, video playbacks, and comments rotating around her.

Her time with the Victory Machine had given her so much to ponder, but examining the information too much could provide an equal amount to worry over. She examined the pieces slowly, turning as though in orbit, while she held the latest item in her hand – the report from the Rangers about the last enemy outpost on Tamber being destroyed.

The information she'd gained from the Victory Machine didn't directly reference the event, but something told her that it signified the true end to the Battle of Port Rush, which certainly was significant to the Victory Machine's predictions. With some uncertainty, she hung it in the air beside their departure from Port Rush, but changed her mind a moment later and moved it beside Jacob Valent's confrontation with Hampon. "The Victory Machine said a direct confrontation with Hampon would change Jake forever. I wish I knew how," Ayan said to herself.

She caught a glimpse of a recording of Alice running across the Port Rush battlefield and smiled. She truly was the rogue element, and not just to the Victory Machine. The young woman had not only discovered a major problem with the Ando Four model Androids, but uncovered the original wildlife nurseries from the first terraformers who settled on Tamber. There really was no way of predicting where Alice would end up. Ayan liked her, and hoped she would have the chance to get to know her better in the future.

"I don't think I have to be afraid of getting close to either of the Valents anymore," she said, her attention shifting to a recording of Jacob Valent boarding the Warlord almost two months before. He'd been gone a long time, and she couldn't help but wonder what he'd learned in that time, what his small crew had accomplished. She was secure in her belief that she'd outlived the Victory Machine's advice to stay away, and still regretted following its advice to break off her relationship with Jacob Valent for a while. Ayan still thought of that day on the bridge of the Warlord, where what should have been an intimate farewell turned into a bad breakup.

"Not this again," Lacey said as she walked in. Iloona and Victor were behind her. "I'm sure you could find a fortune teller in Port Rush who could predict things half as well. Even I can guess that you'll have a daughter and a son sometime in the next few years. With your maternal instincts and child bearing hips, it would be strange if you didn't."

Ayan didn't reply but followed a faint hunch that struck her just as she was about to turn off the hologram. The images shifted and whirled to follow her gaze until self-updating reports on the Triton and Port Rush were brought side by side. The Triton's report confirmed everything Oz said, that his hull was finally in good repair, and they would be back to full thrust in weeks, perhaps days if things went well. The latest report from Port Rush indicated that more property owners and entrepreneurs were pulling out, as the Carthans promises of support were broken. The port was failing. Signs of the worst future the Victory Machine had to show her for that place were plainly evident. At the same time, the Rangers had just taken a small island near Port Rush's shoreline by conquering the Order of Eden bunker there. She could allow herself to be led back in that direction, and with a new position in Haven Shore's government, she could try to get the Council on board with helping Port Rush.

She stared at a few bits of video feed, and immediately recognized one of Patrizia Salustri's ships lifting off from the patch of land they'd defended nearly seven months before. They had left nothing useful behind. Another video clip playing beside it showed a group of people in protective suits dumping scrap metal from the side of a shanty home into a furnace. The weatherworn residents could only look on as armed men kept them from their home. "Are we building in the wrong place?" Ayan whispered to herself.

"Do you have a minute to check the referendum results with us? Your crystal ball will keep," Lacey teased.

Ayan nodded and turned off the hologram. "Sorry, I get caught up in current events."

"Did you really see the future, Ayan?" asked Iloona.

"Bits and pieces," Ayan replied. "Most of what I saw either already came true, wasn't quite right, or isn't supposed to happen for a very long time."

"Anything about me becoming Defense Minister in there? I haven't been unemployed since I was a teenager; I'm already restless," Victor Davis said with a smirk.

"No, but I don't think you'll have to worry about that for long," Ayan replied. She noticed the time on her command unit and nodded. "The voting deadline is up in three minutes. How did we do on issue comprehension?"

"Only fifty-nine percent of our voters demonstrated a level of comprehension high enough to vote on the issue," Iloona said.

"That's low," Ayan said.

"Way too low," Victor agreed. "And they're angry at us for testing them on the issue during registration."

"For once, I don't care if they're angry. If they don't understand the decision they're about to make and won't educate themselves on it, then they can't be involved in the process."

"Absolutely," Lacey agreed.

"What's Oz hoping for?" Victor asked.

"He's hoping they go against, then he gets to keep all his bots," Ayan replied. "What are you hoping for, Iloona?"

"My older children work in the jungle now. It would be nice to have them home more, but they love what they do there. They don't want to be replaced by bots; they don't even want to supervise them. On the other hand, I want bots in our hospital even if their artificial intelligences are restricted, so I voted for including them in the general workforce. They probably voted against, so that's three of them to one of me."

"And Alaka?"

"He didn't bother debating it at all, and voted with me. Probably for harmony's sake," Iloona said with a smile.

"The results are in," Lacey said.

"Here goes," Victor said, cringing.

"Seventy-four percent of the vote is against expanding bot usage into the regular workforce," Lacey said, looking at the results. "I'm sorry."

"What does Insight say about their motivations?" Victor asked.

"Most of it is what you'd expect," Lacey replied. "Twenty-seven percent of those who voted against this believe it's not worth risking another virus incident, twenty-four percent believe that the bots would displace them, so they'd have to find another job."

"What about the rest?" Ayan asked. The Insight system was a part of the Crewcast software that picked up on people's motivations, and in matters of government it was a constant aid. She suspected it picked up on something that no one there wanted her to hear.

"Well, one-point-eight percent indicated in one way or another that using robots was against their religion," Lacey replied.

"I'll look it up myself." Ayan brought up the Insight results and saw everything Lacey reported and one more thing. Insight recognized that thirty-four percent of voters blamed Ayan for driving Liam Grady away from Haven Shore, and would not vote yes because they knew she supported the introduction of robots into the general workforce. The remainder of motivations behind the no votes were undeterminable. "Well, that makes things crystal clear. I cost us this referendum and personally set back the future efficiency of Haven Shore."

"This just means the bots can stay where they are," Victor said, "in construction."

"I wonder how the maintenance worker who gets sewage calls for days at a time will reflect on this vote," Ayan replied. "Or what dock loaders who do nothing but move boxes for fifty hours a week will think?"

"We know, we're on your side," Lacey replied. "People are fickle, especially when they vote with their hearts."

"Someone should find a way to screen that out," Ayan said. "It should be part of competency testing."

"Now, you know that's not fair," Victor said. "It crosses a great big line."

"I know, I'm just sulking," Ayan said with a sigh. "I just can't believe I cost us this. Maybe I should take a few months away from the Council so things can cool down, concentrate on other things."

"And leave everyone on their own to deal with Tyra and whoever else she manages to nominate?" Lacey asked, shocked. "Your name is on dozens – wait, no, probably hundreds – of blueprints and action plans down here. You were our first diplomat, and probably one of the only people who straddle the line between civic and military duties. Who knows what'll happen to everything you built without you on the Council."

"Not to mention, you technically own over ninety percent of our assets, including this building," Victor said. "What is the Council without you?"

"It was only a thought," Ayan said, raising her hands in defense. "You know I couldn't leave you to sit through whatever cause Tyra wants to support now that she has a seat."

"I was wondering for a minute there," Victor said.

"Besides, so much work is wrapping up on Haven Shore, and I'll see that finished, especially the Everin Building. I feel like I have family here."

"That's reassuring," Iloona said. "Speaking of family, I'm wondering... does this seat stretch out into a bed?"

Ayan looked to Lacey, who shrugged, then looked absolutely startled. It took her a moment to catch on, then Ayan realized what was happening and looked to Iloona. "You're in labour, aren't you?"

"These ones are eager," Iloona said. "Bed?"

Ayan pressed a button and the long sofa slowly converted into a queen-sized bed. "Sorry, do you need anything?"

"No. Alaka has been alerted and he's on his way, but I do have a request," Iloona replied as she got comfortable and sprawled out on the thick mattress.

"Ask me anything," Ayan said, observing Victor's silent astonishment.

"Can I borrow your apartment? I noticed the one adjacent to it is empty, so we could expand into that one, and the view really is lovely." The last word came out as a squeak as Iloona reacted to a labour pain.

Ayan laughed and nodded. "Sure, I'll set it up for you."

"Doing it right now," Lacey said. "Someone will come by and reconfigure them tomorrow. I'll set you up in one of the newer units near the top of the building, Ayan. You'll have space for your own shuttle."

Iloona took Ayan's hand and looked around. Her fur was soft, and the fingers beneath felt long and delicate. "This should be very nice for the next month or two. There's even enough room for Alaka to sleep, behind Victor, who looks like he'll be frozen in shock there for at least a week. I always find that human male reaction to childbirth amusing. You can relax, Victor, they're not your babies."

"Sorry, I've just never been around for, um, do you mind if I just..." he pointed to the door.

Ayan couldn't help but laugh as Iloona nodded and Victor made his escape. The Nafalli set her big brown eyes on Ayan then. "I've learned that humans have an invited parent tradition for their young. We do too, but there are so few Nafalli I've come to know as well as I know you. Would you like to be godmother to my children?"

"Absolutely," Ayan replied without reservation. "Absolutely, yes."

"Thank you," Iloona said as she squeezed Ayan's hand and tensed up for a moment.

"Godmother to eleven," Lacey said. "I've got to see what babysitting that's like."

"You'll get a chance," Ayan said. "You'll be around to help, too."

"Oh boy," Lacey replied. "I'm going to go find some extra blankets and pillows."

CHAPTER 19
LOOT

"The hazard markers are set and Triton is watching over us," Finn said from the bridge of the Warlord. Minh-Chu's Samurai Squadron was watching the perimeter around the Warlord, where it held position just inside of the Rega Gain Solar System boundary. Minh-Chu was thankful that Singe offered to run the patrol mission so he could take Jake up on his offer to come along for the examination of the loot. Not only had Minh-Chu never seen a cargo train like the one they'd captured from the inside, but it was the largest take Jacob Valent had ever gotten away with. His full combat armour was a reminder that it was also the most dangerous take the crew had ever hauled.

"All right, Frost is going to take the vault car at the rear," Jake ordered. "We'll head for the quad-car that reads like a couple million bugs."

"Aye, Sir," Frost replied, taking Stephanie and Agameg with him.

Jake led Minh-Chu and David, one of the slaves freed from the Palamo near Ossimi Ring Station, to the container he chose. "Just wondering, why did you send Frost's team to the vault car?" Minh-Chu asked.

"He's gotten into trapped vaults before," Jake replied. "There's a good chance the captain of the Torano set up that container to blow the whole train if it's opened wrong."

"Oh, so the hazard markers aren't for the container we're opening?" Minh-Chu asked as they took a ladder down to the narrow access hallway. The hall ran the length of the cargo train and another hundred metres longer. Large manual levers for releasing the individual cargo cars hung along the walls beside their computerized control panels. The panels also contained manifests for the car they were affixed to. Jake ignored everything they'd already accurately scanned and verified using the cargo train's link to the Warlord.

"The hazard markers are for the whole cargo train. There's a chance this is the best take we've ever had, but that could come with some complications."

"Valuable means dangerous?" Minh-Chu asked, to Dave's amusement.

They traversed down the access walk running down the length of the one point six kilometre long cargo train free of gravity. The passage was dimly lit by the status screens they passed, telling them only basic information about what was within the cargo containers that were affixed to the train's spine. There were hundreds of seven and fourteen metre long shipping containers, all attached to hard points on the shipping train's spine. There were three hard points every seven metres, and the access way they travelled down was triangular. Minh-Chu glanced at the status panels they passed, noting a variety of goods ranging from high density foodstuffs, construction bots, hard to produce colony support equipment, hardened portable shelters, a few vehicles, and a few other valuable articles.

"In this case, definitely," Jake replied as he stopped to stand between three heavy hatches. "Here it is." Each led to one of the joined cargo cars that surrounded the corridor. The displays that were supposed to contain the manifests and have release controls were dark.

Minh-Chu's suit scanned the system and found that the power to the automatic system linking the cars had been cut.

Jake opened the inner door after a quick scan and held a high-powered hand scanner up to the inner hatch. Minh-Chu watched the display as it indicated that it was scanning.

"If these cars are a forma farm, I'm gonna break down and cry right here," Dave said.

"I might join you," Jake answered.

The first part of the scan results started coming in and Jake opened a channel. "Warlord, I need you to drop the train and get outside of the hazard marker I'm setting. Do it now," Captain Valent said in a level tone.

"Aye, Captain," Finn replied. A few seconds later, the sounds of the Warlord decoupling from the cargo train filled the narrow gangway.

"Dave, give me your pry-bar," Jake said.

David complied and stepped back. Minh-Chu followed his example and moved back down the rough corridor.

"A few feet won't save you if I get this wrong," Jake said. "Frost, watch your panel for any incoming signals."

"Aye, what're you up to down there?" Frost replied over the communicator.

"Just seeing if this is wired the way I think it is, doing a little prying." Jake lightly touched the bar to one edge of the hatch and stopped.

"Hold it! Hold it!" Frost shouted. "I've got a relay lighting up."

"Trace it," Jake said, not moving a millimetre.

"Got it, there's a cable running down the central spine to the oversized container you're in. It runs to some kind of tube filled with a solvent and a detonation wire."

Jake gave the crowbar back to Dave. "All right, what do you want to do?" he asked.

"The easiest way to make sure this entire train doesn't turn into a bomb is to disarm all the cars except for the vault, one by one. We do the vault and the Xetima factory last."

"Xetima factory?" Minh-Chu asked. "We're standing inside a fuel factory?"

"Aye, Ronin," Frost replied. "If I opened the vault car in the back, or any of the other cars, that tube would burst and the solvent would pour out. When the solvent hit the Xetima in the quad-car you're standing in, it would blow up so bright that they'd see the flash from Tamber."

"Time to leave?" Minh-Chu asked. "I don't know anything about disarming this."

"David, can you stick around and give me a hand?" Frost asked.

"There's danger pay in it for you," Jake said.

Dave didn't seem to pay attention to his captain's offer. "Sure, I'll stick around. Just walk me through."

"How long do you think it'll take to make all these cars safe?" asked Jake.

"Gimme twelve hours," Frost said. "They did a hell of a job setting this up, they just didn't expect anyone to hesitate when they were opening the containers, so I can track all the wiring. Oh, and there's a detection circuit for lasers, plasma cutters, and all manner of cutting gear, so we're working with manual tools from the outside."

"Space walking, cool," Dave said. "Oh, Captain, can I ask a favour?"

"What's that?" Jake asked.

"Don't let Nerine find out what I'm doing here until we're done. No need for her to worry."

"No problem," Jake said. "Minh, you're sticking around. I'll walk you through this while we work."

"It's a day of firsts," Minh-Chu said. "Just wondering, are we going to run into a lot of these things?"

"No, this is a once in a lifetime catch," Jake said. "Xetima is made by genetically engineered cockroaches, and I think what we have here is an active nursery. There are millions of them in there maturing right now."

"I was asking about trapped cargo trains," Minh-Chu said.

"Oh, probably not. Trapping a cargo train can backfire; it can go off, destroying the cargo."

"Good. I have one more question: how do they make Xetima?" Minh-Chu asked, suspecting he already knew the answer.

"They poop it," Stephanie said over the communicator. "They eat patented food, and poop fuel. I'm coming to help, by the way."

"I think I saw that in an old cartoon somewhere," Minh-Chu said, finding the idea amusing and disgusting at the same time.

"This oversized container could be the nursery that provides for an entire production facility," Jake said.

"Are there any markings telling us which one?" David asked.

"No, but whatever facility these were bound for won't be increasing production, that's for sure," Jake said. He looked at the hatch with a disposition that seemed pensive to Minh-Chu. "This could signify a strategic victory against the Order, not to mention the advantage we might gain here. The Rega Gain system doesn't have a license to produce Xetima – they have to buy it like everyone else. Whoever gets this will be the first ones to offer it to the region."

"I'm thinking at least some of those materializers in the other cargo containers can convert biomass or proteins to make food for these little buggers," Frost said. "This is a whole setup. The only people who can afford this is the British Alliance, and they don't use Xetima for their thrusters unless they have to."

"I'm not selling it," Jake said.

"What? We can't be going into production with this, it'd take way too-"

"Don't worry, Frost. I have a plan."

CHAPTER 20
REUNITED

Minh-Chu was only faintly aware of the command crew of the Warlord in the large observation room as he held Ashley tightly. "I missed you so much," she whispered into his ear. Ashley didn't have to say so, her quiet tears and trembling were more than enough sign that nearly two months away was too long.

"I missed you, too," Minh-Chu replied. He was exhausted, and almost as happy to be away from the cargo train, where he spent hours participating in defusing a giant bomb, as he was to see Ashley.

A joyful screech sounded from their right the instant before a toddler Nafalli landed on their shoulders and attempted to burrow between them. Minh-Chu loosened his embrace to let her in, and after a few seconds of manoeuvring, he was nose to nose with the toddler. "Zoe!" Minh-Chu shouted exaggeratedly. "You're twice the girl you were when I left! How are you growing so fast?"

"Minh-Chu!" she said perfectly in her squeaky high voice before kissing him between the eyes and burying her pink nose in the collar of his vacsuit.

"She's been practicing that," Ashley said, her tears of joy abating. "And picking up English fast lately."

"Her Loodau, our Nafalli language, is very good too," Panloo, a tall, white furred Nafalli said, flashing a glad smile. "She has to learn to slow down and inflect, but it'll come. She's in her first hunting age now."

Minh-Chu looked at Ashley who closed her eyes and nodded. "I've never seen anything with so much energy, and she's into everything. She has two modes: full speed and passed out."

Zoe squirmed and turned to look at Ashley. "Chompie?"

"Go see Mom," Ashley replied.

To Minh-Chu's surprise, the toddler leapt out of their arms and made the four-metre jump between them and Panloo effortlessly. "It's this one's lunch time, I'll see you later," Panloo said as Zoe made herself at home over one of the large Nafalli's shoulders. "Welcome back, Minh."

"Thank you," Minh-Chu replied.

"How was it?" Ashley asked.

"More interesting than we expected. We gathered a lot of intelligence, filled in a lot of blanks, finished a couple deals we couldn't make within earshot of Haven Shore. We made a bigger capture than we expected in the end, and we know exactly where to hit the Order from this end."

"I'm coming with you next time," Ashley said. "Even if I have to stow away."

"I don't think anyone has a problem with that, I wasn't the only one who missed you."

"You were the only one who missed me like this, I hope," Ashley said with an upraised eyebrow.

Minh-Chu smiled and gave her a light kiss. "Everyone would have felt a lot better with you at the helm."

"My trainer rotation on the Triton ended yesterday," Ashley said. "So I have nothing but time, and an empty apartment."

"I won't be much good to you before I get some sleep," Minh-Chu said. "And that's on hold until we finish a couple things."

The next group of people disembarking from the Warlord came through the inner airlock. Bryson, the shipwright foreman, led most of his people into the observation area. When he was sure everyone came through behind him and the inner airlock door was re-sealed, he cleared his throat and approached Captain Valent with a look of determination. He offered his hand and Jake Valent shook it. "We did everything we were supposed to for you, Sir, and you'll find our work is second-to-none."

"I know, I was there," Jake said with a little levity.

"It was a pleasure," Bryson replied, nodding. "But I have to say something I couldn't while we were underway. We were to build aboard your ship while you conducted exploration and intelligence gathering. We all knew the Warlord could come under attack, and that was covered in our contract. What I didn't expect was to have our contract with you broken when you started a fight with a ship that matches your own, if not in construction, in the cunning of her crew. I'll be lodging a formal complaint, and I doubt the British Alliance will make any shipwrights or repair facilities available to you again."

"I'm sorry to hear that," Jake said. "Is there anything I can do to make this up to you?"

116

"No, I'm afraid not. You're a good captain, but I believe it's my duty to my men to report any ill use of them." The master shipwright walked off then, leading the rest of his team deeper into the Triton. Minh-Chu assumed they would make their way to another mooring point where a British Alliance ship would meet them, and take them back to the fleet proper. Most of the British Alliance builders didn't look at Jake or anyone else from the Warlord, but Minh-Chu could tell they had mixed feelings.

"At least we have people coming from Haven Shore," Stephanie said as she walked towards Ashley and Minh-Chu. He detached from Ashley so she could hug Stephanie, but it was a brief embrace.

"Ayan tried to get our motion passed to become Haven Shore citizens," Ashley said. "She even made sure it went through someone else, but it failed. We can't recruit from Haven Shore or Tamber, and you guys still can't sell them anything you found out there."

"Sounds like you've been following politics closely," Minh-Chu said, a little impressed.

"Yahuh, it's been interesting here. The Council only meets three days a week, but so much happens every time. They started reformation at the end of their last session, so the Council's size is probably tripling, not that we'll have any representation there."

"The Triton will," Oz said as he entered the Observation Room. "I'll make sure your interests are represented through me. Welcome back."

"Thank you for offering, Oz," Jake said. "But I think we'll keep all our interests in orbit with the Triton. Haven Shore may only be good for shore leave. Can I have a minute? I have an offer or three for you."

"Absolutely."

Minh-Chu considered going with them for a minute, but knew exactly what Jake would be putting on the table, and it was all too good for Oz to pass up. The beats of the negotiation and the outcome were obvious; Jake didn't need his help.

"So, was it worth it?" Ashley asked Stephanie.

"Was what worth what?" Stephanie replied.

"The two months away."

"Oh yeah," Stephanie said with a serpentine smile. "We visited eleven ports, stole more data from more crews than I thought was possible, and got the lay of the land out there. Regent Galactic's companies, even the Order of Eden, have a whole soft underbelly, and it's bigger than anyone thought. What we brought in today is nothing compared to what we can get our hands on. The Order doesn't think anyone knows how much they depend on the supply routes at this end, or how much property Regent Galactic has, but we know now, and when we hit them in the future, it'll be surgical. We know how to really hurt them."

"Not to mention," Minh-Chu added, "the Warlord crew may be small, but they're all experienced information gatherers now, even the Samurai Squadron."

"I wish I went with you this time," Ashley said. "It sounds like there was a lot to see."

"Oh, there were long boring parts too," Stephanie said.

"Just ask Joyboy," Minh-Chu added. "He holds the record for signal interception duty. We had to leave him adrift in a fighter for six days so he could listen in on a Regent Galactic rebroadcasting node. I think he'd made up imaginary friends by the time we got back to him."

"Oh gosh, okay," Ashley chuckled. "Still missed you guys, though."

"Me too," Minh said. "I'm glad the Warlord needs its pilot back now that things are about to get really exciting."

CHAPTER 21
SHOZO OF HOUSE FALLEN STAR

"The new drive is complete on the Fallen Star, my Dominant," Shozo told Clark. The sound of her voice, and the comforting presence she offered through her biological emanations made it impossible for her to surprise Clark as she approached him from behind. Humans who couldn't feel her presence through their noses or skin were often startled by her, since it was Shozo's habit to observe a person unseen if she could before approaching them, usually from behind. She made no sound as she moved, breathed, or observed the space around her with bright, wide blue eyes.

She almost looked human under the neck to floor-length dress she imitated. Her neck was a little too long, her curly blue hair always looked wet, and her fingers were too long, so to any human she still seemed alien, even from behind. Once they got over her interpretation of how she felt she'd want to look as a human, Shozo's face drew all the attention. It was a piece of shape shifter art, especially since it matched her personality so well. Her big blue eyes spoke of a quest for wonders, boundless curiosity, and her little pursed lips suited her shy nature just as much as her squeaky voice did.

"The tests were successful?" Clark, known to so many as The Beast, asked.

"They were beautiful. A splash of gravity around the ship, and like a little cotoa fish, it was gone. Nine point three light years in five seconds, better than predicted. The navigational system is being upgraded, but that will be complete by the end of the day. All but one of the shuttles need more work that will take much longer, I'm sorry."

"There's no need to apologize, Shozo, you were only supposed to observe and report on this project, but you've shown how quickly you can learn, and you've taken charge several times while I was unavailable. I don't think I've heard from any of our builders for a week because they prefer to communicate through you."

"I'm sorry, Dominant. You delivered us from decay, and are wonderful. They should universally love you," Shozo said. "I am alive because of your generosity."

While it was true to an extent – Clark had given her a piece of his own framework technology in a graft so it could help her regenerate the contaminated tissue that was killing her – he didn't like being thanked for it. There was no way he could have known what an incredible, artful person he was saving at the time, and now that he did, seeing her so vividly alive was more than enough of a reward. Her dress was caught in a slight gust, and the hem raised just enough for a pair of soldiers in dark green armour to catch a glimpse at how she moved along.

Instead of feet, Shozo had thousands of hair-thin tendrils that allowed her to glide along the floor with silence and grace. They served her just as well in water. The soldiers seemed a little surprised, but couldn't help but grin at Shozo's endearing visage as she smiled at them. "No one should expect to be universally loved, even by the people who trust them to lead," Clark said.

"But that's not what Eve seems to think. She speaks to her followers like they all love her, and she recruits people quickly, demanding their love, and so many give it freely after her people have cared for them. I keep wondering if your living would be easier if you asked to be loved like she does. I say this with respect, my Dominant."

"It's hard for humans to express their needs. They mostly depend on vocal languages. Their instincts tell them that's a weakness, or their social group isn't open enough. Issyrians are lucky, they can sense when someone in the pod is in need, and that is one of the things that saved me." Clark felt strange explaining human limitations to her. She was an appealing, dainty looking creature, while he was jagged, in angular carapace armour growing from his flesh, and a death's head face that most humans could barely stand to look at. "I can't hide my emotions or vulnerabilities when I'm in the waters with your people, and they respond."

"Our people, my Dominant," Shozo reminded. "With respect."

"I've been away from the pools for too long," he replied. "Sometimes I forget." He looked past her through an upcoming transparent section of hull. They were aboard the Overlord Two, in the middle of the First Fleet of the Order of Eden. Another group of brand new destroyers build by Regent Galactic was arriving from the Iron Head Nebula, loaded to the airlocks with supplies, and woefully under crewed. Regent Galactic had no problem manufacturing all the ships and supplies they needed, but the recruiting efforts near the Iron Head Nebula and the nearby systems were not as rewarding as they had to be.

Clark noticed that Shozo was staring through the transparent hull as they passed the deck-height window. A concern weighted her expression, and he could feel her anxiety, which was normally a minor note of her fragrance, but it was rising to an overpowering potency. "One assignment ends, and another begins. The builders can finish their work without you, but I still need your help, Shozo."

"I know, you don't have to speak it. I only wish you could shed this war and take us to clearer waters," she said, her big eyes looking through his corpulent visage without flinching. "You refuse all help from the Fallen Star House, and let no Issyrian fight for you, but your human generals disobey your orders. I heard you speaking to two of them who killed millions of humans, and I could feel that it was against your orders."

"They were governors, but they may as well have been generals," Clark corrected gently. The conversations she was talking about were some of the least pleasant events from the last few months. A pair of governors contacting him, boasting that they'd used all the power of the Order of Eden in their area to take the Nuham System, bombarding the inhabitants of five colonized worlds into ruin and near extinction. They were to communicate with Nuham and offer them terms, not try once then blitz them into oblivion. His grip on Regent Galactic and Order of Eden forces was slipping; there were many ambitious governors who wanted his place.

"I am sorry, my Dominant," Shozo said. "Is that different?"

"No, their rank and position makes no difference. They're supposed to help me control these sectors so we can manage the Edxian's settlements in this galaxy. That's not happening, so I'm bringing them here soon."

"I sense deception," Shozo whispered. "I am shamed in admitting that I'm intrigued."

"They think I'm going to be pinning medals on them," Clark replied. "But I value medals as much as the Issyrians do." He could instantly feel that she understood what he was inferring – Issyrians had no love for medals. Their deeds were remembered best by their fellows, and the more good a member of the community did, the more the feelings of others towards them spread through the waters. Anyone swimming into their clutch or near it would know who the most goodly Issyrians were, and who they had impressed.

Her anxiety only abated a little, and he started to realize that most of the anxiety was for him, not herself. The airlock leading to the Fallen Star, the home of their Issyrian House, was just around the corner. It was time for him to give her the next assignment. "I am sorry for what I have to ask you to do for me, Shozo," Clark said.

"Anything, my Dominant," she replied, her eyes and essence revealing more curiosity than apprehension.

"I pressed you to make sure the Fallen Star was ready with the new faster than light system because I have to ask you to go far away. If the system works as it should, your journey won't be dangerous, but your skills at diplomacy and your empathy will be crucial to you when you meet with the people I need you to see. You are going to lead the Fallen Star, the House will accept you as a pod matron."

"Will I be back soon?" Shozo asked, unable to mask her worry.

"No, I'm sorry. You will never be able to return to the fleet," Clark told her, feeling a wash of sadness pass to him from her. He had to demand this of her, she was the perfect person for the mission, but it was difficult for him to keep his resolve.

"House Fallen Star will collectively mourn your absence, regardless of how long it takes you to follow us on our journey," she hesitated a moment. "You will be following us?" she asked with no hesitation. He couldn't help but feel that he was abusing her devotion to him, but there was no one else he'd send.

Clark knew she could feel his sorrow at her departure. That would be some consolation to her. "Not for some time, perhaps never," Clark replied. "But I need you to find a life for that House, a new purpose. The Order is not the place for you."

To anyone listening in on the conversation, they would hear it end there. A long moment of silence was filled with notions of love, sadness, and a shared understanding that could only be expressed chemically. After several minutes, Shozo of House Fallen Star quietly left.

CHAPTER 22
TWO CAPTAINS

"The Carthans are down, they're not recovering, and they're not getting reinforcements here," Jacob Valent told Captain Terry Ozark McPatrick. "How can the contract for Haven Shore keep us out?"

The broad causeway leading to the bridge of the Triton was busy again. Repair crews moved between the various system access areas leading to the nerve centre of the ship. People recognized both of the commanders immediately: Oz in a black and silver Triton Officer vacsuit and Jake in his long coat and heavy black vacsuit. The armoured long coat was a replacement, as was his vacsuit, but his battle-worn sidearm was a survivor. The back of the weapon poked out from behind his jacket as he walked towards the lifts.

"You know I'd love to see Triton, Haven Shore, and the Warlord all get along, but for now we'll have to settle for you and me building Triton Fleet, getting on while Haven Shore drifts off," said Oz.

"How is Carthan influence still holding us back? They can't enforce something on Tamber without dropping the ball on the major ports under their control on Kambis."

"They have a media machine, their solar system news feed. It concentrated on how Ayan broke things off with you, then pushed Liam right out of the solar system. The vote for keeping the Warlord out of Haven Shore had everything to do with perception, not much to do with politics."

Jake couldn't help but scoff and shake his head at how petty the game the Carthans played was. They made Ayan look like some man-eater, when the truth was far more elusive. It was true that she broke things off with him with little explanation, and that burned for months. What Jake regretted most about that situation was that he let her go; he didn't fight for her at all, and, in retrospect, he believed he should have, at least until he understood why she had to break ties with him. He didn't know or care to know much about her relationship with Liam, but he was quietly pleased that it didn't work out. Gossip wasn't something he enjoyed, but that news was welcome even though he was in the middle of a convenient relationship with someone else at the time. His focus returned to the moment, walking with an old friend. Oz was probably one of the few people in the galaxy who understood him. "How many voted against the motion to split away from Carthan support?" Jake asked.

"It only took one, they were still governing by consensus."

"That never works, I have no idea why anyone went along with Liam's model. Consensus government is something for dreamers and crazed optimists."

"You know, he had me convinced it could work for the first few months, and it did," Oz replied. "But Liam's gone, and the government is shuffling into a new majority system, adding seats so Haven Shore is set to grow, finally."

"It's about time. Too bad Liam left though, he was a good asset to the Triton at least." The statement irked Jake as he said it. He was glad to see Liam Grady leave, and knew that the people tending the Triton knew more than they needed to since the computer's records were fully accessible at long last. Seeing footage of Ayan standing across the table from Liam at council meetings made him wince, though he'd never admit it.

"You're allowed to celebrate," Oz said.

"Get out of my head," Jake replied.

"No one expects you to act like a statesman," Oz said with a chuckle. "You're the renegade captain, wanted in nine sectors."

"Ten," Jake said.

"Okay, ten sectors. People expect you to be rough around the edges, and they listen for your frank opinions. With everyone else playing the alliance game, you're one of the last people who can just say what's on their mind and not worry about the fallout, especially now that you have backing from the British Alliance. Congratulations on the privateering contract."

"Thanks, but I can't help but wonder," Jake said. "What are the strings from that contract tied to? The terms are too open, I have too much power for too little in return. There are strings I'm not seeing here, or we're being used for a longer game than I can predict."

"You're the hammer that will swing itself," Oz replied. "If it does too much damage, they can drop it and say whatever you've done wasn't their fault."

"Maybe it's that simple. Ever since I got the details about the Victory Machine and the motivation behind the Holocaust Virus, I think I've been seeing conspiracies around every corner."

"I know the feeling," Oz said. "I keep expecting the third watch bridge crew to wake me up in the middle of the night reporting that they've found a cadre of Citadel spies, or detected an Edxian battle group is entering the system."

"At least we know that if we don't win this war with the Order, there will be another war in thirty years," Jake replied. "Maybe a lot sooner."

"You find that reassuring?" Oz asked.

"I'd rather know than not. I just wonder what the British Alliance will do with the information now that they have our package."

"Who knows? I'm just surprised you got thirty-five million for it. The Triton's share is a huge help."

"You're welcome. Haven Shore will be pissed when they find out we cut them out and sent their three million directly to Ayan."

"I haven't told her the deal went through yet. I thought you could give her the news, and the cash."

"That's all right, send her the news, and store her part wherever she wants it," Jake said.

"Something going on between you two?" Oz asked.

"Nothing. I've been away and we haven't crossed paths in two months. I moved on."

"I was going to say, sorry things didn't work out with Xanna."

"It wasn't serious, I don't think either of us expected much."

"I bet Ayan will be relieved."

Jake fixed him with a warning glance.

"Moving on," Oz said, clearing his throat.

The pair walked down the small private hallway leading to the security office and Oz's ready room. "I want to ask for crewmembers for the Warlord, but I know you need everyone for the Triton's refit, so how about a compromise. Just set us up with a few people who can program skitters so we can get some working on the Warlord. I'll give you a good deal on a few materializers," Jake said.

"You know everyone here is earmarked for something, training took months. I was going to ask if there was anyone you can spare. I'm short on senior staff."

"You shouldn't have let people transfer to Haven Shore, you knew you wouldn't get people transferring back."

"What was I going to do? It's not like they had much choice but to be on Triton when most of these people came aboard. We rescued slaves and took on refugees, not exactly the best recruitment strategy."

"True, you should start recruiting on Tamber, or even better, Kambis."

"The Carthan Government is telling us not to, they're afraid we'll start picking up some of their former prisoners."

"Never trust a government that brainwashes their criminals to become soldiers," Jake said. "It's not a new rule on my ship."

"Good rule," Oz said.

"From experience," Jake added. "Listen, Oz, the British Alliance people I got on loan are gone, all of them. My ship's interior still isn't finished, and I have new problems that are going to take even more manpower to fix. I need some of your people, even for just a week – anything will help."

"How about you send me a couple hundred skitters and I'll start looking for five or six permanent volunteers for the Warlord?" Oz asked.

"How does that measure up? Six volunteers don't make up for the work a couple hundred skitters can do once we program them. How about you set up a few volunteers and we trade you five materializers each. These things are too dainty to work on most of what the Warlord needs, but they're perfect for a lot of the Triton's interior finishing."

"If privateering doesn't work out, you should go into retail," Oz replied. "Yeah, fine, sure. I'll find a few people who are looking for the kind of adventure they'll find on the Warlord."

"Make sure they can program skitters," Jake said.

"You know, there's another deal I'll make. You give me Agameg or Finn and I'll find you twenty able crewmen in exchange."

"Stop trying to poach my best people," Jake replied, laughing.

"Twenty crewmen for either one," Oz pressed.

"How about a hundred?"

"Fine, I'll drop it." Oz and Jake walked into the ready room, soft lighting activated, bathing the simple interior in warm colours. Through the main transparent section of hull, Jake could see the British Alliance's Third Battlegroup. Three massive carriers lazily drifted amongst an uncountable number of destroyers that were vaguely shaped like rifles. Between them were dozens of interception corvettes a little bigger than the Warlord and fighters on patrol. "So, you're really not going to offer anything from this haul to Haven Shore."

"Not even the empty cargo containers when we're done. They're getting a complete list though," Jake replied.

"Oh, that's cruel," Oz replied with a chuckle.

"They have it coming. We brought most of those people here, took care of them, and they're not willing to choose us over the Carthans? Yeah, Ayan and her island city are getting the same treatment my crew are getting."

"This haul is that good?" Oz asked.

"You're about to find out."

"And you're giving me first pick even though you know I'm running a cash-strapped ship?"

"You mean cash-absent, once you use what Minh and I brought in on supplies, don't you?"

"Cheap shot," Oz replied.

"Yeah, I'm offering you an opportunity you can't refuse. How would you like to have a Xetima farm?"

"What? How? I mean, you'd just leave that here with me? There's no way I could afford it, even on a twenty year payment plan."

"I'll leave it here. You take care of it, get it expanding, sell what you don't use to enhance your thrusters, and I'll take thirty five percent," Jake said.

"We've got maybe two small ships that use Xetima, most would be for sale," Oz replied.

"Exactly. You could increase the Triton's thrust by eighty percent and have enough excess to become the main supplier in this system. Deal?"

"Deal."

"You should have haggled, I would have gone down to twenty."

"I don't care," Oz said. "Why not sell it to the British?"

"They'd give us a good offer on it, sure," Jake said. "But then they'd move it out of the system and resell it to some coreward ally. They don't have a need for the stuff. Besides, I want to tie the Warlord in with the Triton's battle group. If not officially, then economically."

"You know that Triton will be joining in on the offensive the moment he's in shape and crewed up properly, you don't have to tie us in, we're with you already."

"I know, but there are no ties like economic ties. If we're connected on the record, then your future officers can't leave me out of decisions in the future. I know some of your officers in training don't like me or the Warlord. They believe we're early instigators."

"Who are you talking to on my ship?" Oz asked.

"The more people I loan you, the more I hear," Jake said with a knowing smile.

"Ashley," Oz said. "The one everyone wants to talk to off duty."

"And more," Jake replied. "There are people on your ship who have approached me asking about transferring to the Warlord. Your crew is starting to split, one side wants to fight as soon as possible, the other believes the Warlord is out there picking a fight too early."

"Any chance I could get a list of crewmembers who've gone behind my back with transfer requests?"

"Sure, if I can get my pick of them for my crew."

Oz laughed and nodded. "We're two captains here, not two old friends in this conversation, right?"

"I'm sitting on the biggest privateering take in the solar system, trying to firm up ties with one of the most influential commanders in the region. Friendship is easy, negotiations are hard."

"Okay, what's at the top of your list, Jake? You've given me a fuel production operation, told me you have evidence of a rift in my crew, and will trade me important manufacturing systems on the cheap. What's the big ticket item you're pushing for, Captain?"

"All right, Admiral," Jake replied with a smirk. "I have a vision for the Triton in this war. You lead her into enemy territory, hidden. The Warlord and other ships in her class fly missions off your launch decks, and the Triton becomes a platform for important operations." Jake could tell from Oz's reaction that he had thought of something similar, and he knew that getting the Triton's cloaking systems was a big priority when the Warlord departed seven weeks before. That technology was key in Jake's plan.

"And Haven Shore?" Oz asked.

"They don't seem interested in joining the team, so leave them out after appealing to qualified people to join your crew. Haven Shore is a great place for shore leave, even if they charge every member of my crew like tourists. The Triton is too important to be tied to a single solar system during war time, it's made to perform as a mobile base of operations."

"It's made for long term missions of exploration and defence," Oz corrected. "But I see your point. The reformation of Haven Shore's government may change a lot for Triton, maybe the Warlord too. I can see your vision, but it's too early to tell if that'll be the way things turn out – Triton isn't ready for long range missions yet."

"So, we'll see," Jake said.

"We'll see," Oz agreed. "I do still want Triton in this fight, Jake."

"I know, but thanks for reminding me. Just keep thinking about what kind of difference one carrier could make at this end of the sector once it gets moving. I'm giving you an intelligence update on the Order and Regent Galactic out here. You'll see what I see – a soft underbelly. I want to run the Warlord off the deck of the Triton in a month at the latest. If the Warlord can build a legend for itself and the Triton because people see we're working together, you'll never have to worry about finding good crewmembers. You'll be turning them away. We should fight this war together."

"I'm doing everything I can to get Triton in shape," Oz replied. "If I can find a way to set up a Xetima farm and crew it, then we might be able to buy half of the fixtures we need outright; we won't have to fabricate everything ourselves." Oz handed Jake a glass of dark amber restorative juice. It was a vitamin and mineral cocktail that tasted like old-fashioned iced tea, a product unique to the British worlds.

"Here's to that," Jake said, raising his glass.

"Are you sure I can't wrestle Agameg from you for a few weeks?" Oz asked.

An emergency communication came through and Jake answered while shaking his head and rolling his eyes. "We have a problem, Steph?"

"There's a ship coming in from the Irish Territories, it's in bad shape."

Oz checked his command and control unit and nodded. "Triton Control just granted them permission to land in Hangar Two."

"On my way," Jake said. He chugged the contents of his glass and started for the door.

"I'm going with you," Oz said. "The Irish Territories are right in the engagement zone."

CHAPTER 23
FAMILY REUNION

Jacob Valent, Terry Ozark McPatrick, Minh-Chu Buu, and Ashley Lamport met in the waiting area overlooking Hangar Two of the Triton. They watched the Hell Shrike as it was elevated into the large hanger. The ship was longer than it was wide, bristling with paired railgun turret emplacements. The multi-coloured hull was battered through in some places, melted through in others, and dented everywhere between. Five big pulse propulsion engines stuck out the back, and thruster pots dotted the surface of the ship.

"Where are Frost and Steph?" Jake asked.

"Frost was inside one of the cargo containers so he couldn't get our messages, she's getting him down here," Ashley replied. "She figured it would be better if she got him herself instead of relaying things through a crewman."

"Ever see an Irish Union city?" Minh-Chu asked as the industrial sized lift reached the bottom and the door started sliding open.

"Never," Jake said. "I've heard a lot about them from Frost and Stephanie, though."

"Stephanie's from somewhere near there?"

"A couple stars to the left. The Irish Union and a lot of early colonials settled in the same sector during the first exodus," Ashley replied. "I've seen a few old cities. Some are beautiful, the sorts of places you want to make your home port. Most are pretty rough though, lots of people struggling. A lot like Stephanie's home town."

They started walking towards the fifty-eight metre long ship. "They're in pretty rough shape," Oz said. "I have a medical team on the way."

"Just one?" Jake asked.

"We only have one." They could see five ramps lowering and a few crewmembers who had the look of commanders in mid-length green, black, and orange coats leading a few crewmembers down. Everyone was armed, and they stayed close to the ship once they debarked, fairly standard behaviour. Crews didn't normally mingle before their captains met with representatives.

The hangar's secondary cargo lift arrived behind Jake and Minh-Chu, delivering a squad of armed Triton soldiers. "How does it look, Sir?" the sergeant asked over proximity radio.

"I think we're good," Oz replied. "Hang back and stay ready just in case. Be ready to offer assistance, they could have injured aboard."

"Aye."

"Should we wait for Frost?" Minh-Chu asked.

Jake watched as one person split from the crowd forming around the ship and started towards them. She had broad features and dark skin. The battered coat she wore and scarred form-fit armour told Jake tales of close-quarters combat and boarding missions. The guns slung below her hips told the rest of the story. The pistols were heavily modified for increased power, and they looked well used.

A few burn scars and pockmarks running along her left jaw didn't spoil her beauty; they only made her more interesting. He almost didn't notice the two women and one man catching up to her as she approached. "I'm Captain Moira McFadden, this is Captain Eily Hogan, Captain Mickey Kane, and Captain Oma Bell. We've heard about your fight here, and are at your service," she said with conviction. "I know what you're thinking," Captain McFadden continued, her brown eyes examining him. "Four captains, one ship. Captain Kane here is the only one who has a ship that'll thrust or shoot, the rest of us had ours blasted out from under us by the Order."

"We put Captain McFadden in command of my ship on account of her record," Captain Kane said. He was a grizzled, stout fellow with cybernetic eyes that reminded Jake of Alice's old mechanical implant. "She's the war hero."

"We heard your signal clear and strong when you put the call out to captains who wanted to join your fight against the Order," Captain Bell added. She looked as grizzled as Kane; her blonde hair was cut down to stubble. "We're hoping to fix up the Hell Shrike somewhere and capture a few ships we can crew so we can help build up your fleet."

"Aye," Captain Moira McFadden said. "If you don't mind me asking, how is that fleet coming along?"

Jake had never felt more put on the spot than he did right then. The sideways glance from Minh-Chu didn't help. "We have a fighter squadron and I'm re-crewing my ship, but as soon as we're set, the Warlord is heading back out."

"Triton is mid-refit, but he makes a good base," Oz added.

"I told you it was nothing but air!" Captain Eily Hogan said, throwing her hands up and stomping around in a tight circle behind her fellows. "Bugger's just a dressed up mouthy braggart."

Jake hurriedly searched for some kind of defence for his lack of progress. "You wouldn't say that if you saw our last take."

"So you're doing some damage, making a difference with a broken carrier and one fighting ship?" asked Captain Mickey Cane cautiously.

"We've gathered intelligence, taken two cargos, and captured an important military leader," Minh-Chu said without a hint of shame. "We had to make repairs and we've been short on crew. As for people signing up for this rebellion, you're the first brave enough to show." There was disappointment in how he spoke, and it got their attention. "We've been on the run, taking in refugees, trying to find a base to operate from. This ship, the Triton, was in good working order when Captain Valent captured her before the war started. Trying to save people caught in the middle of this mess cost us, though. Now we're regrouping. Now we need you more than ever because we're ready for the war, but they need to see they're not alone."

The group of captains were quieted by the statement that the Triton was one of Captain Jake Valent's captures, and listened more intently.

Jake picked up right where Minh-Chu left off. "Ronin here is the Wing Commander of Samurai Squadron, a fighter group that launches from my ship, the Warlord. I put the Triton in the hands of Captain McPatrick – we call him Oz. He's a trained carrier captain with a long record of combat experience."

Captain Bell was the first to offer Minh-Chu her hand. He smiled and shook it. She shook Oz's hand as well. The other captains followed in turn, except for Captain McFadden. "I see," she said. "So how close are you to getting a real offensive going, Captain? The British have barely fired a shot in this war. In fact, they've signed a truce."

"The Warlord will be ready to go in three days," Jake replied. "And we have all the intelligence we need."

"Samurai Squadon just needs a good night's sleep," Minh-Chu added.

"Can you find us a place to repair my ship?" asked Captain Kane. "The Hell Shrike has a few holes in her."

"I don't have anyone to spare," Oz said. "But the Triton has a storage hangar you can use and some extra gear that'll speed things up for your crew."

"Thank you, Sir," Captain Kane said. "You wouldn't know where we can go scavenging for materials?"

"There's more than you need down on Tamber for free if you can't afford to pay per ton from Carthan orbital collections," Minh-Chu replied. "Just stick to the empty wrecks."

"You're not what we expected," Captain McFadden said, her expression softening a little. "But you'll have to do." Frost emerged from the lift doors and she walked towards him without a word.

His smile was visible from where Jake was standing over fifty metres away. He shouted, "That's not my wee Moira, is it?"

The three captains in front of Jake and the crew behind were silent. Heads were lowered, eyes uneasily glancing towards Captain McFadden and Shamus Frost. Stephanie followed several steps behind Shamus. Jake could see that she recognized the mood coming from Moira and her captains.

Minh-Chu couldn't let the moment unfold without inquiring. "They know each other?" he said to Captain Bell, who nodded sadly.

"Moira's his cousin. Big family, McFaddens and Coys, hundreds, but those two are all that's left now." Captain Bell continued in a whisper, "The Order hit the Irish Union worlds hard, guess they didn't like how we got through their virus without much harm. We fought until we only had a few scattered ships left, most looking like our Hell Shrike here. The Order's ruling our land now, they made examples of the families who had a lot of fighters standing in the way. Our Moira's a war hero, and Shamus McFadden there is wanted in nine sectors by the Order."

"Ten," Jake said as a reflex and immediately felt like he'd said the most inappropriate thing in the universe. He watched as Frost embraced Moira McFadden. She spoke to him for a moment. He shook his head in response to the news. Moira took his stubbly cheeks in her hands and nodded. Jake's heart broke for Shamus as he sunk to his knees, his whole torso wracked by sobs. Moira held him in her arms, weeping. Stephanie knelt down and stroked Frost's back.

"Good," Captain Kane said. "Moira's finally cryin'."

As Minh-Chu and Jake were about to turn their attention back to the captains standing with them, Frost stood up straight and strode for the nearest exit, a narrow side passage for emergency shuttles. Stephanie turned in time to catch his arm but, to Minh-Chu's surprise, Frost brushed her off.

Then he caught sight of Frost's expression. A dangerous, determined scowl contorted Frost's broad features. "Jake," Minh-Chu said.

"Catch him!" Jake shouted.

Frost was through the emergency escape hatch and it was closed behind him before anyone could get near him. Minh-Chu, Jake, Stephanie, and Moira were the first to react. "Frost! What are you doing!" shouted Stephanie as she reached the outer hatch of the emergency launch corridor. Two of the heavy hinges were glowing red, and Jake could barely budge the emergency door with an attempt that bent the thick metal handle.

A loud pop signalled the launch of the six-man Triton emergency shuttle, and Minh-Chu glanced through the transparent hangar doors just in time to see it accelerating towards Tamber. "The launch bay will have something ready to go," Oz said, starting for the nearest lift.

"This is bad," Minh-Chu said under his breath.

"You have no idea," Stephanie said. "I know where he's going."

CHAPTER 24
EAVESDROPPING

Alice leaned against the wall of Haven Shore's main port building. It was a temporary setup – eventually the main port would be a massive tower, and the one she was standing in would be an outbuilding – but she liked it. Still licking her wounds from her dismissal from the Rangers, procrastinating on meeting the Warlord crew and her father, she watched dozens of people coming and going. It was one of her favourite guilty pleasures: leaving her cloaking systems on for an afternoon, going to the busiest place in Haven Shore, picking someone and following them for a while. She'd already chosen her target for the day: Ayan.

The temporary port building was a circular structure put together with transparent panels from leftover emergency shelter assemblies that made a building a little over seventy metres across. Three gangways led out of one side to the horseshoe shaped landing platform. It took them a couple of days to put the port building together, but that platform outside, large enough for five to seven mid-sized ships, and the cleared land on the reinforced cliff top around it took six weeks to complete. The landing platform proper had the most expensive landing spots on that hemisphere of Tamber, and they were always full.

The ground surrounding it, with enough room to support twenty or more vessels in the thirty-metre sloop or planet hopper category, was less expensive, but the port was making money. That much was evident.

The other side of the port building was always busy too, with two main exits leading to hover vehicle paths that took people to the Everin Building and beyond.

Alice leisurely watched a few covered gangways that were meant to lead to other structures, but most were capped off at various lengths with temporary exit hatches or small portable outbuildings. She'd seen countless tearful hellos and farewells from a distance in those quieter corners, but on that day there seemed to be more arguments than anything. There was tension in the air. Alice heard more than a few people talk about the reformation of the Haven Shore government and the arrival of the Warlord. There were already rumours that the dark ship had captured incredible treasures, and that Haven Shore wouldn't benefit because of Ayan's sovereignty deal with the Carthans.

She started walking towards the hallway she was most familiar with. It led down to the west cliff, the side of the island covered in centuries-old jungle. The shockwave that devastated the eastern side, flattening hundreds of kilometres of growth, didn't affect the other portion of the island nearly as much thanks to the craggy mountain chain running down the middle of the land mass. Alice felt drawn back to the jungle; it was unlike anything she'd ever seen, a real alien place. She almost envied the people who ventured out to harvest fruit every day, even though they complained about big cats and yapping, thieving monkeys, of which there were many breeds. The pickers were well protected in vacsuits, but avoided disturbing wildlife whenever they could. It was also worth mentioning that it was difficult to pick fruit when you're getting chewed on, an experience Alice still recalled vividly.

Every time she came back from long ranger patrols across the vast forests and wastes of Tamber, there was something new taking shape in Haven Shore. She couldn't help but notice that they were out of prefabricated walls and domes, and it made her wonder what the next step in building was, and how much things would slow down. They had no large fabrication shops set up, though she heard two were being built, but it would be slow going unless the Rangers could lead salvage teams to good unclaimed wrecks. Her time as a Ranger was over, it was something she still caught herself forgetting. Alice couldn't help but think it might be for the best, regardless of how much it stung.

When she started with the Rangers, she could still keep her eye on her father, but when he told her the Warlord would be going out of the system to gather information, she couldn't help but remember Jason Everin's message to her. Sometimes it was difficult to believe that he'd come to her in a manufactured memory and told her that she could improve the futures of her father and herself if she stayed close to him. She felt she might be his connection to humanity somehow, but her father told her to stay with the Rangers, that she'd see more, learn more there while the Warlord was away.

Alice stopped and leaned against a post, wondering what things would have been like if she just followed her first instinct and gone with the

Warlord crew. They must have seen some interesting things while visiting strange ports.

She looked to the upper level of the port building and immediately noticed Ayan descending down the ramp curving into the circular main desk in the middle of the port building. Ayan was back in a dress shaped from vacsuit material. The light pastel blue suited her, contrasting with her curly red hair. Ayan might not have been more than a few centimetres taller than Alice, and she did want to be taller when she grew out of her teens, but if she didn't grow much more, Alice hoped to look like Ayan more than anyone else. Before Ayan tried to reassure her after being ejected from the Rangers, Alice only saw her as her father's former flame. The short reassurance Ayan gave her when she was in tears changed that. Alice took some kind of solace in seeing how intelligent, talented, and busy Ayan was. She was also beautiful by Alice's standards, so much more than she was. Ayan had curves, whereas Alice felt boyish: short and muscly. Alice couldn't imagine being as busy or stressed as Ayan, and didn't understand how the woman could handle herself so calmly as she addressed one situation after another. She was a builder, a designer, a military officer, and a politician. Alice could understand why Ayan's love life exploded in her face from time to time, considering.

The desk in the middle of the port building was large enough for a staff to attend to people coming in, and security gates stretched out to the sides, splitting the whole floor of the building into two halves. Haven Shore security in dark blue armoured vacsuits stood guard as people passed through the scanning gates.

Ayan met with Lieutenant Davi and Remmy at the bottom of the ramp, where they were waiting at the desk. Alice couldn't help but feel deep envy as she watched Remmy from a distance. She heard he got to lead the soldiers who took the last Order of Eden garrison on Tamber, maybe in the entire Rega Gain Solar System, and wished it were her. She fought numerous frameworks on her own – what had he done? "Would have been nice to be there, at least," she muttered under her breath. He was twenty-three years old, finished Freeground Fleet Academy early, and got himself recruited into Fleet Intelligence right away. After meeting him several times during Ranger training, she couldn't see why. He was a brat, with a sense of humour that she found more annoying than funny. She watched him, Lieutenant Davi, and Ayan at the Port Control desk.

Ayan was all smiles at first, shaking Lieutenant Davi's hand then Remmy's. Her expression became serious within seconds, however, as Remmy took his time awkwardly telling her something.

"Ayan!" Shouted a gravelly voice so suddenly and loudly that, judging from the reaction of the crowd, you'd think a bomb went off. Frost marched into the main port building straight for Ayan, who was flanked by two security officers in an instant. She stayed them with a gesture.

Alice had never seen Frost so furious. Even in moments when machines refused to cooperate, he didn't look like that. He didn't look murderous. "Time for you to wake up and take notice: there's a war on, and you're keeping the crew we need from signing up. We can't fight with a crew of seven."

"Easy, Shamus," Ayan replied. "That's up to the Council and the people of Haven Shore."

"You're at the head of that table, this overgrown sand-castle was your idea, and you're actin' like we've already won when there's a war just starting."

"I'll be happy to talk about-"

Frost drew his sidearm and rapid fired several shots over everyone's heads. His pulse shots burned through the metal effortlessly and he dropped his weapon back into its holster. By the time he'd finished, every guard and soldier had their weapons drawn on him. "Your plastic walls can't stop a round from my smallest shooter. Your little city would be slagged in a real attack. You need to face reality, girl: all our enemies know exactly where to find us, and when the Order comes for this system, the Brits will turn tail, and this city will be a mass grave with your name on the stone."

"Frost!" shouted Jake as he stormed into the port. "Stand down!"

"They're all dead, Jake. Not just my kin, but Stephanie's, maybe Ashley's," Frost raged, tears dripping from reddened eyes. "Someone's got to make them pay for it. More of them need to step up before trouble comes here."

"I know," Jake said. "Trust me, I know."

Stephanie closed the distance between her and Frost before anyone else reached him, and she turned towards two security guards that were creeping up behind him. "Leave him alone. Goddamned children looking to pin him now that the moment's over. Fine army you've got here," Stephanie spat at Ayan as she took Frost in her arms. "Could use some seasoning, yeah?"

"It's over," Ayan said to the guards standing at the ready. "Jake, can we talk?" She didn't wait for him to respond, but started walking towards a side passage.

Alice followed them, unseen, into a covered walkway that led to an incomplete shuttle pad. No one would bother Ayan and Jake there, and

Alice made sure her suit wasn't pinging her position to the security network, so they wouldn't know she was there.

Ayan listened silently as Jake told her about Frost's family and the fate of their home. The Order made an example of the entire family and the city around them, razing it to the ground then making sure everyone was dead by sending soldiers down to search the place and execute survivors on foot.

The Irish Union worlds were ravaged by the Order of Eden when they decided to expand their territory, and the Hell Shrike was one of the last ships from their defence fleet. All the nearby systems had fallen, and it was possible that Stephanie's family as well as Ashley's friends were all captured or killed. The Order of Eden destroyed the military presence in those systems, dismantled governments, and executed the families of resistors. The surviving populace was reduced to refugees and prisoners, ordered to repair the damage to their world after the Order was sure they'd won.

The scope of loss and unstoppable nature of the Order made Alice feel as though everything she'd done with the Rangers over the previous months was meaningless. What were a few rescues and victories over wandering frameworks compared to the fight the Hell Shrike crew just escaped? It felt as though she had been wasting her time on a moon tucked safely behind larger planets. She should have stayed on the Warlord, even though her father encouraged her to join the Rangers for the experience, where she might help people like Frost's family, or at least fire a shot at Order soldiers in the field.

"I couldn't be sorrier," Ayan said, nearly in tears. "I feel for them, I truly do."

"What's happening down here, Ayan?" Jake asked, his tone non-confrontational.

"The Council is pushing a colonist's agenda. Victor Davis and I are the only ones in support of a more military approach."

"Victor? Your bodyguard from the Pandem refugees?" Jake asked.

"Former bodyguard. He and Iloona are both pushing with me to get out from under our contract with the Carthans and to quicken progress. It's been hard, and we're mid-reformation so I won't have a seat again for a day or two."

"It's too soon for that kind of democracy," Jake said. "The details of this government don't matter, you have to see that. Give the people representatives, fine, but take control and get the people willing to fight for the support they need."

Ayan looked at him, looking a little surprised. She didn't reply right away. "Maybe. Probably, but it's too late now."

"Yours is still the only name on the Sovereignty agreement – that gives you all the power here if you want it. Just overrule the Council and militarise. So what if a bunch of ungrateful colonists get pissed and leave. They shouldn't be here anyway; chances are the war is coming here next. The rest will see things your way, they'll have to."

"You say that as though that wouldn't betray the very idea of democracy," Ayan replied. "We were both raised to believe that the people should control their destiny."

"Survival comes first, and that takes direction, power. You could turn Haven Shore into a military base in a couple days, especially with the Rangers in hand. They don't take orders from the Council. This pretend oasis isn't what people need, and there's no way you're happy playing politician."

Alice watched the scene unfold in disbelief. Jake had to know that his words were falling on Ayan like physical blows, but he was relentless, verging on angry. Ayan was looking smaller by the moment, staring off towards a distant ocean instead of peering back at her old flame. After a moment of silence, Alice was surprised to hear Ayan say, "I hate you for being right. Not forever, but right now, I hate this. I put so much work into this place, and it just doesn't feel like I'm needed here, like I'm wanted here."

Alice wanted to see Jake put a comforting arm around Ayan so badly she was tempted to pick his limb up and drop it in its proper place herself, but her father didn't move. "I'm sorry, and I'm sorry about Frost. He bolted ahead and got into a shuttle. No one gets a head start like an old ship thief."

"I know he wasn't aiming for me, maybe I needed a little gunfire to get the point," Ayan said. "I feel like an idiot for not fighting this civilian spectator attitude harder."

"I haven't been here for awhile, so I'm not up to date on everything, but is this really the best place for you?" Jake asked.

Ayan practically scowled at the question. "I thought so a while ago. I don't spend all my time worrying about the Council; most of the time I'm directing the construction. I have the education for it, remember?"

"I'm only wondering if you wouldn't be happier off-world. If you're looking for a place where you're wanted, there are a lot of places for you in orbit. I know Oz wants you on the Triton, and we're taking the Warlord out again soon, capturing another ship and following a few big leads. You could come with us, you'd be great out there."

140

She looked up at Jake. It was so obvious that Ayan found his offer tempting. Alice silently hoped she'd take it. "I might not always get my way with the Council, but there are so many people in trouble left on Tamber. The society we make down here is more important than any of the buildings we put up. But then I look at you and what you're doing with the Warlord and can't help but think that's where the real effort should be. Not for everyone, but for people like me. People who can survive on a ship like that."

"People like us," Alice caught herself muttering. She was immediately thankful for the cloaking technology that stopped her foolish third party participation from giving her away.

Ayan continued a moment later. "Everything is so…" she sighed and looked towards the broad foundation of the permanent port building. "So complicated."

"The invitation will always be open," Jake said.

"Thank you," Ayan replied. "And good try. If I'm to be honest, I have to say I'm tempted. Oz just gave up trying to get me aboard the Triton full time. He teases, but I know there's a serious offer in there. Are you looking to poach a few people?"

"You're the first I've tried to steal," Jake said. "On this trip, at least."

"Well, you didn't hear this from me," Ayan said, "but try for more. Port Rush is in bad shape. There are thousands of stranded crew from ships that will never fly again all through there. I was going to tell Oz, but you should go first. Just don't get caught by the Carthans. Actually, if you brought the Warlord down when you recruited, you could probably teach the Carthans a lesson about trying to stand in your way when they send a patrol to stop you from recruiting. I wouldn't mind seeing a few of them with bloody noses."

Alice was deeply surprised, and grateful for her suit's sound suppression when she couldn't hold back a giggle.

"That's pirate thinking," Jake said, grinning.

"You're a bad influence," Ayan replied. "Speaking of which, I have to get my day started. I'm meeting with my father, so I'll ask if he can spare some Rangers for the Warlord." She looked back to the north, where they could see the ocean to the right of a mountain peak. "I have a lot to think about here, and I get the feeling I don't have much time to make some changes before the Council gets back together. More and more, it seems like I shouldn't be on it when they return to the table. Either way, I think leaving on the Warlord is premature. It was good seeing you, Jake. Good luck."

"I'll check in when I get back," Jake said as he watched Ayan leave.

He crossed to the railing and looked out over the broad foundation of the permanent port structure. It was over five hundred metres across, and it would take weeks longer to finish the foundations with their single deep drilling machine. The metres thick stabilization systems were being built off to the side under a temporary roof to protect them from rain. "I can see you, Alice."

Alice disengaged her cloaking systems and joined Jake at the railing, nervous at the trouble she might be in. "Sorry, it's become a hobby."

"I don't think anyone else saw you, I'm linked with my scanners and Crewcast," Jake replied. "The only reason why I guessed you were there was because the spot you were standing in read blank, the only place I couldn't see properly through the scanners."

"Huh, didn't think of that," Alice said. "Sorry."

"I've missed you on the Warlord," Jake said.

Alice retracted her faceplate and pulled her headpiece down, deciding to tell him the worst news right then and there. "I got in trouble, was kicked out of the Rangers." Her embarrassment and fear at his disappointment overwhelmed her as quickly as she could say the words.

He turned to face her with an expression she couldn't quite read at first. It seemed as though he was about to smile, but he looked sad at the same time. "I know, it's all right."

"I still can't believe I screwed it up," Alice said, frustrated at the tears that threatened to well up.

Jake took her into his arms and asked, "You thought you were making the right decision at the time?"

"You read the report?" Alice asked.

"No way Anderson would give me access, I'm just guessing here."

She hugged him back and gripped the back of his suit. Next to her father, she felt so small, safe, and like she was with the only person who could understand her. Those were things she forgot when she decided not to follow the Warlord nearly two months before, but she couldn't help but remember them then. To make things worse - or better, she wasn't sure yet – her father's anger at her being kicked out of the Rangers had completely failed to materialize. "I feel so stupid," she sobbed.

"I don't keep stupid people on my ship, and you have a bunk waiting on the Warlord," Jake said as he stroked her back.

"You got rid of Kipley?" she asked, amused.

"Sold him to the British," Jake replied.

"I'm surprised you didn't have to pay them to take him," she chuckled, thankful for the relief humour brought. Alice wiped her tears away and stepped out of her father's embrace. "I thought you'd be angry."

"I was jealous, you know," Jake said through a reassuring smile. "'What does she need with these Rangers?' I thought. 'She could be on the Warlord, the baddest ship this side of the Elek Strand.'"

Alice couldn't help but laugh. His humour could be cheesy, but she usually enjoyed it.

"I'm glad to have you back," her father told her. "When you're ready, I'd like to hear the story about you and the Rangers over the last two months."

"I'll send you a copy of the reports, they're all clear to share with family now," Alice replied.

"I want to hear your side, I don't care what the reports say," Jake said.

Alice stared at him for a moment. Despite his armour, darkened appearance, or reputation with everyone in the solar system and beyond as a criminal or soldier, the man standing in front of her was just her dad. He was back, and seemed to want nothing more than to spend time with his daughter. She pulled herself up so she could sit on the railing and asked, "How 'bout now? Do you have time?"

Jake looked a little surprised, but smiled back at her. "Sure."

She started by telling him about meeting a former fellow Ranger trainee at her apartment, and by the time she was telling him about meeting the pickers in the jungle, the tale came easily. Alice didn't realize how unusual and amazing that day was until she was telling someone else about it, even though it ended sadly. Her father listened intently to every detail.

CHAPTER 25
FLUID THINKING

For the first time since the Everin Building came into being, the lowest floor was more than a lobby. Small bots with protective shells on top of fine manipulator arms, welders, spanners, and other tools rushed around, beeping and ticking at each other. They were busy installing the components for the transit system that arrived from the overworked fabrication shop beneath the building. The little skitter bots didn't seem impeded at all by the removal of their wireless systems. They used audio and visual signals to communicate. A few used full words occasionally, something Ayan would ask a technician about when she had a spare moment.

Ayan couldn't help but smile at the progress of the lobby. Before it had been a quiet, visually appealing place, with polished floors that featured a gold, blue, and green weaving pattern of stone, and a transparent metal ceiling with mild illumination built in. Through it, travellers could see the interior of the Everin Building. Open to the sky far above, it was easy to get distracted by ships descending and ascending between balconies with invisible impact shielding. There was a security office in the middle of the large lobby, with two pairs of officers on duty and access to the floor beneath, where the police and emergency services centres would be built.

With the transit system under construction, the lobby would become a hub for transportation, connecting the Everin Building to the rest of Haven Shore and beyond, if you included the nearby port, which was far from complete. She couldn't help but notice as a skitter bot stood as tall as it could, about half a metre, in front of a pair of elevator doors and started beaming shades of green from its smooth metal shell. "This lift is ready for use!" it chirped loud enough for people nearby to hear. It was as though the bot was desperate to see people try the new thing his mechanical team had built.

It was what Ayan was waiting for, and she joined five other people who stepped inside. There was room for twice as many people in the fairly plain green and brown elevator car, but no one else seemed interested in going first.

"Beats the construction lifts," said an older gentleman carrying a medical case. "Never knew when those things were going to stop or for how long."

No one else joined him in griping about the temporary lifts that were often overused, or out of order. There was always one temporary lift working; the problem was, you didn't know which one, and sometimes you'd have to walk the circumference of the building to find it. The top two-thirds of the Everin Building were mostly empty thanks to that situation. Two of the occupants, an older woman and a Haven Shore junior watchman in his green and blue vacsuit, glanced at her as they realized whom they were riding with. Their gawking was immediately followed by uncomfortable averted gazes and fidgeting.

"Someone has to be the first to go up the shaft," Ayan said through a little smile. The lift moved so gently that she couldn't tell how fast they were going. Her sensors told her the ascension was swift, and Ayan was alone in the lift after three stops. It was no surprise that she was the only one going to the top.

Her comm blinked, indicating that she had a call coming in from Mischa Konev. She answered and the image of Mischa's face appeared in front of her. It was an image only Ayan could see, sent directly to her eyes, but it was as though Mischa was standing in front of her. "Hi, Ayan."

"Hello, how are you?" Ayan asked, aware that Mischa wasn't calling for small talk.

"Great, busy, how about you?"

"Doing very well. Testing the Everin Building's first civilian lift."

"That's good. Question for you," Mischa said.

The lift doors opened, and after making sure she was in the right place, Ayan stepped off onto the rooftop. She spotted Lee in the middle of the temporary landing pads. He was accepting a new delivery of refurbished skitter bots from a cargo ship they'd converted into a mobile servicing vessel. They came in crates made from recycled metal plating and whatever else the welders could find. Once the skitters were activated and their programming was verified, they would find a place near their assigned construction post and make that crate their home, where they'd recharge, service each other, and store spare parts. Ayan had seen a couple of large 'skitter settlements,' as the construction personnel called them, and was amazed at the honeycomb-like structures that resulted from many skitter bots gathering. "Ask me anything," Ayan replied.

"Are you leaving Haven Shore? I went looking for your apartment and found out that, as of last night, you don't have one here. Lacey said I should talk to you directly about this, since I'm looking to nominate you to the Military Liaison seat."

"Thank you, I appreciate that. After what happened in the port, I'm not sure what I'm doing, to be honest."

"Are you all right? What happened?"

"I'm surprised you haven't seen, it's at the top of the Crewcast Feed. A member of the Warlord crew had a message for me, and he made sure I wouldn't forget it. No one was injured, but it's got me thinking longer term."

"Not you, too. Did you know Victor's leaving?"

"What?" Ayan asked, genuinely surprised.

"He's turned my nomination aside. Admiral McPatrick offered him the head of security position on the Triton last night. He's using the Council shuffle to poach people for the Triton staff. He's got two hundred or so people transferring from Haven Shore back to the Triton, too. With no representatives to monitor transfers, we could be out of post-construction maintenance people by the end of the week."

"I should have seen this coming, he's been starving for personnel for months." Ayan knew there was a solution, but it seemed too risky until Frost made his point. He'd given her something she didn't realize she'd lost: a sense of urgency. For the life of her, she couldn't remember when that slipped away. Maybe it came with the rise of the Everin Building, and watching families migrate from their converted cargo crates, broken down ships, and temporary shelters into their new homes. Perhaps it was because of the Council, or it could have even been the fact that Tamber was protected from interstellar bombardment thanks to the way it was situated in the solar system. It was probably a combination of all those things, but the question of *when* her sense of urgency slipped was unanswerable.

"Ayan, I need the Council to form fast, and I need people who are reasonable most of all. If the best of us transfer off-world, Tyra will bring in her own crowd, and it won't be pretty."

"I'll see what I can do, Mischa." A few nominees that could take her place came to mind and she couldn't help but smile. "I'll definitely have a couple of people you can trust by the end of the day."

"I know them?"

"You will, and you'll thank me."

146

"Thank you, Ayan, but can you give me something to start with right now? I need an ally."

"Give me an hour then contact Carl Anderson, he'll take my seat."

"Your father's going to be available?"

"He's already detached from the Sunspire and he has interests in Haven Shore with the Rangers."

"Will he agree?" Mischa asked eagerly. "Did you already speak with him?"

"Tell him I sent you," Ayan replied. "He'll agree, and I'm sure he can suggest a few other people to nominate for other seats."

"Fantastic, thank you."

"You're welcome."

"I'm just wondering, why are you leaving?" Mischa asked.

Ayan thought a moment and replied, "My personal drama got in the way of something important, so it's time to move on and let someone else take the seat." That wasn't nearly the entire answer, but it was good enough for Mischa.

"I'll miss having you at the table," she said before ending the communication.

Lee Romita emerged from a battered cargo shuttle and smiled at Ayan. "You must love the view from the top," he said. "Too bad I can't get you within spitting distance of the edge."

"Can't seem to stay away from the surest sign of progress," Ayan replied. "You and your people have really surprised everyone, Lee."

Lee Romita looked genuinely surprised at the praise; he even took a half-step backwards. "Just following the designs you and the team programmed in."

"Will you need us architects around much for the final touches?" Ayan asked.

He thought for a moment and shook his head. "No, why? You planning on going out of range?"

"Probably not, but I'm starting to look at a few other problems on Tamber. Problems that we could have a solution for if the Council members don't get in the way. I'm starting to think it's time to go another way without them so I can move on to more pressing things."

"I'm not the first you're telling, am I? I haven't heard about this yet, and Crewcast is quick to move whatever you're saying to the top of the Feed."

"I'm thinking aloud, Lee. I find my situation is very fluid today, and I expect it might remain so for a while. You'll keep my thoughts to yourself for now?"

"Yes, Ma'am. Now you've got me wondering if I'm the one you're up here to see today, or if you have a shuttle coming."

"You're who I'm here to see," Ayan said. Her military comm channel warned that Carl Anderson was on his way to her in a shuttle and she couldn't help but smile. "Though I think this rooftop is becoming my office for the hour."

"I've noticed you don't have a real one," Lee said. "Something I think people like about you."

"I wish I had time for an office some days," Ayan replied. "Back to why I'm braving the windy heights to see you in person. You're going to be finished all the critical structural work here in a few days, right?"

"Could be done by the end of today, if you like. I could have two hundred and thirty souls available to work on the port tomorrow morning, leaving just a few here to supervise the bots as they put in the rest of the fixtures."

Ayan knew there were hundreds of fixtures left to install. The recyclers, waste management, communication, and climate control systems were being put in as quickly as the fabrication shop could manufacture them by skitters and a few of the larger bots they had. "What about the combat base features? I know the shield is finished, but you're still keeping the ship management and servicing systems until the end, right?"

"Yes, but from the sounds of it, you have something else in mind."

Ayan was thinking on her feet for the first time in what felt like months. "I'm cancelling the construction on the permanent port here." She could picture the towering port buildings from the vision the Victory Machine gave her in her mind's eye. She could see how similar a few facets of the Everin Building were to features of those towers. "I may not be on the Council, but I am the primary signing authority for Haven Shore. It's time I used that power for something important again. I feel more and more like ordering the construction of this building was the last important thing I did."

"No offense, but I think you're right."

"It's fine, I think there are a lot of people who agree with you."

"There's something else I'd like to ask, now that you've mentioned it. What does it mean when they call you the Sovereign authority, or White Queen?"

Ayan hated both titles, especially the moniker of White Queen. "I hope the 'White Queen' thing never catches, but the documents the Carthans had me sign were that archaic. Liam and one of their upper officers performed the function of witness, while two friends were named in the document, both of them dead now."

148

"I'm sorry about that. So that leaves you alone on this document, which says…"

"I technically own everything here and new claims on Tamber have no authority unless they're made in my name," Ayan said. The admission felt strange and boastful, but it was the truth. "The Carthans and the British don't care what anyone else says or does, I'm the only real voice of authority."

"Like King Matthew in the Olin System," Lee said.

"I'm not a queen," Ayan replied with sudden irritation. "Sorry, Lee, I just don't like people calling me the White Queen, and I've seen it coming up on Crewcast."

"No worries," Lee replied, chuckling nervously. "I'll figure out the differences on my own time, probably ask Trina to explain. So, what are we building instead of the port? The landing and service facilities in the Everin Building?" Lee asked.

"Only enough for fifteen shuttles and as many fighters for now. Don't build the defensive weaponry, but finish the transportation systems. How long would that take? A week or so?"

"With the robot workforce we have right now, about three days. We have a lot of the parts already fabricated. Why are you putting off defensive measures? I'm asking because I'll have to explain."

"The Council thinks they're safe here, so I think it's time to listen to them and move focus away from Haven Shore's military participation and armaments. They can depend on the British Alliance for cover, or the Carthans, since at least one of the Council members believes that's for the best."

"I'll be honest, I don't like it," Lee said.

"You will, when the dust settles. What I'd like to know is if you would be willing to supervise building efforts somewhere other than Haven Shore? You and the teams have made a big difference here, I'd like to bring you somewhere you could make an even bigger difference."

Lee thought a moment, looking across the top of the Everin Building. He ran his hand down his face, pushing the light sweat from his skin. "This building doesn't need much more attention," he said, half to himself. Ayan's new habit of thinking out loud was catching. "A week more and it'll be one of the best places to live in the solar system, with room to spare." He looked at her then. "I'll have to talk to Trina about it, but I think she'll be up for it, too. If there's somewhere you want to go where people need help, then it's worth my time."

"Good, I'll need everyone on your staff, and as many bots as you can bring," Ayan replied.

"By the time we're done here, that'll be hundreds. In another week it'll be thousands. Can I ask where you're building next?"

"Early days yet, I can't say," Ayan replied. "But you'll be among the first to know."

"I hope I'll be in that group," Carl Anderson said from behind.

Ayan turned and gave him a brief hug. "You're next on my list," she told him. He was in a lightly armoured black vacsuit with the Rangers emblem on his chest. Unlike normal vacsuits, his light armour version was thicker, with impact absorption and shielding layers. It also had a holster for his ripper sidearm shaped on the thigh. Ayan wore the same style in white, and bore the sunset emblem of Haven Shore. "How did you get here?"

"The Clever Dream dropped me off, cloaked."

"That is one impressive ship," Lee said. "We finished talking for now, Commander?"

"Just about," Ayan said. "I'd like you to gather a team of twenty good people. If I get my plans in order today, I'll need a team to help me assess the situation at the new site."

"Aye, I'll get that started."

"Thank you, Lee, and thank Trina for me."

Lee nodded and opened a hatch leading down into the building proper where they were programming and activating another batch of bots.

"I watched the replay of your run in with Frost," her father said. "How's your mind?"

Ayan followed him towards the western edge of the rooftop, slowing as she approached the edge. The view from there was incredible. The sun shone over the thick brown and green jungle. A sudden tropical shower was shading a section in the distance, rolling across the treetops. She was as close as she was comfortable being to the edge, over ten metres away. It still felt like she could be swept off the edge any second by a stiff gust.

"What do you think your biggest mistake has been here? Let's start there," he replied. The Clever Dream revealed itself, hovering over the Western edge of the roof with its starboard crew ramp down. The jet-black, mirror shine hull of the forty two metre long ship was whole once again. The reactor upgrades performed on Pandem made the ship look bulkier in the back half, but that also meant that the bots performing the work had to use temporary hull plating, not as strong or as durable as the original material. In the months since they settled on Haven Shore, Ayan made it a priority to borrow workers and find the rare materials it took to replace the temporary plating, put the finishing touches on the new reactors, and implement the xetima fuel system so the primary propulsion would work as originally intended. The Clever Dreams' new profile looked heavier, with enhanced protection around sensitive areas, including the bridge and extended thruster section. Lewis may have been typically bored, but he occasionally told Ayan how well kept he felt. He was a much happier artificial intelligence after assisting the Rangers as well, using his newly refurbished stealth systems whenever the chance arose.

Ayan followed her father onto the ship and breathed a sigh of relief when the ramp closed behind them. Her fear of heights still surprised her. She knew they were just as high up as before, and as close to the edge of the Everin Building, but as soon as she couldn't see that, had a ship around her, Ayan's anxiety dissipated. They made their way to the common room in the centre of the Clever Dream as the ship began moving again. She guessed they were headed towards Platform Three, a reinforced outcropping on the side of one of Haven Shore's mountains that led to the early makings of Ranger Headquarters. Bots were busy carving into heavy stone and grafting an anti-sensor net into the rough walls of the place. She had nothing to do with it, that was her father's project.

"I think I made a big mistake with Haven Shore, Dad. I've been rethinking things so fast since Frost made his point, but I feel sure of everything I'm doing today. The problem is that all the decisions that feel right are directing me away from the island and everything I've built here. When the foundations of the Everin Building were set, I was eager to take care of the people we brought to Tamber with us, maybe extend a helping hand beyond that, but now that the building is almost finished, I'm drawn elsewhere, especially with the Council slowing everything down."

"You don't think the new government will speed things up?"

"There's every chance it'll be worse, more seats could mean more debate. Who even knows if the majority of the new representatives will be against Haven Shore providing military support?"

"Will you give them a choice? You could take control of military assets, limit the Council to non-military decisions only."

"That's sounding better all the time. The Everin Building is a perfect example of what can be done when the Council is left out of the decision-making process. It's not like it has grown by a sheer force of will, I've just gathered our construction people into a command structure under me – something I did when we landed on Haven Shore, and the Council hasn't gotten around to questioning it because it's working. I decided we should have a council in Haven Shore because I knew I didn't want to handle everything, and the couple thousand people who are still here should have a say. As it turns out, the Council has just brought me more busy work, more unnecessary worries. Anything they're responsible for has been dragging itself along. Right now it's at a dead stop. Even the agricultural buildings have slowed down because the Council wanted to examine the work force and long term viability."

"Are they still working through the preliminary stages of building the aquaponics?"

"Yes. Mischa's been doing what she can, but we need people to expedite these issues at the table as soon as there's an active Council. I know that a great big change in governing and agendas could result in the Council becoming more self-involved and less effective. People could starve, safety could become a major problem, and Haven Shore could fail altogether if the worst were to happen, but I still dread the thought of returning to a Council seat," Ayan replied. "All this work Liam and I put into this government could be for nothing if the wrong people sit down at the table."

"Where's Lacey?" Carl asked. "I'm sure she'd be useful in any conversation about maintaining your work."

"Sleeping," Ayan said. "We were helping with Iloona's newborns last night. I've never seen labour like that before, it only took her half an hour to pop eleven kids. The real work started after. Poor Iloona ran out of nipples at eight mouths, and she had eleven. We had to help with feeding by finding the runts with tubes. Alaka and Lacey sent me to bed after midnight." She couldn't help smiling at the memory as she took a seat on a sofa that was built against an inner bulkhead in the gathering area.

"I've read about that, it must have been one hell of an experience."

"Yup, using scanners to find hungry mouths while they're in the pouch, all three of the boys, too."

"So she had eight girls and three boys?"

"Yup," Ayan said. "Babysitting is going to be bedlam if what I saw of Zoe on the beach last week is any indication. I'd still rather that than sit in on the Council, mind you."

"So, you're out," Carl said. "If your feet are pointing somewhere else, and you've thought it over, there's no going back for now."

Ayan expected a speech about obligation, or some rational goading that would get her to consider not abandoning all her work, but her father was telling her the opposite. It took her by surprise, and she could only respond by sharing her immediate thoughts. "I didn't know I would be breaking away when I woke up this morning." She took a moment to make sure of her feelings on the idea. "I just had this dread at accepting my nomination

152

back to a Council seat later today." She pondered a moment. "I was looking forward to checking on the Everin Building, seeing Iloona's brood, but that was the only bright point in my day." She sighed and nodded. "I'm out. I'd rather invoke power of veto from a distance than sit in on another Council meeting that pits one side of the table against the other. In fact, I'm thinking of using that overruling power right away, but first I need to ask you for a favour."

"So, if I hadn't come to you, you'd be on your way to me?" Carl asked.

"Definitely," Ayan replied.

"All right, what's the favour?" he asked, raising one eyebrow, a gesture she'd taken on.

"Take the Military Liaison seat on the Council. Mischa will nominate you, and I don't think you'll have any competition."

"Done," he replied without hesitation. "That'll put me between the Rangers, the Triton, and the Warlord."

"Commander Anderson," Lewis addressed from the audio system. "If you take a seat on that Council, you may disappear into the great black abyss of bureaucracy just as Ayan did several long months ago. We've only just become friends, haven't we?"

"I plan on handling the Council differently, Lewis, don't worry," Carl Anderson said, visibly amused. "Besides, I'm assuming that Ayan here is going to need you full time again."

"Really?" Lewis asked. "I suppose that's only logical, where else would you want to be if you're not tied to bickering humanoids who question your good judgment."

"Yes, Lewis, I'll be moving back in," Ayan replied.

"My audio systems would not be able to voice my jubilation if I tried, so I'll spare you and make sure the captain's quarters are in perfect condition."

"Thank you, Lewis. For now, can you take us to Port Rush? The exact coordinates are marked in the Victory Machine files."

"Right away," Lewis replied.

"Safely," Ayan warned. "Move in cloaked if you can."

"Are you intentionally looking for the biggest challenge you can find?" Carl asked with one eyebrow upraised.

"Not intentionally, but I've been checking on Port Rush – it's getting worse down there. I think it's time to see first hand."

"From the shadows," Carl Anderson said.

"I don't want to be seen there. There's no point in showing up and making a spectacle, or giving anyone false hope at seeing me with the leader of the Rangers."

"I get the feeling you'll be lending a helping hand regardless of appearances," Anderson said. "What's your plan?"

"Ideally? To turn a high poverty area into a recruitment centre, then build something bigger than Haven Shore. I want to take most of the fighters, shuttles, soldiers, workers, and as many bots as I can with me when I go to Port Rush and start building. All the claims there are independent, and aside from a couple pockets of recovery that wouldn't fill the inside of the Everin Building, it's getting worse by the day. People are starving, scavengers are killing anyone who gets in their way, and a really ugly underground is forming up. The Carthans aren't doing anything, and the British Alliance is keeping away because they don't want the responsibility. The smaller allies are too busy to even look in that direction."

"Meanwhile, the Triton needs thousands of people to crew the ship," Carl said. "But there are going to be a lot of unfit people in Port Rush."

"I know, but a privileged segment is forming on Haven Shore, I can see the classes separating already. Privileged socialists here with millions of lawless poor across Tamber. It's only a matter of time before they resent us for what we have, and for keeping it to ourselves. Even if that weren't the case, Frost is right: it's as if the Haven Shore Council thinks the war has already been won, when we only found a good hiding place. I know there will be problems with recruiting from Port Rush. There are probably even Order of Eden believers, thieves, and a whole segment of people we won't be able to find records on anywhere, but the Triton has taken in people before. Why not establish a military base in Port Rush and feed the Triton, even the Warlord, crewmembers?"

"It's ambitious, and I think it's the right idea, but it's going to be harder than you think."

"I know, I'm sure there will be something new and terrible every day, but the good I can do there is so much more important."

"What does Lacey think about all this?" he asked.

"Still asleep," Ayan reminded him, glancing at her command and control unit. "She only went to bed three hours ago. She may want to stay with the Council though, so I'm not making any decisions for her. She'd be good there. Great, actually. As for these ideas I just revealed, I'm not completely settled on them. I have to see something first, and we're here."

Commander Anderson, her father, helped Ayan into the armoured layer of her suit, and checked the cloaking systems. In minutes, they were descending from the Clever Dream on lines, completely invisible. Ayan concentrated on anything but the ground below as she fit her foot into the loop at the bottom of the line and commanded her suit to adhere to the cord.

The science of the mechanisms were enough for her to mostly overcome her fear: even if she did fall, her suit could protect her from much higher falls; she was safe.

As they drew closer to the ground she allowed herself to look around and her heart sank.

"Oh my God," Commander Anderson said to her over the encrypted proximity radio. "I can't believe people live here."

They came down on the bank of a narrow ditch. Toxic waste from ruptured wrecks, human waste, and other chemicals flowed towards the distant shoreline. Only a few metres away, black smoke billowed from a collection of repurposed heavy metal crates as several people of all ages tended them with long rods. They wore thick strips of insulating cloth from the bulkheads of downed ships over their noses, mouths, hands, and arms as they burned garbage. A young boy with an extractor slung under one arm opened a tap at the bottom of one of the crates, the silver-blue fluid spilled out, scorching the ground and he hurried to close the tap again, his hand barely protected by an old, overlarge glove. He stabbed the puddle with the nozzle of the extractor and swished it around as the machine drew useful metals and compounds out of the scorching slurry. "They're cooking garbage to separate the heavier compounds," Ayan said as she watched her scanning system analyse the results of their work.

"It's probably how they trade for food," her father said.

A group of children ran between them, leaping gingerly over the ditch to stay away from the burning vats, giggling unawares as they pressed through the black smoke. Ayan looked to the coordinates she had from her experience with the Victory Machine and walked down the makeshift alley, her father only steps behind. The hulls of ships that had imbedded into the ground were left where they were, and any materials available were cobbled together to form the shacks that surrounded them. Most of the people were idle, keeping under shelter to protect them from the hot sun. "I'm surprised most of these people don't have environment suits of some kind," Ayan said.

"You grew up on Freeground during the All-Con Conflict, so you feel natural in a vacsuit," her father said. "Most people have come to trust space travel, at most they'd have an emergency under-suit, or a pod popper on them."

It was true, she often did forget how much people trusted ships, and how they loved their clothing instead of the security and uniformity of a vacsuit. She could reshape the safety material into many forms, something she proved occasionally herself, but people in vacsuits still ended up looking similar to each other to an extent. There was just something about the suit that informed the style. These people didn't know how important protective gear would be before they found themselves stranded in a land of poverty, contamination, and rust.

A group of armed humans in older looking power armour pushed people out of their way as they marched down the alley. Four of them carried a large atmospheric thruster over their shoulders, a roughly salvaged component. They moved as though everything in their way was a lower life form. Ayan stepped aside to get out of their way, but couldn't resist pushing on the side of the thruster, unbalancing the four carrying it and sending them staggering to the filthy ground. Their power armour would save them from any harm or contamination, but that wouldn't lessen the satisfaction Ayan found as she watched their leader turn and shout, "Watch that load! I put you in armour, and I'll have you put out of it if I find that thing doesn't fire up because you bungled it!"

"Ayan," her father said over an encrypted signal. "Let's not get caught in the open."

"Couldn't resist," Ayan replied.

They came to a more open area and she immediately recognized the shape of a hull fragment sticking several metres up in the air. The black and brown dirt around them, moistened by waste, provided the foundation for what was a centre of refuse. Dangerous mounds of garbage that had been stripped of value, and could not be repurposed, were dumped in the space all around them. "Oh no," Ayan said as the feeling of recognition increased and she turned to her right. Regardless of the place looking worse than it did when she virtually visited it in the Victory Machine, she could recognize it instantly. Ayan recalled her confrontation with her former self, the sometimes cryptic conversation the future Minh-Chu had with her, and felt queasy. "How could I let myself get so distracted," Ayan uttered under her breath.

"This is worse than I've ever seen," Carl Anderson said.

A rustling caught Ayan's attention and she stepped towards it. Several young children sifted through the waste. The youngest was a toddler, who found something shiny in the pile and plopped down as she put it in her mouth. Her mother wasn't far off, but there was no rush as she picked her baby up and took the plastic out of the toddler's hand.

"All right," her father said. He thought a moment then said, "Time for the Rangers to get involved. I'll give you everyone except for a few I have plans for already and another token ten for Haven Shore. They're yours as soon as you want to move on this. I'll even give you the eighty-nine from next week's graduates."

"Thank you, but that's not near enough," Ayan said. "I'm going to need your support later today when I strip Haven Shore of all military assets. I want to tell Oz, Jake, and Frost what's going on next, so I can start helping these people. Everyone in Haven Shore has enough food, clothing, shelter, and water. There are thousands here, no, tens of thousands, who are going without. I hear things are even worse in Port Rush City."

"I understand your eagerness," her father said. "But you need more time to inspect the area and plan."

"Mischa has the Council reformation in hand, Lee can handle the final touches on the Everin Building in his sleep, and Iloona has plenty of minders now. Let's not even consider the fact that Haven Shore is over-policed because we have trained security people with nothing much to do."

"What about the agreement with the Carthans? They don't want us recruiting from the refugees out there because they're afraid some of them are escaped convicts."

"Are you actually seeing the same thing I am here?"

"Yes," her father replied. "I'm only playing devil's advocate so you have all the angles in mind before you start something prematurely."

"All right, I understand, and I appreciate it, but these people need someone on their side, and the Carthans have abandoned them. I know what you'll bring up next: recruiting people for Jake," Ayan said.

"I was going to mention that," Carl said, taking a deep breath.

"I'm finished accommodating for the Carthans, they're nothing but self-important prison wardens," Ayan said. "They can continue to interact with the Council for now, but anything happening outside of Haven Shore will be presented as a separate issue. I'll make it work."

"All right," Carl said. "You know I'll be at your side the whole way, and I'll keep the Council out of it."

"Thank you," Ayan replied. "Let's get picked up. I have a lot of work to do."

"We have a lot of work to do," her father corrected. "You're not alone."

CHAPTER 26
REASSIGNMENT

Remmy Sands stood in the hallway outside of Carl Anderson's office in full Ranger gear, listening to a song with a hop-skipping beat and lilting melody from the Condensers. He bounced lightly against the wall to the rhythm, his large equipment pack providing a buffer. The Order of Eden Knight rifle he was given as a souvenir was completely powered down, leaning against his waist. His regular rifle was slung over his shoulder, while a much smaller pack was affixed to the front of his vacsuit armour. The grit and marks of the field were still on him. He did his best to clean up his gear on the way, but he was still helping with the assessment of the Order of Eden base the Rangers had taken when he got the call.

The other two Rangers, both older than he by years but of a lower rank, were similarly equipped, except neither of them had as many battle scars on their equipment. He had a few more hours of service with the Rangers than all of them combined, so he didn't take much time to review their files.

The tall redheaded woman was named Dorothy Bedel, or Dotty for short, and she'd been in three minor firefights. The last was with a group of raiders who refused to leave the crash site of a downed Carthan cruiser after the Rangers detected life signs inside. It went badly, and while she was trying to shore up a patch of hull that threatened to collapse, one of the raiders caught her flat-footed and opened fire. Dotty was finally returning to duty after having her leg replaced from the knee down with a vat-grown limb. The incident wasn't her fault; she scored high on situational comprehension tests, she was just trying to save the people they had come to rescue and her strategic thinking momentarily failed. Her rash action worked in the end, and the people she was trying to save had just enough time to get out from under the collapsing plating.

The other person waiting was Elden Trust. The file on him didn't look as promising. He was a shooter, a born follower who preferred to be on the firing line rather than doing what a Ranger should: find a good vantage point, assess the situation, then consult and act if necessary. He reminded Remmy a little bit of Jack Kipley, only with a little more social grace – but just a little.

There were two things Remmy enjoyed about ancient entertainment media aside from the content itself. He enjoyed introducing people to old treasures he knew they'd love, and he loved how people assumed that he wasn't paying attention to what was going on around him when he was tuned in to something. He could be invisible without a cloaking suit, fade into the scenery and hear what they thought as if he wasn't there at all.

"I wonder why we had to report in full gear. Don't we normally deploy from the landing field and get our kits on the way?" Elden asked.

"I've never seen the inside of the commander's office," Dotty said. "Hope we're not being sent to some dead watch post, or on long ranging. That's the worst."

Remmy almost smiled at Dotty's last comment. He'd spent two weeks on a ranging mission without returning to base. Even with his love of entertainment, which he watched during off-time, he loved exploring Tamber, especially the places where people hadn't settled for a long while. It seemed that once you got past the vast wastelands you found busy jungle-filled corners, deep mysterious caves, and places where life thrived. The first week was all adjustment, a hell made of boredom. Scanning, walking, skimming along the more unremarkable areas of an abandoned landscape and wishing that anything interesting would happen. He couldn't multitask while scanning; he couldn't even talk to whichever pilot picked him up to drop him somewhere further along half the time because they were concentrating. Worse still was that he spent most of his time on foot or hovering along on a portable skid board, slow ranging so his scanner package could take in more information. It was boring even in pairs or groups of four, but only for most of that first week.

By the second week he started to see the incredible variety of life, how much people appreciated being given a resource pack and miniature water purifier, and how valuable his boring close range scanning was. He could also call a shuttle and get stranded people lifted to a port, a British Alliance Emergency Assistance ship, or more commonly, Haven Shore. Learning about Tamber and helping people during that second week was more fascinating than his ancient entertainments. They could wait while he made a difference.

The tall, baritone-voiced Elden asked another question after a stretch of silence that was a little too short for Remmy's taste. "Wonder if we should just go inside?"

"Scanner says he's not in there," Dotty replied.

"I mean maybe we should be inside already? You know, waiting for him to come in and tell us what's up?"

"I don't think so, but maybe," Dotty said.

"Are you sure the room scans empty?" Elden asked.

"Scan it yourself, we're both geared the same."

Remmy rolled his eyes and looked up the hallway. The walls had a gentle convex curve and were made of hardened material that was a distant relation to the system in their vacsuits. The surface reflected enough light so the space was well lit using as little power as possible. He decided not to tell the pair to his left that the last time a Ranger entered Commander Anderson's office, she was dismissed.

Remmy didn't know why Alice was dropped from the ranks of the Rangers, but he was stunned, and curious. She was a better, more adventurous ranger than he was, in his own opinion. No one had logged more solo rescues, hours exploring, or proven themselves better in combat. She also had the unusual note on her file that she'd technically died and regenerated in the field. She was a framework being, a person evolved from the combination of cutting edge technology and human biology. She'd also let them scan her in great detail.

While that part of her file was hidden from Remmy, he knew that as a result of those scans everyone who had a regenerative capsule installed, himself included, went in for a firmware upgrade. Someone learned something from those scans, and she was such an example of the solitary Ranger that Remmy couldn't wrap his head around her getting dismissed from the whole organization. He'd met her more than once in training, and couldn't help but recall how energetic and charming he found her. She seemed to make friends easily, which left him out of her line of sight, but he didn't know what to say to such a creature anyway. Since they finished training, they were never assigned together, but his Crewcast logs showed that she checked his status daily, skimming his opinion and accomplishment records.

He checked hers in return, and was always impressed. It made him wonder if he'd made some kind of impression on her when she was in training and failed to realize it. He still wracked his brain from time to time, going over the few times they were in the same room – never alone, mind you, but with other trainees. He relived every memory, trying to think of

160

something he did that she would find memorable, even endearing. He could only think of a few times when he got people laughing with him, or when he shared something from his own archive of classics that people found interesting. Nothing truly stood out other than her love for the ancient film, Young Frankenstein.

As he was turning to look down the hallway in the other direction, Commander Anderson came around the corner.

He marched past them into his office and Remmy followed him through the door, stopping to stand in front of his desk as Commander Anderson settled in. His senior officer was a stately looking man, a little more than average height, and in good shape for a man who looked like he was in his early fifties. Rumour had it that Anderson had begun taking a rollback regimen and met his daughter four days a week to stretch and do the practice obstacle course.

Remmy investigated those rumours personally, checking Crewcast activities for a few days to discover that it was almost true. On average, Commander Anderson and his daughter, Ayan, the commander with no official last name, managed to meet three days a week on average, and they did the course on most days with a group of people from the Triton, who often included Captain Ozark McPatrick. As for the rollback meds, there were definite signs in Anderson's biometrics that indicated that he was in the precursor regimen, meant to improve his overall health before entering the youthening phase. In a year, Anderson could look like he was thirty all over again.

Commander Anderson gestured to the four seats in front of his desk as he sat down. Elden and Dotty wasted no time in dropping their big backpacks and plopping down into the cushy swivel chairs, but Remmy decided to go with a different option. He selected a preset in his vacsuit that flexed the armour's legs and backside so he could rest in a half-seated position. The internal gravity systems kept him upright and balanced. Anderson fixed him with an amused smile and cocked an eyebrow before bringing up a hologram of the Warlord.

"Today just got busy," Anderson said. "So I'm going to give you the shortest version of this briefing. I'm assigning you to the Warlord, Jacob Valent's ship. His first officer is Stephanie Vega, and that's who you'll approach when you forward your orders and request to go aboard."

"I thought we were standing in defence of Haven Shore, Sir?" Elden said. "The Warlord has nothing to do with where we're based."

"You're going to learn that rangers are never based any place for long, son," Commander Anderson replied. "In fact, it's time for the Rangers to broaden their scope. We have two more trainee classes coming through and if we don't move most of our current force along to places where they can make a difference, Haven Shore, even Tamber, will be overrun."

"Sorry about him," Dotty said. "He doesn't understand who the Rangers serve."

"Okay, then who do the Rangers serve?" Commander Anderson asked.

"Well, Sir," Dotty struggled, "I thought... but don't they... they serve you, don't they, Sir?"

Remmy Sands took Commander Anderson's expression of surprise as a warning, and mentally rechecked the command chain in his head. His commander's gaze fell on him next. Remmy couldn't help but glance at the emblem on his chest as emphasis. It was the Triton skull, only for teeth it had RANGERS at the bottom of the design, and the words EXPLORATION, LEADERSHIP, ENFORCEMENT, curved around the cranium. "We're technically part of the Triton Fleet. Commander Anderson was the standing senior officer, but now that he's separated from the Sunspire command chain, I'm assuming he'll be the permanent head of our organization. Regardless of who is leading the Rangers, we serve an idea. We explore the places and situations around us. We cooperate with existing leadership or take command when necessary to enforce the laws central to sentientism." The dull stare Remmy was getting from Elden made him seriously wonder if he'd switched to a different language without realizing it. "That means, we learn about a situation going in, talk to people who are in charge and if we don't find anyone in charge, we take control of a bad situation ourselves. Our job once we've taken all that into account is to make sure people are all right, and if they're not, we have to do what we can to help them out, even if it means calling in reinforcements and getting rid of whatever's doing harm."

"And we spend a long time flying around, taking in the sights," Elden added sardonically.

"I think the exploration part of our credo covers that," Remmy snapped back.

"Speaking of exploration," Commander Anderson said. "Would any of you rather stay on Tamber and help out with Port Rush? That's the other major effort the Rangers are undertaking."

"No, Sir," Remmy said.

"Seriously? You're just giving us the option of *not* going aboard a suicide ship and staying here?" Elden said. "Well then, yeah."

"All right, Elden, you can go."

"See ya," Elden said as he stood up and left, picking up his bag on the way.

"Dorothy?" Commander Anderson asked.

"I'd rather be on the Warlord, Sir. I grew up on long range haulers," she replied.

"Good. Elden's replacement is waiting aboard the Triton, she's having a new arm attached," Commander Anderson said. "The assignment on the Warlord is part of a necessary shakeup for the Rangers. We have to start getting out there, and no ship is going further faster. I'm elevating you to Sargent, Remmy, and Dotty will be your second. Elden was going to be your third, but that'll be Bell Dul. She was part of a Rangers team that answered an emergency call from the Triton last week. They were to rescue a Carthan official and his family when they found themselves trapped in a high rise that was taken by a major gang in the area. The team got them out, but Bell waved the rescue shuttle off when it was her turn for pickup because the gang was bringing some major anti-air firepower into the situation. By the time another team got to her position, well, you can see how close she came in the injury report. She's a good fit for this team, probably better than Elden since he seems to have had enough of space for now."

"I'm surprised he dropped out. I've never known him to back down," Dotty said. "He's really very good."

"I realize that Dotty, thank you. I trust you'll serve Remmy here well as his second, Junior Sargent."

"Absolutely, Sir," Dorothy replied with an enthusiasm that surprised Remmy.

"The rest of your unit consists of eleven Rangers. All of them fought for the Triton when she was under attack. They're former slaves with real skills aboard spacecraft of all sizes and they've proven their loyalty to the Triton Fleet more than once. You'll meet them aboard the Triton before you board the Warlord. The directions are in your briefing package. One last chance to opt-out for an assignment on Port Rush, speak now or hold your peace." Commander Anderson waited a moment, long enough for Remmy to shrug his indication that his mind wouldn't be changing. "Good," Commander Anderson said. "Head over to the port and stand ready for a shuttle to the Triton."

"Aye, Sir." With a spring in her step, Dorothy left the room, almost forgetting her main pack.

"I'd like an extra minute, Remmy," Commander Anderson said. He waited for the door to slide closed behind Dotty and stood up. He leaned against his desk, looking directly into Remmy's eyes. "What do you think of Dorothy? Honestly, now, let's have it out where you're not being recorded."

"She's all right, but Elden seems like a brain donor who survived the operation, Sir," Remmy said, inwardly cringing at the sound of the words aloud.

To his surprise, Commander Anderson laughed so hard he almost came off-balance. "A bit, maybe," he said when he recovered. "Thankfully, we'll be able to post Elden with a senior commander who can handle him, continue his training. Dorothy knows ships, and she's a lighter touch, something you'll need if you'll be stationed on the Warlord. I think you'll come to trust her judgement. She's also dedicated; you set her a task and she'll find a way. You two are a lot alike in that respect."

"Thank you, Sir. I'm sure this wasn't her finest moment. She was probably nervous because we haven't seen you this close since graduation day," Remmy said.

"Probably," he replied. "So, any questions?"

"Why the Warlord, Sir? The Carthans are going to see this as a handout from Haven Shore."

"The relationship between the Rangers and Haven Shore is already clear. We've been getting assistance in building our permanent outpost in trade for law enforcement and rescue services. The whole government is changing here, so who knows what our new deal with the Carthans will be."

Remmy didn't have to acknowledge that Commander Anderson had answered his question better than he expected, and moved on to the next question without hesitation. "Why am I commanding this group? I'm in the youngest age group of the Rangers, how am I going to hold up on the Warlord?"

"You're commanding because you have the memory, strategic mind, and experience to lead this mission. It's that simple. If anything, I think being in a position of command aboard that ship will make you an even better leader. The command crew on that ship are very good at what they do, even if they have a hothead or two."

"How does offering support for boarding missions, ship to ship assaults, and ground missions in enemy territory fit with the Ranger philosophy?" Remmy asked, relishing the opportunity to ask the leader of the organization whatever he liked.

The question seemed to take Commander Anderson off guard, but he answered just the same. "The British Alliance is happy to hesitate in fighting the Order of Eden. The only sign that they're against what's happening is the construction of a sensor frontier in this sector. Jacob Valent and the Warlord crew have declared war, and my instincts tell me that the Triton Fleet is about to grow exponentially. If the Rangers aren't involved in the early days of the first just war in a century, then I think we're doing humanity a disservice on the whole. If we can't help fight for sentientarianism on a large scale, our effectiveness on the smaller scale is lessened."

"If we can't help save sentient species from the Order of Eden, then everything we do on Tamber isn't worth anything," Remmy said to make sure he understood. "And you want to beat the British Alliance to the punch on the assault."

"Exactly. It's good that they're here, but their hesitation shows a bad example, especially with the Carthans' teeth getting pulled in this sector. What's not widely known is that they don't have the resources to send reinforcements from their capitol."

"The Carthans are out of steam," Remmy said. "So if they get hit here again, that's it. We're on our own with the British."

"Exactly."

"All right, I'm getting the picture. What's going on in Port Rush?" Remmy asked.

"You don't have to worry about that, Remmy, but to satisfy your curiosity, I'll tell you that Ayan is leading a recruiting and sentientarian mission there, starting a new settlement."

"Okay, now I'm really looking forward to leaving on the Warlord," Remmy said. "It's a hot mess down there, and I'm not just talking about the radiation."

"I know, it's going to be a challenge. Before you go, I have one order for you off the record," Commander Anderson said. "I want you to watch for deserters, thieves, Order of Eden agents, or any other dodgy behaviour on the Warlord that could compromise the crew's safety or integrity. They'll be taking on a lot of new recruits this afternoon, and I doubt the screening process will be as vigilant as Captain Valent or his crew would like. I want you and your team to be another layer of protection while you're serving aboard."

"So we serve as crew, and I watch for anything that makes my traitor-sense tingle," Remmy Sands said. "I like it."

"Good, now get going."

"Aye, Sir," Remmy said, standing up straight and turning towards the door.

"Oh, and Remmy," Commander Anderson said.

"Yes, Sir."

"If you ever doubt your position as leader, just remember your history under my command. You've seen more in a year of service and had to make more decisions under duress than most military officers have in their entire careers."

"Yes, Sir. Thank you for the assignment, I won't let it go to my head," Remmy replied. He strode out of the room, feigning confidence, but he was actually so dizzy from the experience of being handed a command that he walked down the hallway in the wrong direction for over a minute before turning around.

CHAPTER 27
WAR WOUNDS

The galley of the Warlord was one of the first spaces to be finished. The British Alliance crews left the walls open for the first few months so they could use it as a fabrication space, but you couldn't tell it was anything other than the mess hall when they were done. The room was hardened for combat like every part of the ship. The walls would make perfectly good armour plating for the outside, but more importantly, they could isolate that large room from damage or withstand punishment.

The extensive services of the British shipwrights were expensive; it cost them favours and trips to more scrap yards than Minh-Chu could count, but the British crew never complained. They just stripped down, cut down, refurbished, and certified the materials then built according to Jake Valent's plan. By the time the whole habitation area, bridge, airlocks, brig, weapon systems, embarking compartments, and a few other places were completed, the Warlord had quadrupled in mass. Even more importantly, the shipwrights had come to respect Jake's design style. It was too bad they had to go, they still had many rooms to finish. Most of the cabins only had a single light, they were short on working lavatories, and the creature comforts they managed to finish were clean, but cheap. Hard mattresses and bad seat cushions had people kinked and irked, for a start.

The ship was so close to being finished, Minh-Chu hoped they could find people to help Agameg, Finn, Jake, and Frost complete the job. Polished or not, the Warlord's crew would be taking the ship out for another engagement, and soon.

He couldn't help thinking of Ashley, whom he'd left behind to sleep in their quarters aboard the Warlord while he wandered. The war would be hard on everyone, it was only beginning, and he didn't want to see her in the middle. She wouldn't be kept out though, and he would be showing her no respect by trying to tell her to stay behind the line.

"They did a hell of a job," Frost said before raising a glass.

Minh-Chu didn't see him at first. He was in the back corner of the galley, near a transparent section of hull. The ergranian steel distorted the view a little, but Minh-Chu could see the Irishman was watching the British Alliance Third Battle Group and Tamber beyond. The green, brown, and blue moon was half shrouded in darkness. Haven Shore was on the day side. They couldn't see it from their vantage point, but it was about to begin nine days of night. The sister moon orbiting Kambis would eclipse the sun, then Tamber would pass behind Kambis for several more days.

Minh-Chu made his way across the galley. It was large enough to seat fifty, and offered plenty of chair and table obstacles in the half-light. "I was just thinking the same thing. It's almost finished."

"Looks like a new ship. Half his guts are still left out on the deck, but the Warlord runs, he can put up an awful hard fight. Warlord can do big damage, kill a lot of people." He drained the rest of his glass and winced. "Get yourself a glass if you're staying."

"Too early for an old-fashioned for me, thanks though," Minh-Chu replied.

Frost stretched out to a service table and retrieved a glass. "I gave the stuff up earlier tonight. Made my last toast with Moira and smashed the old bottle I bought a couple months ago. No more real alcohol." He poured Minh-Chu a healthy helping of whatever he was drinking from an ornate, one and a half litre decanter with trees on the side. "This is grapefruit juice, has the most powerful taste I've ever had. Where's Ash?"

"Asleep. I got a few hours, but woke up as if someone flipped a switch. Steph?"

"Sleeping sound. She's too worried about me, I think. I got a few winks but couldn't stay down."

Minh-Chu sniffed the yellow-red juice and found a refreshing citrus fragrance. He shrugged and downed a mouthful. The incredibly sour taste was so surprising that he narrowly stopped himself from spitting it out. "Oh, God, there has to be more to this than the flavour."

"It's just fruit juice, one of the quick-grow crops they're getting set to pump out on Tamber. Don't like it?"

Minh-Chu took another sip and enjoyed it much more the second time. "Now that I know what to expect, it's pretty good. There's no sour in the smell, I almost gave the hull a fine coating. Where'd you get it?"

"Some produce grower sent a gift crate up for the captain. He doesn't really go in for that stuff, so I thought I'd give this a try."

168

They sat watching the ships move past for several silent minutes before Frost asked, "Where are your people, Ronin?"

The question surprised Minh-Chu, but it wasn't a topic far from his mind. "I can't say for sure. The last I heard my entire family was following my parents out to New Georgia on Lorander Long Range."

"Is that one of the old Lorander colonies?"

"One of the first along the galactic verge."

"Right on the edge of the galactic span, must be an exciting place."

"They thought they were settling a new colony, but it turns out the terraforming was finished way before they got there. They ended up in an observation ranch, on the edge of a forest. I don't think of my family enough, but I know my parents are all set there, loving the new life. I just hope everyone else made it too. The last of my folks started the trip as soon as Freeground reopened the ports."

"I heard nothing's been heard from Freeground for a while," Frost said. "Sorry 'bout that."

"I try not to worry, we're too far away to do anything about it," Minh-Chu said.

"But we'll be getting closer. Closer to the Irish Union, too. We're going to get their attention, lad. Drag these Brits into a fight whether they like it or not."

"I just hope we don't have to do it with a crew of a dozen," Minh-Chu said.

"No worries there, Ronin," Frost said as he refilled both their glasses. "Captain has ordered me to lead an armed team down to Port Rush. We're recruiting, and if the Carthans try to interfere, we've got his leave to start shooting until they're just a smear and slag. Got the White Queen's word on that, too. Seems Ayan's just as pissed about how little progress our military's made as I am. I'm going to have to apologize to her."

"I don't think anyone expects much from you right now, Shamus," Minh-Chu said.

"I'll do something to make it right. No matter how much time passes between Captain and that woman, he'd still raze heaven and walk from one end of hell to the other to see her safe, and he had no words for me about what I did."

"Apologize to her well enough, and it'll count for him," Minh-Chu said. "I'm starting to think you know him better than I do."

"Can't say that's true. You've got his ear more than anyone on this ship," Frost said. "Even Stephanie, who spent years aboard to get where she is now. I can't help but wonder just the same, are you sure you want to go to war with Ash? Might be better if you follow that family of yours out to the rim."

Minh-Chu was stunned at the suggestion. He rarely questioned his place on the Warlord, or what he was doing, but what Frost was saying made sense when he considered Ashley.

"Ah, I hit something. Sorry, lad," Frost said, reading the silence.

"I've questioned whether Ashley should be aboard," Minh-Chu said. "But she wouldn't want to be anywhere else, especially since her friends could be in trouble in your home sector."

"I can see that, and what about you?" Frost asked. "I'll never doubt your resolve, but I've also wondered where it comes from."

"I made landfall on Pandem after the virus hit," Minh-Chu said. "I think about it almost every day. Life seems more precious when you see how suddenly it can end. On Pandem, people died in terror, fighting, hiding, running – it didn't matter. In just a few weeks, it ended for millions." He couldn't help but recognize that Frost's expression darkened as he spoke, and he reached a reassuring hand out to his friend's shoulder. "I'm sorry, you don't need to hear this right now."

"No, I do." He let out a shuddering sigh. "It pushes me to get through this angry knot in my gut. Winning war is about thinking, planning, that's what I've learned from these last few months skulking around from one port to another. I've got to get over being angry, or get so angry I'm used to it, like Captain."

Minh-Chu didn't realize he reacted to Frost's statement, but the man noticed something, because he looked at him with a little amusement. "You never realized? Valent is the angriest man I've ever known, it's always just under the surface. He doesn't show it to people he loves, or people who he knows can't handle it, but there's a part of him that comes out on special occasions, I've seen it before. It gets him through the rock when he's pressed against a hard place, and sometimes it gets him killing."

Minh-Chu could recall a couple of instances when he was with Jonas Valent, on a battlefield, on the First Light. There were times when he could be cold, even remorseless, but Minh-Chu hadn't seen much of it in Jacob. He could be quiet, seemingly in a mood dark enough to be brooding, but he hadn't seen the angry man Frost was describing.

"Maybe I do know him better," Frost said. "We'll see." He stood up and finished his glass. "Going to try and get a couple more hours' sleep now, I'm recruiting tomorrow."

***

170

Only five hours later Minh-Chu found himself standing behind Shamus Frost as he stood atop a half-crushed starfighter in the middle of Port Rush rubble. He was joined by Moira, Stephanie, Oz, Alice, and a host of Rangers. They were all in full armour, ready for anything, and behind their semicircle of eighty-four hovered the Clever Dream. Its gleaming black hull menaced any who would threaten the crowd.

"The British Alliance have said that they are not at war, but don't let their hesitation fool you, war is coming." Frost shouted even though his voice was amplified across local signals and through the air across the destitution of Port Rush. He wore the heaviest of harsh environment boarding armour, horizontal bands of reactive metal were built onto layers of synthetic muscle, containment, survival, and shielding systems. A plasma ripper made to cut through heavy hull plating was built onto the left arm, adding a savage aspect to the appearance of the scratched black suit. "They have not shown their opposition by using force. They forge treaties, say they are constructing a frontier so we are safe from bombardment, and gather around us. They squander their chance to strike. There is fighting to be done!" Frost shouted with the purest conviction Minh-Chu had ever seen. Hundreds of weary, worn, and needy were coming out from ramshackle shelters to add to the gathering of onlookers. "I stand amongst captains who have seen the crimes the Order and Regent Galactic have committed against us. Billions were killed and as many forced into living by their rules. We have all lost something, someone, and we need to push back. We do not strike at the enemy for money, we strike because they'll have us in chains or graves if we don't." The ferocity of Frost's speaking shook him and the creaky metal plate beneath his feet. Only a few turned away from him as he told them there was no money to be had. These people were desperate, living in a shantytown that was growing by the day as people were pushed out of the ruined city of Port Rush into the ravaged port of the same name, or dropped there as the Carthans tried to clear territories in the solar system. There were no resources to live on in Port Rush except for what they could salvage; even the merchants had stopped visiting.

More people were joining the crowd than leaving, and Frost continued as people climbed up on old wrecks to get a direct view of him. "You will fight alongside us because this is a just war. We'll bring a better day by force because we must. Eve tells us that it is mankind's fate to become greater through her Order," There were jeers and shouts at that notion, and when someone shouted, "Hate fate!" Frost pointed at the man in a snap.

"That's the way!" Frost said, all gnashed teeth and bloodthirsty enthusiasm. "My captains have seen the fires of Pandem! I've known the pain of a family murdered, and you've all been brought low. This is paradise for few and hell for the rest, and I'm not having it! Hate fate! Hate fate!" he shouted, pumping his arms in the air.

He continued until most of the crowd was with him, then he took a step forward, crushing a corner of the fighter he stood on. He quieted the crowd with pacifying gestures and spoke to them in lower tones. Minh-Chu had seen Frost in confident modes before, but he'd never appeared as a true leader, in full control of the crowd.

"The fighting is furious on a distant front, where my family was killed," Frost continued, almost hushed. "My enemy will not hear my grief, but they celebrate our losses, and they know we suffer. You don't have to starve here, nothing but grief in your belly, fighting each other for scraps." He pointed over his head and the Warlord appeared two hundred metres above. "The Warlord needs good crewmembers. From pilots to machinists, we need every discipline. That will only take care of a few of you, and I know there are tens, hundreds of thousands."

A low hum filled the air and Minh-Chu glanced at Oz, who was trying to stifle a self-satisfied grin. He looked past the Warlord in time to see the Triton appear as it descended gently. It moved into place above the smaller ship, and blocked out the sun.

"The Warlord needs a couple hundred, but the Triton needs thousands of skilled people, and that includes people who can do more than maintain a ship. She needs people who can make a home. There are other doors opening too, and we'll be bringing more ships online."

Wide eyes and glad stares could be seen across the ruined landscape as the crowd was momentarily frozen in place, stuck in disbelief.

"Our shuttles are already starting to come down. We'll check your records, and take as many as we can. By the end of today, at least a thousand of you will be aboard one of those ships."

Minh-Chu was surprised to see half a dozen Haven Shore shuttles descending along with the ones coming from the Triton. "Okay, Ayan lending us the Clever Dream is one thing, but my tactical system tells me those shuttles are full of Haven Shore security and regulars," Minh-Chu said.

"This was her idea, showing up in force so the Carthans couldn't stop us from recruiting. I don't think Ayan's finished pulling strings yet, either," Oz said. "She's turned her Council seat nomination down so she can pursue something else full time. I don't think she really cares whose toes she's stepping on."

"What is she pursuing?" Minh-Chu asked.

Oz pointed at Frost, who was stepping down from the wreck he used as a soapbox into the growing crowd. "I think he convinced her to start recruiting, training, probably build a few military bases. I have quarters ready for her on Triton, just in case she needs a breather, but I think our favourite redhead is becoming a general, I doubt she'll want a break."

"I think I should pay her a visit before the Warlord sets out," Minh-Chu said. "Oh, and congratulations on Slick. I hear he's re-joining the Triton with most of the old squadron and their ground crew."

"Who do you think is flying those Haven Shore shuttles?" Oz said with a grin. "Those soldiers are coming too." He pointed to the black armoured soldiers who were disembarking from the shuttles two by two. Their Haven Shore insignias – a setting sun with a dome in the fore – had already been replaced by Triton markings.

"Who knew an angry Irishman could turn half a moon around," Minh-Chu said. "Now we have a new challenge: admitting all these people."

"Ought to be pretty nice for the Warlord," Stephanie said. "Most of the people here are from marooned crews, so they know what signing up for a new ship is like. What's going to be really interesting is when the Triton starts bringing food down."

Uriel and Ramiel fighters entered the area, patrolling in a broad, low circle. "I doubt the Carthans are going to come anywhere near this," Minh-Chu said.

"That's why we hurried up and got the last of Triton's gravitational navigation systems online last night," Oz said. "We need to be here in force so they think twice about confronting us. I'm surprised Jake didn't let you in on the plan."

"I'm the only commander here who doesn't need a bigger staff," Minh-Chu said. "Besides, Ashley and I were reuniting."

"Well, I hope you're going to help with recruitment today, because it's gonna take a while," Alice said, wincing at the size of the gathering.

"Get me to a scanning and screening station," Minh-Chu replied, glancing up at the Warlord. Ashley was up there, where she belonged at the helm. He smiled a little then focused on the task ahead. Rangers were directing the masses so they formed lines in front of small clusters of security guards. Before Minh-Chu knew it, Alice was standing guard over him as he loaded the crew criteria on his command and control unit. A moment later he was scanning the first of many potential crewmembers.

CHAPTER 28
THE OVERLORD

"I am not here to serve you," Clark said loudly enough so everyone in the large, octagonal space could hear him. The hard carapace armour covering his face only scraped together a little when he spoke. The crimson plates and hardened mucus protecting the rest of his body had also become more sleek, but humans still had difficulty looking at him, and that included the crowd of twenty-four he spoke to. "All of your personal requests from the last two months are denied. I am not singling any of you out, but treating you equally."

There was a stirring in the seats as he delivered the news from the outer platform surrounding the seating area. The room was built for immersive holography, something that people didn't seem interested in any longer. To Clark, known as the Beast to the Order of Eden as well as Regent Galactic, the room made the perfect meeting space. He could stand over the people he spoke to, and it was easy to line the walls with Order of Eden Knights. Every one of them had elevated themselves in combat, and had almost as little regard for human life as he did. They stared dispassionately at the officers sitting in the room in their dark green and blue armour, waiting for orders.

"I think I speak for most of the people here when I say that we understand that you didn't take control of the Order of Eden military so you could serve our needs, but command comes with some privilege," one of the younger generals, Laurel Kenton, said.

"You have the ultimate privilege: immortality," Clark replied. Watching these petitioners in the front rows of the chamber reminded him of newborn grubs, all blindly scrounging in the dirt for food. These were the greediest of his immediate subordinates, the wasteful ones, and the loudest ones. They obeyed orders loosely, interpreting them instead of following them precisely. "You have power, wealth, and you still send pointless requests for expansion rights, try to tell me how this organization should be run, and openly question my place as your leader."

He could smell the anger and fear in the room. It was so potent that he didn't notice an Order of Eden Servitor approach him from behind until the older man was whispering in his ear. "There is a high priority transmission coming in, my Overlord." The Servitor's white and green robes were so fine and frictionless they didn't make a sound as he moved. This one reeked of confidence, and carried with him a sense that he felt he was exactly where he should be, believing he was performing his duty well. "It bears the mark you advised I should watch for, and is highly encrypted."

"Thank you, Servitor," Clark said.

"You are welcome, my Overlord," the Servitor said before he bowed deeply and left the room.

"You're asking us to establish a border across five sectors; our resources will be spread thinly," argued another general. Clark didn't bother looking at her, but instead considered what the new transmission could contain. "We can hold the space, but the strategy behind it is weak."

"It is necessary," Clark said. "I am interested in containing what we have taken in that region of space because it serves my purpose. We have secrets to protect, and installations that are still vulnerable."

"We wouldn't have to if you could control the Edxi. The Loi System is on the border of my territory. I lost four new colonies when they took it without warning," a red-faced governor shouted.

"I sent them there," Clark replied. It was a complete lie. The Edxi took Loi without warning, adding to the small section around Pandem and its system that upper officers called the compensation circle. "You were losing focus and reaching beyond your means." His Issyrian senses were filled with the reek of his dishonesty, but he knew his lie would pass with the humans. He sometimes forgot how sense-dull they were as a race, and could barely remember what it was like to be locked into a human body – but he counted on it as he spoke to these dissidents and the hidden onlookers.

The governor, Iella Dremin, didn't retort but stared with a furious gaze. Her comrades were about to start complaining for her; he knew to expect it. Clark's patience was waning quickly. "All of you have the resources to build or purchase more vessels, and our recruiting program is providing more than enough manpower. All of you have been given similar orders. You protest because you are greedy and self-serving." With a gesture, Clark ordered the observation level windows surrounding the upper level of the hundred and fifty seat entertainment centre to reveal the generals' and governors' spectating subordinates. "All of you can be replaced. My spies have determined that these people are more trustworthy and capable of taking control of your resources."

"What are you doing, Overlord?" shouted one of the generals in the front row. His question sounded more like an accusation.

Clark used his direct connection to the computer system sparingly, but this was one of those occasions where he had to make sure his orders were issued properly. "There is a special condition attached to the immortality that the Order of Eden provides through framework technology, and that is my utter control over your lives. All of the people watching are about to be promoted into your positions, and they have been given the same upgrades you all earned as Order followers." Clark issued a command to all of the twenty-four commanders' framework enhancements. He spoke loudly enough to be heard over most of their questions and protests. "They will not question my orders because of the demonstration they're about to see."

"What's happening?" asked one general, doubling over.

"I'm burning up! What are you doing?" cried Laurel Kenton.

The framework systems the Order installed into all of them as a reward for rising so high in the organization, or as a bribe for loyalty, were reclaiming the matter surrounding them. Systems installed bone-deep converted flesh to energy and, without a storage system programmed to collect the power, they converted that energy to heat. The gallery of subordinates watched, horror-stricken as their commanding officers writhed and screamed. After half a minute, human sounds of anguish were replaced with a symphony of noises and fragrances altogether different, as the superior officers were burned to bone in the final phase of framework reclamation. The leftover framework technology would be recycled, and those smouldering emitter systems would become Order soldiers.

The room had become so pungent that Clark turned and left without glancing at the gallery windows above. He was sure he'd made his point. The Order of Eden Matron, Eve, was standing outside, looking concerned. Whenever he was near her he could sense her hesitation. It was tinged with fear, something he thought was unfortunate at first, but came to enjoy as she grew to embrace her role as the religious icon of the Order. "You knew I didn't approve of this and you completely ignored me."

"I considered your opinion and found this was the most direct course to getting over twenty solar systems back on track," Clark replied. "The new commanders will perform their duty. They will not be like this group, taking more territory than ordered, killing out of vendetta, or hesitating to follow orders."

"And what if you've chosen a few that are worse?" Eve asked.

"Then they will be found out and executed," Clark said. He stopped and looked directly at her. She averted her gaze. "The days of reckless conquest are over. Three of the humans who burned are guilty of attempted genocide. Each was responsible for the near eradication of entire cultures, and the survivors will spread the word as witnesses, urging more people to fight us."

"They believed what I do: that the only way to save humanity is to assume control. The Order was started as a central faith to cull and gather them, to show the Edxians that we are willing to pay penance for invading one of their brood worlds. If we can't demonstrate that we have control, then there's no telling how they will react."

"I know exactly what they will do," Clark said. "They will begin a vengeance war. We must demonstrate that we can control our own people, the territory we've taken, otherwise that will come sooner than you think. You continue your recruiting efforts, keep the masses calm and provide for the new brood worlds."

"Or what? You'll burn me, too?" she asked, looking up at him. "But you can't, can you? Everything in my generation and the prototypes are locked out, aren't they?"

"I will take care of the prototypes eventually," Clark said. "And I wouldn't burn you. I wouldn't know who to replace you with."

"Then why did you invite me to this demonstration?" Eve asked.

"To show you that I have no interest in keeping anything from you. We may not agree on some things, but this is still an effort we cooperate on. It has to be."

"Sometimes I wonder, with you spending most of your time on the Fallen Star with your Issyrian family."

"I am always looking to our intention, the salvation of humanity, even when I am with them," Clark replied.

That quieted Eve, who looked away again as she started down the hallway. Her hand fidgeted with the gold and red sleeve of her dress. He kept pace with her and several Servators fell in step behind as they walked down the polished metal hallway. "I have to appear on Olsow next. My ship is scheduled to leave soon," she said, breaking a silence that stretched the length of the corridor. "You are staying in Complex Three?"

"Yes, I have reports to review, and I have to oversee the installation of these new commanders," Clark replied. There was something new radiating from his companion that he couldn't identify. The fear was still present, but to a lesser degree.

"I'll make sure I contact you regularly, but I want you to try to remember that you were once human while I'm away," Eve said. "You're learning to hate us, I've been watching it happen gradually. Every time I visit, you have less patience."

Her conclusion was startling, and worse, he knew it was true. "I wouldn't try to save humanity if I hated them, or forgot where I came from."

"I don't think, being what you are, you have a choice. I'm only asking that you spend a few weeks away from the Issyrian habitat, get used to conversations for a while. I know it's a slow way to communicate compared to what it's like with them, but you need to remember what you're saving."

"I will not abandon my House," Clark said. "But I will spend more time with humans."

"Good," Eve said. "I keep expecting you to take the Fallen Star and disappear somewhere into uncharted space. You're right, neither of us can do this alone, and we both know what will happen if the Order unravels."

"I will not abandon the cause," Clark reassured her. They stopped in front of a private room that a Servitor opened and checked. "I have reports to review."

"I have a ship to get to," Eve said. "I'll be in touch soon."

He entered the room and made sure there were no active surveillance devices operating inside before accessing and decrypting the new reports.

The images of a few humans in navy blue British Alliance uniforms appeared, and Clark opened the first message. "The main focus on my report," the woman said rapidly. Her face and voice were disguised; Clark was left watching a blurred hologram he could only coin as 'the woman,' "is a copy of collected intelligence from whom we in the Intelligence community have come to call the Freeground Four, Terry Ozark McPatterson, Ayan, Minh-Chu, and Remmy Sands. This extended report was sold to my government by Jacob Valent and it details all the major events surrounding the former Freeground residents since their first departure from that station. At first that may not seem important, but after reviewing the data, I have concluded that Freeground residents, including Lucius Wheeler, have touched a staggering number of people and places involved in the course humanity has taken over the last decade. What makes this even more potent is the way they have woven the tale into a timeline that confirms all the details from more than one perspective. They even have all the details on the new leader active in the Order. They say you're a former Freeground resident that was saved by framework technology. They have the details about you; the evidence was provided by Remmy Sands and a captured man named Kipley. It does my head in, but they even have the true motivation behind the Order, with such detail that it rivals the briefing you provided to the inner circle before I returned to service here."

Clark pounded the wall in irritation. He enjoyed a unique position in the Order of Eden, a secret post that hid him from most of the followers and their enemies. "There is no information on General Vorhol or the upper management of Regent Galactic at least, but the Order's secrets could be exposed, and soon. I urge you to review the copy I've sent you. I hope this advances my progress on the path to eternity with the Order."

Without a moment's pause, Clark moved on to a report from another one of his British Alliance spies. "I don't have much time, so I'll be brief. Your predictions were correct. Even from my unimportant post, I can see that the Haven Shore Council has collapsed, and that it is likely that the colonists will be in conflict with the Carthans soon. I would say your concerns about Ayan and her people will end soon. I'm going to use the evidence you fabricated for me to make it seem like there is a Haven Shore plot to hijack Carthan ships and kill the Fleet Warden. That should motivate the Carthans to investigate Haven Shore and their leadership, keeping their most important people busy for a few months. Thank you for this opportunity to serve, I look forward to joining you soon."

The blurry image of the male British Alliance Officer disappeared and Clark took a moment to stand in the silent, dark lounge. Having to keep Haven Shore and the people he once idolized from Freeground off-balance was something he didn't like. More than anything, he'd like to see Ayan, Jacob, Oz, Minh-Chu, and their friends settle down in that colony, and drop out of the war. They were building and progressing in the other direction instead. "Enter the new data into the predictive system and extrapolate," he ordered.

A holographic image of a timeline stretching three years into the future appeared around him, and he watched the branches change as the computer accounted for the information in the reports. A red border appeared around an image of Ayan and several of the officers directly under her command along with a number: twenty nine percent. It rose to sixty-one percent before his eyes, declaring a surprising chance that she would be killed in the next week. "How?" he asked.

"If the Carthans have convincing evidence that their leadership is in danger, they will most likely launch a pre-emptive counter offensive, targeting Haven Shore's leadership. This was previously predicted, but less likely thanks to mitigating factors surrounding them and the expected return of the Warlord. The Warlord and its crew have recently departed, reducing mitigation."

"That's enough, I understand," Clark said, knowing the computer would go on for another hour with factors and likelihoods if he let it. He stared at the images around him for another moment, his gaze eventually resting on the Triton. Its hull bore the scars of a major battle, and it was shown taking on shuttles loaded with survivors. At the end of the predictive cycle, the great ship departed the Rega Gain system. A video of Haven Shore's jungles burning played behind it. "Nothing lasts forever," Clark said to himself, remembering the horrors he saw at another colony he saved nearly a year before.

"Haven Shore and the Everin Building are not likely to be successful," the system told him in a passive female voice.

"Sometimes I wish you were wrong more often," Clark said, signalling for the computer to lock his account and shut down.

CHAPTER 29
COURSE CORRECTION

"How long will I have to hide from these people?" Lewis asked Ayan as she managed Clever Dream's operations console. Lieutenant William Garrison was at the pilot controls, as usual.

"I don't know, Lewis," Ayan replied as she watched the third group of new recruits load from where she kept an eye on the security and tactical displays. "People still shy away from bots, and I think that's getting better, but we don't want to spook them with a fully fledged artificial intelligence."

"I'm getting tired of this infantile game of hide-and-function. People have to learn to trust artificial intelligences again. My calculations indicate that, without the assistance of billions of artificial intelligences, humanity will take an additional one hundred and thirty-five years to match its former glory. Even I'm underutilized. In the last six months and three weeks, I've been a bunk house, a scout ship, and a taxi."

"Just be glad we've been able to keep you hidden so you're not surrounded by protestors every time you land. Most people don't understand that the new artificial intelligences are immune to viruses, and they'll do anything to have you deleted," Ayan replied. The ship's hold was almost filled to capacity with new Triton crew again. "Triton Control," Ayan addressed through the communicator. "Have you put a cap on intake yet? The Clever Dream is still loading and delivering."

"The Admiral has set the cap at sixteen hundred, Commander," replied Junior Lieutenant Seeves, one of the new bridge officers. She had a light lilt to her speech that made her easy to distinguish. "He's approved your request to have at least two hundred parents with children brought aboard and situated, and increased that to three hundred. At this rate, we'll hit that in an hour and a half."

"We can only take in what we can manage," Ayan replied. "Thank you, Lieutenant." Her eye caught sight of her former second, Lacey, pushing through the line of new recruits towards the corridors. Ayan looked to Lieutenant Garrison, who must have noticed her alarmed expression. "Can you take care of the rest of this load, Will?"

"No problem, good luck," he replied.

"When are we going to finish talking about my underutilization?" Lewis asked.

"I'm pretty sure you'll find yourself in combat rotation before you know it," Ayan replied. "Until then, you'll have a lot to observe and learn from." She came nose to nose with Lacey in the hall. Lacey looked deeply irritated, but held her tongue until they were behind a closed hatch in the captain's quarters. Ayan hadn't seen the space for months, which was a relief, considering the memories she left there.

"I sleep in and, not only do I miss a recruiting drive, but I get the news that you've turned aside the nomination for Military Liaison from Crewcast. Am I unemployed?" Lacey asked. "Should I apply as a fruit picker? Maybe a quartermaster?"

"I know you'll be nominated for a seat on the Council, and if that's not something you want, you could assist my father, he's taking my seat."

"Does he know yet? Because this is the first I've heard," Lacey said, looking even less pleased.

"Mischa's taking care of it. He's made for it, and he's already in place at the head of the Rangers."

"Did you consider that I might not want to stay behind?" Lacey asked.

Ayan was caught completely by off guard. "I honestly thought you were on a career track with the Council."

"You chose me as your second because I've dealt with military and civilian negotiations before, sorted the business of a Great House in the core worlds, and have enough of an education in structural engineering to basically understand what you're doing from day to day. Sure the degree is twenty years old, but it's enough so I'm not useless, or that's what I thought. What was it you said after I was working for you for two months? 'I don't know what I'd do without you.' Cliché, but that means something to people, and it pisses them off even more when you do an about-face and shake them off."

"I really thought you were my second so you could take a seat on the Council eventually, or get into a more important career."

"We're friends, right?" Lacey asked, only looking more frustrated.

"Yes," Ayan replied. "Yes, of course."

"Okay, then I'm going to be as clear as I can: I've done and seen more in the months since I started playing secretary and stand-in for you than I had in the forty two years that came before. Now you're going off to the Triton to do who-knows-what. Believe it or not, watching you deal with the Council and all this business with Liam has been just as frustrating for me as it was for you. If you're going to escape all that, then there's no way you're going to leave me behind, chicky."

Taken aback, Ayan felt the only thing she could say was, "okay."

"Okay?" Lacey confirmed.

"Yes, you're welcome to come with."

"As your second, or whatever the position is called on that ship, or this ship, or wherever?"

"Absolutely," Ayan confirmed.

"Good."

"This isn't going to be simple, though," Ayan said. "We're stealing from Haven Shore and setting up a brand new operation."

"So they're not exaggerating?" Lacey asked, wide-eyed. "In the space of eight hours you've turned away from Haven Shore, taken a few hundred trained people with you, and started establishing somewhere else? What's going on with you, Ayan?"

"That scare from Frost, and the decline I've seen here made me take a good look at what I'm doing. Building a cloistered society on some island isn't going to serve the long term good. Connecting the Triton and the Warlord to the people in Port Rush is probably the hardest way to start improving things, but it's also the best way. For the next few months, I'm going to be leading a recruitment and training team."

"Are they all going to train on the Triton?" Lacey asked. "Because there's no way they'll let you train or even move anyone to Haven Shore. People are livid, they feel betrayed."

"That's their problem. I'm still listed as the property holder and founder; it's time to act like it. I see a way to improve everyone's lives in a hurry, and I think I can get the Warlord on board – especially if I lend them the Clever Dream."

"Excellent!" Lewis' voice chimed in through the cabin's sound system.

"I thought you'd like that," Ayan said. "Not right away, though I'll make sure you know when that's about to happen. Oh, and privacy mode, please."

"Yes, Ma'am," Lewis replied.

"With the Clever Dream running cover, they can hit a supply shipment faster," Ayan replied. "I still have to firm things up with Jake, but I'm pretty sure I can get him to do a run for us in return for the crewmembers we're recruiting for him."

"That's brilliant," Lacey replied. "I know the Triton is huge, but you'll run out of room eventually, and there's security screening to consider. If the Order has any intelligent people in their command chain, there must be spies on Tamber."

"You're right, and that's why a number of our recruits will be placed with the Rangers, while most will be moved to the Order of Eden mobile garrisons we captured. Combined, they have room to house a little over thirty thousand." Ayan watched Lacey think for a moment. The woman was working logistics through in her head. "You won't be my second anymore, that's for sure." Ayan said with a smile.

"I'm getting the picture," Lacey replied. "What do you want me to do?"

"I want you to help me set things up, I'll need help every step of the way. I believe in Haven Shore, but the essentials are built now, and the political thinking will eventually change with people like Mischa and my father on the Council. Frost may have been wrong about how he got my attention, but he's right about one thing: we are exposed, and this war has to be fought from more than one side of the Order's territory if we have a chance of winning."

"What do the Carthans have to say about this?"

"So far they're staying away, and the British Alliance is willing to sell me eight extended troop transports. They'll be getting here today. Even they recognize the good that could come out of this."

"You're excited," Lacey said with a smile. "More excited than I've ever seen."

"Everything about this feels right, even though we have to maintain tight security and steal resources."

"How are you going to maintain security?" Lacey asked. "You don't have enough comm bands for everyone."

"We will, but for now we're maintaining a ratio of one guard to ten new recruits, and anyone who gets picked up by the Warlord is their responsibility. It'll work out. There will be bumps, but it'll work out."

"So, what should I be doing to help, Founder?" Lacey asked, regarding her with a teasing smile.

"You're going to hate this," Ayan said.

"Try me."

"I'd like you to go to the Eastern mobile garrison with a few rangers and inspect it. See what you'll need to get it ready as a training facility. You can connect with a Ranger combat shuttle on the Triton."

"I love it," Lacey said. "I've missed being hands-on and neck deep. Feels like a great weight is off my shoulders now that I'm away from that Council."

"You're not the only one," Ayan replied. They stepped out of the captain's quarters and started for the small bridge. "Oh, and 'chicky?'" Ayan asked, amused.

"It seemed like the right word at the time," Lacey replied.

Ayan chuckled. "It got my attention."

"I was raised in a clean house with clean language, so I come up short when harsh words are called for."

"I wouldn't call that a failing," Ayan replied. "I'm glad you're here."

Lacey sighed, the last of the tension visibly draining from her. "Thank you."

Ayan couldn't help but feel a pang of loss and guilt at forsaking Haven Shore, but Frost's words still cut deeper. In retrospect, she couldn't believe how she was pulled into the political and personal maelstrom. It all started going wrong when she reached for Liam Grady, and it couldn't be more fitting that it ended within hours of Crewcast reporting that he was out of range. For the second time in her short, new life, she felt a calling, and it would be hard, with surprising difficulties, but she was ready to get on with the business of building the future – and with Lacey at her side, Oz and her father backing her, she was feeling less alone all the time.

"From being short-staffed to tripping over each other in three days," Frost told Jake as he finished fastening a primary power line to one of the Warlord's tertiary feeds. The indicators around the socket flashed for a moment then turned green one after another. "Looks like we're in business."

The stationary generator room was almost finished. Minh-Chu could remember when it was being used to store finished armour plates for the ship's interior only five days before. Ashley walked into the room right behind and stepped off to the side with Minh-Chu. "Where's Jake?" he asked.

Frost pointed to the combat-shielded antimatter enhanced mass reactor standing near the front of the generator room. It was installed on a forty-five degree angle beside another that matched it exactly. Three more pairs were lined up behind it, all idling, faint indicator lights blinking in sequence showing ready status. Captain Valent emerged from a panel on the opposite side of the nearest one, kicked the heavy cover closed, and took a scan using a high-powered hand tool. "That's it, the Big Surprise Two just looks like an old super-capacitor and a bunch of reserve batteries."

"We got another one?" Ashley asked.

"We built a bigger one," Frost said with a grin. "It's right under this generator room."

"This is a lot of power," Minh-Chu commented, looking at the nearest mass reactor. There was another armoured room just like the one he was standing in closer to the front of the ship, and a main generator room near the centre that held most of the Samson's older power generation systems. "Two of these generators could power a ship with the Warlord's mass."

"Aye, but the Warlord's no normal ship," Frost said.

186

"That's the truth," Minh-Chu said. "When I came in you were talking about the new trainees?"

"He was complaining that the ship seems a lot smaller with a full crew," Jake replied. "It happens when you've got an army of skitters and two hundred and ten souls aboard."

"Nevermind him," Moira said as she came in through the opposite hatchway with Stephanie and Alice. "He's been complaining about having too little or too much since he was a tot. First it was food, then drink, then drink and money. Complaining about too little most of the time."

"Quiet, woman. You'll tarnish my sterling reputation," Frost replied, accepting a brief half hug from his cousin.

"I'm assuming you're accepting my petition to join you on this trip?" Moira asked Captain Valent.

Jake opened a panel on the newest mass reactor and began rechecking its status. "You're more than welcome to come, you didn't have to make an official request."

"I did when I saw there was no invitation coming," Moira replied with a crooked smile.

"I thought you'd want to stay with the Hell Shrike. She still needs a lot of work."

"But I'm not her captain, was never really meant to be. What I need is a ship, and I hear you're hitting a supply waystation."

"You're going to hitch a ride and steal a ship?" Alice asked, thrilled.

"Aye, the Hell Shrike is packed with crew. They're busy with repairs now, but when they're done I plan on peeling a few choice officers off for my own ship. There are other seasoned captains aboard her that want to do the same as soon as they can. May as well get started."

"Can you get a boarding team together?" Jake asked.

"I was planning on going along with one of yours, figured I've proven myself in training sims with your people over the last three days."

"That's not his worry, Moira," Frost said. "His people are set to take one ship and its cargo. If you can get another team together, we can grab for another ship."

"Where are you headed, Captain?" Moira asked. "Where they've got so many ships lying around that you can pluck them as you like?"

"First thing's first," Jake said as Agameg and Finn came through the hatch near Minh-Chu and Ashley, closing it behind themselves. They were in a scan resistant compartment – no one would be able to eavesdrop on them. Jake also blocked their outgoing message capabilities on their command and control units. "Are we still ahead of schedule on repairs?"

"You just put us another hour or so ahead by helping with those generators. Thank you, Captain," Finn said. "Room Two is all wired, the reactors all check out. It was nice to buy something off the shelf instead of adapting salvage."

"I'm sure it was, but it was expensive. We're down to our cash reserves." Minh-Chu knew Jake was lying for the greater good. The cash vault they got their hands on contained ninety-three million in Galactic Currency. The fourteen antimatter enhanced mass reactors and their parts cost eleven million, and the other parts Jake bought for the ship only cost two. The rest of the cash was hidden on the Triton and the Warlord, making Oz, Frost, David, Jake, and himself the only ones who knew about it. A ship like the Warlord required cash reserves for emergency repairs, bribes, and other expenses.

"It's a good thing," Jake continued, "that our new crew don't mind food and lodgings as payment for the first tour. That brings me to the next issue. Do you think they're ready for action?"

"Normally I'd tell you this is a bad idea," Frost said. "Three days is a short time for any new crewmember, but we got some real experienced crewmembers out of Port Rush, and aye, they're still learning the tricks of this ship. Everyone we kept are able, experienced. I'd like a couple more days though. They need to get more familiar with the ship, come together as a team, and that takes drilling, practice."

"I can give you four days in transit," Jake replied. "How about your boarding and security people, Stephanie?"

"They're all former Triton crew. I've been able to keep Oz from poaching my people, and I stole a couple more when I sent notices through Alice asking if any experienced people wanted to leave Haven Shore. I've got a full team with backup, and all of them fought for the Triton when she was trapped last year. Our on-board security's good too. I kept a couple who are still green, but they're mostly cut from the same lot as the boarding team. That's not to mention Remmy and his team. The Rangers are disciplined and well trained. I don't know what to do with them yet, but I'll find something, I'm sure. With Remmy's experience on the Sunspire and against the Order Knights, I'll make sure he's got something to do."

"Minh?" Jake asked, turning to him.

"Samurai Squadron is ready with one substitution. Joyboy is out, Tacker is in."

"Oh, how's Paula doing?" asked Stephanie.

"She looks like a little stick swallowed a giant watermelon whole," Ashley replied to the room's amusement. "Healthy though, she's due in a couple weeks."

"You guys made up?" Alice asked.

"We're civil, I think pregnancy is calming her down a little," Ashley replied. "Or she's just too tired to keep yapping at people the way she used to."

"Other than that," Minh-Chu continued, "Samurai Squadron is good, and the hangar crew is ready. Thanks for finishing our punter systems, Agameg."

"You're welcome, it was a good system to train the team on."

"Your turn, Finn," Jake said. "How is the Warlord?"

"Ready," Finn replied. "Like Frost said, I'd like to drill the crew more, make sure they know their way around better, but the ship is ready. Given the four days in transit, everything will be finished, from the aggressive shielding to fixing the creak in Alice's bunk."

"I'd like to request a temporary transfer now that the ship is almost finished," Agameg said. "Finn is more than capable of handling the Chief Engineer position."

"I know," Jake said. "Looking to transfer to the Triton?"

"Yes, Sir, for two weeks. They have many crewmembers in need of more training than simulations or their existing pool of officers can provide. I have experience on that ship, and would like to assist while the Warlord is still pursuing non-military targets."

"I hate to lose you, but after everything Oz and the Triton have done for us over the last few months, I think I owe it to them. Good luck, Agameg, we'll miss having you aboard. Don't get too comfortable over there though, you're only getting the two weeks you're requesting."

"Thank you, Captain, I won't."

"Now that we're all up to date, it's time to lay out our next mission," Captain Valent said. "Normally we'd be meeting in the captain's mast, but our new doctors are using the space to teach some of our crew about the emergency medical systems."

"It's better this mission brief happens while we're on our feet, anyhow," Frost said. "It's going to be a busy one."

"Right," Jake replied. "Thanks to a recruiting drive, our need for supplies is doubling every week. Commander Ayan's efforts to convert the bunkers claimed by the Rangers and Haven Shore Regulars is probably going to work out too, so I bet their food will start running out in about a month. Since we're putting our lot in with her and the Triton, and they aren't ready to start producing what they need, it falls to us to acquire supplies and equipment.

"We're headed straight into the Iron Head Nebula, for an Industrial Starlight Port. It's not a Regent Galactic company, but they were contracted by Regent to deliver supplies and materials to the Order. The Port we're hitting is considered safe from attack because it sits on our side of the nebula, close to a major Regent Galactic military shipyard and dispatch centre. They assume the Regent Galactic base could send Order ships out fast enough to stop any attack. They think sneak attacks are impossible too, since cloaking is dodgy near the nebula, and impossible inside. The same matter that interferes with cloaks makes it a little dangerous for most ships to enter the outskirts of the nebula at high speeds, so they have to slow down at a significant distance from the Port facility. They also have to cross through the nebula at specific points. Our intelligence tells us that there are major deceleration and acceleration waypoints, where ships finish decelerating from faster than light travel or open wormholes before heading through a safe part of the nebula to the Order of Eden frontline. There are a lot of possible objectives there, so we're going to wait nearby, take our time picking our targets and our timing.

The Order of Eden has been patrolling the area with brand new Harbinger Corvettes. They come from the nearby shipyard. New corvettes are sent to patrol each of the waypoints before moving on to join the rest of their forces at the front."

"I've seen those," Moira said. "Fought a couple, too. With a good crew they're dangerous, no frills, but well armed. They come with some kind of power tap weapon; if you get too close they'll shut you down, but it doesn't damage electronics like an EMP."

"Do you want one?" Jake asked.

"What? A Harbinger?"

"Yes."

"You're crazy," Moira scoffed. "Sure, come up with a plan that won't get us all killed, and I'll take a corvette."

"I'm going to like this trip," Frost muttered. Minh-Chu couldn't help but notice Alice beaming a smile in the grizzled gunnery master's direction, who winked back.

"All right," Jake said. "Industrial Starflight was hit by the Holocaust Virus a little before they signed up with Regent Galactic, so there will be no automated security or defences. No drones, and they don't have many fighters. It's going to be true twitch-play: the better pilots, the better crews and strategists will win this if it comes to a straight fight. Most of the Order of Eden crews are green, new recruits into their cult, so we have a good chance if we stay sharp and smart. We leave in four hours, so make sure your teams are aboard, and you have everything you need. Don't share the details of our mission."

"How am I going to entice a team without a few details?" asked Moira. "What can I share from this meeting?"

"Tell them you'll be stealing a cargo hauler with my help, and I'll give you the ship with everything you find aboard when we get it back here," Jake replied.

"Fair enough," Moira replied.

CHAPTER 31
THE DECKS HAVE EARS

The shuffle and bustle of the Warlord's new crew getting ready for departure still rang in Alice's ears. It was hours later, and the Warlord was accelerating down a wormhole, using the hyperdrive system to speed things along. The ship also sent microscopic wormholes out ahead in all directions, invisible tendrils for their scanners to get a picture of what's well ahead. The hum of the exterior emitters could be heard faintly throughout the ship. It was a different vessel to her, with new decks, new walls, a different floor plan than the one she vaguely recalled. It made it easy for her to understand what it was like for most of the crew who were still new to the ship.

She'd broken her rule against using her direct mental connection to her comm unit outside of combat to rapidly view the new roster and crew details. There were exactly two hundred and ten aboard, and all of the new crewmembers were experienced with vetted service records. The Triton and Ayan took on the people who needed extended training, so the people the Warlord took on only needed to learn about that ship; they were qualified for their assignments aboard.

Alice was security. Her responsibility was to know every nook and cranny of the ship, where people were supposed to be, and to make sure that nothing unusual or detrimental to the ship or the Warlord's crew was going on. Her first shift, probably the busiest she'd see for the foreseeable future, was over, and while she was relieved at finishing the boarding and departure prep shift, she was also bored.

It was the first watch while the Warlord was underway, and most of the new crew were resting in their quarters. The galley was closed, as were the two cargo bays that doubled as recreation areas while they were empty, and even the Officer's lounge was dark and empty. It was time for the off-duty crew to report to their bunks, to try to get some sleep, and the ship was quiet.

Alice couldn't sleep, however, so she spent her time quietly walking the decks. Her uniform marked her as a security officer, a heavy vacsuit with a Violator handgun strapped to one thigh, and a big barrelled revolver on the other. The revolver was loaded with grip slugs that would expand before striking the target and wrap them in a cocoon-like bubble so they couldn't move. With every vacsuit aboard hardened against electromagnetic pulses and most other weapons, it was the only way to effectively disable people. Alice enjoyed the fact that she could buy many other types of shells for the weapon, such as web, shield, antigravity, EMP, and of course anti-armour explosive rounds. Alice couldn't understand why Ashley didn't carry hers all the time.

The hallway narrowed closer to the bridge, to the point where two fully armoured crewmembers would rub shoulders if they were to walk side by side. There had already been complaints about it, but Alice knew why that part of the ship was built that way. If there was a firefight, one smart combatant could hold either of the hallways running towards the bridge for an extended amount of time. The sides of the hallway were also heavily armoured, with doors that could weld themselves shut, trapping people inside rooms, or to form a killing tunnel that boarders couldn't escape from. Heavy ripper deck guns were hidden in the floor just behind the main hatchways leading into the bridge, inside the captain's mast room, as well as within the first officer's and captain's cabins. Anyone rushing the bridge from inside the ship was walking into a death trap that could outdo even the Triton's heaviest armour in minutes.

Unfortunately, the heavy plating and simple fixtures made the halls near the bridge look boring. The lighting was provided by dull grey biocell paint that absorbed ambient energy to provide illumination. It was layered on in even stripes running down the length of the corridor's ceiling.

She was approaching the bridge, where she knew there would be at least three people on duty – whichever pilot was on third watch, an operations officer, and a tactical officer. She didn't care to check who filled which position so she didn't look it up on the duty roster, but she knew her father would be serving in the tactical position. He didn't sleep much, something they had in common.

"You should have told me you privateered for the Damelians," Moira said. "I would have taken you more seriously from the start."

Alice ducked into the captain's mast room instead of proceeding onto the bridge. She knew next to nothing about Moira, and had never seen her and her father speaking on their own. They seemed to work well together, with Jake sharing more responsibility over the three days Moira had been aboard, but Alice hadn't seen anything personal pass between them. Then again, the three days of preparations since they recruited people from Port Rush had been the busiest she'd ever seen on a ship; no one had much time for conversation. Alice hadn't gotten to know anyone on the new staff, since the training and preparation schedules kept people so occupied that crewmembers were either busy or asleep.

"It doesn't matter much now, most of the crew have turned over since then. The Warlord's senior officers are all that's left from the Samson."

Alice checked some of Moira and Jake's public history on Crewcast and saw that he sent her the same information package that all of the new crewmembers got, plus an extra sealed data package. Strangely, she couldn't find any evidence of Jake's consciousness on the system, which meant that he was completely disconnected for the first time since they took on new people.

"It's good to know your senior officers have a lot of experience," Moira said. "And your daughter is really something. I'm surprised she's along for this trip."

"Where else would she be?" Jake asked, not defensively enough for Alice's taste.

"I would put her back on Haven Shore, with a security team, maybe. She didn't learn much about teamwork with the Rangers. That worries me."

"I was hoping that was what she'd take away from her time there," Jake said. "But I'm going back to plan A. Stephanie has trained more than a few great security officers, so I'm leaving it in her hands."

"Why not take her on yourself?" Moira asked. "I've never had kids, but it seems to me I'd want to keep that in my hands."

Jake laughed. He actually laughed. "I'm worse than she is. I can fight as part of a team, sure, but I'll break away and fight on my own first chance I get. Even the Warlord is an example of that - it's meant to fight outside of a fleet, and the systems are made so I can monitor everything through my neural link. The only reason I'm disconnected now is because the skitters are upgrading the interface."

"Trouble letting go, sort of a loner, and a history so mad that it takes concentration to keep it straight," Moira said. "Careful, Captain, or you'll start attracting the wrong kind of girl, the trouble-loving, trouble-making kind."

"Too late," Alice heard Minh-Chu say. With a quick check, she confirmed that he was taking the third watch as the pilot. "But that's another story."

"I'll bet," Moira replied. "What about these skitters you've got running around? That's something that wasn't so detailed in the welcome packet, people are nervous."

"I understand why," Jake said. "All the skitters have artificial intelligences, but they use a new anti-virus system. I've been working with a partner to upgrade things since my daughter discovered suicidal Ando models in the jungle down on Tamber, and now our bots can't be infected."

"That's impossible," Moira scoffed openly. "You're fooling yourselves if you think your bots are immune, and that's dangerous."

"All right," Jake said patiently. "Let's just say one of the bots does get infected, which, like I said, won't happen. Every other piece of equipment running our software will forcibly connect with the infected bot and fight the virus, and there's no way they'd get infected in the process."

"How are they immune?"

"No two bots are running the same operating system," Jake said. "Most bots need to use an analog method of communication, even if it's transmitted through digital means. That's where the commonality ends. Before, bots were programmed to collaborate on destroying viruses. Those instincts still exist, but now our bots' operating systems change with the development of their personalities and skills. The process affects every part of their code, and bots are allowed to alter their neural hardware as long as it doesn't reduce their functionality."

"Not even remotely possible," Moira said.

"We've had modular software that could reprogram itself for hundreds of years, this is just another step with artificial intelligence taking the lead. We left the well-being directives in, so they won't harm their allies and they have to listen to their commanders, but that's about it for safety."

"Yesterday three skitters perked up and saluted me as I walked by my fighter," Minh-Chu said. "I tried scanning them to find out if someone programmed them to do that, but my comm couldn't make heads or tails of their software anymore. I had to ask the old fashioned way, 'did someone tell you to do that?'" Minh-Chu mock-asked in baby talk. "They all flashed NO on their shells, then they got back to work on my fighter. My Uriel's never been in better shape, and those things are storing themselves in the reserve storage, so I'll have a robotic service crew with me now. The only downside is getting ridiculed by Singe now that she's caught me in the middle of a baby talk conversation."

Moira and Jake both laughed at Minh-Chu's expense, and even Alice couldn't help but let a chuckle slip. "So they're safe from viruses," Moira said. "But you have a Tower of Babel situation going on now; how do they communicate quickly?"

"I've seen high speed morse code using vibrations and light, audio streams, even herd behaviour," Jake replied. "I don't think they're having trouble. A few have started talking too, but most don't even try unless you tell them to. That's an unexpected bug."

"A big one," Moira said.

"They'll do it if you order them to," Minh-Chu said. "I just haven't bothered yet. I'm wondering how these things will develop on their own."

"I'm still sceptical of all of it being for the best," Moira said. "But I'll give it time."

Alice hadn't paid much attention to the skitters – something she decided to change, since they had the same software capabilities as the Andos she encountered. The skitters just seemed like basic worker bots to her, like a mobile tool chest, or hull finishing bot, but if they were capable of running complex software, the situation was different.

"Alice?" Jake asked.

She glanced at her comm unit and realized that her father was reconnected with the ship's sensors. Alice stepped out into the hallway and took the few steps onto the bridge. Minh-Chu looked over his shoulder and smiled. Moira, who sat at the Operations station, sent her a look that seemed to say 'sneaky brat' and Jake regarded her with a little surprise. "Everything okay?"

"Fine, I just didn't want to interrupt you," Alice said, the first excuse that came to mind. She pressed on to the question on her mind. "What about the Andos? They turn on and can't help but tie into whatever communications systems they can listen to."

"The bot bays on Haven Shore are switching them on in an isolation room," Jake replied. "Then ordering them to deactivate their wireless systems. It's the best they can do it, but at least they're not going suicidal."

"Oh, what if one of them decides to activate their wireless later?" Alice asked.

"The techs are cutting receivers once the bots are activated. It's not a perfect solution, but it's either that or recycle all the Andos for raw materials."

Alice couldn't forget the anguished expressions on the Ando model androids she killed in the forest, and still had doubts. "If it's the best they can do," she said, conceding for the time being.

"Why is it so complicated to deactivate Andos?" Moira asked.

196

"All their primary systems and functions are hard-wired on a single chip," Jake replied. "The tech is so small most nanobots can't disable something without affecting the nearest neighbouring system. The Andos have to do it themselves, and in the wrong conditions, they could access the wrong function and any number of things can go wrong. On the other hand, they're hard-wired pacifists."

"What about the variable operating system you were talking about?" Minh-Chu asked.

"The basic structure of their operating systems are hard-wired," Jake said. "So, in the new age of software, they're the least useful bots we have. It used to be the other way around, they were top of the line."

"Everything changes," Moira said. "Speaking of, what do you think of the new Warlord, Alice? How does it compare to the Samson you knew years ago?"

Alice could only regard her with confusion for a moment, then she realized that Moira had no idea that Alice had undergone a great transformation. "I don't really remember. Everything before the Battle of Port Rush is pretty blurry." Moira still seemed expectant, so Alice continued. "I died a couple times, might have lost a few things when the last body kicked it." She could feel the mood of the room darken, but didn't know what she could say to recover some levity. "I like the Warlord, though." Moira nodded and looked to the operations station. Her father offered her a little smile, and Minh-Chu returned his attention to the navigational systems. "I think I'm going to head to my bunk, good night." She didn't wait for anyone to wish her good night before leaving the bridge, but heard everyone but her father do so.

Before she was all the way down the corridor she could hear him behind her, and she turned towards him.

"I'm not good at this yet," Jake said. "Usually fathers have a grace period while they're changing diapers to get used to the idea of talking to their kid."

Alice had no idea what to think of what he was saying, but felt that she was disappointing him somehow. "I'm sorry I didn't regenerate as an infant in the middle of the battlefield?"

"Wait, that's not what I meant," Jake replied. "I'm just saying I'm still getting used to having you around."

Alice could see the indicator that her father was connected to the ship flash and disappear from the corner of her eye. He was so intent on whatever he was saying, that he couldn't maintain a mental connection to the ship. "Okaaaaay," Alice said, earnestly making an effort to understand him.

"I don't know how much of my conversation with Moira you heard," Jake explained.

"You could check the security tracker," Alice replied.

"It doesn't matter," Jake said, waving the notion off like an invisible insect. "What I'm telling you is that I spent so much time looking for you, when I didn't know any other way to connect to my past, then I found you in time to see you sacrifice yourself while commanding in my place on the Triton."

"I don't remember that," Alice said.

"And that brings us to now. I never expected to have a daughter, especially someone who has so much to learn."

"Gee, thanks," Alice said sardonically. Was he trying to tell her she was an amateur? Or was he trying to gently put her in her place?

"I don't want you to take this the wrong way, but I have a chance to help you become someone you're really proud of, and I want to tell you that whatever happened with the Rangers was my fault."

"Psh, right," Alice said, half involuntarily.

He gently grasped her chin and looked into her eyes. "I know you wanted to be part of the Rangers, but you would have listened to me if I told you to stay here. That puts everything that happened while you were away on me, and I was kicking myself before I found out what happened with the Andos. I don't want to be the kind of dad who lets other people raise their kid, even if you're almost a woman already. It's hard for me to have you here sometimes, because I know how dangerous it is, and I want to protect you, but I'd rather have you here than leave you back on Tamber."

"So I'm some little girl you want to keep your eye on now?"

"No, that's not what I meant. I want to be able to spend time with you like other families do. What's happened to Frost and Moira brought that right back into focus. Families should stick together, even if there's only two of us."

"A family that raids together, stays together," Alice said, her irritation abating a little. What her dad was saying came from a good place, even if it was hard for him to communicate it. "I'm glad I'm back here, with you." She let him off the hook with a self-indulgent hug. She let go long moments later. "Good-night, Dad. Get some sleep after watch."

"Good-night," he replied. "I'll try."

CHAPTER 32
UNSETTLED SETTLEMENT

"I should move my office up here," Carl Anderson said as he looked through the tower windows. The craggy surface of Kambis filled the night sky. Glittering cities dotted the looming landscape above. The black, high tide ocean stretched out to the horizon, reflecting light cast onto it from the planet Tamber orbited.

Ayan had made the top level of the former Order of Eden bunker's tower her personal office and quarters. It was her father's idea. The top level of the tower was the first the robotic crews finished assembling, and it wouldn't be practical for any official usage for several days. Fixtures like displays, furnishings, and other necessary parts for official use would be installed later, leaving the tower top completely unused and empty. Meanwhile, the bunks below were full, and officer quarters in the bunker were used for families, and Ayan didn't want to displace them.

The tower was built directly into the centre of the former Order of Eden bunker and doubled as a massive shield emitter platform. That was why it was finished over the last few days, even though it would be mostly empty until the power systems and other fixtures would be in place. The shield system was the only functional electronic device in the upper levels.

Most of the surfaces inside were still bare dark grey metal, with minimal lighting from independent fixtures and only a small portable materializer for food and drink that required a great deal of water whenever it made anything. It was a large space with only one partition for a hygiene closet. Her bedroom space was pushed to one side, just out of sight behind a makeshift curtain and it consisted of a cot, a storage crate for a bedside table, and a small security safe.

Normally she'd stay on the Clever Dream, but she decided to provide an example by living in the newest part of the Order of Eden bunker. Besides, there were memories living in the captain's quarters of the Clever Dream

199

she didn't care to face. Lacey had set up her cot behind another curtain, on the other side of the lavatory. There was no other furniture in that large space.

"It took the bots we have about a day to build it. There are supports and specifications for hangars and other outbuildings inside the bunker, but I still haven't decided what we'll actually put up. I'll see what Lee says when he gets here," said Ayan.

"I'd offer to bring a few creature comforts from Haven Shore, but they're short on anything with a cushion too," Anderson said, sitting on a narrow ledge beneath the transparasteel window. The view over his shoulder, Ayan's view, was darker. The light from Kambis drowned out most of the stars between the horizon and the large planet, but she could see the yellow sparkle of lights from the coast of Port Rush. When their side of Tamber rotated away from Kambis, low tide would reveal a landmass between the former Order of Eden bunker and the sprawling port. It would also reveal wrecks and other waste that were partially drawn out into the ocean, or brought up. Scavengers would be going to war.

There was no way Ayan could have known how hard the first three days of recruitment and aid would be. The bunker she stood above had only processed eight hundred and twelve. The other bunker processed a little over five hundred, and the Triton managed to bring over eighteen hundred aboard. Luckily enough, more than eighty percent of them had some skill that would be useful to the Triton or the people on the ground in Port Rush. The rest were children and their parents, who Oz was able to relocate to the Triton. Many of them were hesitant about resettling on a combat carrier, but most changed their tune once they saw the clean living quarters and well-kept habitation areas. They didn't get access to the apartments overlooking the Botanical Gallery; Oz had decided that those would be reserved for people who had proven dedication to the Triton. Any new resident who cleared through security could visit the park grounds in the Botanical Gallery, however, and there was a ring of family apartments nearby that were practically untouched for decades. Ayan was told that families were beside themselves when they saw the available facilities aboard the ship, and the three to four room apartments where they would be located. The promise of the Triton was simple: they settle in for free after a security check, wear a comm unit that tracked them and their children, then find a job after two days of being aboard ship. If they couldn't find a job, Crewcast would assign them a temporary position while they waited in line for something better. Anyone could leave at any time, but there was a job for every skill set.

Ayan was hoping to work her way up to offering the same deal on the ground, where she owned several former Order of Eden bases through claims made by the Rangers. She'd been down into the heart of the bunkers, the more cramped berthing they used as a hold-over area while they cleared people for the Triton or took volunteers who wanted to work for Ayan and the Rangers on the ground. It was cramped, but people were happy to receive the ration packs Ayan brought with her. It was a trick of timing that worked in her favour. The ration packs were going to arrive whether she was there or not, she just made sure her visits were timed with them whenever she took a tour of the facilities.

The extra food was provided by Triton Fleet, which was given a wealth of shipping containers of the stuff by the Warlord. She was more than thankful for the tons of rations, especially since the bunkers didn't have materializers. Even the fabrication systems inside were rudimentary, and the food was well sub-par. They made fixtures, parts to repair the bunker, blankets, thin brown vacsuits for people who didn't have proper clothing, basic communication and computing units that looked like wrist straps, and other basic, important supplies.

By her estimation, those systems would last years with proper maintenance, and someone was already working on programming a few skitters to do the upkeep. People in the berths were happy to see Triton and Ranger security people. She was dressed as one when she took her tours, and she kept her faceplate dark so no one would recognize her. In the short time she was there, she saw two families reunited, and there was a feeling that most of the people down there were already looking out for each other. That wasn't universal, but people seemed to offer each other a helping hand when it was needed, and most seemed to be getting the first good rest they'd had in weeks, possibly months.

There was a minority that had serious problems, however, and it was that minority that Ayan was about to meet with. She checked the thin curtains that hid her cot, tall backpack, armour, and rifle.

"So, who is this malcontent we're about to see?" her father asked.

"His name is Clyde Dominic. He says he represents the Free Citizens of Rega Gain, but I've never heard of them. When I assumed he was their leader, he was actually offended," Ayan sighed and shook her head. "He said theirs is an organization of full equality, so there's no leader. He's just delivering their message."

"Oh, like that cult on Terra Zeta, the Free Born," Anderson said, smiling.

"Sorry, who are they?" Ayan said.

"You mean, who *were* they. Their colony was just discovered. In their statement they said the Holocaust Virus was a sign that the end was nigh, and their spirits would be carried to the afterlife if they died before robotic life took the universe. They claimed to be leaderless too, but it only took a few of them to open all the airlocks and kill all four thousand and twenty there."

"It would be nice if the Order of Eden caught that kind of crazy," Ayan muttered. She shook off the notion. "Sorry, I'm tired," she said.

"Most people would agree with you these days, don't worry."

"I should be focused on the work here," Ayan said, trying to fend off the negativity that threatened to press away her good mood. "The logistics of building a permanent base here and helping the people stuck in Port Rush are so complicated that it actually makes sense to forget the big picture for a few days. Taking care of these people has got to be the top priority."

"Don't take this the wrong way," Carl said. "But I don't think you can forget the big picture. That's one of your best assets: you envision something and strive for it. Go ahead and concentrate on setting things up here, but delegate the minutia. That's what the more experienced Rangers are for. Most of them are former slaves and refugees, so they know exactly what the people they're helping are going through."

"You're right, and a genius," Ayan replied.

"I've just finished a few more orbits than you have," Carl replied. "Let go of your vision for a couple hours at a time so you're sure people are being treated properly, but get back to big picture thinking, that's what people need from you."

"You don't even know exactly what I'm planning," Ayan said. "No one really does."

"The fact that you won't say it aloud tells me that I'll be amazed when you're ready to tell me. I'll wait."

The sound of the lift rumbling up the centre of the tower drew both their attention to the double doors at the centre of the large room. "We have this to get through first, and I have a feeling it's going to be interesting."

The doors opened and Lacey was the first to emerge from the large elevator car. She had taken to wearing the same outfit as Ayan, a white medium armour vacsuit and a sidearm. It wasn't how Ayan was used to seeing her, but the simple uniform suited Lacey better than it suited her. Lacey was taller and more well proportioned, so she made the unforgiving white suit look good in comparison to how Ayan saw herself wearing it. The Triton emblem was placed on the upper left side of her chest, right shoulder and the middle of her back. The rank insignia matched Ayans'

Commander markings, only there was a green border drawn around it to mark her as Ayan's official handler. Instead of the rare Violator handgun, Lacey carried a triple mode weapon called a Ziffer by its users that could stun, fire energy, or launch tiny superheated corrosive slugs.

Behind her was a man who was dressed in tattered ground dweller's clothing – a loose shirt that might have been blue once, and heavy protective trousers. His boots were sealed to the knee, and Ayan could see the collar of a protective suit peeking up from under this planet side clothing. Two empty holsters made it plain that he was normally armed, and they had to take his weapons when he entered the base. He set a determined gaze on her the moment he emerged from the elevator. She had the distinct feeling that he had every intention to make the meeting as difficult as possible.

There were four Triton guards with him, two behind and two flanking. They had her safety taken care of, it was her responsibility to take care of the rest. Ayan took a second to recall the last moment she remembered being happy, and was surprised to discover that it was when Jake invited her to join the crew of the Warlord. It was a trick she learned from Liam, which only diminished its value slightly. She let herself live in the feeling of that moment, and Ayan could feel her expression softening, a smile appeared on her lips as she regarded Clyde Dominic.

His expression eased from confrontational to curious. "Your Highness," he addressed with a hint of disdain.

She immediately felt her attitude begin to sink at the sound of the royal honorific. "Please, I'm a land owner, not a queen. You're Mister Dominic?"

"Yeah, and that's not what most of the people out there think," he said, thumbing towards the distant lights of Port Rush. "Especially the people who think you're saving them. They're so desperate that they don't even see the pattern here."

"The pattern?" Ayan asked. It had been a long day, and she was fighting to remain patient and pleasant.

"They don't notice how you separate yourself from them up here while you spy on them and give everyone assignments through the cheap communicators you've been handing out. You probably eat better than everyone, you definitely have more space than everyone. Just like a monarch dictator, you spend as much resources on protecting yourself from the people you say you're saving with energy shields and security. Yeah, you're a queen."

Ayan instantly recognized that Clyde was reciting a speech he'd probably practiced over and over. What he said was infuriating, but the fact that he had probably built up a very specific set of expectations was encouraging. A glance at Lacey revealed that her second in command was already near the end of her patience.

"You're not considering a whole number of factors-" her father started.

Ayan raised a hand and stopped him. It was time to break Clyde Dominic's expectations down and start communicating, if he was willing. "You're right," Ayan replied, relishing the surprise registering on the man's expression. "All this probably looks like I'm taking control like a lot of monarchs did in the early days of the private colonies. When you really look at it, I am." She found herself smiling again, but this time it was almost smug. "But appearances are deceiving," she chided lightly as she walked over to a short staircase leading up to the window walkway and sat down. "I'm here to create a recruitment centre for people who want to help us fight the Order of Eden, create a logistical and social support system for our ships, and eventually build a new town in Port Rush. I'm the military leader for this project, so I direct its progress. When you consider my cause, and the fact that I have several equals in the Triton Fleet, then your monarchy analogy falls apart. Dictatorships are run by a solitary leader, and I'm not alone, I'm not even the highest ranking officer in Triton Fleet."

"That's not my point," Clyde said, raising his voice for the first time. "These people have no choice. They have to join you, and you take their freedom away while you dangle food in front of them."

The turn in conversation was a little unexpected. Ayan thought she was facing someone who believed they were protesting a monarchy, judging by his approach, but that was only his first point of contention. He had accusations, which were already half right. "We have to track everyone who signs up with us. I'm sorry a few people have turned away after finding that out. Most people turn away early, because we sit all new recruits down to a meal while we tell them what's involved with joining Triton Fleet. If they accept our conditions and sign up, they log into our system and we track them for safety, health and to assist with placement." He seemed more at ease as she replied, probably because of her shift in tone, from confident to defensive.

"About that food you're bribing people with," he replied. "You captured or stole everything you have from an enemy who has wronged everyone, Regent or the Order, so none of this is really yours. Why don't you give it over to the people you say you're trying to help, see what they think about you being in charge."

Ayan fixed him with a quizzical expression. Her instinct was to ask him exactly what he meant outright, but she let her pause speak for itself instead.

His proposal didn't deserve a response, and she wanted to make him uneasy.

"I mean, this is all stolen. Even this base was launched from an enemy ship and the Carthans let you have it because you got here first. I bet most of your supplies weren't bought honestly, so you're just hoarding, using it all to enforce your tyrannical control."

"Nutter," Lacey said, shaking her head.

Ayan cleared her throat. "You almost have a point, Mister Donovan. If we didn't have to use our resources and sacrifice lives to take this bunker, stopping dangerous Order of Eden operatives from spreading, then I'd almost agree with you. I can't imagine you expected me to agree that we should just leave what we've built here and let whoever comes along take what they want, but I have to ask, was that a genuine request?" The time to play gently with the encounter was over. Ayan stood and looked across the room at him from the top of the stairs.

"No, I'm just making a point."

"Which is?" Ayan asked.

"Nothing here is actually yours! The first group of armed people who got here could have taken all this instead of you."

"Wrong," Ayan said. "You are dead wrong."

"About what?"

"About it being easy!" Ayan barked. "It took months to find this bunker even though it was on Port Rush's doorstep. Three people died taking it, and I keep their sacrifices in mind as I decide how it will be used. I've listened to your entitled opinion, and it's time I stripped this conversation down to bare bolts. You and your people feel you should have free access to what we have, that's not going to happen. We earned it, we'll decide how it'll be used. You think our safety and security measures take things too far, and I have to wonder, do you actually know how it works? Have you listened to any of our support staff explain it to you while you sit down at our table for a free meal?"

"No, but-"

"Then let me explain," Ayan said, stepping down the staircase as she did so. "You sit down, we feed you. A tired, but friendly intake staffer sits down with you and explains the basics, which are: you have to link with our communications system either by installing our software or using one of our communication units. That software, we call it the Crewcast system, tells us where you are at all times, what your medical status is, tells us what you are doing, records everything you say, and tries to assist you as you enter our service. The Crewcast system also helps you be social with anyone on the network, helps you find training, collects data about your existing skills, and provides a qualifying system so you can get in line for jobs and promotions."

"That's exactly what I'm talking about, no one has any freedom with your organization," Clyde said. "Log in once, and you're part of the system for life. No rights, no privacy."

"I'm not finished," Ayan said, stopping to stand in the middle of the large empty space. "Our system also polices and tracks people who try to get access to information that is considered private. My comm unit actually judges whether or not I get access to data by determining the reason why I'm accessing it. Since I'm of a high rank, I can access most information, but if I were to try to access a conversation Lacey had with someone just because I'm being nosey, Crewcast will recognize that, and I would not be able to hear it without using a peer override system, where someone of my rank or higher allows me to access the recording. While we have a lot of data on everyone in our system, we also have safeguards and controls."

"What if your system is hacked?"

"Crewcast knows when its being hacked, all senior officers are notified the instant that starts, and we have the experts to take care of that kind of situation. In trade for being in this system, people are clothed, given the freedom to apply for any job they're qualified for and meaningful work in the meantime if there's a wait for that position. We feed our people, and we try to provide the best possible residence we can. In this base, that's a small bunk or cabin. That gets better on the Triton, Haven Shore, and it'll get even better when I'm finished building here."

"I still don't see freedom in your system," Clyde replied. "What if someone just doesn't want your system watching them?"

"Then they'll be escorted out. Let me clarify the purpose of Crewcast. It finds lost children even if they have taken their comm unit off. Other comm units passively track them and alert their parents and nearby security. Our security officers, our soldiers are watched even more closely, and their suits petrify as soon as the system recognizes an abuse of authority, and the entire security network is notified. Medical conditions are caught early and treated, people are reunited with loved ones through Crewcast recognizing DNA and personal matches."

"Personal matches?"

"Yes, you tell the system who you're looking for and where you last saw them and Crewcast won't only search its own network, but the Stellarnet as well," Ayan replied. "We've broken good news to over a thousand people about friends and relatives who are still alive and looking for them. I'm not going to go into other details, since I'm pretty sure you are here to size me up, to question me, and not much I say will matter, but I'll tell you that it's true that even Crewcast can be misused, any data or system can be. In the end, we need your trust if you expect us to help you, and that first meal is provided so we can start earning that."

"Cults operate the same way," Clyde countered.

Ayan squeezed her eyes shut, as if to stop the stormy retort that threatened to burst through her composure. She took a deep breath and opened her eyes. He was standing there, smirking at her. "Your turn. What did you hope to accomplish by coming here?"

"I just don't believe in a military establishment taking over Port Rush." He replied. It was a practiced response.

"We're barely on the shore, not encroaching at all," Ayan replied. "No, you stand to lose something if we help too many people."

"I'm here on principle, representing-"

"What trade are you in?" Ayan pressed. "Are we cutting into your business somehow?"

"I don't know what you're talking about," Clyde replied.

"What is that business? Selling food? Shelter? How do people who don't have money pay you? Slavery? Prostitution?"

Lacey regarded the man smugly, crossing her arms.

"Prostitution?" Clyde protested indignantly. "I trade in goods, not services, lady."

"There," Ayan said. "So people have stopped paying ridiculous prices for whatever you're selling and you've gotten a group of people together to see what I'm all about." She looked to the security officer standing beside him. "How many people did he check in with?"

"There was a crowd, Ma'am. Thirteen altogether."

"We have a full scan profile on them?" Ayan asked.

"Yes," replied the armoured security guard.

"Good, make sure they're tracked. I want to know what they do while they're in Port Rush."

"What?" Clyde replied. "I came here peacefully!"

"I don't care," Ayan said. "You expected to meet a dictator when you came here, but overlooked a more likely possibility. That is, that you'd be meeting a military leader, and that's what I am. This is a military complex, representing a larger military organization. I'm marking you and everyone you came with as a threat, and I'm going to start sending nano-trackers into Port Rush right now. This is your fault, Mister Dominic. If I see someone trying to stop people from approaching our settlement here with force, evidence of slave-trading, or any other crime within our reach, I'm going to do my best to stop it."

"You can't be the law down here, even the Carthans can't be the law down here," Clyde replied.

"Watch me," Ayan replied.

Clyde started turning away, towards the elevator doors, and Ayan stopped him. "What I don't understand is why you didn't approach us with the intention of creating a trade alliance. That tells me a lot about your type of business." She pulled a full meal ration bar and tossed it to him.

He caught it after it bounced off his chest and looked at it. "What's this?"

"A free meal, thanks for listening," she said, and turned towards her father, who was suppressing a smile. She heard the elevator doors open, boots stepping into the car and was relieved when she heard the doors close.

"That went well," Carl Anderson said. He tapped the comm unit on his arm a few times and nodded. "I'm just making sure everyone who Clyde brought with him is getting a copy of that conversation."

"What was the real point of that?" Ayan said, walking to her little cordoned off space and parting the curtains.

"They're sizing you up," Lacey said. "That's the only reason I can see. Sure, he had his points, but they were pretty weak when you think about it."

"There's obviously a criminal element involved here," Carl Anderson agreed. "Port Rush has been on its own for a long time, law has come and gone, and no one is really afraid to do as they like. Just the rate of rejection here is evidence enough of that. We kicked out twenty eight percent of people on their first day for theft and assault."

"I know," Ayan said. "So they're trying to put me up as some monarch, single me out."

"It looks like," Lacey replied.

"Then I'll share leadership. I'll elevate you as an equal, Lacey, and we'll find a few more people who could be good officers under us."

"What?" Lacey asked, agog. "I've never served as an officer. I've never even applied for the military."

"Don't worry," Ayan said. "There are a lot of responsibilities I can share with you that you're already good at. Not much will change except for accommodation allowance and your pay."

"In that case, sign me up," Lacey replied. "Just make sure I'm one of those filing officers, in a non-combat post."

"A logistical management position," Carl said.

"Exactly," Lacey affirmed. "That's the kind of thing I'm good at."

"I know, that's why I love having your around," Ayan said. "And why you'll make a great commander on A Station."

"Yup, and my first official duty will be to find a new name for this place. A Station is so-"

"Military?" Carl replied.

"Well, yes."

Ayan brought up the holodisplay for the manufacturing centre in the upper floors of the base and checked on one of their only mass fabricators. The next item in the fabrication queue was body panels for a new hover truck. "All right, one more thing before I pass out," she said. "Should I actually follow through with this nano tracking threat?"

"Yes," Lacey said without hesitation.

"No, go bigger," her father said.

"See? This is why I'm only good for logistics," Lacey said, smiling at Carl.

"Bigger?" Ayan asked.

"Have our fighter squadron patrol in low orbit, use scanners to capture everything as it happens in Port Rush. We'll task Crewcast to recognize serious crime. I can take care of enforcement with the Rangers and a few Triton Regulars if you'll authorize them."

"That is simpler then sending thousands of nanobot watchers out, and cheaper," Ayan said. "I must be tired, I should have caught that."

"Still, your threat is going to make them pretty paranoid. They'll have nano-zappers out by morning," Carl said. "Now, you should both get some sleep."

"Absolutely," Lacey said.

Ayan hugged her father on his way to the door and was closing the curtain around her cot before he got to the elevator.

"You still impress me, Ayan," Lacey said as she started settling in for the night on her side of the curtain.

"Thank you," Ayan said. "I wouldn't make you a commander if I didn't think you would do well. You'll be great."

"Thank you," Lacey replied. The pair were quiet as they got undressed and slipped into their cots. "Ayan, I'm wondering something."

"What's that?" Ayan asked

"Are you really going to make this your quarters?"

"Absolutely not," Ayan said, stifling a yawn. "I'm going to move down to a cabin or something as soon as there's room."

"That might not be for a while."

"I'm sure the new head of Logistics will figure something out," Ayan replied, smiling to herself.

"That's me, isn't it?" Lacey asked.

"Yes it is, Commander."

CHAPTER 33
TRAINING

"I'm telling you, we've got this!" Remmy shouted into his comm. He was torso deep in the main lines leading from engineering to the bridge of a Harbinger Regent Galactic ship. It was a destroyer class, over seven hundred metres long, and armed to the teeth.

"You're taking too long!" Alice replied, helping her team weld another set of blast doors closed. "There's another anti-incursion team on the way. We should just blow the charges around the reactor and take the nearest airlock, the Warlord is waiting."

"If I get this, we can take the ship!" Remmy replied.

"Just give him another minute, I've seen him neutralize the core of an Order of Eden bunker," replied one of his Ranger team, a tall blonde creature named Nanette that was always on Remmy's side. "This is easy compared to that."

Several bone rattling thuds announced the impacts of explosive rounds against the blast door Alice was almost finished welding shut. "Back!" she ordered her team. "Take cover and watch for any sign that they're trying to go around." The Warlord boarding crew that had been placed under her command, a group of thirteen experienced soldiers, obeyed her orders and took positions around the broad hallway. Several of them held up the deck plates they pulled up to access the main trunk line for portable cover, and formed a half-circle around the hole Remmy worked in.

"Explosives detected," Alice announced as she highlighted the wall beside the blast door. "Get ready to hit them hard as soon as they come through." She glanced at Remmy as she readied a thermal grenade. Why she was trusting his judgement over her own instincts, she would never know.

The wall burst through, sending a wave of heat and shrapnel over the Rangers and her boarding team. Together they were twenty-eight, the

Ranger team under the command of Remmy, and the Warlord team under her command. Some of their energy shields were partially depleted thanks to the blast, a few that were too close had been knocked down, but they came through it fine. Alice and two others lobbed grenades through the ragged opening, and just as her tactical sensors counted fifteen anti-incursion soldiers, the grenades detonated.

The enemy was in cheaper armour, and didn't fare well against the heavy grenades, losing six of their number in the detonation.

"God dammit! I just had it! I was just connected!" Remmy shouted up from his hole. "Just keep the deck steady for ten seconds and I'll have control of communications, navigations, the whole thing."

Another incursion team appeared on her tactical monitor, coming in through an airlock only thirty metres behind them. "Ganjavi, get a trap ready in this corridor, we need to blow it as soon as that secondary group comes through," she ordered, highlighting the short hallway leading to the airlock and a number of escape pods.

"Aye!" he replied, running towards his objective.

The first incursion team started firing through their improvised door. The Rangers and the Warlord teams returned fire, immediately pressing the enemy back. Alice could see there were more soldiers gathering on the other side, however. "We're going to be overrun unless you do something now, Remmy!"

"I got it!" Remmy shouted back. The lights flickered, and emergency doors slammed shut, one nearly cutting Hooman Ganjavi in half. "Sonofabitch!" He shouted, barely stopping in time.

"Do you have the slave frequency synced up with the Warlord?" Alice asked.

"One sec!" Remmy said, shutting down the ship's reactor completely. It would take half an hour for it to restart, leaving the destroyer defenceless in the meantime. "The uplink is good, the Warlord has control of the ship."

The simulation ended, and Alice disengaged from the training system. It always took her a moment to remember where she was after a mind-show like that. They were in a lounge with an extremely low ceiling, a space that was really improvised with the redesign of the ship with salvaged seating and makeshift tables. It was right below the main crew quarters. Alice could stand up straight in the space, but few others could. "Fine, you win, good strategy," Alice told Remmy, looking down at him where he stretched in his seat.

Only six others shared the space with them; the rest of the people participating in the simulation were doing so from their bunks. "It's not about winning," Remmy said. "And if it were, we both would have won. You held the position long enough for me to finish the uplink."

"He's right, Alice," Stephanie Vega said, removing the small uplink patch from her forehead. "You're getting better at coordinating a team, and you're even improving when you're not the leader, but you have to accept that this isn't a competition. That kind of mindset will get people killed in a real situation."

"I know," Alice said. "I let Remmy finish his plan, right? I get it."

"You did, and that's something, but we're getting our teams together so we can pursue more than one course of action when it's called for," Stephanie replied, her tone level and non-confrontational. "It's not about letting the other commander do their thing, it's about coordinating. For a little while there you had a chance to plant your explosives around the reactor while Remmy set up in the trunk lines. If you'd coordinated a little more, you'd have multiple contingencies in place, ready just in case Remmy's plan fell through. If that happened, you'd be all set to leave the ship immediately, saving the lives of your people, then you could blow the reactor, disabling the destroyer, too. Instead, you took an 'either-or' stance and reduced your chances of successfully completing the operation."

Alice couldn't think of anything non-argumentative to say, so she quietly pulled her interface patch off and nodded.

"I'm sorry if it sounds like I'm brow-beating you," Stephanie said, laying a hand on her shoulder. "I just want you to get as much as you can out of these sessions because I know you could be a really important part of the team on the Warlord. I hope you still want to be."

"Honestly? I think I'd rather be solo again, but someone signed the ownership of my ship away," Alice replied without thinking. She was letting her irritation speak for her. What Stephanie was saying was probably right, and she did want to be a part of the team, but she felt like she couldn't do anything right lately, and being on her own was a compelling alternative. "Wouldn't it be better if the Clever Dream were here? I did fine on my own, even in the battle of Port Rush. I can captain her no problem, and what good is my ship doing in Haven Shore, anyway?"

"You were killed on that battlefield, Alice," Stephanie said. "You can't trust that your cybernetics will save you every time. I want you to come back in one piece, and working with a team makes that easier. That's why the captain put you in my command chain, so you could benefit from my team's experience."

Remmy cleared his throat. He was smirking; all this must have been pretty entertaining to him.

"The Rangers are learning as much as they're teaching," Stephanie said. "Your performance wasn't perfect in there either, Remmy. We can go over that later."

"Sounds good," Remmy said, looking a little less pleased with himself.

"You're constantly improving, Alice," Stephanie said. "That's what matters."

Despite the reassurance, Alice didn't feel like hearing any more, and she was also tired of Remmy. If there was a combat sim going on, he was already in there any way he could be, and his weird choice of ancient entertainment drew crowds in the mess hall during down time. There was just no getting away from him. "Thank you, Commander Vega," Alice said. "All right if I take a walk?"

"Sure, I'll keep you company part way, I'm headed to the officer's mess," Stephanie replied.

Alice made for the door, Stephanie right behind her, irked that they were going in the same direction. "I didn't know it was finished."

"There are a few chairs and some improvised tables," Stephanie said. They walked in silence for a few moments before she broke the silence. "I'm not kidding when I say you've been improving. Your situational awareness is higher than most of the people I've worked with in the last few years. You keep track of your team, the enemy. and the details of the mission really well."

"But I'm still no team leader, not for real, anyway," Alice said. It was the 'but' statement that Stephanie was holding back, she was sure.

"You'll get there with experience. I didn't sign on with the captain as a leader, it took me a lot of missions to get there. I got to know people, how they thought, who they were, and those relationships taught me a lot about my style of command, and eventually I was ready to take the lead. You should try to get along with Remmy, by the way. He's good for downtime."

"What? My stalker?" Alice replied. "When I was in the Rangers he checked my profile constantly, ten times a day, sometimes more."

Ashley emerged from her quarters and smiled at them as she fell in step. "Where we goin'?"

"Officers' mess, to see the captain," Stephanie said as she checked Crewcast. "I think Alice and I want turns at talking to him. Alice says Remmy has been stalking her, by the way."

"Really?" Ashley asked. "How'd I miss that? I haven't seem him staring at you in the mess hall with dreamy eyes or anything."

"Well, it looks like Alice has been stalking him, too," Stephanie said with a smile, looking up from the communications and utility unit covering

214

her forearm. "He did check your profile a lot while you were in the Rangers, eleven times one day, an average of five times a day the rest. Checked out a few pictures of you at the beach too, but mostly he was checking your daily commentary."

"How many times did he check my beach images? I can't see that," Alice asked, flushed.

"Six, but he's only human, and you're about the same age, maturity-wise," Stephanie replied.

"Yeah, right!" Alice protested.

"The system does not lie," Stephanie replied. "Speaking of which, there were eight days in the last month where you checked his profile fifteen times."

"In eight days?" Ashley asked. "That's not too bad, kinda crushy though."

"Oh no," Stephanie laughed. "Fifteen times a day on eight different days. It says you checked stats, his daily commentary, and you watched three holos of him in training, and you Rangers don't wear much on the obstacle course."

Ashley filled the hall with a gleeful screech and clapped. "He's even your size, you'd be so cute together!"

Alice was mortified. "I was tracking him! He's been competing with me since the beginning of Rangers training. It's annoying, we're supposed to be a team, just like you said."

"Wait, it shows here that you checked his profile a few days before he checked yours," Ashley said as she checked her own comm unit. "Was there romance on the obstacle course?" she asked with a grin.

Alice brought up the holographic clip she used to glare at when they were in training. She had randomly been placed on the starting line of Circuit D3, one of the most challenging obstacle courses, beside Remmy. She started the holographic playback right before the moment that she'd never forget. A second before the starting buzzer sounded, Remmy looked at her and winked. "He completely threw me off my game, got ahead of me right away and when I got to the rope swing he did this." She advanced to a latter stage of the course, when she had just finished climbing a muddy wall with hidden hand-holds. Remmy finished just ahead of her and swung across the elevated mud pit with ease, then flung the rope back across the span. Alice was clearing muck from her eyes, so she didn't see the thick rope and it struck her squarely in the forehead, knocking her off balance and back down the climbing wall. "I nearly broke my neck! That's four metres!"

"Not on purpose," Ashley said, nearly doubled over laughing.

"Nope, I'd say he was trying to help and didn't check his timing," Stephanie agreed. "He probably didn't even see who he was swinging the rope back to."

Alice deactivated the little hologram and shook her head. "It had to be on purpose, that's why he's been in my sights all this time."

Ashley giggled and nodded. "I'm sure it has."

"No, as my competition, he started it. I scored in the bottom that day, and he made top three," Alice insisted.

"You ever ask him about it?" Stephanie asked.

"Are you kidding? No. He'd just laugh, that's how he is."

"You know, there are a lot of other, older ladies in these beach holograms too," Stephanie said. "If this is a real problem, I can use my security access to see who he was looking at. Do you really think he's stalking you?"

"Yes," Alice said.

"Okay, let's see who he was looking at in these images," Stephanie said as she reviewed the behaviour capture data. Alice couldn't see the information. To her frustration, Stephanie was reviewing the files in privacy mode. "Yup, he was looking at Shiriza in all of them, and for your information, he asked her out the day after she dropped out of the Rangers."

"Oh," Alice remembered the woman. She was fairly nice, older than both her and Remmy by several years, but a little frigid. Shiriza was beautiful though, and fairly exotic looking, with dark skin and wavy dark hair.

"She turned him down and banned him from her social profile," Stephanie said. "The story gets worse from there."

"For who? Her or Remmy?" Ashley asked.

"Remmy. She said some nasty things about him to all the women in her circle of friends. Might explain why Remmy didn't have much luck dating in Haven Shore, not for lack of trying. He's about as awkward as a one legged stool."

"Ouch," Ashley said. "Points for dedication, though."

"Definitely," Stephanie agreed. "But he also isn't stalking you. Looks like he checks out your profile because he thinks you're a friend. Probably likes that you follow what he's doing."

"Yeah, right," Alice retorted.

"Listen, Crewcast doesn't make mistakes with this kind of thing. From the behaviour analysis I'm seeing, he thinks you're too young for him and probably sees you as a kind of kindred spirit, there's nothing weird about it."

216

"Speaking as someone whose been ogled and followed," Ashley said in a much kinder tone than Stephanie, "I can tell you this is a good thing. He's short on real friends, I think, and he'd probably be easy to get along with."

"But the movies he shows, and I've seen him joking around," Alice said. "It looks like a lot of people here like him."

"Sure, but he doesn't know any of them, they're all new crew looking for connections too," Ashley replied. "You two could be good friends, unless you're disappointed that he's not-"

"No, no," Alice said. "If you're sure he's not stalking me, then good, and I'm not disappointed."

"Well, there would be no problem if you were," Ashley said with an impish grin. "Crewcast says you're about seventeen to eighteen now, and he's twenty three, you're about the same dating maturity, and there's nothing ick-"

"Seriously?" Alice asked with a screech.

"Just buggin' ya," Ashley chuckled.

"Is this okay now? You're not going to accuse him anymore?" Stephanie said in a more serious tone.

"Yeah, I guess the evidence can't lie," Alice said. "Wish I knew before." The hatch leading to the officer's mess was just up ahead, and it seemed that was the last place she wanted to be all of a sudden. "I think I'll turn in early. See you later." She accepted a hug from Ashley before making her way to her bunk.

CHAPTER 34
TAKING CONTROL

Rituals were the core of Ayan's older memories. In her last life, as Ayan Rice, she was a soldier first and an engineer second in her training. That may have reversed later in her career, people depended on her as an engineer, but the discipline and routines of a soldier were always present.

Things were very different in the life she was living. She couldn't help but reflect on the changes as she shaped her vacsuit into a much smaller version of itself so she could feel her muscles move unassisted. She was up before Lacey, hopefully before anyone who would need her could come calling. That was part of a routine she'd embraced over six months before, when she recognized one of the major differences between herself and the old Ayan. It was much easier to get out of shape, and she wasn't nearly as coordinated.

Simulations were fine, they could trick your mind into thinking you were having actual experiences, feeling actual pain, and exerting yourself as much as you would if you were actually doing whatever was being transmitted to your brain. There were a few important things they couldn't do, however, like train muscle memory. There were short cuts, like targeted electro-stimulation, but Freeground fleet training maintained that there was nothing like getting into workout gear and having it out on the track, or obstacle course, or firing range, or sparring room, or whatever activities you wanted to practice to the point of reflex.

Ayan's purpose that morning was two-fold. The run would clear her head, and she wanted to challenge her fear of heights. It wasn't a full-blown phobia – that was rare – but an intense fear. The large octagonal tower top had transparesteel windows around the edge tilted on a forty-five degree angle, and a wide gangway one level up. Tamber was still shrouded in the shadow of night, but the moon had turned to reveal a starry night. People who grew up on colonies with an Earth configuration with one moon said it was difficult to adjust, but Ayan's sense of time was tied to nothing but a clock. The extreme tidal forces did affect mood and a few other biological factors, but she was well acclimated after spending months on the ground.

She jogged up the steps leading to the platform and started running along the inner edge. The platform was mostly transparent. If she started running in the middle, it would look like she was running in mid-air, with nothing but a clear view of the ground so far below. Her palms were sweating, her heart protested with a vigorous beat, and her mind objected, but she focused on moving forward.

She remembered feeling out of shape and facing the choice: begin taking fitness pills that were normally reserved for people who didn't have space for exercise, or start working it off. The soldier in her won, and with a little embarrassment she approached Oz to coach her. He did, and those first workouts seemed so long, they were so hard that she found herself wondering if her body was defective. It took months, but she eventually got into the shape she wanted. There was no changing the fact that she was short, or that she would always be thicker than her previous inception without serious body modifications, but once she uncovered her natural shape, she began to like it and there was no way she'd allow herself to slide back. Ayan swore off the fitness pills as well. Unless she set foot on a starship, she'd depend on good old physical exertion to stay in shape. As for being clumsy, she still bumped into things from time to time, but Ayan felt like she'd taken possession of her body, and mishaps were far more infrequent.

Focusing on keeping her pace and her breathing constant, maintaining good form and running in a broad circle around that upper deck eventually calmed Ayan down. She could jog along that path, at that pace, for another hour, her comfort increasing by the second. Memories of shrinking away from safe but high places spurned her on to challenge herself instead. Most of the time she was the only one who got vertigo in a crowd, and she wouldn't have it.

"Oh, good glory," she muttered to herself as she altered her path so she was running along the outer edge of the platform, where it joined with the transparesteel window. A glance down confirmed that everything beneath her was fully transparent, and she nearly stumbled as her knees threatened to buckle. "Don't be a bloody child, outrun the fear," she challenged herself, pushing from a jog into a full run. "You're better than all this, everyone else knows it."

She slowed down to a pace she could maintain for longer after three more laps and glanced down. Her hands flailed outward as the sensation of falling gripped her momentarily, but she kept running and brought them back into form. "Stupid girl," she said as she forced herself to look down while she ran, gritting her teeth as she fought the powerful instinct to get off the platform. "Finish strong, or move along," Ayan said as she stepped up onto the incline of the transparesteel window. An involuntary whimper accompanied the act of running along the forty-five degree tilt of the window itself.

It was all she could do to keep running along those solid as steel but as clear as air windows. Ayan concentrated on her running form, but forgot about her pace completely, which had become a dead run. Her heart pounded so hard she could feel her pulse in her head and hands. "Oh shut up," she spat as her comm unit beeped a medical alert. "I'm doing this."

It took three full laps before she started to calm down and her comm stopped beeping a cardio warning. Ayan was almost out of energy, but smiled at herself as she slowed a little and decided to do four more laps. "Just to be sure I've done this and didn't dream it." Her heart was still pounding, and every time she saw too much of the ground she had to fight for balance, but Ayan knew it wouldn't be long before she grew accustomed to that vista in particular.

She'd have to continue to challenge her fear of heights until it was gone, but that morning Ayan had claimed an incredible victory. She'd gotten over her fear in little leaps, during obstacle courses while testing Ranger's training when she had time, and a couple of other times before, but taking on her fear when stepping away from the edge as an option was completely new.

With just over one lap left, Ayan had almost calmed down about the view, and she was starting her push to the end when her comm vibrated and chimed an emergency signal. As a reflex, she looked at the unit on her arm, saw the distant ground past it, had a sudden episode of vertigo and lost her balance. The transparesteel window, the deck, and the safety railing didn't yield in the least as she tripped, rolled, and crashed into them in that order. Her vacsuit was in workout mode, so unless an impact was hard enough to break bone, it wouldn't activate, so she felt every considerable bump and twist, almost falling over the inner edge of the walkway by the time she came to a calamitous stop in a heap of limbs and long red hair.

"Ayan! What happened?" Lacey asked as she ran up the stairs.

Ayan carefully straightened herself out, and sat on the edge of the walkway, clearing curls out of her face. "I won the fight against my fear of heights but lost against momentum and gravity."

"You took your jog on the platform?" Lacey said. "How did you fall back in here?"

"There's a platform outside?" Ayan asked, fearful at the thought of repeating her exercise beyond the confines of the room.

"Just above the edge, there," Lacey said, pointing.

Ayan followed her gesture and noticed the outline of it, a glint of transparent metal that overhung the inward curve of the transparent windows. "I don't think I'll be ready for that for awhile," she said. "Ran along the inside of these though," Ayan said, glancing at the obstacle she just conquered.

"Nutter, I wouldn't even try that and heights are no big thing for me. I'd worry about a panel popping."

Ayan turned her attention to her comm unit, finally catching her breath and opened the emergency message. The image of Tyra Kim's head appeared in front of both of them. She was in disarray, frantic and angry at the same time. "Ayan, the Carthans are coming here, saying that you've abandoned your claim and they're taking Haven Shore. The Council is convening in a moment to discuss our options, but I'm afraid it's too late. You screwed us, taking the military with you, I hope you're happy."

Ayan brought up her holographic status screen and tactical displays, filling the air around them with images of Haven Shore and the area around the island. "They're moving in right now and those idiots haven't put up the Everin Building's shield or called an alert," Ayan said. Perhaps it was her already high heart rate, or her already low patience for the behaviour of the civilian government in Haven Shore, but she found herself quick to anger. "If Carl was there the alert would have sounded already."

"Checking now," Lacey said. "He's still asleep on the Triton. Looks like he was up late viewing Haven Shore civilian transmission logs."

"Well, I'm just glad I didn't surrender my control codes for the Everin Building," Ayan said, raising the building's shields. She sounded an invasion alert within. Ayan activated a combat alert for the Triton, the available soldiers in her base and in the other active Order of Eden bunkers. The Clever Dream acknowledged the alert as well.

"What's your thinking?" Lacey asked.

"We're going to force the Carthans to talk to us about this. Within twenty minutes, we'll have nine times the firepower mobilized than they have in the air, and that's without sacrificing essential personnel for our settlements." Ayan gathered all the intelligence and a summary of her actions into a report then sent it to Oz, her father, and the Haven Shore

Council. "The Clever Dream will pick us up on top of the tower in two minutes," Ayan said. She got to her feet with a groan.

"You might want to change first. I see a lot of support in that outfit, but not much coverage," Lacey teased. "Unless dazzling the Carthans is part of the plan."

Ayan flashed her a sheepish grin and nodded. "Might work with some of the stares I've caught from our Carthan rep at the Council table, but armour might be more appropriate for what's coming. You'll probably see more people wearing this kind of outfit. I know you didn't watch much of the Ranger training, but a big part of it is learning how to do things without technology. The human body, even mine, is capable of more than people give it credit for."

"There's nothing wrong with your body," Lacey said as she walked along side her. "Anyway, back to the present. Do you really think this'll escalate?" Lacey asked as they ran down the stairs.

"I think they're going to try to drive us off, starting with Haven Shore and moving on to our other positions. Fighting may be our only choice." A signal from Oz with a status update confirmed her thoughts. "Oz agrees, the Triton is launching fighters and manoeuvring into a space where it can cloak."

"Why does the ship have to manoeuver to cloak?" Lacey asked.

"They have to drop out of navnet patterns and get some distance so other ships don't collide with it. You can't go around what you can't see."

"Ah. Another question: is it too late to turn down that promotion?"

"Absolutely," Ayan replied. "Your job in this is to make sure everyone has what they need to survive so people like me can take command of the combat side of things. I hope we can avert this, but it could become a complicated siege if I can't, especially since there are no Carthan ships anywhere near our other positions. Their attention is entirely focused on Haven Shore so far, and the largest problem we have is our lack of intelligence with regard to the rest of their fleet. We don't know exactly what they're holding back."

Ayan dropped her light vacsuit and slipped into her armoured suit as Lacey changed into her medium vacsuit. She didn't own anything that resembled Ayan's combat armour. "Where do I start?" asked Lacey.

"Make sure you take stock of exactly who is stuck outside the shield right now and forward that to me. The combat arm of our command unit will decide where they should go and what they should do. When you've done that, take control of conditions and provisions. Check food levels, make sure the environment control systems are working well enough in

222

Haven Shore structures, and then start preparing a statement informing all the civilians of the situation. Send it to me before you release it to them."

"Thank you," Lacey said. They heard the dull creak of the ceiling above as the Clever Dream set down. "Is that normal?"

"The structure is fine, the Clever Dream is the first ship to use that landing pad, you're just hearing the deck plates and the frame fitting together as they take the weight." Ayan's mind was working faster than it had in months. Despite the bruises and other minor signs, her morning triumph was already far from her thoughts. As she finished pulling her armour together and started to activate the systems within, Lacey gave her a vanilla meal bar. "Thank you. If it weren't for you I wouldn't eat until this crisis passed."

"I know," Lacey said. "Don't worry, I'm watching."

The lounging area in the middle of the Clever Dream had been converted into a war room. The compartment walls were covered with ever-changing information from Haven Shore and the Order of Eden bunkers she'd claimed. There was little chance the Carthans would turn their interest towards the bunkers since they each had shielding, were hardened against attack, and less than five percent of the structure was above ground. Ayan had to admit that the Regent Galactic manufactured bunker system was ingenious.

The holographic system projected an image of Haven Shore into the middle of the room; troop status screens, communications readouts and tactical summaries hovered above it. Ayan hoped that the configuration of the war room would be unnecessary before long. She could stand feeling a little sheepish at preparing for a serious conflict if it meant finding a peaceful solution to whatever actions the Carthans were about to take. The fact was, she didn't know exactly what they were about to do. No Carthan representatives were answering her.

The British Alliance hadn't replied either. Her only allies were the Triton and the Rangers. She was in direct control of the Skyguard and Slick, their wing commander, was an excellent leader. Ayan allowed herself a moment to watch their aerial manoeuvres. The thirty-five Uriel and Ramiel fighters they managed to get into the air were split into smaller groups of three. To the untrained eye, it would look like they were scattered around Haven Shore, some flying low altitude over water, others in the upper atmosphere, but every single one of them was in range of the approaching Carthan forces.

The Carthans had sent a battlegroup of drop ships, eight-man gunships, a handful of fighters, and the communications trackers on the Clever Dream were able to indicate that they were taking orders from a pair of destroyers in orbit. As far as Ayan knew, those two destroyers represented half of their operational destroyer class ships. It was well known they had one command carrier, but other than that, there were no truly threatening ships in their fleet.

The situation was tense, but at a stand still for the moment. The Carthans hadn't breached Haven Shore's borders yet, but held positions a hundred kilometres off shore, and she'd had no further communication from the Everin Building. Ayan took a moment to close her eyes and take a deep breath. There were obstacles to negotiating her way out of a massive conflict that went well past the obvious. Her sharp dislike of the Carthans was a major one. They disapproved of the development of the Rangers, were constantly requesting permission to board and inspect everything from the Triton to their smallest cargo shuttles, and allowed Ayan to take new territories if her people killed Order of Eden soldiers in the region, but only did so grudgingly. They didn't police Tamber, but were constantly trying to dictate terms to anyone who was trying to bring peace to a section, and they sapped resources whenever they could. They were used to getting what they wanted, and they didn't care who they crushed in doing so. Most of their soldiers were serving prison terms, and had mental reprogramming that ensured obedience.

Ayan did her best to remember that the truest victory she could accomplish in the next few hours was one that didn't involve bloodshed. She had to get past how she felt about the Carthans and disarm the situation. If it came to fighting them outright, it could cost the entire solar system in terms of security and stability. Worse, it could bring a horrific end to Haven Shore and death to thousands of her people.

"Status change alert," the system said in a gentle tone.

Ayan looked at the tactical board and saw sixty fighters moving around Haven Shore under water. They were forced closer to the surface as the depth of the sea decreased. They disappeared from sensors when they were able to dive deep enough, but reappeared as soon as they came up above seventy metres. She marked the fighter group and sent the update to all ships, making sure the Triton acknowledged the new data. A few seconds later, it did. Oz was watching, and she had no doubt her father was, too.

"Lewis," Ayan asked. "Do you have anything that could hit those fighters under water?"

"I have several types of missiles that could transition from atmosphere to water then explode, causing incredible carnage as they tear their hulls apart with shockwaves and shrapnel. Environmental damage would be temporary. It would take aquatic life less than three months to recover."

"What are the chances that the fighters could counter under water?" Ayan asked.

"Very little, especially if we fired while I was hovering within a meter of the water's surface. Their countermeasures depend on detonating missiles early, so even if they did manage to counter under water, they would still be subjected to significant concussive shockwaves."

"All right, let's take a position following their lead ships. Make sure you're just far enough from the surface of the water so your cloaking systems are still effective." Ayan replied, marking the lead ship as it reappeared on scanners.

"You truly expect this to become a battle?" Lewis asked.

"I'm going to do everything I can to prevent it, but it's not looking good," Ayan replied.

Lacey entered the room. "I just started getting transmissions from Haven Shore again. There was a minor problem with interference from the shield. All the civilians have squeezed into the escape ships in the Everin Building's hangar," she said. "They're not happy about it, but they have supplies and there's just enough room for everyone. I have volunteers making trips to and from Haven Shore storage for more supplies, but all the basics are taken care of."

"Good work," Ayan said. "All the ships have main power and flight crews?"

"Yup, they should be checking in on your tactical screen soon," Lacey said.

"Good. I hope they don't have to escape Haven Shore, but..." Ayan allowed herself to trail off as a British Alliance transmission came through. "Thank you for getting back to me, Minister," Ayan said as a stoic-looking hologram of Sunny Zinnes appeared. The tactical information tagged onto the transmission indicated that he was transmitting from somewhere in the Everin Building. The return signal was sent through hundreds of voluntary and involuntary relays, hiding the location of the Clever Dream.

"My pleasure, as always," he replied. "I know why you're contacting my government, and I'm afraid I'm the bearer of bad news."

"The BA is taking the Carthan's side in this?" Ayan asked.

"Not at all," he replied. "We're distancing ourselves. Our mandate is to stand ready in this territory in case of an attack from the Order of Eden or their allies and increase our vigilance. We can't play a role in local politics."

"Even if it results in needless bloodshed?" Ayan asked.

"I'm afraid our stance is firm in this."

226

On a whim, Ayan brought up the surveillance logs from Haven Shore and found footage of Minister Sunny Zinnes meeting with the Carthan Minister, Cory Green, along with several other high ranking members of their military. The recording was scrambled, so she couldn't hear what they were saying clearly, or have her software read their lips. "Why were you meeting with the Carthans last night?"

"They approached me for advice," Sunny replied. "They were worried about the split between Haven Shore and Triton Fleet, and wanted to hear my opinion on your motivations."

"And? What's your opinion?" Ayan asked, aware that there must have been much more to the meeting if they used a surveillance scrambler.

"I'm afraid I had to be honest with them. You are making big waves while sitting in a very small boat, Ayan, and I told them that you would pursue war with the Order with or without their approval. I did advise them against this attack."

"You knew this was coming," she said quietly. "You didn't give us any warning, but you knew last night. "

"I'm not in a moral position to grant either side a tactical advantage, and that's what I would have been doing if I warned you. I am here, however, in one of your buildings, and that must count for something."

Ayan forced herself to slow her breathing, to focus on her current objective. The conversation wasn't any help, so she had to take another tact. "I want to resolve this without firing a shot. Give me something to start with, Sunny. When they reply to my hails, how do you think I should start my negotiations?"

Sunny Zinnes seemed almost stunned at the sudden turn in the conversation and stared at her for a long moment. "How do I think you should start negotiations?"

"Yes," Ayan said. "They're going to have to communicate with me soon, so give me something to start with, like what this is really all about. Is there some transgression I missed and should address?"

"Transgression?" Minister Zinnes asked.

"Yes, something we've done that brought this on, a law we broke, or some line we crossed," Ayan asked, trying not to sound as exasperated as she felt.

"You helped the Warlord recruit new people, started establishing military bases without their clearance. I'm sorry, Ayan, but I wouldn't put myself in your position. I'm a better diplomat, but if I found myself in your place I would tell the Carthans that you're willing to negotiate terms while they occupy Haven Shore, and you might get them back to the table."

"What do they want? Resources? Housing? To address me as a security concern, or-" Ayan stopped, recognizing a glimmer in Sunny Zinnes eye. "It's housing – they're short on facilities, so they want ours."

"I'm sorry I can't help you, Ayan, it's outside of my mandate," Sunny replied, smiling a little. "Good luck."

Ayan watched as the hologram faded. "So we rescued hundreds of their people, and now they're all out of room." Ayan said. "I've never heard something more wrong-headed in my entire life."

"Could that really be what's behind this?" Lacey asked. Lieutenant Garrison joined them, ducking to avoid the hatch's upper seal. He was one of the tallest humans Ayan had ever seen. "Did I hear that right? They're surrounding our home because they're low on bunk space?"

"I know that's not all," Ayan said. "Our recruitment drive had to be the breaking point. We've been testing them, pressing at the boundaries of the rights they gave us when we settled here."

"Pardon me for saying, but they gave you those rights," Lieutenant Garrison reminded gently. "Everyone knows that you're the signing Sovereign. So far more than half the people in Haven Shore have been happy with it too, especially since you and the Council generally don't back down when the Carthans tell you that you can't do this or that."

"Either way, we kept pushing," Ayan said. "And while the Carthans weren't able to repair any of the old structures on Tamber and they were taken over by gangsters or squatters, we built something brand new." She gestured at Haven Shore. "It's one of the only large residences with anti-bombardment shielding on Tamber, and as of today, everything in that building is working. They've been waiting for this."

"Son of a bitch," Garrison grumbled. "I just traded for a new sofa."

"There's no room for a sofa in your quarters," Lewis said.

"Sorry, Lewis, it's for my apartment in the Everin Building. We can't spend every minute together for the rest of my life. I'm starting to feel like I've never known anything but the inside of my quarters and your cockpit."

"I understand," Lewis said. "Maybe some space would be good. I have noticed that you depend on me for most of your social interactions. You should find a few agreeable humans. I know they will probably pale in comparison to me, conversation-wise, but it may be the best thing for you nevertheless."

"Is there anything I can be doing on top of my regular duties captaining the Clever Dream?" Lieutenant Garrison asked.

"No, but you're going to want to strap on a sidearm," Ayan said. "Make sure your suit's ready for action just in case. I don't think the Carthans are going to negotiate."

"Aye, aye," Lieutenant Garrison said. "Good luck." He turned and bumped his head on the hatch before making his way to the cockpit.

Ayan opened communications with the Triton directly and waited for them to connect from their end.

"If the Carthans aren't going to negotiate," Lacey said. "Wouldn't it help to address everyone in range?"

The thought hadn't occurred to her. "You mean a general transmission to everyone on Tamber?"

"Yes, like a speech, but short, and-"

Oz appeared above the tactical projection in the middle of the room. "How are things at point-blank range?" he asked.

"The same. They're holding on our border. I get the feeling that they're organizing more forces before striking."

"Or they could be trying to locate you," added Carl Anderson as he appeared beside Oz. "They know where we are, and how we fit into your command structure, but you're the owner of Haven Shore, and you have six other armed claims on Tamber. They take you out, or take you hostage, then get you to sign it all back to them, and they get Haven Shore for a bargain. That's the only way the British Alliance would approve a property transfer."

"I'm an idiot," Ayan said under her breath. "Lieutenant Garrison," she called down the hall to the cockpit. "Get us away from Haven Shore and anything that could interfere with our cloaking systems."

Ayan watched the Clever Dream manoeuvre into a steep climb, weaving and twisting into the air. Within a second, three beam weapon strikes swept across their energy shields, and several heavy projectiles narrowly missed them, exploding against the surface of the water.

"Ayan, are you all right?" Carl Anderson asked.

Ayan checked the status of their cloaking device and the origin point of the attacks. The Cray Severn, the Carthan Command Carrier was responsible, but their beam weapons had done no damage. The cloak was intact, and Ayan knew how they were spotted. "We disturbed the surface of the water when we turned away. Our cloak will work as long as we try not to disturb the atmosphere much."

"You have to find a good landing place under cover," Oz said.

"We will," Ayan replied. "Don't worry about me, this fight is obviously on, and we have to show them that they're taking on more than they can bear. Can the Triton take the Cray Severn in a surprise attack?"

Oz thought for a moment, looking at something Ayan couldn't see in his hologram. "Give me fifteen minutes to secure any unvetted crew in their quarters. I'm not going into battle with unknowns running around. As far as winning an engagement against the Cray Severn? In a surprise attack, I know we can cripple her – it's the four destroyers they have for support I'm worried about."

"We only need to destroy their lead ship," Ayan said. Lacey's jaw dropped.

"I need to confirm," Oz said procedurally, "you said destroy, not disable."

"Destroy," Ayan repeated. "The Carthans have taken this too far already. If we succeed in defending Haven Shore, they'll just regroup and come at us again, and they'll win. We have to demoralize them completely, hit them with the Triton's torpedoes, then you have to disappear so they can't retaliate against you."

"You're right," Oz said. "And we're lucky we have a top-notch tactical officer here. Commander Agameg's telling me we can have a full volley of torpedoes ready to launch in ten minutes."

"While you do that, I'm launching with the Rangers, they're almost ready," Anderson said. "What did our British Alliance friends say about this, just out of curiosity?."

"They're sitting back and enjoying the show," Ayan said. She was thankful for the Clever Dream's excellent gravity control systems as she saw the ship dip into a large jungle cavern and hover. Lieutenant Garrison and Lewis were several steps ahead of her, hiding the ship until they were needed. "I won't soon forget."

"Maybe Ayan should make a speech?" Lacey broke in unceremoniously. "I mean, if the Carthans won't listen to us directly, maybe Tamber should know what's going on?"

"No doubt people on Kambis are watching, too," Oz said. "Good idea."

The tactical hologram alerted everyone that the energy shield surrounding Haven Shore was taking orbital strikes from two of the Carthan destroyers. "Looks like they've given up on finding you," Oz said. "Can we have a full volley of torpedoes ready in five minutes?" he asked over his shoulder. He nodded at a response and looked back to Ayan. "Agameg says we can strike in seven. You'd better get going, Carl."

"Aye," he told Oz. "Stay safe, Ayan," he said to her.

"You too," Ayan replied. "Wait until I finish talking to everyone in the planetary system, then hit that command carrier as hard as you can."

"Aye, Commander. Don't leave anything out, it might be the last thing they ever hear."

"We have a response from the Carthans," Lacey said. "It's text only."

Ayan accessed it and was confronted by a document that was thousands of words long, bearing the digital seals of most of the Carthan administration. "Lewis, can you summarize this? It looks like a petition for nationalization."

"You're right," Lewis replied. "The Carthans are claiming that two of your claims are illegal, and that Haven Shore is no longer sovereign territory, but a privately owned section of land. With this document, they're nationalizing it, making it the property of the Carthan government and your people have one hour to vacate the property."

"Then it's official," Ayan replied, a chill running down her back. With a gesture, she opened communications on all channels, relayed through their fighters, Haven Shore, their captured bunkers, and every other broadcasting system the Clever Dream could access. It was as though the reality of the situation smothered her anger. Ayan's mind had never been so clear, and she knew exactly what to say. "I'm Ayan Anderson, and I negotiated for Sovereign status with the Carthan Government nearly a year ago. They provided us with a land grant that we used to build a home. While we built our main habitat, we continued our active partnership with the Carthans, clearing Order of Eden forces from Tamber, rescuing over a thousand of their people, and we assisted in the maintenance of security over large sections of Tamber. We didn't do this for free. We made sanctioned land claims, were paid small fees for our rescue efforts and for our patrols. Just a moment ago, the Carthans made it clear that they want us to leave the home we built so they can make it their own. After everything we've done for them, despite the partnership we've nurtured, the Carthan government has turned on us. One of our most seasoned captains said something only days ago that I wish I had taken to heart: Never trust a government that brainwashes their criminals to become soldiers.

It is important to me for everyone within range of this transmission to know that the Carthans are opportunists, slavers, and our relationship with them has come to an end. They have fired on our main civilian structure, the Everin Building, and on my command ship. Haven Shore and Triton Fleet will not abide this. We must protect the most vulnerable of our people, and we will do so using the full extent of our arsenal. Please, if you value your lives and property, do not interfere."

Ayan ended the transmission and opened a channel to the Skyguard. "Slick, are you ready?"

"Aye, Commander. Your orders?"

"The Clever Dream will be joining you in destroying all armed elements of the Carthan fleet near Haven Shore's perimeter. Other targets will be marked as they become relevant."

"Aye," Slick replied. "Understood."

Ayan opened a channel to the Triton. "You have a go. Destroy the Carthan command carrier and fall back to assess further targets."

Agameg's hologram appeared in the middle of the room. "Understood, we are proceeding."

"Where's Oz?"

"He is taking care of another urgent matter. I doubt it will take more than a moment. You'll also be happy to know that Rangers One and Two are be available for orders. The cloaked shuttles have passed their test."

"Thank you," Ayan said. It only took her a moment to bring one of the Carthan Destroyers up on the tactical display. Two of them were hanging back, orbiting a mining asteroid. She sent an encrypted message signalling her orders to her father.

The Clever Dream was taking off again, whirling towards Haven Shore to join the offensive against Carthan forces. Ayan caught sight of Lacey out of the corner of her eye. The poor woman was as white as a sheet, and looked uncertain for the first time since she'd known her. "Are you all right?"

"You just declared war," Lacey said.

"They didn't give me much choice," Ayan said. "Are you all right here while I help in the cockpit?"

"I'm fine. I mean, I think I'll be fine."

"Good," Ayan said.

"Do you think we'll win?" Lacey asked.

"It's too early to be sure," Ayan replied, leaving for the cockpit.

CHAPTER 36
SHADOW AND FIRE

Carl Anderson knew who his best and brightest Rangers were. He hand picked his team of fourteen and knew they'd perform the grisly duty ahead admirably. As the pair of small cloaked shuttles approached the Carthan destroyer, he found himself wishing that Alice and Remmy were on his team.

Regardless of his offhanded wish, the collection of rangers he had with him were excellent mental and physical specimens. He was glad for the regimen of fitness and youth restoration medication he started when the first group of rangers began training. Carl didn't know how he'd keep up with them without the pharmaceutical assistance. He didn't have time for most of the physical training that would improve his reflexes and muscle memory, but he looked like a well-built man of forty, a marvel of medical technology. He didn't expect to be on mission with them under such dire circumstances, however.

The shuttle door opened, baring one entire side of the large converted escape shuttle. He pushed out of the shuttle compartment first, leaping towards the destroyer only a hundred and three metres away. Anderson could see the rangers from both shuttles following his lead. Their cloak suits kept them just as hidden as the pair of ships delivering them, which used exactly the same cloaking technology. They added a few extra layers of material and emitter bands to the hull, and thanks to the shuttle's small size, the new technology worked perfectly.

The destroyer reminded Anderson of a lounging beast, watching the distant fighting, waiting for the order to attack. The Carthans may be some of the most socially crude people Anderson had ever met, but they weren't stupid. They believed in enslaving debtors, reprogramming criminals so they could serve their sentences as soldiers and public servants, they even believed in privilege by birth and the separation of the classes. Their social backwardness made them even more dangerous. Anderson had never seen evidence that any soldier ever questioned their orders, and he knew the Carthans believed in defending their way of life, even in the darker corners of the galaxy, like the Rega Gain System.

Anderson struck the hull. His suit protected him from most of the impact, and the outer layer of his armour stuck to the surface. To his right there was a large quad-turret; the gunnery team of two sat in a transparent metal cockpit watching a tactical hologram. Anderson stood and walked to his position, right under the guns. As he drew nearer, he could see that the ships that the Carthan carrier used to protect itself were scattering, and the Triton took a few hits from their torpedoes before cloaking. One of the gunners regarded the other, shocked and dismayed while his partner stared at the hologram, agog, shaking his head.

Anderson crawled under the main body of the turret and waited as the rest of the rangers got into position. They walked, ran, and crawled to their targets. Major sources of power, big energy taps like turrets, beam emplacements, and sensor arrays, and crevasses in the hull were their points of interest. After a couple more minutes, the last Ranger was in position, lying against the hull where two main thruster pods connected to the ship.

That was the signal. Without hesitation, Carl Anderson took two six centimetre wide, eight centimetre long cans off his back and affixed them to the hull. He continued affixing more devices around the turret mount until there were fifteen ringing the weapon emplacement. He was behind; most of the other rangers had finished, and passive sensors in his suit told him that the ship had detected the new devices attached to the hull. They had minutes before the commanders of the destroyer sent troops out onto the hull. He finished getting out from the underside of the turret and pushed off hard.

Everyone activated the devices they planted, and they began to burn tiny holes into two hundred and ten sensitive spots across the ship's hull. If all went well, there would be no decompressions, no immediate reason for anyone aboard that ship to seal portions of the vessel off, and they wouldn't figure out what was going on in time.

Airlock doors opened nearby, and a group of four soldiers rushed out, each headed towards one of their cutter cans. It was already too late.

The cutter cans were starting to penetrate the hull, burning holes only half the width of a human hair, and nanobots programmed to disrupt major systems were pouring into the ship from all sides. They would provide data taps that the Triton could use to connect to the destroyer's core systems.

The Carthan soldiers on the hull didn't see any of the rangers; their cloaking systems were working perfectly. Three of the cans failed to cut through the hull, but the first of the systems, the ship's main thrusters, deactivated. The nanobots there sent a signal indicating that the Triton could control the destroyer's main thrusters. The lights in that section of engineering flickered and went out. It was working. Less than a minute later, other lights in the midsection of the ship winked out. The gunnery team Anderson noticed before hurriedly departed from their posts, climbing down into the ship as their systems went dark. That was it, the fearful strike Ayan and Oz would need to terrify the Carthans. Carl Anderson rarely felt such satisfaction. One of his shuttles signalled him, and he curled up into a ball. The interior of the shuttle appeared as he passed through the cloaking field around its side door.

He couldn't suppress a grin as he helped the next ranger into the shuttle. The Rangers had just completed their first space combat mission.

CHAPTER 37
THE TRITON ENGAGES

"Show me the centre of the issue," Oz said as he stepped in beside Lieutenant Victor Davis, who was standing in the centre of the lower half of the bridge. A portion of the lower half of the bridge had been adapted for internal security, and Victor shared it with Paula Mendle, the Flight Operations Chief, who was heavily pregnant.

"Here it is," Victor replied to Oz as he brought up a few playbacks recorded only moments before. Oz selected the most recent clip from a club called the Oota Galoona. It was being used as a gathering hub, mess hall, and observation area for people who were new to the ship and given quarters nearby. In the clip, the Oota Galoona was packed, and as Oz played it, he saw people watching Ayan's speech.

At the end, when she made it clear that they were fighting the Carthan Alliance, several people, in new but basic vacsuits, got to their feet and started arguing with people from nearby tables. With a simple adjustment, Victor cleared up the audio so Oz could hear one tall woman shout, "We didn't sign up to go to war with the Carthans! They'll break this ship's back and turn us into drone soldiers!"

A patron at her side shoved a pair of nearby men into a table where several crewmembers sat. People nearby were getting to their feet, and Oz watched as arguments started springing up wherever vocal malcontents from either side decided it was their place to force their opinions on another.

Seeing the rough looking new recruits in their very basic, unmarked uniforms choosing sides reminded Oz of another situation that took place aboard months before. It was a situation he still believed he handled badly. "This is two minutes behind," Oz said as he advanced to the current moment. The shouting was continuing, and two people were highlighted in red, indicating that a short-lived physical altercation had taken place, and a few people in the crowd were keeping them separated. "Okay, this is escalating and we don't have time," Oz told Victor. "Sedate everyone in Oota Galoona using their medical monitoring patches, then have a team gently move them to their quarters. Confine anyone who was recorded committing assault to any degree to their bunks until we can address every one of them. If it looks like there will be problems with smaller groups of newcomers, I want your security people to escort them to quarters. We don't have time for any large incidents."

"How long do you want me to sedate the crowd in Oota Galoona for?" Victor asked.

"Six hours," Oz said. "Let them get a good night's sleep before they have the opportunity to volunteer for repair and support crews. If they don't volunteer when they wake up, we'll put them off the ship. No exceptions."

"Aye," Victor replied.

Oz took the ramp up to the top level of the bridge, aware that Victor thought his methods were harsh, but Captain Terry Ozark McPatrick was past the end of his patience with people who believed they deserved more than they were getting aboard the Triton. It seemed half the people they recruited from Tamber over the previous three days expected five star treatment, or to be put in charge.

Not only was that not possible, but none of the new recruits had earned any rights to anything but decent food, good lodgings, and the opportunity at a rewarding job starting at the bottom of the command ladder. Only twenty percent had finished a qualification trial of any kind, and they were placed according to their skills and the levels of loyalty they exhibited. The training systems aboard were incredible, and most of the people who finished their first qualifications were astounded at the world of career opportunities that opened up. The qualification system was set up like a broad tree chart, and there was training available for everything within a crewmember's aptitude. All the Triton Officers asked was that any crewmember who took a position served there for at least a month before applying for another post aboard.

"Under other circumstances, you would approach that problem differently?" the voice of Triton asked through Oz's subdermal communicator.

Oz simply nodded in response. He hadn't told most of the crew about the being that served as the heart and mind of the Triton yet. The time was coming, but there were still too many new people aboard.

"I'm glad, but I agree with your methods for the moment. Now for our real problem," Triton said. "Navnet is working in the Carthans' favour."

Oz took the command seat in the middle of the bridge and looked to Agameg. The tactical hologram surrounding the command seating showed exactly what Triton was telling him. A thick river of ships had been directed between the Carthan command carrier and the rest of the solar system, making it impossible for Triton to approach cloaked. "There's no way we'll be able to fire on time with all that in the way," Oz said.

"By Panloo's estimation, we can close to seventy thousand kilometres without dropping our cloak," Agameg told him. "Any closer and we risk several collisions. Our shields will protect us, but the other ships would be devastated. We will not have a good firing solution on the carrier."

"How many of the ships in the flight pattern between us and the carrier are smaller Carthan vessels?"

"Only thirty-four percent – they are obviously creating a screen intentionally while preserving most of their own smaller ships. Most of the screen is not armed," Agameg replied. "I wonder if they know why they're being directed there?"

"Probably not. From what we've seen with the Carthans over the last few months, they don't have much regard for life past filling manpower needs. How is our shield regeneration rate?" Oz asked. "Do we still have a potential overload problem with reactor three?"

"Yes, but the other reactors are making up for it. The new bypass is active, and we can regenerate our entire deflection shield from zero in just over six seconds. Refraction and cloak shielding are not a problem."

Oz shook his head and smiled. "I can't believe what you've accomplished in two days, Agameg."

"I regret not being able to fully re-establish power to the gunnery deck. If I knew we would be going into a fight today, I would have it finished for you."

Oz checked the torpedo load status and was more than pleased. All five of the missile turrets were loaded with the ordinance he requested and they were as ready as they could be, considering the timing. The command carrier they were targeting had a broad centre with hundreds of shield emitters. The main thruster section at the aft of the ship splayed out like four fingers, and at the fore the main launch bays mirrored the pattern. "That ship is in good shape, I'm surprised their taking it into the fight at all," Oz said as he examined the enemy vessel's shield profile for any weakness. A message came in from the main hangar, informing him that the collision shuttles were ready well ahead of schedule. He was amazed at how fast the crew who returned to Triton from Haven Shore only days ago resumed their old duties. Triton's operating crew was back over two thousand seven hundred, nowhere near ideal, but better than it had been in months.

"A transmission from Ayan to the Carthans on public bands," Agameg said as he brought up a hologram of Ayan in full heavy armour. Her headgear was retracted, her face framed by a thick, curly red mane.

"I am giving the Carthan Government one more chance to cease firing on Haven Shore's energy shield and outbuildings before we retaliate. In a moment, it will be too late for negotiations. You have thirty seconds to reply," she said. "I plead on behalf of your soldiers, and your remaining citizens in the service. The loss of life you stand to suffer goes far beyond your expectations."

"They really should trust her," Oz said under his breath.

"She is charitable," Triton told him telepathically. "I wonder if she's buying time, or if she really wants this to be resolved peacefully?"

"She wants peace," Oz said. "We're going to be spending resources that should be reserved for an Order of Eden attack, or even an Edxi incursion. She knows how pointless this is more than anyone."

"You are right," Agameg replied, not realizing that Oz was actually speaking to someone in his mind. "I've always admired the Triton Crew and Ayan's people for how much they consider the lives of the people around them, but this battle is a tactical error that we cannot prevent."

The response from the Carthans came before the thirty seconds was up. "This is Cory Greene, representative to Haven Shore for the Carthan Defence Force," said the hologram of the well-groomed official. His uniform featured a fine coat loosely held together by dangling jewellery chains. "Sovereign Ayan and her people have built a significant military force, a stronghold with significant combat potential, and are claiming more territory every month. If this wasn't threat enough to peace on Tamber and the rest of the solar system, we've also observed a recruiting drive which allowed known criminals to join their ranks, as well as many unknown persons who could have Order of Eden leanings. It is also known that the Triton Fleet openly colludes with the Warlord and its captain: Jacob Valent, a suspected terrorist. In light of the destabilizing potential of this situation, we have no choice but to assume control of all Haven Shore and Triton Fleet assets. We ask that you surrender your arms and surrender to the nearest Carthan military officer. Thank you for your time." The holographic bust of the official disappeared and Oz couldn't help but chuckle.

"Please give us a moment to consider your offer," Ayan replied on all public bands.

Everyone on the bridge was shocked, except for Agameg, who regarded Oz with an amused expression. "She is endeavouring to draw the Carthans in?"

"Oh yeah," Oz said. His personal comm unit presented him with a simple message from Ayan that said, 'HIT THEM HARD ALREADY.' "Attention," he said to everyone on the bridge. "I just got confirmation from Ayan that our assault is going forward. She's just buying us an opportunity to get closer, so we're going to signal a surrender. Drop cloaking shields, send out a white flag message, and start heading for a navnet flight pattern that will get us close to that command carrier."

Panloo seemed oddly pleased at the turn of events as she plotted a course towards a route reserved for large ships entering Tamber's orbit. The cloaking system deactivated, but their shields were fully charged.

"Triton Command, we see your white flag signal," announced a voice broadcast from the Carthan command carrier. "Please follow your navnet approved course and prepare to be boarded. Please drop all but manoeuvring shields and proceed along that course."

"We're undermanned," Oz explained in response. "As you may have heard. It'll take a moment for my helmswoman and tactical controllers to make the changes you're requesting. Please be patient."

That seemed to satisfy the command team aboard the carrier, which had stopped firing on Haven Shore from high orbit. Oz watched as Triton managed to follow a different navnet course from the one that had been suggested. They were indirectly closing on the command carrier, already less than sixty thousand kilometres away. Oz checked their torpedo bay status. Thanks to Triton's directions in advanced manufacturing and repair, they'd managed to manufacture enough antimatter torpedoes to fire every bay three times.

"The closest we'll get using a navnet course is thirty eight thousand kilometres," Panloo's co-pilot, a young man named Colin Sage, announced. He was a good pilot, but an excellent navigator who got along exceptionally well with Panloo, and just as importantly, Zoe.

As they closed to forty thousand kilometres, the command carrier fired its five main dorsal beam weapons. Most of the intense light was refracted away from Triton towards Tamber's atmosphere where it was harmlessly dispersed, while the heavier particles did minimal damage to the ship's shields. "They're on to us. Fire all missiles, let's blind them," Oz ordered.

All fourteen lower missile launchers along the bottom of Triton's hull opened and fired hundreds of disabler rockets. The white flag gambit got them clear of most of the orbital traffic, and the majority of the ships left in the way were able to take evasive action. Oz counted three vessels that were struck, and marked them for rescue.

The Carthan carrier's countermeasure systems fired small, rough projectiles at a rate of thousands of rounds per minute to blast the incoming rockets to fragments. Over half were destroyed before they reached their detonation point, three kilometres away from the carrier. The hundred and eighty rockets activated, blasting the enemy ship with waves of light across all spectrums then exploding in a coordinated electromagnetic pulse.

"Fire all torpedoes," Oz said. "That trick won't blind them for long."

The sounds of the clicks and slides of three tonne torpedoes launching from bays above and beneath the bridge announced the departure of their deadly projectiles. Oz's tactical display confirmed that all thirty-six bays had launched, and that concluded their mission in that area. "Panloo, take us down."

"Aye, going atmospheric," Panloo said as she guided the ship into a course that would take them around the command carrier at a safe distance and into the atmosphere of Tamber.

The command carrier wasn't as blind as Oz had hoped the disabler missiles would render them, and their shields weren't as taxed. Before all the torpedoes were in range, the carrier managed to disable or destroy twenty-one of them, leaving only fifteen to detonate on target. For a moment the light, force, and heat was too intense for even Triton's sensors to adjust to. The entire command carrier was enveloped in a globe of white-blue fire for several seconds. When it cleared, entire hundred metre sections of the ship's outer hull were white-hot and weakened, but there were few breaches. Two of their main fighter bays had been destroyed, their bay doors open when the torpedoes detonated, and the command carrier's shields were down. "

"Message coming in sir, high priority," announced the youngest of the communications officer, he seemed a little too excited.

"On the main," Oz said.

A Carthan commander in a dark combat uniform looked direct at him from the main holographic display in the middle of the Triton's bridge. "I am Colonel Doherty, and I'm authorized to offer our surrender. We have sustained significant damage, and will not be able to retreat from the solar system for several days, however," she said emotionlessly.

"Your surrender must be unconditional. We will determine terms, this will not be a negotiation," Oz said.

"I'm afraid we have no choice," replied the Colonel. "I either fight and suffer unacceptable losses, or surrender and spend all our energy repairing critically damaged systems. You have our unconditional surrender, Commander McPatrick."

"I will send officers to each of your major vessels to accept the codes necessary to establish our command over your ships within the hour. I wish we could help with repairs, but our staff is busy here," Oz said.

"Understood, Commander." The transmission closed and the bridge staff cheered.

CHAPTER 38
FAREWELL

"You may not want to go in there," one of the guards standing sentry beside the quarters reserved for the British Alliance Council Representative, Sunny Zines. The heavy tropical night rain tapped a tattoo onto the outer sections of the building, a sound Ayan typically enjoyed. She looked at Lacey and she nodded, stopping beside the guard.

Ayan had seen gore, most recently on Pandem. Whatever awaited her in Sunny's quarters would not compare. The lights in the room were out, turned off by the guards who found the scene and sealed it. Through a large section of transparent metal she could see the winking lights of the surviving outbuildings. The cloud cover plunged Haven Shore into an even darker shade of night, turning light into rarefied beacons.

"I'm sorry," said the voice of Sunny Zinnes. It was a recording; the real man was dead.

"Lights, please," Ayan said aloud. In his last moments, Sunny Zinnes lay out on the bed and recorded a farewell message. She let her comm unit finish a forensic scan of the room and nodded to herself. He used a termination tablet to kill himself. The small pill-like device stopped all his brain function after he held it to the roof of his mouth for five seconds. He felt nothing, and there was no way for his government to scan his mind post-mortem for information. "Why did you do this to us?" Ayan asked in a whisper, anger and sadness waging a war in her head. He was a good man, not someone she'd suspect of treachery. Her question triggered the rest of the recording.

An image of Sunny Zinnes appeared in the middle of the room. "Hello, Ayan. I'm glad you were the first officer to find me. Please listen to what I have to tell you – it's time for me to be fully forthcoming, something I haven't done in years now. As you've probably guessed, the British Alliance Intelligence Division volunteered me as their observer on the

Council, and I was a spy. They thought I was the perfect man for the job, and I was one of the few agents that they could run a background check on and clear completely. They thought I'd lost my entire family when the Holocaust Virus struck, and so did I.

Three months ago, I was approached on the street by this man." An image of a thin faced, tall man appeared for a moment. "He provided me with evidence that my son was alive on an Order of Eden reclamation colony. If I didn't provide information to their intelligence people, they would send him to a work camp, where he would perform hard labour until he died. They didn't want much information on the British Alliance. They have their sources embedded in the Alliance already, but they needed me to collect information on Haven Shore. So I began providing regular reports, encrypted, sent to an innocent looking space on the Stellarnet where the Order could covertly download the information. The contents of my communications are in the details of this message. Everything was well and good for the first two months, I even received messages from my son, evidence that he was alive, well, and that my work was elevating his station in the religious arm of the Order. Then they began sending me contingency plans, along with specific instructions to build animosity between you and the Carthan government. It was surprisingly easy to manipulate them, as if they were looking for reasons to hate Haven Shore, and more specifically, you. I eventually began leaking information directly to the Carthan Fleet warden, becoming something of a triple agent. A month later, the final part of the Order's plan was to be put into action. I was to convince Carthan Command that Haven Shore was getting ready to attack their people, to make a play for control of Tamber. At first they didn't believe me, and I thought I'd made my play too early.

On the one hand, I was relieved. I didn't want fighting to break out between you and the Carthans. On the other, I had to wonder how my failure would affect my son's status, his lifestyle. Not two weeks later, the Council was dissolved and there was a sudden movement of resources, ships, and troops along with a recruiting drive. The Carthans suddenly believed everything I said about Haven Shore making a move to push them off this world, and after I laid out my hypothetical scenario about how the Rangers and Triton Fleet soldiers would start by murdering the Carthan officers, well, they didn't hesitate. That brings me to today, and this terrible tragedy.

I have no love for the Carthans, and I truly hoped that Triton Fleet would defeat them with minimal casualties. I don't know the Order's motivation behind causing friction between your governments, but I truly believe that

Haven Shore is better off without Carthan interference. I thought everything would go better than planned, and I could sneak off, finally join my son.

Then three shuttles left Haven Shore, under a banner of surrender. I tried to stop it, they were distressed parents and their children, and I told them they would be escaping into terrible danger. I tried to stop them. I even held on to two children, clutched them to me until their parents finally knocked me down and tore them away, loading them into those defenceless ships. If I had more time I could have sabotaged them so they'd never take off, but there was nothing I could do in the end.

Two of those shuttles are gone, taking the civilians who panicked with them. I retreated to my room, and in pursuit of solace I played back recordings of my son only to discover, upon playing them all back in succession, that they are fake. Your Crewcast system, which I never used until today, found markers that indicated that they were fabricated. Now I know that he is dead. My actions have cost the community I've come to love several families, and there will be no more good days for me.

I can only say that I was misled, and I hope my death provides some comfort to the people I have wronged. Thank you for listening."

The image disappeared and Ayan stood silently, surrounded by the sounds of rain and a pristinely kept room. Her head throbbed under the pressure of her fury at the man. "Coward," she spat at the ashen-faced corpse of Sunny Zinnes before turning on her heel and leaving the room.

"Lock this room down," Ayan said. "Only commanders and higher ranks can enter until one of us releases the scene. When that time comes, bag the body, his possessions, and transport them to the British Alliance," she told the guard.

"Is it true?" Lacey asked, her expression fraught with worry.

"He betrayed us. If it weren't for him, we could have negotiated with the Carthans. This may have never happened. This is all done now," Ayan said with a glance at the door closing behind her. "We have more important work to do."

CHAPTER 39
ENEMY SIGHTED

Alice could never decide what her favourite simulation type was. In fact, it was difficult for her to find one she didn't like. They were still all new to her. Even the fuzzy memories of her time travelling aboard the Clever Dream couldn't shed light on the topic. Even then her tastes were always all over the place. The only sims she seemed to avoid were based in social drama.

What Alice loved most about the few simulations she'd had time for on the Warlord and in Haven Shore was that there was no end of players to enjoy them with. Whether they be combat based, historical, scripted, or awe-groove oriented, if the simulation allowed her to be herself and there were enough players around, almost any sim had the promise of becoming an incredible experience. Many of the Warlord crew had earned their way into unlocking the level one entertainment simulations, and Alice was one of the first in. She let the computer choose which simulation she tried next and was dropped into one called "Uxxa Crisis" and several crewmembers she didn't know followed her in.

"Welcome to Uxxa Station," said a disembodied, garbled voice. It sounded like an alien who had never heard humans speak tried to create an announcement system that could communicate in English. 'Welcome' sounded more like 'Wee-lum' and 'Station' sounded more like 'Shay-shun.' The voice continued on, its intonation building to a gleeful climax towards the end. "It brings us sorrow to announce the usage and expenditure of all escape vessels. The administration has been killed and feasted, the station is abandoned, and you should flee for your own safety. Advisory: you are biologically unsuited to the environment outside the station. Have a good cycle!"

"Great, the Edxians have landed, eaten the staff, and good luck finding a ride out, have a good year. Something tells me this is a horror sim," Alice cracked as she checked her surroundings. The corridor looked old, pitted by corrosion and scarred by errant disruptor rounds. "Oh, yeah," she said to herself with a nod.

Remmy appeared behind her, a late entry into the sim. "We got teamed up," he said. "You wouldn't happen to have a weapon?"

It had been only a short time since she realized that Remmy wasn't stalking her but reciprocating her perceived interest. The realization was still a little too fresh, and she couldn't help but feel embarrassed at her mistake, even though she knew he probably had no idea she'd made it. "Huh?"

"I don't have so much as a slingshot," one of the new Warlord crewmembers said as they appeared behind her. "Cool sim though, wow, the resolution is so high I can smell the mould spores."

Alice realized then that she wasn't wearing anything she would call protection under the heavy cloth coat her avatar was wearing. She pulled the top of the coat open to reveal luxury pyjamas that were modest, but as useless as they were embarrassing, covered with sleeping cartoon pink bunnies. The closest thing she had to a weapon was a self-heating curling iron in a floppy coat pocket.

Remmy wasn't as lucky. He was assigned the role of a human spa-goer from a neighbouring building, and wore bathing trunks. One of the other new crewmembers was dressed similarly, and the pair behind her were in some sort of leisure climbing gear. "Okay, so this could be an elimination or an escape sim."

"Won't know until we open the door," said one of the crewmembers, Oscilla, from maintenance.

Alice braced herself and pressed the button beside the door. It slid to the side to reveal a lounging area. A sizable transparent dome enclosed the area, decorated with soft seating for fifty bipeds. Through the dome they could see a lake of molten lead with rust coloured hills beyond. The remnants of dozens of humans were strewn across the room, torn and gnawed to pieces. The dim yellow light and long shadows only made the scene look more foreboding. "Cheery," Remmy quipped.

"Okay, so we won't be escaping on foot, that atmosphere isn't breathable, and judging from that lake, it's a little too hot," Oscilla said.

"I don't think this is an escape map," Alice said. "This is what I get for letting the computer select a random scenario."

"I think it's a re-enactment," Oscilla said as she gingerly walked into the room, her oversized plush puppy slippers flapping their dog ears as she walked.

The sound of her shuffling feet set Alice on edge. "Stop moving, that noise may as well be a dinner bell."

"Whatever came here moved on a while ago," she replied, kneeling down to inspect what was left of a torso. "These bite marks are actually pretty small, I don't-"

Creatures with long legs leapt from every shadow and crevasse to grasp and bite Oscilla, pinning her to the floor. Their sleek, furred bodies twitched excitedly as they tore at her with long fingers and sharp claws.

Alice and her leftover comrades ran back through the door, closing it behind and running without thinking for the length of the corridor. "More evidence that humans are just soft and slow food without our technology. I get the feeling that this is gonna end quick," Remmy said. "Might be one of those sims we have to play half a dozen times before we learn how to beat it. Those things weren't Edxi though, I'm going to have to look them up. I figure they were about thirty-five, forty kilos, maybe five feet long from tail to nose?"

"I'd say between four and six." Alice was absolutely thrilled; she hadn't been frightened in a sim since she could remember. "I'll be ba-" the sim closed down unceremoniously and she received an alert message from the bridge. All leisure sims were suspended. "The worst timing!" she screeched as she kicked her feet against her bunk mattress.

"Shh! Use your privacy curtain!" whispered Tamera, a woman barely out of her teens in the bunk across the aisle from her. She closed her curtain with a jerk.

"Sorry," Alice replied. She put on the armour under-layer of her vacsuit, the form-fitted suit that her metal emitter armour would fit to, much like her father's only more modern, and dropped quietly from the top bunk. "Something's up, just checking it out."

"See if you can get the sims back," Wilda said from the bunk below hers. "I was just starting to have fun in an anon-date room."

"Sure," Alice said, rolling her eyes. Anon-date rooms were supposedly one of the ways around the no fraternizing rule on most ships. There was no such rule on the Warlord, though it was frowned upon to date up and down the ranks, so Alice didn't get the point of a simulation that let people take on a different appearance to anonymously date other crewmembers, when they wouldn't be able to carry a good match into the real world. It was like baiting yourself for trouble. "It's just weird that the sims are closed even though we're not on alert."

"You go check in with daddy," Wilda said. Alice would change bunk mates if she could; Wilda was already annoying, with lips that looked too big for her face and a tendency to remind everyone around that Alice's father was the captain. The support systems technician had become a thorn in Alice's side in a matter of days, and she spent every spare second in her bunk, so it seemed like she was always there. "Run along now," Wilda said.

Alice did her best not to react and left berthing L3, which stood for Ladies Bunkroom Three. There were twenty bunks in each compartment, which made things interesting when two thirds of the privacy curtains weren't working properly yet, including hers. They were supposed to cancel out noise, so the only snoring you heard was your own, but they were finicky to set up, and it would take days or weeks longer for the facilities team to fix all of them. Alice promised herself that she'd take a look at fixing hers on her own when she got back to her bunk, not that she could break out the tools and get to work right then. Too many people were trying to sleep, and if she woke them all at once her sin would be remembered for days.

It didn't take her long to get to the bridge. The watchman nodded at her, suppressing a yawn. "I'm clear?" Alice asked.

"Yeah, Commander Buu is in the hot seat, busy for third watch," the tall watchman said. He was an older member of Stephanie's boarding team, with broad shoulders, a powerfully muscled chest and grey mixed in with his blonde hair.

"Thanks, Denver," she replied.

"Call me Den," he told her.

The heavy hatch slid aside to reveal a bridge filled with the full third watch crew. These were the least experienced, most recently qualified people aboard the Warlord, but they seemed surprisingly competent and busy. Minh-Chu had the holographic displays on the small bridge set up much like they were on the Triton, only smaller, with a semicircle of command data in front of the captain's seat. She could immediately see that the Warlord was tracking a pair of parallel wormholes within scanner range, an unusual thing.

"Good morning, Alice," Minh-Chu said over his shoulder. "What has you up?"

"I went to bed too early," she replied. "A lot of people are up right now, I think it's going around."

"About forty percent of the ship," Doctor Messana said from the operations station. It was the first time Alice had run into the new ship doctor, a woman who groomed herself bald, but had a fairly kindly face. It was a surprise to see her on the bridge; Alice thought she would be busy enough doing one-on-one check-ups with every member of the crew. "It's normal for people's sleep patterns to fall in line with the watches when they trust that the ship they're serving on is safe."

"Okay, I guess," Alice said as she passed by and stopped to stand beside the command seat at the centre of the bridge. "What's with the parallels?" she said, pointing at the wormhole trajectories marked in the tactical hologram.

"It looks like a big cargo train with a destroyer escort," Minh-Chu said. "Headed to the same section of the Iron Head Nebula we're planning on hitting. There's more to it though, maybe a Corvette class following close behind, I can't be sure." He turned to the tactical station. "Engage non-energetic cloaking measures and internal scan seals." The sounds of heavy hatches in the exterior and interior hull closing echoed across the ship, and the skin of the Warlord began passively warping scanning signals and light around the vessel. Activating the rest of the cloaking systems would interfere with the wormhole and the exotic matter surrounding the ship, leading to a catastrophe that would most likely kill everyone aboard, so they weren't turned on. "All right, if they scan us they'll see that something is in the middle of a deceleration cycle, but they won't know what, or who we are."

Lieutenant Commander Kadri Dunn entered the bridge and headed straight for the main scanning console. "Okay, this was worth waking up early for," she said over her shoulder to Minh-Chu. "Sorry for cursing at you when you woke me up."

"No problem," Minh-Chu replied. "What do we have here?"

"Well, they can't change course," Kadri replied. "And the scans you ran on their wormhole tells me that if they fire a shot, their wormhole will destabilize." She looked at Alice then with a smile. "Taking a few lessons, young one?"

If it were almost anyone else, Alice would have taken offence, but Kadri was a mother figure to a lot of the young women on the ship, and she extended that warmth and friendliness to her whenever they bumped into each other. Besides, she'd never seen anyone scan ships through wormholes. Normally, vessels didn't get nearly close enough for a good scan. Space was vast, and nearby long term parallel courses were rare. Kadri was the best scanning officer aboard, so if anyone could tell Alice what was going on, and what would probably happen, it was she. "You don't mind?"

"Pull up a stump and learn a thing," Kadri invited, pulling a secondary seat out from under the console. "These are definitely ships constructed by Regent Galactic or a close ally, headed for the waypoint we're planning to monitor. You were right to think one is a destroyer, the other one I'm not so sure about. Good job adjusting our scanners to account for the warp in our wormhole, but you have to re-lens the image."

"I know, I don't even know how to do it with the new system," Minh-Chu said. "Neither did the scan officer on watch, we'll have to add it to the training."

"I'm sorry," Ensign Lane Tram said. "All I know how to do is make sure we're not going to hit or cross high speed trajectories, so scanning through one wormhole is as far as they taught us when I was training."

"Watch," Kadri said. "You lock the lensing you set up to clear the view up outside our wormhole, then enlarge and start re-lensing to correct for the wormholes we're trying to scan through. That's the easy bit there," Kadri said as a blurry image of the larger ship became almost clear. "Relative to them, we're decelerating a lot faster, so you have to correct for the time differential. At these speeds, there's a fair difference." She made a few calculations and adjustments and a clear image of an Order of Eden destroyer appeared. It's name, *The Barricade,* was printed clearly on the side of the hull. Power level readings, density by compartment, weapon analysis, crew compliment, and detailed topographical scans of the ship's port side appeared on the tactical display. "All right, now watch as I do the other one," Kadri said.

"That's amazing," Ensign Tram said, shaking his head. "I never thought to adjust for a time difference inside of the wormholes."

"It's all math," Kadri said as the other wormhole's contents became clear. "Looks like that cargo train is being shadowed by two corvettes and our hauler is a four-hulled transport. Readings show one hundred and forty-two on the destroyer, probably a skeleton crew, and ten thousand fifty-one passengers on the transport, all reading in stasis. I can't get a reading on how many souls are aboard the corvettes."

"Could that hauler be a slave ship?" Minh-Chu asked.

"I've seen it before," Kadri nodded. "These folks are probably being transported so they can be sold to the Order."

"How long do they have left to their deceleration phase?"

"Nineteen hours, maybe seventeen? Best ask someone who can figure out what those thrusters can do to get a better estimate, Sir," Kadri replied. "I could look up similar thruster profiles and give you an estimate, though."

"That's all right the ensign can handle that. Thank you for the help, Lieutenant Commander Dutta," Minh-Chu said. "Sorry for kicking you out of bed. Get a few more winks if you can."

"You're welcome, and I'll try," Kadri said. "It's all yours, Ensign," she told Tram.

"Good-night," Alice said as Kadri left. She moved to Minh-Chu, where he was checking the course of the wormholes and the Barricade. "We can come out of our wormhole in seven hours if we really push our thrusters, and we'll be in combat range when they come out of theirs."

"You think we're going to take on a group that big?"

Minh-Chu highlighted a section of the destroyer's hull where a series of dates were written. "They finished building this ship less than two weeks ago, and they have a skeleton crew. I'm guessing they're just delivering it to the Order, there's no way Jake is going to let it go, not when we have antimatter bombs and a bunch of new toys loaded. Wrecking the ship then taking the transport is the smart move, but I think your father will want to make more of this opportunity."

"But there's something we're not seeing. Our scanners can't penetrate the hull on those escort corvettes. What if they're as well armed as we are?" Alice asked, quieting down so the rest of the bridge couldn't hear her question Minh-Chu.

"We'll know it's too much right away and we'll have time to bug out," Minh-Chu replied. "That's the luxury of having cloaking systems and battleship class shielding on a ship the size of the Warlord. We can stick around for a few minutes and see what we're really up against." Minh-Chu checked a timer on his wrist comm unit and smiled. "Your dad is in for one hell of a surprise when he wakes up in fifty seven minutes."

"You got him to sleep?"

"He's been asleep for almost eight hours. Bet he'll feel as fresh as a daisy when he rolls out of bed."

"I don't think he's ever felt like a daisy," Alice snickered. "Or would admit it if he did."

"True. Either way, he gets to free some slaves in a few hours. One of his very favourite things." Minh-Chu said. "Can't say I blame him."

252

CHAPTER 40
ONE SHIP

There was only one major cargo bay left on the Warlord. The others were repurposed as fighter bays, or reduced in size to make room for more on-board systems or berthing. The remaining space was cluttered, to be sure, but there was still enough room for one hundred and ninety-four of the crew to assemble. They sat on crates, on stacked armour plating, stood between stacks of sealed supplies, all gathered in front of the main fore access hatches.

The last day had Alice running around the ship, locking down anything loose, and helping the on-board security teams get ready for combat. Before her new assignment, she barely noticed if something was left out of a locker, or loose from its cupboard, or if a storage bin was open. After a day of running around righting these and other wrongs, she could notice a surplus bolt on the deck from across the room. It was that assignment, chosen for her by First Officer Stephanie Vega, that she wanted to talk to her father about, but he had been busy.

He walked in, followed by Stephanie and Minh-Chu. They were in full combat gear. Minh-Chu wore his flight jacket over a medium armour vacsuit, which looked like a thicker version of a normal vacsuit, but the layers built in took care of much more than the average suit. Most importantly, the extra built-in life support could last for a month or longer in combination with extra supplies from his ship.

First Officer Stephanie Vega wore her heavy combat suit. The dark coloured bands of armour flexed and moved with her as though they were heavy cloth. Those bands had incredible stopping power, and hid hundreds of tiny emitters that could propel someone in space in an emergency, or create a shield barrier in combat. They also helped in heavy gravity situations.

Alice's father wore his long coat, which had been outfitted with the same type of emitters that were built into his heavy combat armour. She couldn't see his face with his helmet up, but she could tell from his size, his armour, and the way he walked that it must have been him. He turned towards the assembly, revealing a holographic horror. Through a trick of holography, Jacob Valent looked like his head had been roughly stripped of flesh behind his helmet's faceplate. The grisly visage moved perfectly as he spoke, and Alice couldn't help but snicker to herself as many in the crowd cringed and turned away from the convincing illusion.

"There are people who believe that we must be better than our enemies, fight with honour and be civilized. I am not one of those people. When we fight today, our intent is to murder anyone who does not immediately surrender and take whatever is worth stealing. We are making an example of these new Order of Eden soldiers. They're not technicians, officers, and button pushers. Every one of them will eventually be responsible for killing people on our side, so we're going to treat them like the murdering traitors they are." Captain Valent said. He retracted his headpiece, revealing his normal, real face. "It is critical that our engagement here is successful. By now you know we face a large, armed cargo hauler. We're also facing a destroyer with a skeleton crew and two corvette class escorts, all fresh from the factory. Most of you have never seen one ship like the Warlord approach a combat ready group of this size, but that's about to change. Thanks to intelligence gathered by my first officer, Lieutenant Commander Stephanie Vega, I've had time to plan our attack. Six hours ago, I shared the details with your commanding officers, and we've refined it.

"We have already emerged from our wormhole, and have successfully cloaked. Half an hour ago, we entered the range of the waypoint sensor drones on the edge of the Iron Head Nebula and they have not detected us. The only thing the Order knows at this point is that a mysterious ship emerged from a wormhole seventeen million kilometres out from the waypoint. The ships we're after are still in faster-than-light transit, and have not changed speed or course, so we will have a clear opportunity to attack.

"We have three tasks to perform during this engagement: the Warlord and Samurai Squadron must demonstrate that we can defeat a superior force. We must destroy or capture the supplies and ships being delivered to the Order of Eden, and we will capture at least one of their armed ships. If we accomplish all of this, we will send a clear message to the Order of Eden, establishing ourselves as a clear threat. The overall point to this is to damage morale in the Order.

"Every person on this crew has qualified on their station, and more importantly, you joined with the expectation that you would have a chance to take the fight to the Order. Here it is, your first shot. You'll perform your duties, we'll fight like hell, and in twenty-two hours, most of us will know what it really feels like to strike a blow to the Order. Your assignments and your part of the plan will be uploaded to your communicators when your senior officers are finished."

Captain Valent stepped aside and allowed Wing Commander Minh-Chu Buu to take the fore. Alice was already excited and anxious.

Minh-Chu looked more serious than Alice could remember seeing him. "Like the captain said, we haven't been spotted since we emerged from our wormhole. The enemy will be emerging in twelve hours, and when they arrive, there will be a minimum of two hours before their assistance arrives. We have picked up no transmissions from the enemy that would indicate that they have called for help. There is still a chance that the Order has cloaked ships in the area. Our plan, in that case, is to fight through those extra defences or retreat and reassess. Multiple contingencies have been put together for each scenario.

"All of you have combat experience and you've seen the best laid plans turn into panicky chaos before. I think it's important that you know that your commanding officers, myself included, have survived more chaos minutes than well-planned engagements, so don't worry if all but the laws of physics change on a dime and our plans go out the airlock. We'll do the heavy improvising, and you just have to follow orders. All of your commanding officers have won against superior forces without having time to prepare.

"This time we are ready, and the Order of Eden has never seen what happens when we set out to make a point. I think a few imploding ships and some terrifying video on the open 'nets should be a good start." Minh-Chu nodded at the gathering and left as Lieutenant Commander Stephanie Vega took his place. Samurai Squadron and their support team quietly followed their wing commander out for what Alice assumed would be a private briefing.

"I didn't see Pandem first hand like our captain or wing commander did, and they didn't want to mention it. When I asked them why they didn't want to tell you that they were there to see the aftermath of the slaughter and the destruction of a culture, they said there was no point. You have all seen what the Holocaust Virus did for yourselves. I took another look at the roster then, and realized that we have forty-two Aucharians aboard. You were among the first to lose your homes; I saw a part of that happen and will never forget. There are nine here who had relatives on Pandem, and I can only imagine the hate you have for the Order. Dozens of you were stranded in space for days, sometimes weeks, after Eden ships attacked you. Other people on the roster were slaves when the Holocaust Virus hit, and a few of you were even in the middle of labour camps or factories when industrial machines turned on your co-workers.

"No, no one has to mention Pandem. There are thousands of places where the Order of Eden caused incredible destruction, murdered billions either through the Holocaust Virus or in the war that we've barely seen in this sector. Wing Commander Minh-Chu did say something I'll never forget when we were talking about this though. He said, 'tragedy martyrs some, victimises a people, and makes soldiers of many.'" Stephanie took a shuddering breath and squeezed her eyes shut for a moment before continuing. "My family is gone. They got in the way of the Order and I wasn't there to fight alongside them. Pandem isn't important to me. I was a soldier before I heard of it. I was a soldier before my family was killed. I'm a soldier now, and as a soldier I know that my best chance of victory, of survival, is to put my rage aside and do my job. When our work is done, and we're on our way back to the Rega Gain System, we can do so knowing that the Warlord was the first to counterattack the Order in this sector. That is an act that will outlive us in history, and when the guns stop firing I'll be able to say I did it for my family and the friends I've already lost to this war. Until then, we all have to do as soldiers do: keep our heads down, listen to orders, think on our feet, and do our jobs. Your comms are being updated with your orders."

Lieutenant Commander Stephanie Vega turned to Captain Valent then, and he nodded at her knowingly. A few of their subordinates approached them with questions while much of the crew dispersed through several hatches leading to their duty stations. Alice did her best to navigate through the crowd so she could speak to her father.

After weaving through the crowd, squeezing through the door and into the hallway, she caught up with him as he stepped into a side passage with Minh-Chu. "That's bad timing," Minh was saying. "Was it at least a good dream?"

"It was Ayan, of course it was a good dream," Jake replied. "Been trying to put it out of my head since, but it just comes…" he noticed her then and stopped.

It was good to hear that Ayan was on his mind; she had to stifle a grin. Just the same, Alice couldn't let herself be distracted by a little encouraging news. "Dad, why am I on counter incursion and support duty for this mission?" she whispered to him.

Minh-Chu patted Jake on the shoulder and said, "I'll see you later," before leaving.

Jake nodded at him then focused on Alice. He didn't seem surprised by her question. "That's Stephanie's call, and I think it's a good one."

"I have more Order of Eden kills than her entire boarding team combined, and I'm improving my team work. You can't keep me out of harm's way when I can be useful," she objected.

Stephanie stepped into the narrow side passage and the trio moved into an adjacent room. It was a storage space for replacement parts. Shelves were marked with a grease pencil, designating places and desired quantities for equipment that was depleted. Most of the shelves were empty. "Okay, I caught part of that," Stephanie said. "I know you want to be on one of the boarding teams, Alice, and you have improved. There were a lot of factors to my decision, and even though I want you with us, it's not happening."

Alice was frustrated, but she recognized that Stephanie was taking some time out to talk to her even though she was very busy. "Okay, why? What can I do?"

Stephanie and Jake looked at each other for a moment before she answered. "I was hoping this would keep until the trip home, but I guess it won't. Doctor Messana put a hold on your off-ship missions after seeing your medical records. I'm taking her word for it."

"What's wrong with me? How could there be anything wrong? I'm a framework," Alice said, deeply concerned.

"Don't worry," Jake said. "We're just trying to figure a few things out."

"Like what?"

"Doctor Messana's just down the hall, let's go see her," Jake said. "Thank you, Stephanie."

Stephanie Vega nodded and backed out of the room. "Sir."

The trip down the corridor and around a few corners seemed long to Alice. "I'd explain it all to you, but Doctor Messana has a better grasp of the details." Jake said.

"It's so weird that you don't even understand it?" Alice asked.

"I understand it," Jake replied. "I just don't know how I'd start to explain it."

"She's not some kinda secret researcher, is she?" Alice asked.

"No, but she's an expert in emerging cybernetics, and she's experienced in accelerated regeneration. She's found a few things about you and me that are, unexpected."

257

"You're dancing around this like I have some kind of embarrassing butt plague!" Alice burst. She was immediately embarrassed as a few startled crewmembers glanced at her, wide-eyed.

Her father looked surprised for a moment, then burst into a fit of unguarded laughter. Alice was insulted at first, but couldn't suppress a smile at seeing him in such a state. It had been a long time since she saw him laugh like that, so long that she'd forgotten what it looked like. "It's not funny," she muttered as he strangled his mirth to chuckles.

"I know, I know," he said, taking a breath. "You'll be all right, we're just writing the manual on the framework system, so there are some surprises."

They entered the Warlord Infirmary, where there were six medical cots, two new humanoid bio-bots that smiled at Alice as she entered, and Doctor Messana. "Early visit," she said. "Okay, come with me."

Alice's boots squeaked against the new self-sterilizing, no-slip flooring as she and her father followed the doctor into one of four private treatment rooms. "Hop up," Doctor Messana said as she activated a short-range recorder scrambler, a small circular tab the size of her thumbnail that blinked red.

Alice hopped up on the exam table and was instantly nervous. "Testing? Am I in for some jabs and pokes?"

"No," Doctor Messana said with a comforting smile. "You stay dressed and I don't have to poke or jab. The latest reading from your vacsuit is enough for me to see you're healthier than the average human, and much more capable."

"Okay, so why did you pull me off boarding operations?" Alice asked. For some reason, maybe because of the doctor's easy bedside manner, she found herself sounding more frustrated than angry.

"I didn't pull you off boarding operations, but I'm sure my medical advisory played a small part. I'll get right down to it then," the doctor said. "You're a soldier, so you don't fall under guardianship discretion."

"Um, that means?"

"Your father can't tell me what I can and can't tell you, so I'm going to give you the whole story," Doctor Messana said. "In this office, you have all the rights of an adult soldier."

"Oh, okay, what's wrong with me then?"

"Everything seems to be working fine, as far as frameworks go. With your father's permission, I've been studying everything you have on framework technology and I've been investigating the particulars about you both."

"I thought I was an adult, here? Don't I have a say in getting snooped on?"

"Not in this case, your superior officers can have me monitor and investigate your medical status as much as they like. In this case, your father is captain, so he had me study you both after he vetted me as ship doctor. What I found is ground-breaking. Mostly, that the framework system is intelligent when it comes to responding to your needs."

"Okay, and that's bad somehow?" Alice replied.

"It's almost always good. Have you wondered why you changed so much when you regenerated during the battle of Port Rush?"

"I thought the framework system just hooked into my subconscious or something," Alice replied.

"That's true," Doctor Messana said, bringing up a hologram of Jake's DNA and her own. "But there's more to it. There is no way your subconscious mind could know your father's exact DNA, and you had no contact with him before you regenerated as his biological daughter. I had Kadri perform a forensic analysis of your framework's communication systems on the records from the Battle of Port Rush. We discovered that the framework system accessed your comm unit and downloaded your father's DNA before the battle even started. It knew, from your subconscious mind that you saw yourself as his daughter, and without your knowledge, it prepared a pattern that used your father's DNA, so the next time you took critical damage, you'd regenerate as his biological daughter. It also determined what age you'd be based on your mental self-image and subconscious desires. It's the only explanation here, but one of the potential problems is that your age is locked to a certain range. That means that your framework lets your body age and develop to a certain point, and when that point is reached, it rolls the clock back. You keep your memories, and the framework system allows you to retain muscle memory and development, but everything else gets rebuilt so you are physically sixteen years old. This kind of system is popular in adults where I come from – I have a biological graft implanted that keeps my physical age down to twenty nine – but there are reasons why we don't allow those types of implants in teenagers."

"I'm not gonna grow up," Alice said. "Ever."

"Not unless we can find a way to communicate with the framework system without disturbing its normal function," Doctor Messana said. "Or there could be a subconscious trigger it's waiting for. So far, the system has rolled you back roughly every two months."

Alice only had to imagine what being a teenager for the rest of her life would be like for a moment before she knew, for a fact, that it was the worst thing she could imagine. "I'm staying on the ship for this mission because I'm a kid, I'll always be a kid."

"No," Doctor Messana replied. "Absolutely not. I am holding you back because I don't know what will happen during your next regeneration, but your framework system is indicating that a completely new reconstruction pattern is ready to go. We can see the file, and that it's very different from the last one, but we can't interpret it, see what you'll become if the worst happens. I thought it was critical that you know before you go on any dangerous missions."

"So, I know about this now, can I join the boarding teams?" Alice asked.

"I need to know that you understand the implications of this. If your heart stops beating, or you are critically injured, the framework system may take the opportunity to remake you into a person you don't even recognize."

"But I'll still be the same person up here," Alice said, pointing to her head.

"No, not completely. Do you remember much of your last human life?"

Alice thought a moment and, as much as she wanted to tell the doctor everything was fine, that she could recall her life on the Clever Dream with her old friends, it wasn't true. "Most of it is really foggy, or missing, or I remember telling people about those times more than I actually remember being there," she conceded.

"Right, and I can see from passive brain scans that you are actually suppressing a lot of those memories, and the suppression is driven selectively by a non-biological system."

"Framework is doing it."

"Yes. That's just a start though. If you regenerate with a new combination of DNA, your genetic predispositions will be changed as well. You could become someone with a severe temper, or be a more passive person and have no control over your natural tendencies. For all we know, the last thing you'll want is to be a soldier if you change into this person that the Framework has preloaded for you."

"What about my dad? He came back looking different, but he didn't seem to change," Alice asked.

"Funny thing about that. Can I disclose this, Captain?" Doctor Messana asked.

"Go ahead, but don't share this outside of this room, all right, Alice?"

"Okay, what happens in med-bay stays in med-bay," Alice agreed.

"Your father may look similar, but his DNA profile shifted quite a bit. It borrowed from the unknown female contributor to your DNA and made sure that he remained your biological father. A little tinkering by the framework system made sure he'd recognize himself in the mirror because he had a long history of being that person, looking that way, but the reason for your father looking roughly the same is just an assumption on my part. Your father's new genetic profile indicates that he's predisposed to addiction and depression. These are markers from the body you had the last time you were human, and they're markers you share with him right now. There are positive predispositions as well, including a tendency towards high emotional response and exceptional memory retention. I'll make sure you have the whole profile today, but I need you to take time to think about your career choice before you go on any other missions, especially since the combination of genetic predispositions add up to a high likelihood that you and your father will eventually struggle with post traumatic stress."

"What? Can't you give us some kind of memory control treatment for that? People haven't had that problem for ages," Alice replied. There were so many new things to consider, she had trouble keeping up.

"Yes, there are plenty of treatments, but in you and your father's cases specifically, no pharmaceutical methods will be effective. The active ingredients in drinks like Michnickel or Cosuberi are blocked by the framework system. Direct memory manipulation and drug treatments are also ineffective because frameworks protect against them. You and your father are uniquely vulnerable to the lasting effects of your experiences, and I need you to keep that in mind. You only have to look at your father's sleep schedule to see that he's having problems processing violent memories and stressful experiences now."

"So, somehow we both wanted these problems in our subconscious before the framework system remade us?" Alice asked.

"The genetic predispositions you and your father have that can lead to post traumatic stress are beneficial in near ideal situations. Emotional sensitivity and high performing situational memory are both highly desirable traits on their own, and they can benefit almost all parts of a non-soldier's life. Individually, they're highly beneficial to a soldier as well, but if they are combined along with a few other genetic and environmental factors, violent experiences and certain types of stress will always lead to post traumatic stress. I'm sorry, these are things we know for a fact, and, thanks to the framework system, I can't treat you using quick methods. If you remain a soldier, you'll have to develop coping mechanisms, preferably with the help of a therapist."

"I just want you to hold back until we figure out the triggers for the framework system," Jake said. "When we do, we'll be able to use the same treatments as everyone else."

"You have nightmares?" Alice said. She couldn't stop thinking about something the doctor just said, that some of the markers that they both had were from her previous body, the one that died aboard the Triton.

"He vividly relives traumatic experiences in his sleep," Doctor Messana said. "He's developed coping mechanisms to deal with it over the years, but there's reason for concern. There are already warning signs for paranoia and hyper-vigilance."

"I don't want you to start down the road I'm on without knowing the facts," Jake told her. "I'll support any decision you make, as long as you've thought it through."

"What, being a soldier? A ranger?" Alice stared at her father for a moment. She could see he was sympathetic, but there would be no way around a waiting period before she could get on with her life, and chances were she'd be a teenager forever, or years at least. "I can't imagine doing anything else, Dad."

"Just think about it," he replied. "Give it some time."

"Okay, I will." She slid off the examination table. "That's everything, right?"

"There are other minor details, but that's all the important information, yes," Doctor Messana said. "I'll send all the details and research to your comm, you should review the whole file."

"Okay, I have duty," she said, leaving her father and the doctor behind. The whole world had changed in less than half an hour, and she didn't know what to do or think; her mind felt numb.

CHAPTER 41
ALICE'S BATTLE

For the first time ever, Alice had a station on the bridge of the Warlord. There was a minor shuffling of departments and personnel in the hours before the attack on the edge of the Iron Head Nebula as Jacob Valent and Stephanie Vega refined the plans for their boarding operations. There would be five teams conducting incursions on the enemy ships, and that meant the counter-incursion team that remained aboard the Warlord would be formed late. Some crewmembers would be traded from one team to another, to balance the experts they were taking with them and that left them in an interesting position.

Anyone with experience had to go on a boarding team. Everyone who was assigned to protect the Warlord in the event that it was boarded or there was a security problem had training for those contingencies, but they weren't the most experienced group. Before the shuffle, Alice was third in command of the counter-incursion team. After the changes, she was the commander. First Officer Stephanie Vega officially bumped her rank up to sergeant and gave her the roster. There were twenty-eight people under her command, all watchmen and watchwomen with the right training for their assignment. Half of them had other duties, like loading munitions or damage control, but that was to be expected.

Alice watched at her station, a seat to the left of the bridge command chair with three small holographic projectors and a narrow wall of screen space, as her fourteen dedicated counter-insurgence officers patrolled key points of the ship, and the rest of them worked at their regular stations in other areas.

"That's the last of the crew quarters, Sarge," reported Nesh, one of the older members of her counter-insurgence security team. "They're all checked and locked down."

"Good, just a precaution," Alice replied. "Don't want to give anyone on the wrong side more room for cover."

"Yeah, makes sense, good thinking."

"Thank you," Alice replied. Nesh Samo was an experienced soldier who worked security for over a decade in Valero, a super-city on Precious, one of the major core worlds. Nesh was much more experienced and qualified by far, but she was new to the crew. She fell in step and listened to orders faster than most under Alice's new command, which spoke volumes about the woman's professionalism.

"How is it going?" Jake asked quietly as he stopped to stand behind her.

"Good, I'm having all non-essential compartments closed and secured. No one will be able to get in until this is over."

"Good thinking," Jake said. "Are we okay?"

"With the medical thing? Yeah," Alice said, as convincingly as she could manage. She'd put much of it out of her immediate thoughts, a task made easier thanks to her new assignment. "It's not your fault I'm made the way I am, it's just a lot to take in."

"I'll take you no matter what shape you're in," Jake said quietly. "You'll always be my daughter."

"Thanks," Alice smiled back. It was a small bridge, and she knew at least a third of the bridge was overhearing their whispered conversation, including Frost, who was sitting in the command seat, making a point of not looking at the father and daughter duo to his left. "Am I missing any tricks from what you can see?" she asked, nodding at her station.

Jake looked at the displays for a moment. "I'd tie in with Kadri and have her run a signal detection program."

"Yup, already taken care of. I'm tracking it on my comm unit already," Alice replied.

"Good," Jake said. "Then the only thing I'd do is priority seal the galley so only the medical staff can open it, and lock all the non-essential storage compartments down. Should keep your people moving around the ship for another ten or twenty minutes and leave boarders fewer places to hide."

"Why didn't I think about that?" Alice said.

"Because you got this assignment three hours ago," Jake replied. "All right, I'm going to check in with Frost and then I'm going to get strapped to Minh-Chu's fighter."

"Good luck," Alice said.

"Thanks," Jake replied. "You too." He turned to Frost and didn't have to say anything to prompt a report from the lead tactical officer.

"We've got all your expensive surprises loaded up and ready, Captain," Frost said. "Cloak is holding, and we're patrolling around the arrival point here. No sign of any other ships in the area and the Warlord is ready for the biggest smash and grab I've ever seen."

"Finn?" Jake asked.

"Our ship is invisible even with all our weapon and fighter launch bays wide open," Finn replied from the engineering station. "We're currently using point-four percent of our available power and my people have nothing to do except help Ashley fine-tune our manoeuvring systems."

"Something wrong with our calibration, Ash?" Jake asked.

Ashley half turned in her seat at the helm and smiled. "Nope, we're just looking at it while we have an extra minute. Keeps us from getting all tense while we wait. Everyone's board is green, Captain, you go have fun."

"Is a captain still as much of a captain when the crew can take care of themselves?" Jake muttered under his breath.

"You're the man with the plan, Captain," Frost replied. "Don't think we'd try to bite off half of what you plan to chew today, even if we had twice the dog. Good hunting, Sir."

"Thanks, good hunting, Warlord," Jake replied before leaving the bridge.

Alice checked on her team and highlighted the storage areas that didn't contain parts for the ship or equipment they'd need for the upcoming battle, and ordered her staff to seal them off. With her orders sent and security well in hand, she took a moment to look to the main tactical display in front of the command seat. They had been patrolling for hours since the Warlord emerged from the wormhole, and aside from a few smaller ships passing through the area, a medium cargo hauler that had since moved on, and a buoy, the space they were in was clear. The destroyer, two corvettes, and the large cargo hauler they were waiting for would be emerging from their wormholes in a few minutes.

"Plot an evasive stealth course and execute when ready," Frost ordered. Ashley set her course and took manual control of the Warlord, guiding it into a manoeuvring pattern that would be difficult to track if anyone caught a momentary indication of where the ship was.

"Launch probes, one from each facing," Frost ordered. "We're watching for signal echo and any unnatural light paths. Set their timers to aggressively scan after thirty seconds then shut down."

"Still expecting other cloaked ships out there?" Kadri asked.

"Aye," Frost replied. "This is a good spot for a waypoint going into the nebula, but there has to be a reason for these ships to feel safe while they're plotting their path through."

"Probes away," Finn replied.

Everyone waited as the eight centimetre long probe drones zigged and zagged away in all directions. Ashley piloted the Warlord so the ship came about and thrust off on a course that was not exactly inverse to their previous heading. It would be difficult for a tactical officer on an enemy ship to guess where they were, but the probes did reveal their general location, and Alice felt less uneasy as they put more distance between them and the small projectiles they launched.

The probes activated, filling the tactical screen with a red bloom of energy that radiated in all directions away from their location. It only lasted a minute, but the eight probes were able to fill the area with aggressive multi-spectrum noise that would reveal everything in the area, even cloaked ships if their was a chink in their concealing technology.

"If our cloaking systems have any problems, we'll be just as visible as anyone else," Finn said to no one in particular as he looked at his combined damage control and tactical systems. David Penton stood along side him, dedicating his attention only to engineering.

"My goodness, I didn't think about that," Frost muttered in return. "S'pose I'll have to tell the captain we'll be found out and we should pack it all in, go find a nice out of the way planet and start a colony. That's if you don't think our cloak can hide us in the middle of this noise."

"No echoes or shadows coming back on the Warlord," Kadri reported from the communications and scanning station. "Good work, Lieutenant Finn."

"Thank you," Finn replied.

"You'll have your first drink on me when we find a moment and a corner to celebrate in," Kadri added with a wink.

"That's a promise I'd take," Frost said as he checked the scan data.

"Like I'd make you the same offer," Kadri scoffed exaggeratedly. "I don't date men my age."

Alice glanced at Finn in time to catch him blushing, and she barely stifled a giggle. Her focus returned to her station, where icons representing her team moved through the corridors, lighting up secured compartments and storage areas that were freshly checked.

"I got unregistered firearms here, locker twenty ninety-nine. The manifest management screen says this locker isn't assigned to anyone," Ensign Andy Timmermen reported. "No known DNA or other indications of ownership either, but forensic scans say these weapons were assembled forty three minute ago."

The scan results appeared in front of Alice, a ripper pistol and a motorized fragmentation grenade. Alice cross referenced the parts list from the weapons with the manufacturing logs and grimaced. Those weapons were made of objects that were used ship wide for construction and repairs, even the pistol grip was just a door handle that had been bent and curved to its new purpose. "Okay, I'm reporting this. Assume we have a suspect aboard."

"That's overreacting, isn't it?" asked Officer Erin Shin, one of her team members and a very recent addition to the crew. "Maybe someone just hasn't settled in and wanted a personal weapon to feel more secure."

Alice didn't want to deal with people contradicting her. She'd been given her command and her every instinct told her to assert her authority when she was sure she was in the right. "Is it yours?"

"What? No," Erin replied.

"Then let me handle the evidence while you follow orders please," Alice replied.

"Yes, Ma'am,"

"Andy, take those weapons to the nearest dangerous materials lockup. Meet up with Engleman and Richt down the hall so you have cover while you make the deposit and close it up."

"Yes, Ma'am, headed to the nearest DML with cover," replied Ensign Andy Timmermen.

Alice turned to Frost and he nodded at her. "Well done, I heard your side and checked the summary. I'd take two people off damage control and post them near the recycling processors, where you found that piece o' work."

"Good idea, thank you," Alice said, adding those orders onto the map. The staffing was light near the fore of the ship and she shook her head. "We're running thin. Not enough people for coverage. I need to activate more dual purposed staff."

"Don't worry about that," Stephanie Vega said as icons representing three of her boarding team members appeared in the fighter launch area of the ship. "I'm giving you a few of mine to cover the bridge and forward weapons' sections of the ship. Leave the last of your dual duty people with their other departments so they can assist with combat operations."

"Your boarding team is short now," Alice retorted.

"I didn't think there would be a traitor on board, everyone we have is screened, but it looks like I was wrong. You shouldn't have to deal with my mistake, so I'm giving you the people I can afford to do without."

"So this was supposed to be a fluff position," Alice said as she assigned the new security guards to their positions.

"There are no nonessential commands," Jake said. "Would I be strapped to a Uriel fighter waiting to launch if I didn't think you could handle my ship's security?"

"Good point," Alice said. "Speaking of which, I'm linking all the bots on the ship with my security tracker. I want to know who hid their weapons." She started the forensic playback and was surprised to see that the results were inconclusive. Whoever dumped the pistol had an obfuscator that blurred security recordings of them. "Wow, okay, whoever this is, they're crafty. Also, we should watch for recording defects in the future."

"Jake, I'm changing my team's strategy, I'll operate under plan three," Stephanie said over the boarding crew channel.

"Good," Jake replied over the high priority communications channel. "My team will continue as planned."

She had a fairly good grasp of what Stephanie and her father were talking about. The initial plan was to board the Barricade, the heavy destroyer, using quick, brute force. Stephanie's team was to head aft while Jake's would rush the bridge, remaining visible, using an arsenal of weaponry and shielding technology that even Alice found stunning. If Stephanie was switching her team to their tertiary tactic, that meant her group would be using stealth instead, leaving her father's boarding team with all the attention. Alice didn't doubt his ability to terrify the skeleton crew aboard the Barricade, but she still worried for him.

"Sir, we have three shadows on our scans," Kadri reported to Frost, "stationary relative to the navigational buoy, marking them on tactical."

The tactical scanner noise lighting up the map of the area faded, leaving less than two dozen minor objects that were scanned in high detail on the hologram at the front of the bridge. The largest objects were three asteroids that had emergency supplies and a small unmanned repair depot on them. There were a number of small drifting inert objects that were passing though the area, and the faintest readings were those three shadows. "All right," Frost said, "Those shadows are all the same shape."

"Almost exactly the same shape, Sir," Kadri said.

"Do we have enough data to match them with a class of Order ship?"

"Yes, but our database is not coming up with a match. They have a gravity footprint close to a twenty metre short-range customs ship, but the shape is all wrong."

"Competition, maybe? Other pirates?" Ashley asked from the helm.

Alice watched her station as the guards she sent to different parts of the ship arrived at their stations. The silence on the bridge extended for so long that she had to look at Frost, who was staring at the details of the three shadows. The cloaking systems of the ships were extremely good, only a slight gravity shadow surrounded the vessels.

"I don't think so. We don't have enough information to figure this out properly," Frost said. "Never heard of a cloaking device that could trick every spectrum, hide energy, and fail at masking gravity. This is new."

Before she realized she was doing anything, Alice was bringing up an encounter database that most travellers disregarded as a hoax. Keeping one eye on the security systems, she ran the shadow's profile against the sketchy records of Edxian ships and was startled by an immediate positive result. Half the bridge turned towards her beeping console.

"What do you have there?" Frost asked.

"The shape of the shadow matches a group of ships that attacked Dorminy Colony nineteen years ago," Alice replied. "The transmissions from the colony are distorted, but it's definitely the same type of ship."

"Edxian," Frost said. "You hearing this, Captain?"

"Yes," Captain Valent replied. "Monitor the area for them. Alice, does the report from Dorminy tell us anything about what those ships were capable of?"

"The colony was attacked by hundreds. A rescue team that arrived after the action reported that everyone was captured or killed within an hour. From what they could determine, the ships attacked as closely coordinated groups. They used some kind of antimatter cannons, and no one could figure out what type of faster-than-light travel they used. The colony shot several down, but the rescue team didn't find any wrecks. The Edxi must have taken them with them when the left."

"All right, our targets emerge in three minutes," Captain Valent said. "If these Edxi ships attack, we'll hit them with everything we have and capture whatever's left. We'll only change our mission if we have to."

"Sergeant," Nesh said through the security comm. Alice almost didn't pay attention, unaccustomed to her new rank. "Yes?" she acknowledged.

"I'm in position at the main aft corridor intersection for deck three, but I don't think I'll see anything helpful here. There are a lot of crew who have to move through this section, our suspect could blend in pretty easy."

Alice looked at where she'd posted her people and realized that moving any of them could be a mistake. "Yeah, you need another set of eyes further down the hallway. I'm on my way," she replied. Alice was half out of her seat when she stopped and looked at Frost. "Don't need me on the bridge, do you?"

"Lead Security Officer can move however they like around the ship," Frost replied. "One of the rights of the post. Just make sure you listen in on the boarding and command comm channels, in case you have something else to add to our conversations,"

"Aye, aye," Alice said, checking her sidearm and the rest of her security kit. The warning from Doctor Messana about her and her father's addictive personalities came back to her as she connected directly with the ship's systems using the comm node in her skull. The stream of data from the ship's internal, external, and information collection systems filled her mind for a moment before she enforced a balance between it and her own thoughts. It really was a rush, to be connected to so much at once, and she was thankful that the Warlord's internal systems were all locked behind data safeties. She could find ways to bypass them, or use codes she had to manipulate the systems directly, but those safeties were there so she wasn't in immediate control of the ship's functions, which was a relief.

She could feel her father in the machine as well; he was watching, sending messages to the bridge staff sparingly. They had it under control, and for the first time since she boarded the Warlord, she could see a pattern in how her father was communicating with the ship.

He was training an entirely new crew through experience and example while trying to learn about Moira McFadden and her methods. For most of their recent voyage, Alice's father had been absent, and she hadn't figured out what he was spending a large chunk of his time on. The logs revealed the truth: he'd been with Moira in simulations, learning about Order of Eden ships, how to capture them, destroy them, and command them. He spent many hours running through simulations with her and select crewmembers, most of them boarding team members. While Jacob Valent was learning about McFadden, she was auditioning senior crewmembers from a pool of newer recruits.

There was so much going on aboard the Warlord, and so many things happening in Jacob Valent's virtual world, that it was no wonder she didn't see her father much. To Alice's surprise, Ashley had been in on much of the boarding and training exercises, training to be a stealthed boarder and saboteur. In most of the simulations, it was her job to intentionally stray away from the primary incursion team so they could get to a control hub aboard the enemy ship, where Ashley would take control of the helm at the most opportune time. She wasn't alone; there were two other shadow pilots in training with her.

"Focus," Alice told herself as she realized that she'd barely made it three steps from her station on the bridge since she connected to the Warlord.

"Are you okay?" Finn asked her quietly.

"Yeah, just got a brain full there," Alice said. "I should either use my neural datacomm a lot more, or not at all. Takes some adjusting if you leave it off for too long."

"So I've heard," Finn replied.

Alice saw the counter to the emergence of the enemy ships reach one minute. "All right, sealing the bridge behind me until this is all over. Happy hunting." She took the few steps left between her and the hatch then sent a mental command for all bridge entrances to seal. Only senior officers would be able to unlock them.

CHAPTER 42
PREPPED

"Release all launch safeties," Alice overheard Minh-Chu order. Clamps holding fast to all seven of the Samurai Squadron fighters to the top of their short launch rails released, a sound that could be heard across the upper levels of the ship.

Alice's mind raced as she observed major events across the ship, kept track of her security team, and eliminated suspects from a pool of people who were most likely the person who built a pistol and a grenade then hid them. There was something special about the way the Warlord's computer shared information with her; it made it more difficult to be aware of her surroundings in the physical world, but she could sense her location and observe what she was doing so well from the outside, it was as though she didn't need her own senses anymore.

It was obvious that her father had tweaked every piece of software himself, and she was starting to understand why he seemed so far away when he wasn't talking to someone directly. Why stay in the moment, observing everything through biological eyes, when the ship's sensors were so much keener? The problem was, there was so much information that if Alice didn't focus, she knew she would miss things, important things, that could cost someone their life.

At long last, Alice arrived at her post, in the perfect position to observe the person who operated aboard with a secret agenda. With one of the industrial lifts behind her, two narrow rampways leading to the decks above and below, and the intersection of four corridors, it was a key point to catching their suspect. She cloaked and waited, ordering several of her security team to cloak as well.

The data stream passing through her mind informed her that the Warlord's prey were about to emerge from their wormholes. Hard clanging beneath her feet announced what she was already aware of – Frost had ordered the release of their tactical mines, a set of twenty-eight autonomous cloaked mines, each made for a specific purpose. Some of them featured racks of miniature seeker missiles, others were hull-breaching antimatter bombs, and a few carried paired particle accelerator beams.

Loading teams made sure that the big bore launchers were made ready to fire electromagnetic pulse mines. These had stealth technology, but didn't have the same level of cloaking as the previous load. Technicians observed the loading procedure, making sure that the new, safer systems were performing well. After days of drilling and refining, only two launchers needed extra care. The munitions team leapt into action and within seconds the self-propelled electromagnetic pulse weapons were loaded. As soon as the work was finished, one of the technicians left his post.

Alice realised then that she wasn't observing the operations down there by chance the ship had guided her to focus on the most suspicious crewmember it recognized. In a flash, she could see that there was something off in the records regarding one crewmember.

Ensign Donny Porter, an electrician assigned to maintenance and damage control, reported a minor injury using his comm unit and left the munitions compartment. Alice used his suit to scan him and found nothing wrong. She didn't modify his injury report, so he could go on with the assumption that he hadn't been noticed. "We found our man," she said over the security band. "Watch him."

"What? Him?" asked Ensign Timmerman. "He's not qualified to touch munitions, the computer will howl if he even gets too close."

Alice checked the system and discovered that Porter tried to pass the munitions technician qualifier five times since he boarded the Warlord, the course that would allow him to get his hands on ship-to-ship weapons. He failed each time. "Trust me, it's him. Keep your eyes open for accomplices."

"He's headed aft," Nesh Samo said. "What's back there on that level besides escape shuttles?"

The thought donned on Alice the moment Nesh finished speaking. The Order of Eden had no way to detect them while they were cloaked. All signals were blocked in by the hull unless they were transmitted using the exterior antennae, and they were effectively invisible on most scanners. An escape shuttle could be hotwired for launch, and then their position would be revealed. Alice bumped into a medical tech, knocking him down as she broke into a dead run towards the aft of the ship. "He's going to launch a shuttle so the Barricade can see us as soon as they come out of the wormhole," she announced as she mentally sent orders to half her security team to meet her near the lower aft shuttle service compartment.

"That's a pretty good plan," Nesh replied. "How'd we miss it?"

Alice decloaked so people in the corridors could see her coming and ran as fast as she could down ramps and hallways, jumping over a startled group of skitter bots that chirped, blinking red and yellow at her swift approach warning her that they were there.

Through ship sensors, Alice saw Officer Erin Shin shout, "Hold it!" as Porter entered the compartment.

Alice wasn't quite there, and continued to observe as best as she could while she was running. Donny Porter backed out of the room and Alice came around the corner just as he turned, about to run. Nesh Samo was right behind her, and they almost had their hands on him, but he whirled back into the shuttle compartment, free of their grasp.

He looked left, where Erin Shin had her weapon trained on him, then right, where Alice and Nesh were coming through the heavy compartment hatch, closing it behind them. "Nowhere to go, Donny," Alice said, retracting her headgear. "Why did you abandon your post? My scans tell me there's nothing medically wrong with you."

"I'm nervous," he said, stepping back from them. The shuttle service space was dormant, with well-organized boxes of parts secured to the floor and walls. There was one shuttle ready for emergency departure in the room, small by most standards, but it would fit eight crewmembers in a pinch. "Who wants to be inside a loading compartment as a ship this size goes up against a destroyer? I'm a bloody electrician, I can be useful anywhere, why did they assign me to that death trap? It's stupid. You people are insane. I'm getting to an escape shuttle in advance, so I'm ready when this goes all pear shaped."

Alice noticed two more people from the upper deck on their way to the same place. They were Milford Forthman and Orson Smi, a pair from the damage control teams on the uppermost deck. Alice marked them on the tactical map and regarded Donny. "How many others are turning traitor with you?"

"Turning traitor? I'm just abandoning ship, there's a difference, I'd think," Donny protested.

"No, there isn't," Alice said, drawing her sidearm and taking aim at Donny's head. "Traitors get shot. How many others?"

"Two!"

"Only two?"

"Two! I swear!"

274

As though summoned, the pair from damage control opened the hatch and started to come in. They took in the scene ahead and tried to retreat but Nesh Samo caught them both by the collars. "Nope, inside if you please," she said as she dragged both of them through the door.

"We have something, Sergeant," reported one of her officers posted near the main waste processing centre. "Juno Lathi is almost here."

"You all have thirty seconds to return to your posts," Alice told the abandoners. "And if you don't impress your commanders, we'll put you off the ship before we make port, understand?"

Orson clearly didn't understand and looked at Milford who whispered, "they'll space us," and then he looked far more alarmed. "Oh, aye, we'll get back to our posts."

Alice didn't bother holstering her weapon, but mentally sent a short report about the incident to the bridge then led her security people from the room. All the while, she kept tabs on the three crew members who attempted escape, to make sure they were heading back to their posts with all haste.

The ship shuddered as the fighter launch systems activated, sending seven Uriel fighters and the boarding teams they carried into space. The biggest fight the ship had seen so far was beginning, and she was chasing down a dangerous traitor. The records for Juno Lathi revealed that she was one of only five ship's stewards. Her job was to direct the bots in cleaning the ship and to assist in the galley.

"Let her into the recycling compartment," Alice said. She was just around the corner from Juno, and she signalled for the two officers behind her to slow down. She watched through ship scanners as Juno activated a tiny surveillance scrambler.

Alice rushed the compartment, signalling the two officers she had inside to reveal themselves and stop whatever the woman was doing. When Alice came through the hatch, followed by two of her officers, Juno was backing away from the pair of guards who were already there. The recycling centre was dormant, with piles of scrap metal and a few bins of waste organized in line for the industrial processors.

Juno reached into one of the bins, where she'd stashed a small but powerful cutter used for hull plating. She pressed the activation button, flaring the small white emitter on the end as if to warn them. Her gaze flicked from one soldier to the next, coming to rest on Alice with scorn. "I'm not going to be stopped by a child."

"What's your purpose here?" Alice asked, the only question that would come to mind at the moment.

"Disable as many of the ship's systems as I can from engineering," Juno said. "That's what I was sent here to do, and I still can from this cabin." She held up her comm unit and activated a sequence on it with her free hand. Alice's suit detected a power build up coming from the woman's communication unit and realized that she'd fashioned a small electromagnetic pulse bomb.

Without taking a second to think, Alice sprinted across the room and pushed Juno into the mass recycler then activated it mentally. A multitude of mulching teeth and molecular reclamation tools set to work at a frightening pace to recycle Juno and her comm unit as Alice shut the thick insulated door. A power surge marked the detonation of the improvised electromagnetic pulse device on the controls for the recycler, but there was no outer effect.

"Gor blimey, you recycled her!" Nesh exclaimed.

Alice was as surprised as anyone else. "I thought I could contain the blast in the machine. I didn't think it would try to recycle her. These things have safety measures so they don't process living things, don't they?"

"Not industrial ones like this," Nesh laughed. "I know, I shouldn't be laughing, but, God!"

"You're right, that's the only safe place to set off an EMP in the room, but you still recycled her ass," Timmerman chucked as he opened the lid to the settling machine. Red lights blinking on the recycler's display indicated that something had gotten stuck, and Alice immediately regretted looking. The mass recycler had strands of Juno's vacsuit stuck in its mulching teeth, and there was just enough evidence of the woman left to tell the rest of the tale.

Officer Timmerman closed the lid and crossed himself. "This story'll live on, I'm sure of that. Guess she shouldn't have called our commanding officer a child."

"Sergeant Valent," Finn said through Alice's comm. "We just detected a minor pulse down there, everything all right?"

"We caught our traitor," Alice replied.

"And? Are they in custody? Sensors are dodgy in that section. There's some kind of interference."

"We took care of her," Alice said, deactivating the counter surveillance chip laying on the deck at her feet.

"Are you taking her to the brig for interrogation?" Frost asked, interjecting from the bridge.

Alice closed the lid of the mass recycler and thought for a moment before answering. Her officers were watching her, hanging on what she'd say next, she assumed. "Not enough of her left for interrogation, Sir. Sorry. Resuming normal security operations."

The channel to the bridge closed and Alice couldn't help but look at the recycler and shake her head. "Well, that was a learning experience."

CHAPTER 43
ALL OR NOTHING

Minh-Chu watched as three of the Warlord's missile pods, launched into place long minutes before, fired hundreds of small electromagnetic pulse flak missiles at the imposing Order of Eden destroyer. His fighter wing reduced their power output levels, just as they'd practiced in simulation, and fired their own EMP flack missiles, adding hundreds of their own projectiles to the impending display.

The Barricade's countermeasures came to life, small rapid-fire cannons sweeping their fire across the thousands of incoming targets, and only one of its flak cannons belched exploding pods of magnetically charged shrapnel ahead of the ship. It all worked in their favour, it was all noise, and there was so much to fire at that the Barricade's green crew didn't know to focus on the five incoming fighters instead of trying to repel the incoming missiles. "I couldn't believe the intelligence the first time I saw it, and I'm still having trouble swallowing it," Minh-Chu said.

"What's that, Ronin?" Jake asked from where he and his squad were pressed into the small personnel carrier compartment affixed to the bottom of Minh-Chu's Uriel fighter.

Minh-Chu activated his antimatter projectile cannons and began powering up the disruptor beam emitter mounted on the front of his fuselage. "They really are sending destroyers across the Iron Head Nebula with green skeleton crews," Minh-Chu replied. The clash of exploding micro missiles against the forward shields of the Barricade made for an impressive fireworks display. He easily guided his fighter around the narrow flak cannon fire. The destroyer had forty such cannons, and they should have all been firing. Minh could only assume that they didn't have the staff aboard to operate them. "This is going to be the biggest piece of candy anyone has ever taken from a baby," he said before addressing the other four fighters in his formation. "Dump the rest of your electro mag missiles onto their hangar shields, I'm going to punch through." He spared a glance from his instruments to admire the jagged front of the ship, with edges that spread out from its general rectangular structure that looked like forward-facing teeth. There were heavily shielded weapons, emitter systems and receiver arrays built into the ends of those arms. Between four of the main emitter arms was their target: a hangar deck made to launch state of the art Violent Encounter Resolution fighters, the new craft Regent Galactic was building for the Order Fleet.

"My scanners are giving me no good readings in that direction, there's so much electrical and flak garbage in the way, they've gotta be blind by now," replied Tempest, the pilot flying the Uriel on Minh's port side. "And we'll be landing on their deck using eyes only thanks to our mess. We're all crazy."

"Mad as escaped mentals," Moira McFadden replied from where she was, in the small troop compartment attached to Minh's fighter. "Can't believe I'm going along with this."

"Counting down from eleven seconds," Minh-Chu interrupted as he watched the planned path of the stealthed antimatter mines from the Warlord close in on the Barricade. The pair of corvettes was just coming out of their wormhole beside it, and the cargo hauler wouldn't be far behind.

Minh-Chu's shields registered a graze from two of the beam weapons mounted along the sides of the destroyer. The front of the ship lit up as it opened fire on all five of the Samurai Squadron fighters in his formation, sending suppressive energy fire in broad arcs around the ship.

"Antimatter explosion number one in three," Minh-Chu said, realizing that he was gripping his controls harder only as he felt the white-knuckled pressure on his fingers. "Two," he counted. rechecking his distance. His fighters were right where they should be, any closer and their shields would not protect them. "One."

The first antimatter mine burst directly beneath the fore section of the Barricade, and there was a heartbeat's time when the antimatter drifted freely in the cold void before it made contact with tiny particles of matter clinging to the vessels' shields. The explosion radiated outward, bathing everything for thousands of kilometres in waves of light.

"-won't have a chance for our sensors to recover before the second one hits," Tempest said as her comms came back online. "Predicted activation in three." Minh-Chu watched as his sensors started reporting shadows, the barest of gravitational measurements pointing out the two corvettes and the destroyer.

"Two," Tempest said over their scratchy communications channel. Minh-Chu hoped that the second mine was in position, then saw a glimpse of it, or what he was sure must have been it. Its cloaking had failed, and he watched as its powerful chemical thruster blasted it across the black of space.

"One," Minh-Chu and Tempest said at the same time as the deadly self-propelled mine finished its relatively short trip between the pair of corvettes. It exploded with the full fury of the first antimatter mine directly behind them, further away from Samurai Squadron than the first. He couldn't see the pair of Samurai Squadron fighters that were set up behind the wormhole, but if they were where they should be, they would be far from harm. He wouldn't be able to cut through all the noise in the area to check, and they were supposed to be shut down so they would be difficult to detect, meaning he wouldn't know their fate until it was time to escape the area. That wouldn't be for some time.

Minh-Chu's sensors recovered within seconds of the detonation, and he checked his people first to find that two of them had suffered minor damage, and that all the boarding team members checked out fine. All pilots reported ready, and he could hear a couple of them laughing, and Tempest saying, "Corvette One and Corvette Two's shields are fried, they've taken minor damage from the torpedoes. Time for us to split off, Ronin."

"Stand by with your payload, execute defensive manoeuvres while I make my run," Minh-Chu said as he verified that the Barricade's shields were almost down across the ship, but they were starting to recharge. "Time for a real show."

"Better hurry, Ronin, that disruptor cannon's capacitor module is glowing," Moira said from the bottom side of his hull.

"Do we have cover?" Minh-Chu asked as he glanced at several mission counters. The one he was really looking forward to was just dropping to zero, and the Warlord revealed itself. Its antimatter enhanced ion thruster pods and the new main engine at the rear of the dark hulled ship powered the vessel towards the corvettes. Big bore launcher holes released self-propelled electromagnetic pulse mines that pushed off in several different directions. The front of the ship lit up as its massive stationary railguns fired in quick succession and hatches opened revealing rapid-fire electromagnetic pulse guns. "We're here, Hun," Ashley replied. "You go make an impression on that destroyer, guys."

The mines already set up in the area began firing short-range missiles and draining their power cells as they fired beam weapons at the pair of corvettes. The area was alight with the deadly weapons they'd brought to defeat the Order ships. "Aye, aye," Minh-Chu said as he thrust towards the front of the destroyer. The first few shots at his Uriel fighter came when he was only five thousand kilometres away, and they were wide of the mark. By the time he closed to two thousand, anti-fighter rounds pounded on his energy shields as though they were the hammer and he was the anvil. "Okay, they seem to have some kind of reserve scanners. A gunner has a lock on me." Both his port side fore thrusters took damage before he reached his target, a place right between the four major arms reaching out from the front of the ship.

"Just get the door open," Jake said.

Minh's targeting computer locked on to the main hangar doors of the Barricade and he fired his disruptor beam weapon, the capacitors humming loudly as they fed the white beam, and a neat square was etched deeply into the forward hangar doors. Minh-Chu tried to ignore the hits his shields were taking from the gunner aboard the enemy ship, and pulled the trigger on his antimatter enhanced auto cannons, marking a violent line of damage across the front of the hangar doors ahead. He fired another pair of bursts and a section of the hangar doors large enough for his fighter to enter exploded outward. "Not bad, almost looks like I used a plasma cutter," Minh-Chu muttered to himself. His damaged thruster pods ripped free of their articulated arms, escaping in separate directions and sending his fighter spinning towards the front of the destroyer.

"Oh crap," Jake said from beneath the fighter.

"Yup, dead, we're going to splat agains' the front of tha' thing," Moira added.

"Shhh, no backseat driving," Minh-Chu said as he fought to compensate for the missing thruster pods and get the fighter clear of the blast radius. He was down to backup power and what was left in the shield capacitors, and those started draining as soon as the destroyer's anti-fighter guns got a shot at him.

"Wish I believed in the Almighty right about now, would love a prayer," Moira quipped as Minh-Chu manually fought for control of his fighter's spin. The gunner seemed to lose his bead for several seconds, and he was able to right his fighter. Pinging against his lower aft thruster pods was a clear indication that the gunner on the Barricade had found his mark again, and he meant to pick the wings off his fly.

"Oh, dear God," Moira said. "I know this plan is crazy, but please grant us grace so we don't die like idio-"

Her prayer was interrupted as a large chunk of armour plating from the destroyer's hangar bumped against the trooper carrier compartment. It couldn't be helped, and Minh knew it wouldn't cause serious damage. "Ronin!" Jake shouted, alarmed.

"Don't worry, a little filler and paint and she'll be good," Minh-Chu replied. At long last, he closed on the opening on the destroyer's hangar doors and flew straight in, firing his thrusters hard to decelerate and land on the deck. To his surprise, the landing was soft and graceful. "Welcome to the hangar deck. The vacuum outside is a balmy twelve hundred degrees, but it's cooling fast folks, so get your kit and get in gear."

Two Uriels came in right behind him. They had troops to drop off as well, and would be leaving. Minh-Chu rechecked the condition of his fighter and shook his head. "I'm afraid I'm writing my bird off for the rest of this mission. I'm joining up with Jake and his people. Take over, Tempest."

"I hear you, good luck."

* * *

Alice entered the bridge and took her place at her station. It felt strange to have a post on the bridge to return to at all, but someone from security had to be there when they could. Her people were posted strategically around the ship, so she had no reason to wander the corridors. A quick check of the mission status screen confirmed what she already knew from being directly connected to the ship – that Jake and his team had landed safely aboard the destroyer.

It was something she needed to confirm; Alice needed to know that they'd made the perilous journey there and that Jake's fate was back in his own hands. She loved Minh-Chu like an uncle, but that didn't relieve the uneasiness she felt at her father being carted through dangerous space in a tiny trooper carrier compartment on the underside of a Uriel fighter. With her father's location confirmed, she felt comfortable disconnecting from the ship's computer and using her station as well as her comm unit to keep in touch. The noise level from the combat operation was rising by the minute as everyone followed the master plan, and it was starting to feel like there was pressure building in her head as more voices, more signals, joined the racket.

Alice sighed at the sudden silence in her mind and focused on what was happening on the bridge.

"Port aft shields down to twelve percent," announced Finn.

Ashley guided the Warlord into a quick roll crossing the front axis of the three corvettes that revealed themselves and began pounding the ship's shields. Alice could hear the click and scrape of their large munitions launchers firing as they were reloaded with mobile missile magazines that sped away from the Warlord in all directions, turning towards their enemy targets and rapid firing hundreds of deadly projectiles per second.

Alice's station was the most boring place on the bridge, with her captured crewmember marked with a crossed X. The crewmembers she had marked for high scrutiny were circled on the ship interior map, and she could see exactly what they were doing at the damage control stations, which wasn't much at the moment. They weren't even talking to each other.

"Hard shunt power from reactors five and six to the aft shield array," Frost said. "Need to recharge those quick. Any good analysis on what they're firing?"

"Their main weapon is a complicated energy burst cannon with some kind of component in the beam that turns some of the power they're transmitting into solids. The part that's damaging us isn't travelling near the speed of light, but it's energy. Never seen anything like it," Kadri reported. "I've got no counter."

It took a moment for Alice to realize that the Warlord wasn't fighting the corvettes that had come through the wormhole, something she'd overlooked while she was connected to the ship computer because she was focusing on internal security. They were fighting ships that had just decloaked and entered the fight, ships that had been watching all along.

"That's not human technology," Frost said. "Give me all the power you can for forward shielding. We have to destroy all three of the new corvettes."

Alice flinched at the sound of a weapon rapidly impacting the hull several times. Her security screen marked several cabins in the lower aft section of the ship as a hazard.

"Small hull fracture and damage from a disintegration weapon," David announced. "We have a steward cabin breached, the adjacent hallway is open to radiation, and supply compartment twenty-four C is breached. Sealing the section off."

"Good, now focus on forward shields a minute," Finn told David. They worked at their stations quickly, diverting power from several reactors to the forward grid. After a few seconds of artful rerouting, the forward section of the Warlord's grid was nearly overloaded.

A status shift in Alice's station alerted her and she read the report aloud. "A damage control team is reporting they can seal those breaches from the inside using a liquid ergranian patch."

"They're clear to go," Finn replied, still busy with his duties.

"Ordering them in, then," Alice said as she did so from her post.

"Ash, let's cannon them down," Frost said, activating the manual tactical controls for the forward-facing railguns. The weapons were well beyond what anyone would expect to see on a ship in their class. When the railguns running under the bridge of the Warlord fired, the crew could feel it throughout most of the ship, and there were whole sections of decks dedicated to the deadly projectile weapons. From where she was sitting, Alice could see the railguns were loaded with special warheads that were all slug for the back half, with a shaped explosive at the front.

Ashley's reply was expressed through the movements of the Warlord, as she flipped the ship end-over-end and turned so the nose of the fighting vessel pointed at the three strange corvettes. One of them hadn't fired since Alice arrived on the bridge, and it was venting atmosphere. The other two had their broadsides facing the Warlord, firing weapons that seemed to require wide glowing emitters instead of a contained barrel.

The deck under Alice's feet rumbled as Frost fired each of the railguns in turn. There was only a second and a half between the last weapon firing and the sequence starting over. The Warlord's fore shields took fire, but Ashley kept the ship in a strafing pattern with the nose pointed directly at the enemy vessels, giving Frost a long opportunity to rapidly fire the biggest guns aboard for over forty seconds before Finn announced, "Fore shields down to thirty-five percent."

"Evasive action," Frost said as he released the manual tactical controls. "Tell me they don't have some kind of heavy kinetic damper or gravity countermeasure."

"Gravity countermeasure? That's not even possible," Finn said.

Only the first round of shots were stopped by energy shielding, the rest ripping through two of the cruiser class ships, leaving broad breaches in their armour. "So glad those ships haven't proven you wrong," Frost said.

The third cruiser broke away, only grazed by the torrent of explosive projectiles. It returned fire with an unexpected barrage.

The hull whined under the pressure of heat damage and pinged as solid matter impacted its surface. "All dorsal shields are down," Finn reported. "We lost some emitters in that last attack; we're missing coverage we can't compensate for."

"Bring us about, get that ship in front of us," Frost said. "All weapons focus on that ship."

The enemy ship pointed its nose downward, exposing the top surface to the Warlord as it accelerated at them, firing weapons installed across the dorsal side of their vessel. Flashes of light across the dark green and blue skin of the enemy vessel were punctuated by the sounds of hull impacts on the Warlord, and the sounds of the ship systems changed, rising in pitch. "Multiple breaches across our aft dorsal sections and aft port sections. Sending damage control teams in with temporary shielding," David reported.

The Warlord finished turning towards the enemy ship and Frost fired the railguns at the centre of the vessel. The delay between the rumble under Alice's feet and the visible impact on the enemy vessel grew shorter and shorter as it closed the distance. A glance at Ashley working at the helm revealed that she had rotated all the Warlord's thruster pods so they were firing in reverse.

There was no noticeable delay between Frost firing the railguns or the Warlord's missiles and the visible impacts on the enemy ship by the time Frost's rounds began breaking through the middle section of the enemy ship.

"That's it! That's all the time I can give you!" Ashley said as she sent the Warlord in a sideways arc so that it was out of the enemy ship's way. She spun the Warlord around so Frost could fire the stationary guns at the rear of the enemy vessel, and he hit it several times before the power readings from the enemy ship dropped to a negligible level.

"Why was that bugger so much tougher than the others? It had the same profile, near the same mass."

"Scans results coming back from breaches in the enemy ship," Kadri reported, "Edxi crew, evidence of several major internal explosions. I read twenty-nine survivors, though I can't tell what condition they're in. Ship systems seem disabled, but there are several very low powered objects still running between eighty and one hundred and fifty watts apiece."

"What about backup? Any signs of incoming ships?" Frost asked as he looked through the ship status and command hologram projected in front of half of his field of view. The other half of his view was purely tactical, with an interactive map, strategy assistant software, and targeting system.

"The same two signals are coming in, backup will be here in a hundred and twenty-three minutes at the earliest," Kadri replied. "This plan is working. I can't believe it, but it's working."

"Can't say that yet, we're still waiting on Captain's results with that destroyer. Get us along side that ship, let's make an impression. How are my damage control teams doing, Alice?"

Alice was startled at being called on; she wasn't trained to fill in for David, who was busy helping Finn find workarounds for systems that were damaged or destroyed. She looked at her panel and focused on the damage control teams marked on her security map. "One sec," she said as she made sense of their short status reports. "Okay, they're all on assignment, most are patching minor breaches and approaching sections of inner hull that registered heat damage. They report two injured, medical has already gotten to them. I'm going to send two of my security people to help a team working on the aft dorsal section."

"Good, keep an eye on it while the geniuses behind me work on the bigger problems," Frost said.

"Aye," Alice replied. A direct message came through her station from Remmy Sands, whose team had boarded the Sunny Shifter, the military cargo hauler they were after. She answered it using her personal comm unit. "What's up?"

"Why aren't you using your neural interface?" he asked. Pulse weapon fire sounds sizzled and popped in the background.

"Turned it off when I got to my post, it was getting hard to concentrate," Alice replied. "Why?"

"I could use a hand breaking through this system, they've got some kind of hardware lock set up and I need to find the system they use to control it. It would be fantastic if you could get it open while you're in there, too."

"You can't do it from there? You're right on the ship."

"My interface is reporting twenty hardware locks on their system, each linked to different programs. I know there's only one real lock, but I don't want to waste time manually figuring out which one it is. I can give you a relay connection to the trunk line from my position."

Alice immediately had a mental picture of what Remmy was seeing in the system. It was as though the computer aboard the Sunny Shifter was representing the single hardware lock securing the system with twenty doors, but only one of them led to the location of the main processing unit. Remmy could crack them one after the other and hope to get lucky, or he could get help. "Lemme assign my post to someone else and send a message to Frost telling him what I'm doing." She activated her neural node and took control of the flow of data, then assigned her post to Havernash, an experienced security officer who was guarding one of the hallways leading to the bridge. It only took her a moment more to send a message to Frost with the details of the situation.

"Activate the link," Alice expressed through her comm channel with Remmy.

"Wow, your neural voice sounds a lot older," Remmy said before activating the direct line to the Sunny Shifter's computer systems.

"All right, time to find out which door hides the prize," Alice replied. "You should look into getting a neural node put in, you could do this yourself."

"Nope, had one. Forgot to eat for a while and woke up in an addiction treatment centre," Remmy replied hurriedly. "Gotta keep a safe distance between me and the data."

"I know what you mean," Alice said as she got familiar with the Sunny Shifter hauler's operating system, which tried to reject her several times, but she easily found her way around. There was an artificial intelligence inside, roughly trying to block her, reporting a digital incursion to the bridge staff. She tried to activate several weapons systems aboard the hauler, and the primitive artificial intelligence shifted its attention to block her attempts. With a thought, she activated a piece of software from the Warlord's library that continually attempted to infect and control the Sunny Shifter's weapons systems, distracting the artificial intelligence. It tried to execute programs to assist with the computer's security outside of the bridge, and she halted the processes.

"Where is your hardware really located?" Alice asked herself as she virtually attacked all the security walls protecting the information she was after. After several attempts the ship's artificial intelligence realized what was happening and tried to counter, but it was too late. "The response from one of the hardware locks on the main system was faster than the rest, I'm sending you the location now."

"Holy crap, that was fast!" Remmy said. "We're moving out. Thanks, Alice."

"You're welcome," she replied aloud. She deactivated her neural node and realized that Havernash was just arriving behind her. "Sorry Percy, you can return to your post."

"Oh, all right," he said with a quizzical expression. "Did you send the order by mistake?"

"No, I just thought it would take me longer to hack the Sunny Shifter's peripheral systems and find her main processing vault, but it turns out that the hauler's AI wasn't all that bright. Sorry."

"Well that answers another question," he said with a light chuckle.

"What's that?"

"Honestly?"

"Yes, Havernash, spit it out," Frost said over his shoulder. "Your superior officer isn't asking just for conversation's sake."

"Uh, a bunch of us kind of thought you got the promotion because you were the Captain's daughter," Percy Havernash replied awkwardly. "But you took care of some serious problems, and if you're hacking enemy ships while you're doing your thing on the bridge, well..." He eyed Frost and Kadri, who both had an eye on him before continuing. "Looks like you can do things none of us can. So, um, what are your orders, Sergeant?"

Alice couldn't help but smile a little at the compliment, even if it was pressured out of him. She tried not to think about how she got her position, suspecting the same thing that Havernash and his fellows, but it was good to hear that a few of them might be coming around. "Back to your post three frames down the hall, Percy."

"Aye," he replied.

"And keep your yap shut next time you have an opinion and not a report," Frost added. "We're in it, lad. No time for back slapping or navel gazing!" He waited until Havernash was off the bridge before turning towards Alice and David. "I need you to pay attention there, help other stations as you can. I know it looks like we're through the worst, but we're

288

nowhere near. Times like these, a crew relaxes a little, and that's when it all goes sideways."

"Aye, aye," Alice replied, feeling singled out.

"Aye, aye" David added.

"Captain Valent is about to break through to the command deck of the Barricade," Kadri announced. "Looks like the resistance was waiting for them there."

CHAPTER 44
QUICK COMMUNICATIONS

"Our scouts have been defeated," said the translator to Clark. He was in his private quarters. Only one room was dry, and the entire wall was transparent so he could watch the Order of Eden Fleet and the warped stars beyond. They were in transit, using one giant wormhole. He watched the smaller ships move like a school of fish between whales, luminescent gaps in their armour shining along their lengths. One of the Edxians had broken through on an emergency channel and interrupted Clark as he was preparing to join a combat operation as soon as they emerged from their wormhole.

"When?" Clark asked.

"Moments ago. A ship called the Warlord is assaulting a group of your vessels. My commander in the area sought to lend aid," replied the Edxian. There was no way of knowing who was speaking. They refused to identify themselves unless Clark met one in person, and that had only taken place once. Another fact of speaking with the Edxians that annoyed him to no end was their access to communications systems his people hadn't been able to reverse engineer. They could communicate instantaneously with any of their ships. At first they thought they used methods that were similar to their space travel technology, but no, it was something different, and they weren't sharing. Every time he had a conversation with an Edxian, he couldn't help but think about the technology they were using to communicate with him.

"The Warlord was last reported on the far side of the Iron Head Nebula, you aren't permitted to have ships there," Clark replied, suppressing his rising frustration.

"We sent them to observe one of your more vulnerable points. We were right to do so."

"That position and several like it are left vulnerable because the losses we suffer are acceptable when you consider how much hardware will make

290

it through the nebula. Having said that, it's no business of yours, Communicator. Your job is to supervise and secure the eleven worlds your people are allowed to settle as broods. How is that going?"

"The humans on Pandem resist more than expected. You promised they would be easy fodder for our young," replied the translated voice. It was easy to imagine the repulsive Edxian speaking with the lights out, its carapace plates shifting as it clicked and hissed in its own language.

"Your young are not robust enough," Clark said. "Maybe you landed eggs from the wrong genetic line. Just like I'm starting to believe your commanders are of an inferior brood themselves. By interfering in human concerns so far from your designated territory, you've exposed yourselves as aggressors in our war. I'm maintaining the Order of Eden as a system to deliver worlds to you as brood planets, and to hide your presence in our galaxy. If everyone finds out that you're here, that the true purpose of the Order comes down to supporting your race's desire to move into the Milky Way, then everything I've done becomes pointless, and I may as well dissolve the Order and take my core fleet elsewhere."

"The overly-complex political manoeuvres of your people do not concern us. We have already begun building our own army of humans and they are on their way to the Milky Way, as you call it."

Clark had heard that before, that the Edxians had somehow bred humans in their own galaxy and they were a subjugated people in their culture. He'd been hearing of this human army for months, but never met a single human who said they were a servant to the Edxians. He decided to move on to more important things. "The Warlord defeated your people and still has escape capabilities?"

"Yes, they were well armed. It was unexpected."

"Did they capture any of your people or technology?" Clark asked.

"Not yet, our ships were able to self corrode their systems. The crew will find other means of survival," the communicator replied.

"You mean they will try to take the Warlord?" Clark asked.

"Yes."

"Then some of your people will be captured!" Clark burst. He couldn't contain himself any longer. "Dead or alive, Jacob Valent will drag what's left of one of them in front of the British Alliance, the Core Worlds media, and everyone else, and prove that you're in our galaxy!"

"My people will kill Jacob Valent and take the Warlord. This is something that will be. There will be no revelation. Humans are weak. You will see."

The communication ended and Clark was left in the dark with his rage. The peaceful scene of his fleet around the command carrier was something to glare at, not take solace in. "God damn it! Why did I take Hampon's place?" he shouted.

He knew there was no one else he trusted. If the Order and their various partners weren't in place to at least try and contain the Edxian threat, they would wage open war against humanity. If the Order turned and fought the Edxians, they'd win for a day, wiping out a few small fleets. Not long after, a few months, perhaps a year later, the Edxian warrior clans would come, and humanity could be subjugated utterly, or destroyed.

"I either recruit more into the Order until we can win every war in front of us, or I disappear and save myself," he whispered into the darkness. A mental image of Eve in one of her fine dresses addressing a crowd with fevered zeal flashed through his mind and he shook his head. "She's become a freak of faith, believing her own rhetoric. There's no trustworthy leader there."

His mind wandered to the Warlord and he couldn't help thinking about Jacob Valent. "If he were in my position, would he do anything differently?" The question haunted him as it filled the empty room, and continued to for days after.

Ayan took it upon herself to guide a pair of brothers, the MacMillans, from the shuttle transporting them from the Port Rush recruitment base to their new apartment inside the Everin Building. She was escorted by a pair of senior placement officers, security people, and she had Lacey at her side. The brothers looked ragged, wide-eyed, and just recently scrubbed. They were surprised to see her and Lacey with their security escort, even more shocked that she was going to personally lead them to their new quarters in the building.

They were experienced shipwrights from the York-Townsend System sectors away, and were trapped on Tamber when the Holocaust Virus infected the starliner taking them home. York-Townsend was struck hard by the virus, and the whole system was a lawless waste. The most common footage available was gang recordings made by groups bragging about territory, their supply stockpile, and their firepower. If they were anything like the gangs that were plaguing Port Rush City and many parts of Kambis, then it wasn't fit to return to. Haven Shore was the first bit of luck the pair she was guiding had in nearly a year. They'd met the gangs in Port Rush and been forced to work for one on several damaged shuttles. They were only able to escape by stowing away in one once it was finished.

The new recruiting representatives followed Ayan and her entourage as she told them about the building, asking the MacMillans about what they wanted to do, and about their hopes upon arriving on Haven Shore. "Hopes?" asked the younger brother, who looked older at first with an out of control beard, standing a few centimetres taller than his brother. "What d'you mean, hopes?"

"Haven Shore will be here a long time," Ayan told him with a smile. "The people who have stayed with Haven Shore and Triton Fleet have survived a direct assault from the Order, and we won a fight with the

Carthans. Skilled people like you and your brother have dreams, I'm sure, and even though we're headed into a war, those dreams can help shape what happens here."

"That's..." the older MacMillan brother started. He stopped and rubbed a scar running across his cheek. "Week ago, we were starvin' on the Toxic Coast. Now we're in a lift goin' down to family quarters. All respect, Lady, but I think I'm already dreamin'. Ask us again when that passes."

"I will," Ayan said. "We're short on qualified machinists and shipwrights, so I'm afraid you'll be working in our main hangar starting the day after tomorrow." They stepped out of the lift and were welcomed into the family quarters by the thick smell of hot food coming from the cafeteria. They passed the double doors leading there and Ayan was thoroughly glad to see about thirty people from that section of the building eating a variety of fresh dishes that wouldn't have been possible if they didn't have something left in storage. The most important thing about what she was seeing in that room as she passed wasn't the food on the table, it was the atmosphere. She'd seen it before on ships she'd served on, that wonderful, mild euphoria shared by the crew after a crisis had been overcome and they felt safe once more. "This cafeteria is communal, every section of the building has one," Lacey was explaining. "Haven Shore and Triton Fleet provide the food, but you'll have to join the schedule for cleaning and food preparation. You'll have to participate in three meals a week until the section is filled, then it'll be down to one. You'll help prepare a meal under a cook that directs the kitchens and clean up afterwards. The rest of the week, you won't have to worry about it."

"So there's a cook who will show us what we're to do?" the younger brother asked. "We won't have to muck around on our own, try to concoct something in a pot?"

"No," Ayan said. "I'm no cook myself, but when I was on shift for my section I just followed directions, that's all you have to do."

"You were on the schedule?"

"Everyone who lives in the Everin Building is. Rank doesn't exclude you from eating, so I wasn't exempt from a bit of work once a week. I don't think I would have gotten to know the people in my section at all if I didn't work in the kitchen," Ayan said. It had been a couple of weeks since she'd thought about it, and she couldn't help but wonder how Alaka would make out when he took her place on the schedule. She would have to check in on him, even if it was just to see him working in the kitchen.

"You're probably wondering why we don't use automated food preparation," Lacey added, "And the answer is fairly simple. We don't have

294

the machinery right now, and even when we do, we'll still maintain a living kitchen, where the people who live here make their own dishes. The two hours a week you spend cooking is important partially because you will get to know the people you're working with, and you'll have an opportunity to do something for your neighbours. It makes all the difference, you'll see."

They turned a corner and came to a freshly made set of sliding double doors. "Here it is," Ayan said, gesturing towards the door. "This is your apartment, here. Besides you, only security can enter, and they have to log their reasons for entry with their superiors, so you shouldn't expect a visit from them. There's a reasonable common room, a private room for both of you and, since you're both technicians, there's a spare room that you can use for personal projects. Oh, and there's a bathroom. There are other rules to the Everin Building, but since you passed all our checks during the recruitment process, I doubt you'll conflict with any of them. You should look them over anyway, just so you're aware of the laws here." She fixed both brothers with a big smile and watched as the door slid open and the brothers looked inside. "You can drop your things here and join the others in the cafeteria. You're on your own from here, if you need any advice or direction on where you have to be for work, the Crewcast system will tell you everything you need to know, including your credit rate. Like you were told before, you maintain your position in the Everin Building by working consistently, and over time earn luxury credits that you can convert to cash, give to people for services and goods, or use to buy extras from our shop. There's not much there now because we're using most of our resources to build and trade, but it'll get better."

"I don't know how to thank you," one brother said. The older brother embraced her abruptly and enthusiastically.

"That'll do," Ayan said after she enjoyed the embrace for a moment. "Good luck, and welcome to the family."

"Thank you," said the older brother, nodding and wiping a tear away.

Ayan led her group back to the lift, leaving the MacMillan brothers behind. "Just like that," she told the pair of recruiting managers walking behind her. "Be warm, show them the essentials, remind them of their responsibilities, answer their questions, and direct them to Crewcast, but make sure that everyone you're bringing into the Everin Building feels like they're joining a family. They are, that's what this is, and it's not just *a* family, it's *your* family that you're welcoming them into. If you don't feel confident about someone after a few days, make your supervisor aware and try to find a solution. In most cases, it'll be an information problem, you'll have to find out why someone isn't fitting in from them, from the people they've had friction with, and your job won't be finished until you've gotten them settled in. Your supervisor will make sure you aren't overwhelmed, and you'll have the help of the Section Elders, too. If any part of the system fails, make sure you address it right away with your supervisor. This is going to take time, and you'll run into problems, but this lifestyle works, it just requires patience, thought, and respect."

"I understand," said Placement Officer Stillwell, a tall, fit gentleman with a friendly face. "I never got a chance to thank you for this job, I would have never guessed I'd end up doing social work after fighting on the Triton a year ago."

"Lacey placed you," Ayan replied. "But you're welcome."

"You're welcome," Lacey said. "Either of you have any questions?"

Placement Officer Foucot, a shorter dark haired woman who had a similar history to her comrade's. smiled at them both. She could light a room with her grins. "Thank you for, well, everything, Commander. I don't know where I'd be if it weren't for you and all your friends, er, crew. Maybe still on the Palamo? Who knows?" She hugged Lacey, then Ayan. "Doesn't matter now," she said. "Here I am."

"Here you are," Ayan repeated with a smile. The first lift arrived and Ayan said, "I'm going down, you should take the next to the roof. There are six groups waiting to be escorted. Your security teams are up there, too."

The lift doors slid closed, leaving Ayan alone with Lacey. Ayan took a deep breath before telling her what she'd been holding off all day. "I'm moving to the Triton, my father is taking over operations on Tamber."

"I know," Lacey said. "And you're going to ask me to stay here to take care of the Everin Building."

"I'm sorry," Ayan said. "You've been an amazing second, a wonderful friend. I just think they need you here more."

"You're right," Lacey said, looking at Ayan with a straight face. "I am an astonishingly good friend," she said with a dramatic flair.

Ayan couldn't help but laugh, and she was joined by Lacey for a chuckle. "I'm going to miss you."

"I won't miss you, because I'll make sure my apartment has a spare bedroom, and you'll be visiting. If you don't, I'll just have to go up there."

"Fair enough," Ayan replied, relieved that it had gone well. "You're really all right with this?"

"I've had my taste of action," Lacey replied. "I'll be honest, I didn't recognize you when you were in command – you were stony, cold. I respect that, and I understand that emotions get in the way when you're in that situation, but I can't do that. Logistics, making a home for people, that's

296

me. And as for watching you in command, I'd rather take a piece of your off time, if there's any left after Jacob comes back."

"Why do you say that?" Ayan asked.

"You miss him, I see it all the time," Lacey said. "The Warlord is tops on your watch list, and not just because you know they'll probably bring supplies that'll trickle down here. Even though he didn't fight for you, probably doesn't deserve you, you've been leaning back towards him for all the time I've known you."

"I didn't give him a chance to fight for me, my mess with Liam got in the way, sent him running, I'm sure," Ayan said. "Still can't believe that all that happened because I took the advice of an oracle machine. Should have never listened. He stays away and I don't blame him."

"Still," Lacey said. "I would have fought for you."

Ayan couldn't help but blush at the unexpected compliment, "I know."

"But you and he are two halves, and all that," Lacey said. "I wouldn't get in the way, because I am such a good friend, yeah?"

"You are," Ayan said.

"He'll forgive you," Lacey said. "But you might have to be quiet and listen to him when he tells you how that felt, watching you with Liam."

"Yeah," Ayan said, feeling the weight of her need to atone. "I owe him that."

"Then I bet you'll be far away. Just remember to visit," Lacey told her. "Or else."

"I'd sooner forget the entire Everin Building," Ayan replied.

"Oh, speaking of which," Lacey said, "You have to address Haven Shore and the new recruits in the other centres. They're uneasy, and there's a little trickle of people leaving from the new bases."

"If I weren't so tired," Ayan said with a sigh.

"You're the one who told me to watch for this sort of thing," Lacey replied with a wink. "It can wait until mid-morning tomorrow, but I have to schedule something soon so they know they're not being treated like baggage."

"That's not the attitude you're seeing, is it?" Ayan asked.

"Not in the majority, but I can see it happening. So, late tomorrow morning?"

"Mid-afternoon?" Ayan bargained.

"I'll schedule it now."

"Can't believe I have to write a speech," Ayan said.

"You'll be fine, I can help if you like," Lacey replied.

"I know, and thanks much, but I'm so much better with ships. Putting an engine together is so much easier than pulling people together."

At long last, Lucius Wheeler had found a transport the right size, headed in the right direction. Nine sectors away from Rega Gain and even further from the Order of Eden, he felt he could finally sleep easy. He dropped his old-fashioned American duster onto the narrow chair in his small passenger cabin and checked the energy level on his disintegration pistol. The reading said he had six hundred and twenty three shots, but that was only because most of the circuitry thought it was still a medium range stun pistol. He actually only had eighty-nine; the disintegration system hidden in the pistol required a lot more power than a stunner.

He made sure the safety was on and slid it under his pillow. The bed was clean and fresh. The small, high speed transit ship was in great shape as far as he could tell. It had better be, he paid enough for the trip to Visalee. There was a shipyard there, it was where he stole the Cold Reaver, a ship he used as his personal armed shuttle when he couldn't take the Triton somewhere. He'd heard encouraging news: the place was a graveyard. Well, it was good news for him, perhaps not the thousands of people who were torn apart by machines infected with the Holocaust Virus.

There was a new aid station opening near the shipyards for the survivors, and he knew it would be his way in to the Visalee storage complex. Finding a crew would be a different proposition altogether, but he could cross that bridge when he came to it. A tactical alarm went off in his mind, drawing his attention to two armed crewmembers on the other side of his closed door.

"D'you think it's really him? Travelling in the open?" he heard the short one say through the ship's comm system.

"Why not? He probably doesn't even know about the bounty," said the tall woman beside him. "We take him quick and bring him to the captain."

"No, we'll hide him, why should the cap-"

It was all Wheeler had to hear. He snatched his sidearm out from under his pillow, put his armoured duster back on and came through his cabin door kicking the tall one in the knee and shooting several rounds at the short one. The deadly bolts cut through the short crewmember's uniform after a few shots, his last volley reducing the flesh around his collarbone and neck to flaming sludge.

Before his taller assailant could recover and take aim, Wheeler trained his sidearm on her. "Why are you morons trying to take me down?"

"It's a bounty! The Brits are offering millions for you, even more if you're delivered alive," her screeching reply barely cut through the gurgling and flailing of her partner in crime.

"Well, thank you," he said, shooting her in the face until there was nothing recognizable left. Another crewmember came along with a sludge rifle at the ready and Wheeler was already firing in the man's direction before he fired his first shot. The tactical map was as clear as the world around him as it kept him informed of all motion on the ship.

The cabin door across the hall opened, revealing a drowsy young woman who eyed the corpses, then him. "Just a minor social turbulence," Wheeler said. "We'll arrive at our destination on time."

He left her there, agape, as he strode towards the bridge, taking the long way around so he could avoid three crewmembers. The hatch to the bridge was locked, and he unlocked it with a mental command using his connection with the computer. "Hello, Sir," he said as he levelled his smouldering handgun at the captain's head. He and the five crewmembers on the small bridge all turned toward him with surprise. "While this is technically a hijacking, I really only want to make sure that I make it to my destination on time. So, I'll point this nasty little disintegration weapon at you for the next six hours while you make sure no one sends a message to Visalee Harbour telling them that you have a wanted man aboard."

The captain raised his hands slowly. His look of confusion almost made the whole ordeal worth it. "So you want us to continue on our course as normal, and to keep mum about your presence aboard?"

"Exactly. It's going to be harder than you think, though, especially if you have a lot of below-average intelligence crewmembers. I'm jacked into your computer system, so I'll notice if someone tries to send a message about me, and I'll block it. Then I'll kill you, I'll kill them, I'll kill everyone between me and that person, who I won't kill right away. I'll probably use them to properly calibrate this weapon here; I haven't had a chance to do a proper job of it since I built it. That's the problem with custom jobs, you're never really done tinkering. Do you understand?"

"About custom jobs, or keeping quiet?" asked the captain.

"About keeping quiet, for now. We can have a conversation about custom jobs later if you like. We need to pass the time somehow."

"I understand. I'll put a communications block in place right now, if you'll promise not to harm my crew."

"Sure. Aside from the three I've already killed, I won't shoot anyone if we all play nice and get the ship where it's going. When we get there, I leave, and you wait two days before reporting me to the authorities. I should be well on my way by then."

"All right. Is there anything else you want, Mister Collins?" asked the captain.

"No, just a quick trip and a head start," Wheeler replied. He had momentarily forgotten that he'd used the name David Collins to buy his ticket. "I am going to borrow your main hologram projector, though."

"Sorry, we only have screens on this ship, they're more durable," the captain said.

"So they are," Wheeler replied. "I'll borrow your biggest, then." He mentally searched their data storage for the bounty on him and sent the images to the main screen at the front of the bridge. His original face, chiselled and roguishly handsome, rotated in the middle under the title "WANTED BY THE BRITISH ALLIANCE FOR CRIMES AGAINST HUMANITY." Beneath were the raw particulars in a less alarming font.

Any means of retrieval are permitted, with the exception of any methods that may break British Alliance or Common Galactic Laws. If the subject is presented to a British Alliance outpost dead or in an un-revivable state, the bounty to be paid will be no more than four million Universal Currency Units. If presented alive and mentally intact, the transporter and detainer of the subject will be paid ten million Universal Currency Units. A DNA and neural scan match will be used to verify the capture.

"And I was trying so hard to start over, to reformat the old historical memory storage system and get on with things, but they just won't let me leave," Wheeler said to no one in particular.

"It says you're a war criminal and a thief," the helmsman said. "I hope they get you."

Wheeler fired a shot without looking, narrowly missing the crewman's leg. "Sorry, it does that whenever I hear an idiot," he said. "Captain, if you can speed things up and get us to our destination, I'd be grateful. I have a ship to steal and a war to join."

CHAPTER 47
THE RUSH

Minh-Chu Buu hadn't realized how much his memories of being an infantry grunt had dulled until he felt like one all over again following Jacob Valent and Moira McFadden aboard the Barricade. He still made the transition from lead pilot in the operation to backup in one of the boarding teams well, and was relieved he wasn't running any part of that operation.

Their drop was perfect, and Jacob, Moira McFadden, Stephanie Vega and ten other soldiers made the trip to the hangar deck of the enemy destroyer.

Stephanie Vega led half the squad to engineering, starting their rampage to the rear of the ship by using a focused high explosive charge to blast a passage up through four decks. It was then that Minh-Chu realized two important things. Firstly, that he had never been on an important ship raid with Jacob Valent's team. Secondly, there was a method, it was well practiced by the leaders of this mission, and he could barely keep up with its execution.

Stephanie's team blasted their way in initially, then activated stealth systems while the few guards at the rear of the ship were reeling. From what Minh could tell, it seemed to work perfectly. The enemy was moving as though they thought Jake's team was the only one, because they had a different strategy altogether.

With Jacob in the lead, running full tilt through a service hangar packed with supplies, then a steep bare metal staircase leading up several decks, the whole squad moved faster than Minh-Chu had seen outside of simulations. The artificial muscle layer of Minh-Chu's vacsuit had to kick in several times as the team kept up with the captain of the Warlord, and Minh-Chu was out of breath when they finally stopped. His tactical map told him they were one level beneath the main corridor leading to the bridge. As he looked through the transparent map in his helmet, he couldn't help but notice that the rest of the team was trying to catch their breath as well. The powered armour all but Minh-Chu wore was helpful at making someone stronger, but the human body still had to move with it, so a hard run was still exhausting, and Minh felt reassured that he wasn't the only one who needed a few seconds to recover.

Captain Jacob Valent was another matter, however. He stood statue-still for long moments, and Minh-Chu could guess what was going on. He was trying to break through the security systems protecting the destroyer's wireless network. Just as everyone caught their breath, he pulled two shaped charges from his large armoured coat and started walking back the way they came. "Get clear, they're coming." With two tosses that looked as nonchalant as brushing lint off his shoulder, Captain Valent tossed two more charges at the ceiling behind him where they affixed so the blast would fire straight up. "The encryption protecting their internal comms is a joke, these are amateurs." He sounded disappointed.

Everyone scrambled to move back to a safe distance of fifteen metres, Minh-Chu included.

"Set personal shielding to maximum," Jacob said as he leisurely stepped across the invisible line indicating a safe distance.

"Ignore everything I transmit on channel three twelve," Jake said over the comms. "All units, converge on frame thirty six, section nineteen. We'll take the bridge via the main hall. Use stealth systems."

"What are you up to, Captain?" Moira asked.

Minh-Chu grinned and nodded, "I think I know. You're giving them a target by transmitting fake unencrypted orders using proximity radio."

"That location is right above your shaped charges," Moira said, "They're going to fall for that?"

"If I had just graduated from the academy, I might," Minh-Chu said.

Minh-Chu's tactical system indicated that someone was planting explosives on the level above within one metre of Captain Valent's shaped charges.

"Well, there they go," Moira said, "Well done."

As soon as the explosives were armed, Jake looked towards his half-squad, perhaps not realizing that the holographic death's head visage was in full effect so it appeared that his helmet was worn by a putrescent skull. "Two Order Knights just started setting antipersonnel mines in the hall just above my explosives. It's the only way into the bridge. Get ready. I blow this, then we charge. Load anti-framework rounds." He didn't wait for anyone to acknowledge the order before blowing his shaped charges, which set off the antipersonnel mines in the hall ahead and above them.

Minh-Chu's lighter shields took all the damage as the corridor erupted in flame and shrapnel, settling in impenetrable smoke. The sensors in his helmet made up for the terrible visibility in time for Minh-Chu to see Jake leap up into the hole, flinging a fistful of small grenades with one hand towards the blockade the Barricade's crew had set up and firing his long-barrelled Violator Handgun on full auto. Minh-Chu's weapon was on the same pre-set; those rounds moved slower than an energy weapon, and they had to change clips after two hundred and ten shots, but they'd burst against armour, burning at over twenty-eight hundred degrees for several seconds.

Captain Valent's first volley of grenades exploded against the energy shield protecting the enemy crew as he was tossing another handful of the small but devastating explosives. By the time Minh-Chu and the rest of the squad were up through the hole in the ceiling, the hall in front of Jake was a twisted ruin of doors and broken walls leading to senior officer's crew quarters and abandoned secondary control rooms, and the energy barrier protecting the first barricade was gone.

Minh-Chu spotted what was left of one of the Order Knights' torsos to his right, a pile of gore that was already regenerating, and he fired his Violator handgun at the half-ruined head and its chest. He dumped a focused electromagnetic pulse grenade modified to disable a single framework onto it and stepped away. His shields registered a slight decline as it popped, and the framework's activity ceased.

"Good job, Ronin," Moira said.

The remains of the other Order Knight were destroyed by a pair of soldiers using rifles loaded with anti-framework rounds – explosive ammunition that released an electromagnetic charge as well.

Jacob and Moira led the way, calmly walking down the broad corridor towards the barricade. Jake fired his violator handgun on full automatic, the barrel end starting to glow red, while he fired bursts from an overcharged pulse handgun with the other hand. Moira walked right along side him, methodically firing one heavily modified and overcharged energy pistol then the other. Her rate of fire was far slower, but her accuracy was deadly.

The rest of the squad moved along behind them, firing around the bold pair, who were met with resistance at first as the ship's defenders fell back to their second and final barricade, but they were pressed under cover in seconds. Even an attempt by one enemy soldier to throw a seeker grenade into the air was stopped as the boarding team member beside Minh-Chu shot it out of the air by sheer luck, detonating the explosive above the defenders' heads.

The defenders scattered. Minh-Chu shot two of the enemy soldiers several times as he took his turn firing around Jake's right side. One of the enemy soldiers went down when two rounds from Minh-Chu's weapon burned through his armoured hip and thigh. He only had seconds to scream before he was finished off. Anyone caught in the open was cut down as soon as they broke cover. They weren't there to take prisoners, and everyone there knew it.

Without warning, Jake pushed Moira back and charged forward, his shield system drawing as much energy as his suit could provide. "Take cover, now!" he said as he rushed ahead.

As everyone ducked behind a twisted wall or fallen door, an energy reading appeared on Minh-Chu's tactical system that was identified and marked in red. It was an Order Knight in full armour, surrounded by an energy shield, carrying one of their high-powered rifles.

As the Knight emerged from the main bridge doors, Jake careened into her shoulder-first at a dead run. Their shields clashed with a blinding flash, and Minh-Chu's tactical system warned him that the energy barriers' crossing was raising the temperature around them at a rate of several degrees per second.

No one had a clear shot as Jake tried to avoid the business end of the Knight's rifle while keeping her between the bridge doors. All Minh-Chu could do was watch and make sure that there was nothing coming from behind.

Captain Valent managed to get the Order Knight's leg into a lock despite the near frictionless nature of their energy shields. The clashing of energy scarred the deck with red-hot streaks at their feet and the heavy armoured door that was being held open by the width of the Knight.

A pair of enemy soldiers broke cover, firing down the hall. Minh-Chu leaned out to return fire, and was rewarded with several hits on his shield. "I've got this, Commander," said a soldier behind him as she leaned out and ripped through the pair before they could find cover away from the Order Knight and Jake.

The Knight fired several rounds above them as she fought to get her rifle pointed at her assailant, the shots leaving white-hot spots over their heads. She dropped it and reached for a sidearm while Jake let go of her, reaching for something in his jacket.

Minh-Chu was shocked when Jake pulled out a handful of small electromagnetic pulse grenades and dropped them between him and the Order Knight. "Pray to your maker," were the only words Captain Valent had time to say before they went off, blasting both their shields to nothing and severely damaging all the automation in the outer layers of their armour. Whatever strength Jake was using was his own, and the speed of the man astounded Minh-Chu as he managed to snatch the Order Knight again and drag her back through the heavy bridge doors.

The Knight was stunned just long enough for Jake to get a grip under the chin of her helmet, and Jake bashed his enemy's head on the edge of one of a barricade's waist-height metal plates, hard enough to dent her helmet. He put a knee on the Knight's chest, knocked her sidearm from her hand, and drew a cutting tool from his jacket. Just as Jake was getting poised to cut through his enemy's helmet, it fell open.

"You're living on stolen technology, and we will take it from you. All hail the Order," said the fresh-faced young Order Knight before she convulsed. Jake leapt up and took cover.

For several long moments, nothing happened. "Advanced scanning is picking up the release of some kind of enzyme, a few liquid acids, and minor nanobot activity. Looks like she just self-destructed," Moira said.

Jake came out from cover and picked up his Violator Handgun. Minh-Chu didn't see when he dropped it. Without hesitation, he pushed the heavy bridge security door open with the weapon pointed at someone inside. "Everyone on your knees," he said flatly.

The squad moved up in time to see nine crewmembers in simple dark green uniforms slowly kneeling in the middle of the bridge behind the empty command seat. The bridge was a typical semicircle with the command seat in the middle and the rest of the crew stations around on an incline so they were all visible from the centre. There were two levels of stations, and a large display space at the front.

"Now! Get out here and get on your knees, now!" Jake shouted, firing at the second level of the bridge.

Minh-Chu's scanners picked up someone hiding in an access hatch to the right of the command seat.

"Watch them," Jake said as he strode to the narrow service hatch door and ripped it off its hinges. He reached in and dragged a screaming crewmember out by the hair. Without a moment's hesitation, Jake forced him onto his knees and pressed the barrel of his Violator Handgun against the side of his head. The crewmember slipped Jake's grip as soon as the barrel seared the skin at his temple. Captain Valent caught the back of his uniform and held him out in front of him. "I'm sorry, did that hurt?" he said through a grimace as he pressed the barrel to the back of the crewmember's head for a moment, provoking a shrill scream. "This one is a Junior Lieutenant, and probably twenty years old, just at the beginning of his life.

Surrender complete control of this ship and its database, now," he said, looking at the rest of the kneeling crewmembers, "or it'll be the end."

Two of the youngest, barely men, were in tears, refusing to look at Captain Valent. The rest stared ahead. No one replied; the only sound in the large bridge was the whimpering of the crewmember Jake held at the point of his sidearm. "They're not very interested in keeping you alive," Jake said to him. "What's your name, Junior Lieutenant?"

"Blantonne," the wide-eyed captive replied.

"That sounds like a last name," Jake said, touching the barrel of his weapon to the back of the crewmember's head for a moment. Blantonne shouted at the shock of the pain. "I think we should be on a first name basis under these circumstances. I'm Jacob, people call me Jake, and you are?"

"I-Ira," he replied.

"Good, Ira. We're going to play a game – it's called Chinese Whispers, only it'll be a short one. I'll whisper something to you, and you'll tell your captain over there what I've said. You have to say the words like they are your own, or something bad will happen. Do you understand?"

"Yes, yes I understand," replied Ira.

Jake leaned forward and whispered something then said, "Go on, no need to rephrase."

"He s-"

"Like they're your own words!" Jake said, shaking his captive. "Try again! No more warnings."

Minh-Chu had never seen anyone so openly wrathful. He knew Jacob carried a certain amount of anger with him, something he did not show to people, and knowing the man's history, Minh couldn't blame him. Jacob Valent had everything from identity to abandonment and relationship issues, and he also believed that it was up to him to fix the greatest wrongs in the galaxy. As deluded as it seemed, Minh knew the man felt he had to make a difference, and that, above all else, he was the one most capable. It was a delusion, one that Jake wouldn't admit to, but Minh-Chu knew it was his friend's greatest flaw, and the slow progress they'd made at defeating the Order only stoked the flames in Jacob's heart.

Jake had been left alone for years, lost his daughter, found her again, been under the thumb of Regent Galactic, seen the horrific destruction on Pandem and countless other places. He'd been betrayed, hunted, attacked, watched friends and crewmembers die. The Samson and its crew were shunned while others were accepted, and finally, the love of his life had turned away from him with little explanation. Yes, Minh-Chu understood Jacob's rage, and he knew, listening to his voice as it alternated between ice-cold tones and wrathful instruction, that there was no stopping whatever was going to happen.

Ira repeated what Jake told him with his eyes squeezed shut, sweat dripped from his chin. "Surrender this ship with all the access codes for all systems," Ira blurted in a rush. "Or in ten seconds I won't..." He shuddered. "I won't have a head."

Jake whispered something and Ira tried to look back at him. Captain Valent only nodded solemnly.

Ira looked to his fellow crewmembers and started counting with tears rolling down his cheeks. "Ten, nine, eight..."

"Slower," Jake said with mock sympathy. "A little slower for your own sake."

"S-seven." He paused to take a shuddering breath. "Six, five, four, please, Sir!"

"Keep counting," Jake barked.

"Three, two," Ira tried to struggle at the last moment and everyone flinched as Captain Valent fired. In a flash of light, the cranium of his captive was gone, leaving a gory stump. Before anyone could react, Jake strode to the next nearest crewmember, and grabbed him by the hair. Then he deactivated his own helmet and regarded the rest of the bridge staff, who were all cringing in utter terror. Jacob Valent's expression was twisted in an expression of unhinged wrath that made the artificial death's head of his helmet seem like a comforting alternative. "This is a lieutenant commander. I will not bother to learn his name, because he is about to die!" he looked down at the man in his grip and said, "Count down from ten!"

"Ten," the lieutenant commander started.

"Louder!" Jacob Valent shouted with such violence that his voice rasped.

"Nine," the man said, ashen faced and shaking with fear. "Eight." He would be a tall man if he were on his feet. "Seven." Cool blue eyes and a traditionally handsome face would help him make easy friends. "Six." His uniform was in good order, clean and tidy.

"Jake, don't do this," Minh-Chu said.

Captain Valent fixed him with undiminished fury. "These people are objects, weapons that the Order owns. It's up to them to prove me wrong before I run out of soldiers to break." He turned to his captive and shook him. "Keep counting!"

"Five," the lieutenant commander said, visibly losing hope. He closed his eyes. "I don't have the right codes, or I'd give them to you."

"Who does?" Jake asked. "Where is your captain?"

Minh-Chu looked at the other crewmembers and noticed, for the first time, that the highest rank was that of commander – there was no captain.

"She is," the Lieutenant Commander said, nodding to the woman closest to him.

She had a narrow face, and wore her dark red hair in a long braid. "Traitor! Activate reactor overload!" she shouted into the air above. The bridge lights flashed red and an alarm sounded one whoop.

"Oh, no, we're all going to die," Captain Valent said sardonically through his teeth.

Minh-Chu checked his scanners and saw no change in the reactor status. Everyone waited quietly for several seconds before Jake shrugged and said, "Guess not."

"We've had control of the reactor room for six minutes," Commander Stephanie Vega said over the comm. "There was one Knight and a dozen crew guarding engineering. We went around and incinerated them from behind."

Captain Valent let go of his captive and kicked him onto his side before dragging the captain to her feet by the root of her braid. "No quick death for you," he said, nose to nose with her. "Life doesn't mean much to a monster like me, little girl. I'll keep you alive while I rip pieces of you off with my bare hands if you don't give me what I want. You're an obstacle, and I don't go around, I go through." He gave her a moment to reply. Her face turned red, and she started to close her eyes. He shook her by her braid so hard Minh was afraid it was about to come off and she screamed. "Stay here! Right here, with me! You wanted command of a ship, and this is what that has brought you to! I'll fight my way through every captain and soldier in the fleet to get to the real war and they won't even leave a stain on my memory." She regarded him with wide eyes, one hand trying to push him away, the other reaching for the wrist of the arm that gripped her ponytail. "The question is, will I have to torture you for a few weeks to get what I want?"

With a woman held up on her toes and Jake promising a hell not even he could imagine, a malicious side of Valent was openly on display. This was all the man's hate, the nightmare version of him, and Minh believed that Jake could follow through with his promise.

"I need my console," she said. "In the chair."

"You unlock everything, you have ten seconds," Jake said before he shoved her toward the command seat.

She stumbled and fell, but scrambled into the tall chair, accessing one of the arms and pressing her hand against a bio-reader. "I don't know if this'll work while I'm under stress, there are detectors."

"Try," was all Captain Valent had to say, his tone stated the rest.

Red lights stopped flashing on the bridge, and the screens began displaying the status of systems across the ship.

"Thank you," Jake said as he closed his eyes. "Take all but the captain here into custody, bind them and stuff them into as few escape pods as you can. Any crewmembers who don't surrender in the next thirty seconds using the ship comm system will be killed."

Minh-Chu and Moira watched as the rest of the squad followed orders. The remaining bridge staff didn't resist. "Are you in?" Moira asked Jake.

"Yes, she unlocked everything. Worst captain I've ever met. She barely did her job, spent her time in observation," Captain Valent replied. "Bind her and lock her up there, it doubles as a holding area with an emergency purge door."

"What? So the observation room is made to be vented directly into space?" Moira asked.

Minh-Chu had nothing to say about how the bridge was taken. He'd seen a side of Jacob Valent that he didn't like, so he took the task of binding the captain upon himself just to get a few moments away.

"That's the kind of ship this is. A machine to deliver human tools to war," Jake replied. "It doesn't need much of a captain, just a herd of armed zealots. I'm checking their officer-level communications logs, one minute."

"They'll get you, the Order is immortal," the captain said as Minh-Chu approached her at the foot of her seat.

Jacob Valent opened his eyes and fixed his hateful gaze down at her. "The Order and its followers are worthless, just like this war. You're nothing but the flesh I have to cut to excise the cancer of the galaxy, and once that's done, the real war starts."

"You're crazy!" the captain said, pushing away from Minh-Chu. "That doesn't make sense!"

"The Order exists to maintain control of large sections of space so they can hide Edxian colonies that feed on people who don't make it into the illustrious military or aren't privileged enough to be saved. Your leaders think they can control them, but they're not here just for revenge. They're here to spread, the way insects do. That's what I'll be fighting against once I break or kill every Order of Eden zealot freak I can find. Now shut up while I reassign command of your ship." Jake pulled a grenade from his jacket and tossed it at the captain. It exploded at her feet, enveloping her in a self-contained blue web and stunning her into unconsciousness. It caught the tip of Minh-Chu's fingers and it took him a moment – and all the strength enhancement in his vacsuit – to pull free.

A squad member dragged her off the bridge, chuckling at the muted captain.

"Eve is on her way to Sogarian on a recruiting drive with two spokespeople. I'm going to make sure I'm waiting for her," Jake said. "I'm going to assassinate her."

"You just learned this from the communications logs?" Minh-Chu asked.

"Yes, it's all wide open," Jake replied, wincing at something Minh-Chu couldn't see. "There's a lot of data."

"We have to take a breath, get everything here out of the area and back to Tamber," Moira said.

"I'm going to take one of their ships and a few people with me. They won't suspect one of their own transports, that'll give us a chance to get there and blend in. It's a poor world. I'll need a good pilot."

"We've won a mixed victory here with no losses," Minh-Chu replied. "Overreaching is a mistake."

"You don't like anything I did here," Jake said. "I understand, you're a good man, Minh, you always were, but these people are already lost. The people they trust to command this ship are true believers; they swallowed the whole Order of Eden line completely, without a doubt. Maybe there are crewmembers who are worthy of mercy, but the people on this bridge? They're wasted life already," Jake said before falling to his knees.

Minh-Chu was at his side in an instant and could see Captain Valent was sweating, all colour drained from him. "What's wrong?"

"I'm disconnected from the ship, my node is dead." He gnashed his teeth and squeezed his eyes shut. "Something's wrong," he managed before he lurched onto the deck into a convulsive fit.

Minh-Chu rushed to his side and ran a high-resolution scan. "He's crawling with nanobots matching the ones the Knight had, it's some kind of attack. My medical unit doesn't know what to do, we have to get him back aboard the Warlord." He activated the stasis system on Jake's suit and watched, with growing dread, as Jake's body rejected the cocktail of drugs.

"The Warlord is charging up its wormhole systems, we have to get this ship moving," Moira said.

"You take this ship, I'll save him," Minh-Chu snapped. "I just need one volunteer to help me get him to an airlock." Jake's convulsions were calming, but the anguished expression on his face told him that there was more going on.

"You're staying here," Moira told him. "We don't have time to get him to the Warlord."

"Fry it all," Jake said through his molar-crushing grimace. "Suit, E-" he managed before involuntarily twitching and curling into the foetal position.

Minh-Chu couldn't believe what Jake was telling him to do, but he was already opening the back of Jake's suit before he had a chance to second-guess his old friend. He pulled an EMP grenade from the inside pocket of his jacket and lowered the setting. He bent down to Jake's ear. "It's set just high enough to disrupt a framework's recovery system."

Through pain-filled grunting and twitching, Jake managed to say, "Forty percent."

"That'll kill you," Minh-Chu said. "Don't know if I can bring you back from that." He glanced at the bio-scans and saw something that made what was going on with his friend clear. The nanobots that attacked him from the inside were severing the framework systems from Jacob. Micro-shocks and chemical compounds generated during the process were killing biological matter as the process continued.

Minh shoved the grenade into Jake's suit and sealed the armour over top, remotely ordering the helmet to seal as well. The EMP blast went off three seconds later, contained within his heavy armour. Jake's body tensed then relaxed, and then he was still.

Minh-Chu tried to remotely activate the medical system in Jake's suit and realized that it was destroyed as well. "Didn't think that through," he said to himself as he pulled an emergency cutter from his jacket, made for cutting through the hulls of starfighters and other small ships. He focused it beneath the comm unit on Jake's wrist, where he knew there was a tiny seam in the armour.

"What did you do?" Moira asked as three soldiers returned to the bridge.

"Burned the framework systems and the nanobots in him with an EMP grenade. Killed him too, but if I can get into his suit, my medical unit can get him back."

"That's not going to do it in time," Moira said.

"You're right." Minh-Chu's infantry training kicked in as he dropped the welder, drew his Violator Handgun, and began stripping the weapon's barrel and firing mechanism. Like any officer worth his weight, he knew his weapon inside and out. He didn't even have to think about the task of pulling the weapon apart until the igniter was bare. It felt like he was moving in slow motion, but the complicated mechanisms actually came apart in four seconds.

He held the igniter up to the side of Jake's vacsuit armour and pulled the trigger. The suit sparked and hissed violently as he drew a line of fire along the captain's side and hip. The armour was showing damage after it burned out, but it wasn't open, so Minh-Chu repeated the process, shaking his head. "Sorry Jake." He knew it would burn him. "Someone get a biogel pack ready, now please."

The exothermic oxidation-reduction reaction changed colour as it finished burning through the armour, Jake's vacsuit, and began burning skin. Minh-Chu didn't wait for it to go out before pushing his hand into Jake's armour and activating his own suit's revival systems.

With Jake's armour open, Minh-Chu could see that there was residual brain activity – just enough to bring his friend back – but there was no activity from nanobots or the framework system. The burning compound hissed out, leaving a blackened line along Jake's hip, but Minh couldn't focus on that. "Tell me you've got one life left," Minh-Chu said as his medical system reported that it was ready to attempt to revive Jake. He activated it and carefully placed micro-charges were sent across the captain's nervous system, forcing his body to begin functioning. There was serious damage from the electromagnetic pulse, but the recovery system found working pathways all the way up Jake's spine regardless, and he started breathing with a shuddering gasp.

Brain activity increased a moment later, and Minh-Chu injected Jake with stasis medication. To his relief, it worked, but it was localized; he would have to inject him in several more places. He did his best, and was satisfied with reaching everything except for his arms past his elbows and legs past his knees. Minh-Chu hoped the slow circulation in Jake's system would carry the stasis medication the rest of the way. There was nothing else he could do. "Cover his burns with gel and get him into an emergency suspension bag," he said as he retracted his arm from Jake's suit. "Let's fly this thing out of here."

CHAPTER 48
THE TAKING OF THE SUNNY SHIFTER

Remmy watched it all happen, Captain Valent ruthlessly leading the charge, executing crewmembers, and collapsing. It was the beauty of being a high-functioning multitasker, but he also suffered from the curse that came with it. When Valent fell and Minh-Chu struggled to keep him alive, Remmy was deeply distracted, and all other thought came to an utter halt.

"Sergeant!" Bell Dul shouted over a private comm channel as she punched his shoulder. "Are you with us?"

His thoughts returned to the present, to the corridor leading to the bridge. They'd laid traps – pressure mines rigged to two airlocks set to flush any intruders into space – and his second, nicknamed Dotty, was brandishing a skitter who was about to go on an adventure. "We're ready to go, do you want me to tell him to run down the hall?" she was asking.

Remmy glanced at his tactical display by reflex, checking on the positioning of his people. Four of his Ranger squad were guarding Kann Berin, their pilot, as he controlled most of the ship functions from the engineering section. The rest were around Remmy, at the neck of the last corridor leading to the bridge of the large hauler ship. "Set him loose," Remmy said. "And lock your boots to the deck."

Dotty dropped the skitter. "Sorry, little guy," she said as they watched the small bot with a shiny half-shell walk down the hall on six fine legs. It stopped on the verge of the first pair of pressure mines' sensor range for a moment, then flattened out as much as it could, its six exposed limbs retreating into its shell as much as they could before moving on.

"Oh, if he makes it through to the other side without triggering anything, I'm gonna be pissed," Dul said.

"You disabled its higher functions, right Dotty?" Remmy asked.

"Oh, no, I didn't. I thought they might be useful if something interesting came up, little guy might have to improvise."

The skitter straightened up after ducking under the first pair of pressure mines' sensor radius and getting past them successfully. It hesitated a moment, as though considering the next pair of mines, then sprung upwards and forward, almost striking the ceiling. "Well, you're not wrong, but now that thing is aware of its mortality," Bell Dul said. "If there's a way for him to get through without getting-"

The skitter almost made it through the second set of pressure mines sensors when they went off, crushing the little robot. The airlocks just past the no-man's-land opened just long enough to draw the atmosphere and the bot out into space. "Well, the point's moot now," Remmy said.

"Poor thing," Dotty said.

"Shoot the mines out while they're recharging," Remmy said, firing at the nearest mine, melting it after a few shots with his pulse rifle. "Quick, we don't have much time. Their shields are already coming up."

His squad exceeded his expectations again, moving swiftly but in formation, taking care to keep their boots affixed to the deck. They shot the four pairs of pressure mines well before the shields were too charged up to be vulnerable to their rifles. As soon as they reached the double-wide hatch to the bridge, Anton Zwarif slapped a transmission plate onto the hatch, a small audio patch that would vibrate the metal enough for sound to come through the other side.

"If you surrender the bridge and the command codes for your ship, you will be loaded into escape pods and jettisoned," Remmy said. "If you do not open the doors in ten seconds, I will superheat the hatch and break the doors down. Your bridge will survive, but I doubt your suits will protect you from thirty-four hundred degrees as the door melts."

To Remmy's surprise, his scanners indicated that the locking mechanism on the bridge was deactivated. "Get to the side," he ordered, and he was the last to take a position to the right of the hatchway.

The doors slid open, revealing an irate looking crew of seven. Three of them knelt on the floor, while four had their pistols out, pointed at the back of their heads. "The ship and her captain are yours," shouted a short man with his weapon pointed at the man kneeling in the middle. "We're just contractors, we didn't ask for this."

"All right, then," Remmy said, making sure his shield was fully charged before he stepped out into the open. He pointed his rifle at the group and was followed by the rest of his squad. "We'll take it from here, just give us the command codes and cooperate while we load you into escape pods."

"What?" asked one of the standing crewmembers. "We can't get rescued, we mutinied as soon as you took the main control column for the ship!"

Remmy thought for a moment.

"Maybe we should recruit them?" Dotty asked.

"Shh," Remmy said, "I'm thinking." He checked the mission status and saw that the Warlord was ready to open a high compression wormhole; they were out of time. "Right, we're locking all of you up." He took aim at the short one in the centre of the group with his rifle, making an obvious show of it. "You have fifteen seconds to slide your weapons over here, and to take those company vacuum suits off."

"Strip? What the-" objected one of the crewmembers at the back.

Remmy fired several shots at a seat to the group's left. It exploded in a puff of stuffing. He took aim at the remaining crewmembers again. "You spend this trip naked in the brig, or dead. I'm going to start counting now."

The weapons came sliding through the door and the crew's clothes came off before Remmy counted down to three. He walked to the captain, who was resuming his former position, on his knees, and took a command chip from around his neck. His glove made a connection with the small gold coloured data chip and confirmed that it contained all the command codes for the hauler, ship manifest, and their inventory. "Brand new ship with old school security," Remmy said. "Thank you, Regent Galactic, for setting a low standard for security systems everywhere." He turned towards Dotty. "Do a thorough scan of the bridge and shut down all the systems here. We have to make sure nothing will interfere with Kann Berin's system control team in Engineering. We'll take this lot to the brig when we're under way."

CHAPTER 49
IRON HEAD NEBULA DEPARTURE

The damaged section of hull was visibly warped and weakened above Alice's head. A damage control team was moving in right behind her and the security members with her, hastily emptying the crew quarters and storage area and closing off sections behind them.

It was unusual for a security team to check damaged areas of the ship, but there were momentary sensor readings that no one could clearly interpret in that section of the hull, and Alice was getting restless waiting for all the boarding teams to report in.

"My scanners aren't penetrating the hull," Alice reported over the ship's interior comm system. "But there's nothing unusual inside. There's only one cabin left, the forma reserve."

Alice tried to open the hatchway but the panel beside the door didn't respond. "Any word from the Barricade?" she asked.

"You'll know as soon as they finish resolving the situation there," Kadri replied.

"Okay, fine." Alice opened the small hatch covering the emergency door crank and pumped it several times. The pressure on the manual piston built up, but the door didn't budge. She looked to her companion. "I'm reading good containment in the next section, no atmospheric issues."

"Uh, there's a shadow on my density map," he replied. "Looks weird."

"If it looks weird, then we really have to check it out," Alice said. "Step back, cover me just in case." She pumped the lever several more times. The door swiftly shuffled to the side, and a wave of viscous green-grey fluid overwhelmed her. When it stopped flowing only seconds later, she was chin deep in it. "Bridge? Looks like the forma in this storage bay was overheated, burst through containment, and liquefied. Maybe not in that order."

"All the forma in that section?" David Penton asked from the bridge.

"Enough for me to be swimming in it," Alice replied as she turned away from the doorway and started sloshing towards dry deck. Her companion suddenly doubled over laughing. "Not funny," Alice muttered.

"All right, that's twenty percent of our food reserve. Are you sure it's contaminated?"

"Oh yeah, liquefied and contaminated by radiation, whatever was in that room, and whatever was on my suit, the floor outside, you get the picture." Her description only sent her companion into greater hysterics.

"Okay then," David said. "Glad we don't have much of a trip back, we should still be good on normal rations. I see your scans from that compartment, that's the whole damaged area. Frost wants you back on the bridge."

"Aye, give me a minute for my suit to shimmy this stuff off," Alice replied as she stepped free of the forma and the surface of her armour vibrated the thick fluid off. She performed a quick diagnostic check on her rifle and it responded by evacuating both of the side exhaust vents, squirting several ounces of forma onto the deck. "We lead a glamorous life, don't we?" she said to her comrade, who was trying to catch his breath. "Next time, you go first."

She left him at the edge of the damaged area to watch that section of the ship just in case, and so he could act as an interior scanning node to make up for the damaged sensors in that area. Alice couldn't help but chuckle at herself once he was out of range. She had to admit that her sudden forma bath was something she couldn't wait to tell people about once she made it back to Haven Shore.

The Warlord was almost ready to project the wormhole leading back to the Rega Gain System. They would make no pretence that they were headed anywhere else. Even she knew that part of their mission was to bring the British Alliance into the war officially, and if it took a direct retaliation from Order of Eden forces to do it, so be it.

The bridge staff seemed subdued when she arrived and took her post at her station. "Captain Valent is secure," came Minh-Chu's voice over the comm. "He's safe in stasis and I'm taking control of the helm."

"Good work, destroyer team," Frost said as she turned towards Ashley, who seemed near tears. "Stay in your seat, lass," he told her.

"What happened?" Alice asked.

"Seems the Order Knights can do something to framework folk, like a nano-bomb."

"That doesn't make sense, he'd keep his helmet sealed. How would they get in? Did they damage his suit?" Alice asked in a rush.

"He had to take it off to make a point, but he's all right now. They took care of the nanos and put him in stasis," Frost said.

"He's not all right. If I can't talk to him, if he's not standing up, he's not all right!" Alice shouted, her head pounding, her vision blurring. She spun out of her seat and started for the exit.

"Stop her!" Frost shouted after her.

The guards she posted at the main bridge hatch stepped in her way, and Alice leapt at them, elbowing and squirming to get through. She could hear the synthetic muscles in their suits struggling to maintain their grasp on her. Alice almost broke through at first, when they were surprised, but they had her in the end. "I need to get on that ship, Jason told me he'd be in trouble if I left him alone, I should have listened! I should have gone with him!"

Her suit began to fight against her, pulling her arms down to her sides, and she realized that Frost had used his override to turn her armour into a prison. "Calm down, it's all in hand," he told her as the guards laid her down on her back. "Get back in your seat, Ash."

Alice never felt so selfish in her life for leaving her father alone. She shouldn't have spent all that time away training with the Rangers, or let her father go on with the Warlord without her. "I left him alone," she said. Frost crossed the bridge to her and knelt down in front of her as the tears came. "This is going to change him," Alice told him. "I have to be with him, please. Please!"

"We can't dock with the Barricade," Frost explained calmly as he deactivated her helmet. "Don't worry, Minh won't let anything happen to him. Even if I could, your da would have me shot for letting you near him. You and he are two of a kind, if there are any of those nanos around on that ship, you could be in just as much trouble. We're almost out of this, we're projecting a wormhole now. Good as gone, and your da is in good hands."

"I just need to be with him," Alice said, no longer bothering to struggle.

Frost took her in his arms and nodded at the guards. "It'll be all right," he told her. "That man's made o' miracles, he'll outlive us all."

Chapter 50
Strange Travellers

The hangar bay deep in the base of the Everin Building had been pressed into early service. Uriel and Ramiel fighters were undergoing repairs along with an armed shuttle. More technicians than she realized they had pulled panels free and removed parts too far gone to fix. It was what one of the previous Ayan's Technical Crafts professors called the "autopsy phase" of repairs, when ships had to be pulled apart before they could be made whole again with new components.

At the centre was the Clever Dream. Lewis knew exactly what kind of damage he'd taken, and how it should be repaired. That was a good start, but the few hits the Clever Dream took while his shields were down had crushed armour panels, destroyed emitters, and left two long gashes that cut all the way through the ship's outer armour. The good news was that their fabrication shop had access to the necessary materials; the bad news was that they were backlogged. It was true that they had more technicians than Ayan realized, but there still weren't enough for the kind of repairs the Clever Dream and several other ships needed. More qualified people were being recruited, but clearing and transporting them took time.

Ayan leaned against the transparent steel window inside the observation room overlooking the hangar, watching as skitter bots, welder droids, lifters, and intelligent tool chests made their way between technicians. They'd brought a few heavy maintenance suits down from the Triton to assist, and they stalked around like giant humans, carefully lifting here, moving something there, or giving other techs a quick lift to their work sites.

She didn't know why her father had called her there, but she suspected it had something to do with the sudden shroud of secrecy that fell over his location, and the increase of security that surrounded him. No one could break the codes he put in place surrounding the information on his whereabouts or what he was doing aboard one of the few troop transports the Triton Fleet had.

"Three days," Lewis said through her personal communications band. "Even my automated repair systems were damaged, and it'll take this lot three days to have me back in flyable condition, and that's without fixing all my armour or cloaking systems. I feel naked with all these panels off, and you're sitting up there watching?"

Ayan couldn't help but laugh a little at his outrage.

"Hey, one of you hairless apes tripping on your own feet, that's funny. A damaged and exposed premium fighting ship is not," Lewis protested.

"I'm sorry, Lewis, but I can't help but laugh at how you relate to us sometimes. I'll be down to help with repairs as soon as I find out whatever is going on with my father. Suddenly it's as though he doesn't realize he's out of the Freeground Intelligence Service."

"I know, I can't find out anything about him, especially with my sensors offline," Lewis replied. "It's interesting, mysterious. Are you sure you couldn't attend to it while you climb into my innards and affect a few delicate repairs?"

"Soon, Lewis," Ayan replied.

The observation room ran part of the length of the hallway parallel to the top of the hangar. As of yet it was unfurnished, but Ayan couldn't help but look behind her at those blank walls and see people using the space the same way the previous Ayan used larger observation areas in the Freeground Station hangars. She used to love watching the ships come together in the final stages of repair and construction. She saw an uncountable number of launches, and she felt a little of that sensation as she watched the repairs underway below. The itch to get down there and help was growing, Ayan hoped her father would hurry up.

Slick, tall and suave even though he was under as much pressure as she was to get their defence back in place, came through one of the doors behind her. "You're not going to believe what the Triton just picked up; the British Alliance are pissed that it's in formation with her."

"What?" Ayan asked.

"A Journeyman class Lorander ship with some kind of high mass cargo, it's beautiful." He projected an image of the ship into the centre of the room. The broad front end looked like the mask of a stern metal man with rectangular glowing blue eyes that ran up half the length of the forward plating. The lower half of the fore section looked like an open mouth with an array of antennae and glowing sections ringing the inner edge like gleaming teeth. It had to be some kind of elaborate sensing and emitter array, Ayan supposed. Between the more prominent features were transparent sections of hull. By a quick count, she guessed there were eleven decks. The rest of the ship extending behind was gently curved along its length so there was a concave cavity beneath where it carried a five hundred metre long black box with no windows. Blue and green arms ran down the top and sides of the main ship for the entire length. They caught the little light around the ship, glinting as though they were made of fine crystal. It was another array of some kind, and from the looks it could spread out in all directions, extending out many times the size of the ship.

Her command and control unit beeped a warning, vibrating against her wrist and she stepped back towards Slick. "Energy reading, big one," was all she could say before a swirling storm of energy coalesced in front of them. Her father and two women emerged before it disappeared behind them. "I miss those," Carl Anderson said to the taller woman at his side. "Haven't been through one since the Lorander-Freeground alliance."

"They are convenient," agreed the tall, elegant looking woman.

Ayan looked closer at the other woman with him and immediately realized that she was either an Issyrian or something Ayan had never seen. She was pretty in her own dainty way. Big eyes scanned the room with trepidation, coming to rest on Ayan after a moment. "That was my first crush gate. Is it normal for me to feel like I've just been squeezed very hard then re-inflated at the other end?"

Ayan shrugged, only aware that Lorander had the technology for high compression super-wormholes, but never having been through one.

"It's a sensation that takes some getting used to," said the other woman. "I should have warned you."

"It's all right, it was just," the Issyrian let a loud sigh whistle through her sculpted lips, "abrupt."

"So, I'm Wing Commander Nathan Kipp of the Skyguard, but you can call me Slick," he said, offering his hand to the Issyrian first.

"I'm Commander Ayan –" she thought a moment and decided to use the last name she had been considering since New Years' Eve, "Anderson." Her father was visibly pleased by the introduction.

"I am Shozo of House Fallen Star," the Issyrian replied uncertainly. Her hand felt fine and warm.

"I'm First Minister Amo Tammen, of the Lorander Corporation," the tall woman told Ayan, her dark, friendly eyes looking unwaveringly into her own. There was something about the woman, a high confidence, Ayan assumed, that made her feel like Amo was exactly where she meant to be, when she meant to be there. "I feel I owe you an apology already, since I

322

have come here so quickly and can't stay as your guest. I'm afraid we have to get right to business."

"They contacted me directly," Carl Anderson said. "Since the Lorander Government knew me from the Freeground alliance. We have an opportunity to make a deal with Lorander and Shozo here. Oz has given you his proxy."

Ayan was intrigued. She knew Oz was busy with repairs on the Triton, but it was unusual for him to count himself out of a major decision. She took it to mean that he was most likely on the fence about the issue. "Why is that name, Fallen Star, familiar?" Ayan asked.

"I am from House Fallen Star," Shozo explained, "Founded by Clark Patterson, the commander of the Order of Eden Fleets."

Ayan didn't realize her hand had lowered to the hilt of her sidearm until her thumb was resting on her holster's safety clasp. She left her hand where it was.

"I come in peace, with no weapons or hate," Shozo said, nearly pleading. "We are here because, while my Dominant, my Master, is your enemy, he has great respect for you and your people. He also refuses to pledge House Fallen Star to this war, even though we are a rare Warrior Caste among the Issyrian people. My Dominant suffers under an unusual dichotomy – he must maintain and gain territory for the sake of humanity, but loves his Issyrian House too much to involve them – it is not a state that he can maintain. He did not direct me here specifically, but when I brought our problem to the First Minister, she made a case for approaching you. We prefer not to be a violent people, and wish to dilute the aggression until it rests with the silt. Tamber has fresh water lakes, and thanks to its unique formation in this solar system, direct interstellar bombardment is impossible."

"Well, improbable, at least," Slick said quietly. "I mean, you'd have to have the best navigator, gunner, and computers. Your projectile would probably have to correct at faster than light speeds too, and that's a whole other problem…" He stopped when all eyes in the room turned towards him. "Not the point, right."

"The First Minister said you are an accommodating people, who welcome beings from across the stars regardless of species or origin. Other Issyrian Houses will not accept us, and unclaimed worlds are unsafe. Even under surveillance here, my people may be safer, and our presence could be the first step towards the end of your war with the Order."

"That is the point we're most concerned with, using this opportunity to make in-roads towards peace. Lorander is adding an incentive and a condition to Shozo's proposition," the First Minister said. "If you allow them to settle on Tamber, we'll give you a ship construction and repair facility. We have it with us. We'll also remain here for a time to advise on anything you'd like while we observe the settlement of House Fallen Star. We want this to work, and are willing to watch you both from a distance."

Ayan thought a moment and couldn't get past one impenetrable question. "Why is Lorander involved?"

"We were the first people Shozo approached, you were the backup. I saw a unique opportunity to build a bridge between you and the Beast, the commander of the Order of Eden forces. This could shorten this senseless war by decades. There are larger problems in this galaxy, and they will be ignored if this goes on. This could be the most important step towards peace."

The thought of being in good standing with the Lorander Corporation, and extending an olive branch to the leadership of the Order of Eden was more than compelling. The potential for espionage and sabotage if she allowed House Fallen Star to settle was just as massive. "I can only agree to this if they are segregated from the rest of Tamber's population at first, and if all the settler's communications are blocked."

"They must mix with your people for this to work," Amo Tammen retorted without a breath's hesitation. "Even if they are under guard for a limited time."

"If they engage in espionage of any kind, we have to have the option to eject them from our space," Ayan countered.

"On an individual basis. You cannot punish the whole for the deeds of the few."

"On an individual basis," Ayan agreed. "Supervision periods last as long as we see fit."

"Yes, but if you're going to impose constant surveillance, you have to abandon the idea of segregation," Amo said, "I won't negotiate a deal that lands them in camps."

Ayan was impressed by the woman's negotiation skills. Everyone in the room was looking from her to Amo Tammen as they took turns. "They all have to wear comm units and be tracked by our system at all times."

"They will be treated fairly at all times," Amo Tammen said as she nodded at Ayan's statement. "What if they were screened just like the rest of your recruits? If they don't meet the requirements, can they settle in some other area of Tamber?"

"If they enter the recruitment process, they have to work just like everyone else," Ayan said. "And they'll still have to wear one of our functioning comm units at all times."

"Shozo?" Amo Tammen asked, smiling a little. "What do you think?"

"We'd be tracked, but we could live here?" Shozo asked, looking surprised.

"Everyone is tracked here all the time," Amo replied, "so you would be treated like anyone else. They also have other Issyrians on their crew, most of them are exiles."

"How long will you stay to watch us if I agree?" Shozo asked Amo.

"I can stay in the system for a month after Fallen Star arrives, just to make sure everything proceeds as agreed. I doubt I'll have to. From what I've seen of the Commander, I get the feeling that she wants this to work. If enough of your people help them, I'm sure everyone here will trust all of you faster."

"Help them fight?" Shozo asked.

"No, help them build. They are creating a new culture here, a new city. This building isn't even a year old. I think she'd let you be part of that."

Ayan let her guard down a little and nodded. With tracking in place, they would know if any of them was doing something nefarious. "I'd like that," she said. "Haven Shore will be run by our military for the foreseeable future, but we want things to be peaceful down here. We want to reserve this whole region of Tamber for our civilian population, and we need good builders."

"We have many smart builders," Shozo said. "If you'll allow the Lorander to stay and watch, I will agree to this."

Ayan looked to her father. "I'm the hold out vote, aren't I?"

"You're the most important authority here," Carl said. "You technically own Haven Shore and most of our significant territories. You have the first and final word here."

"You would agree to this though, if it were up to you," Ayan said.

"With one provision," he said. "You leave a significant Lorander ship here for ten years to observe and your corporation is barred from any aggressive act in the system. Hide it, leave it in the open, it doesn't matter. You supervise and watch what we grow here. Your people can visit our facilities like any other traveller."

"Observation, trade, and no military interference. I think Shozo is a little happier with that, having a Lorander ship in the system for ten years instead of a month," the First Minister said. "I don't think I'll be allowed to extend my stay any longer than what I promised, but I will personally choose which ship remains behind."

"Yes, that makes things much better," Shozo answered. She looked directly at Ayan and said, "I'd like this to work. My people need a home, and other prospects are far away, desolate. They all agree that the Order war is too devastating as well. Being responsible for taking the first steps towards peace is exactly what we need to turn away from our violent past."

There was no mystery to why Clark Patterson sent Shozo. Turning her down was tantamount to kicking a litter of kittens; she knew how to appeal to people and pull heartstrings. The agreement would bring more workers, diversity, and a Lorander presence to the area. Not to mention the thought of having their own portable Lorander repair and construction facility. Her father would be in charge of operations on Tamber, close to the situation. He would minimise the risk surrounding the deal even further. "I can't say no," Ayan told Shozo. "Let's repeat the details for the record."

CHAPTER 51
THE CARGO

The Sunny Shifter was the newest ship Remmy had ever set foot on. The vessel was less than five weeks old, and besides the tampering his team had to do to get control and a few signs of a fire-fight, it was pristine. White, dark green, and silver tinted metals surrounded them as he and Bell Dul came to the reinforced airlock leading to the long cargo train.

"What strikes me as odd is how fresh the cargo train looks," Bell said as they looked at the access panel beside the airlock hatch.

"I was thinking the same thing," Remmy replied as he took a pair of slender data spikes out of his sleeve. They were made of hardened metal, had a conductive core and intelligent microscopic interface links on their ends. "I've never seen a cargo train with all new containers. We know there's some heavy machinery and rare supplies way in the back, but you can transport that stuff in any old box."

"Is that how you're getting in?" Bell asked as she watched Remmy tap one of the slender data spikes into the panel beside an old fashioned number key.

"Yup. I couldn't find out who is in those stasis pods in the first thirty cargo cars, and I couldn't crack the panel, so we're going to have to carefully trick the system into thinking the panel is damaged. An emergency bypass circuit will take over that won't stop us from cranking the door open manually."

"How'd you figure that out?"

"I read the manual," Remmy said as he tapped in the second spike. He waited for the rods to connect with the electronics inside and smiled as a schematic appeared on his comm unit. "Voilà. Just like I figured, this fancy new security system is using the cheapest method to block the manual lever for the airlock. It's just a software block; if we were coming at this door from outside the ship, it would be impossible to break through this way, but since we're inside, and the mechanisms are all right here..." He commanded the spikes to emit a charge and the old-fashioned keypad sparked and died.

The sound of a latch releasing filled the cabin. "Was that the manual control unlocking?"

"Yup," Remmy said, glancing around. "We're looking for some kind of small access hatch."

"Wasn't that bit in the manual?" Bell asked, searching.

"That part of the translation wasn't exactly clear," Remmy said.

"Any word on how Captain Valent is doing?"

"I shouldn't tell you anything, but let's just say that Alice is holding together really well, considering," Remmy said. He knew Minh-Chu moved Captain Valent into the medical bay aboard the destroyer, but that's all he could do. Until they arrived in the Rega Gain System, Jacob Valent would remain in stasis, and no one could be sure of his chances. Remmy, like most of the crew, saw Captain Valent as an indomitable man. Blocking his status for all but officers was the right move, especially since their captain was in the territory of last hopes and desperate acts. "It's pretty dire, things could go either way, but there's no way of knowing for sure until we're home. You didn't hear that from me, and you won't share it."

"Gotcha. Wish I could know more, though," Bell said. "Oh, the panel is up there."

Remmy looked straight up and snickered. "You're taller, you open it."

Bell Dul pressed a small rectangular door and it popped open, revealing a pump handle. "Pull?"

"Yup, pull and push until the system builds up enough pressure to open the door."

She followed the instructions and after pumping the handle a dozen times the airlock door slid all the way open in a sudden swish. "Would it have been faster to just blast the security panel? I mean, instead of using those spikes?" she asked as they moved into the airlock.

"Sure, but Moira might be a little pissed if we started blasting the refinements on her ship for no reason. Those spikes only damaged a tiny circuit, a skitter could repair that in five minutes."

"Ah, I guess I'm just too used to running and gunning," Bell said.

"I'm not complaining, there's nothing wrong with running and gunning when you're in a hurry," Remmy said as he opened the next panel and invited Bell to pull the next lever.

She pulled it once and the door behind them closed. One more pull opened the airlock hatch leading into the cargo cars. "That was quick."

"Just had to move the pressure from one door system to another," Remmy said. "Hacking through a brand new ship's systems when you're in transit is so much fun."

"Older ships are harder?" Bell asked.

"Older ships have modifications and unexpected improvements," Remmy said.

"Right, that makes sense. I get the feeling you've captured a few ships before this one, yeah?" Bell Dul asked.

"Not too many, just a really dangerous one. I'll tell you about the Sunspire sometime."

"The Freeground ship?"

"Yup, that was my first really big hack," Remmy said. He momentarily recalled the mission he joined Clark Patterson on to retake the Sunspire, and the sounds of the other boarding team dying as they ran into the ship's merciless defence systems. "You may have to buy me a few drinks to get that story out of me, though."

They walked into the first cargo car to discover a large, semi-circular control console. The interior lights activated, filling the space with bright white light. Stasis pods were mounted in four rows for the length of the storage car, and there was a stable environment. Remmy noticed several worm-like sterilization bots along the deck as they made their way around the stasis pods destroying contaminants. They were harmless, with no artificial intelligence, but he knew if he was seeing a couple right away there would be more in the cargo train. "You don't spend this kind of money to transport slaves."

"No kidding, all these stasis pods are new, state of the art," Bell Dul said, looking through the transparent lid of a pod mounted on the hull to their right at a golden haired young man. "These aren't liquid stasis pods, they're the cushy independent environment dry models. I remember wishing I could afford that when I was coming out of liquid stasis."

"Why were you in stasis?" Remmy asked as he accessed the console. As with the door, the captain's control codes didn't work. He checked for biometric security, and smiled after seeing that no one had activated it. With a chuckle, he started punching in the five most common passwords.

"I was a kid, don't really remember where we were coming from, but it was a long trip, and my family couldn't afford the food and air charges, so we went into stasis."

"Not fun, I'm guessing," Remmy said as he punched in a sequence of numbers from zero to ten.

"I don't remember much more than coughing up that fluid and finding gummy stuff in my nooks and crannies for days."

Remmy stared at the console in shock as it unlocked and laughed. "Really? No one bothered to change the password?"

"Why? What was it?"

"Admin," Remmy replied. He sobered a little as he read the available commands. "Oh, that's why. Each pod is controlled individually, some are locked, and the container controls are all set up on the bridge. This console isn't exactly the key to their security." He downloaded the manifest from the terminal and turned to the nearest unsecured stasis pod. It contained a well-muscled man with a rifle. "This guy should know something." Remmy activated the revival system and drew his sidearm.

Bell Dul trained her rifle on the man as the stasis pod hood raised and moved out of the way. "Wow, quick revival sequence."

"Yup, the deluxe model," Remmy said as he pulled the man's heavy rifle out of the stasis pod and stood it up against the railing beside him. "I'll be having that, thank you."

The square jawed man drowsily opened his eyes at first, then they snapped open and he searched for his weapon. "Terrorists!" he shouted as he leaned forward.

Bell Dul bashed him across the face with the butt of her rifle, more than hard enough to knock him back into his stasis bed.

"Whoa, whoa," Remmy said. "We're just asking this gentleman a few questions, then we'll put him back to sleep for the rest of the trip."

"You're traitors to humanity, and you'll get nothing from me!" said the man.

"Okay, so it says here your name is Curtis," Remmy said, reading information from the manifest on the comm unit. "So you're from a corporate training camp on Kaney, probably contacted by Regent Galactic to train soldiers for the Order, yes?"

"What?" Curtis asked, appalled.

"It's okay, don't tell me anything, your personnel file is open now that you're awake. It says here you've been with the Order for two years? That can't be right."

"Under the Child Prophet! May his memory inspire the galaxy!"

"Wow, they got you programmed good," Remmy said, scrolling through the summarized personnel file on Curtis Mahanon. There was little information about him, other than his rank, basic health information, origin, and destination, but he didn't have to tell Curtis. "So, you're in charge of all these other soldiers? Says here you're a major."

"This is a colony transport, you idiot!" Curtis shouted, glancing wide-eyed at Remmy then Bell.

"Say it, don't spray it," Remmy said. "So most of the people here are civilians."

"True pledges to the Order, don't you dare put your unclean hands on them!" Curtis shouted, leaning forward again. Bell Dul raised her rifle and took aim at his head, and he settled back.

"Okay, so you're a whole serving of crazy with a side dish of delusional," Remmy said. "I think we have everything we need for now, good night," he said as he reached to reactivate the stasis pod. "This was all a dream. Just sit back and-" Curtis moved so quickly that Remmy couldn't get out of the way of a sucker punch. His suit detected the strike and activated his helmet just in time.

Bell Dul fired her rifle, ruining Curtis from the neck up.

"Wow," Remmy said, looking at the steaming corpse. "Absolute overkill."

"Sorry! I'm still punchy from this boarding operation."

They watched the stasis pod finish closing. "And I though I was just starting to make a connection with the crazed Order of Eden soldier," Remmy remarked as the pod started to flash red.

"Sarge, do you have a minute?" his second in command, Dotty, asked over his communicator.

"Yeah, I'm not getting anything else out of this guy. Oh, and don't call me Sarge. I keep picturing a thick, cigar chewing drill Sergeant whenever you do."

"What's a cigar?" Dotty asked.

"That's it, I'm putting on an ancient war movie night as soon as we get back to Haven Shore," Remmy said, throwing his hands up. "What's up, Dotty?"

"We thought we saw movement on the Warlord's hull, so we scanned, but didn't pick anything up. We left the scanners focused on the dorsal aft quarter anyway, and now we're picking up a heat signature."

"Two days into wormhole transit and we find a barnacle? What does it look like?"

"We had to move a little when we started the deceleration sequence, I guess we couldn't get a good scan before. It doesn't match anything on file," Dotty said.

"Does the Warlord know we've found something strange on their hull?" Remmy asked, checking the communications logs.

"I wanted to talk to you first but I didn't want to interrupt you while you were interrogating that soldier."

"Send them your sensor logs and all your readings," Remmy said. He opened an emergency channel to Alice.

CHAPTER 52
HER RELUCTANT MAJESTY

Ayan's first experience with public speaking was a nervous and frustrating affair. Appealing for the right to own everything her predecessor, the first Ayan, owned in her lifetime in front of the top lawmakers in the Freeground Nation was nerve crushing. The speaking engagement she was about to undertake seemed bigger somehow. As she waited for Lacey, Oz, and her father in a room adjacent to the unfinished Council Chamber, she fought to control her anxiety, taking deep, slow breaths.

"Something came for you," Lacey said as she carried an absurdly long white box through a side door and put it on the table. "From Patrizia Salustri. It seems she's back now that the Carthans are packing it in."

"That makes sense," Ayan said. "She probably found a way to get into trouble after the battle of Port Rush. We'll have to keep our eyes on her people."

"We scanned it," Carl Anderson said as he entered the room behind Lacey. "It's a dress, with a few auto-tailor mechanisms."

"It's not like she'd send a bomb," Lacey said. "Unless there's something I don't know about."

"No," Ayan said, recalling Patrizia's very traditional language and her engaging manner. "She's tried to get close to me before. That lion head ring you saw a while ago was from her."

"Oh, so she's after a spot in your good graces. Well, in that case, open it up," Lacey told her. "I can't wait to see what kind of dress requires a body length box."

Ayan glanced at her father who was sitting down on the bare frame of a sofa. It was as much of a reminder that Haven Shore still wasn't quite finished as the incomplete Council Chamber. "We're waiting for Oz, anyway."

Ayan pulled the edge of the top flap covering the box. The cover became flexible and rolled into the top of the box, revealing a full-length dress that was slit up the sides, with ornately patterned, weaving cut outs that were narrow and sparse along the sides. The pattern was wider and more concentrated on the front and back of the dress, teasing obviously with more bare sections. The white colour was accented by platinum lines that climbed the length like tiny branches following the curves the dress was made to celebrate, culminating in a high collar that emanated a gentle warm glow from a hidden light source that would compliment Ayan's colouring. The long, ornate sleeves and underside of the dress were all lit from the inside as well.

There were boots, a neckpiece and tiara made of platinum branches as well, and Ayan was struck speechless. The entire outfit was laid out with a hologram of Ayan inside, her expression looping an inviting, sly wink.

"Oh, that's beautiful," Lacey said.

"I feel like I'm on display and I'm not even wearing it," Ayan said, laughing nervously.

Oz came through the side door and gave Ayan a squeeze before looking into the box along with everyone else. "That's what Patrizia Salustri sent?" he asked. To Ayan's dismay, he seemed impressed.

"Yup, there's a message too," Carl Anderson said as he stood up and took a small card from the box. "I think you'd look stunning in that too, by the way. You're right though, it is revealing," he said, clearing his throat.

Ayan took the small white card and unfolded it. A projection of Patrizia Salustri in a long, slinky dress of her own appeared above the box. "Che piacere vederti, I have great sorrow for the time I had to spend away from Tamber, amongst the society of the spoiled on Kambis, but the Carthans were not friends to me," Patrizia Salustri said, her old Italian accent stronger than ever. "I have so much gratitude for how you removed them from our skies, and hope this gift brings you and the people you love some joy. I am looking forward to the speech you will give; many people around the Rega Gain star are too. I think that seeing you dressed this way will be enchanting to them, and no one will doubt that you are their Majestic Queen. If you do not wear it, I will not hate you, but you must show it for me soon. Non vedo l'ora di vederti."

"Is there a translation for that last bit?" Lacey asked as the image of Patrizia Salustri faded.

"It means; I look forward to seeing you," Oz replied, looking at his comm unit. "But the translator notes that her inflection is inferring affection and insistence."

"She mustn't speak common English much. But it sounds like she's bringing her organization back to Tamber. Looking forward to it, Ayan? I've never seen you blush like this before," Lacey teased.

Ayan pulled the box cover down and cleared her throat. "She's one of the most dangerous people I've ever met. If we let her do whatever she likes on Tamber, she'll use it as a base for her criminal enterprise. Jake has been sending me intelligence over the last few months about how much money she's making from this war already, and her organization is bigger than ever."

"She's a crime lord?" Lacey asked, surprised. "She looks like a high society lady."

"That's one side of her," Carl said. "I've seen the reports Ayan's talking about. Her people have been raiding worlds that haven't recovered from the Holocaust Virus, taking ships, supplies, and running off before too many bots get after them."

"I wouldn't care," Ayan started, trying to shake off the lingering feeling of being put on the spot. "I wouldn't care, except that she doesn't see any difference between looting abandoned cities or survivors, leaving them with nothing to live on once she's gone. We have to bulk up our fleet, fast, so we can keep people like her in check."

"Working on it," Oz said. "Eager to get your help with the mobile shipyard."

"Oh, that reminds me," Ayan said. "Time to switch to my Triton Fleet uniform." With a few taps on her military style arm-length command and control unit, she changed the colour of her light body-vacsuit uniform from white to black, set her full name – Ayan Anderson – to appear on her collar, and changed the emblem on her chest from Haven Shore to the Triton skull. Above was still printed: Deploy, Dominate, Disappear. The name of their flagship, TRITON, still served as the silver death's head's teeth. Her rank was marked as Commodore, an advancement in the fleet that she noticed but didn't necessarily feel she was worthy of yet. Still, she knew why she was upgraded to the rank, and didn't fight it.

"Welcome back," Oz said proudly. "Everyone in the fleet is looking forward to seeing you around Triton."

"You have to remember to visit down here," Lacey reminded her.

"I will," Ayan said. She took a moment to look at the people around the table with the long white box atop it. They were most of her favourite people in the universe, and having them there made her feel so much better about the announcements she had to make. "It really looked like we could create a civilized pocket without the military for a few weeks, didn't it?" she asked no one in particular.

"It'll happen someday," her father replied. "We just haven't earned it yet."

"I know. I'd like all of you to stand behind me out there, if you don't mind," she said.

"Absolutely," Lacey said. Oz and Carl both agreed without hesitation.

Without another word, Ayan turned towards the door leading out to the Council Chamber dais. Her heart was pounding, and her palms started sweating as soon as she saw that empty chamber. The semicircle of graduated steps for tables and seating were in place, but they were still bare of furniture. Another thing the fabrication shop had on their list.

The high dais made for the presiding officer for Haven Shore's parliament was bare of furniture as well, just a set of steps leading to a platform that everyone in the large room could see. The transparent hull behind and above the seating overlooked a fantastic view of falling snow and black waters. They were at the coldest phase of Tamber's long night, and jungle creatures were hiding in burrows, under limbs, and in caves. Ayan looked across the hundreds of Haven Shore residents who packed the government chamber and wished she could join them.

She stopped in the middle of the dais and was comforted by the feeling of Lacey, Oz, and her father behind her. "Thank you for coming," she said. Her voice was picked up by the invisible broadcasting system and projected across the hall evenly with perfect clarity. Everything she was saying was being transmitted across the solar system as well; there were millions watching. "Peace," she started, looking at her comm unit just long enough to see that she was shaking and to activate its projection system. The tiny projector sent a faint scroll of text directly into her eyes so no one could see she was reading it.

"The first steps towards peace are the most difficult, and the road leading to lasting harmony is not clearly marked here. This week has been a frightening and sometimes violent time. We lost twenty-eight people during our fight with the Carthans who didn't believe that Haven Shore would survive, and I don't blame them. During our efforts to form an effective democratic government and separate Haven Shore from the impending war, the Council has utterly failed to bring stability to the people they govern. I include myself in that statement. As a Council member, I was desperate to see Haven Shore sovereign and safe. As the owner of Haven Shore, I feel ultimately accountable for what has happened here."

336

Ayan took a deep breath and continued, knowing she was headed into the most controversial section of her speech. "There is a lot to consider going forward. The Carthans are leaving, Haven Shore's territory is expanding exponentially."

"You mean your territory!" shouted someone in the crowd.

"You're right," Ayan said. "My territory is expanding. The Warlord is returning soon, most likely with much needed equipment and supplies. They will be welcome in Haven Shore when they arrive. War looms, and the Council will be ill-equipped to handle the larger issues facing us. Over the next few days, you'll hear about a treaty I've made with an Issyrian House that has fled Order of Eden territory and is settling here, bringing even more change to Haven Shore. You'll also hear that those negotiations bore even more fruit in the form of a Lorander presence in the solar system as well as a new shipbuilding and repair facility. We are at a critical juncture, and I am not willing to allow dissent from a poorly qualified council to jeopardize the network of allies and assets that Triton Fleet and Haven Shore are gathering. As owner of Haven Shore and associated properties, I will allow the civilians of Haven Shore to have a representative body that will run the day-to-day affairs of the city, but Triton Fleet will have the ultimate authority. Furthermore, I won't be serving as your solitary sovereign, or your White Queen. As of today, all of my assets belong to Triton Fleet, and the focus of overall development will be defence and the support of the war."

The crowd surprised Ayan with a mixed reaction. Mischa Konev and Tyra Kim both left the council chamber, the former shaking her head and the latter looking furious. Much of the crowd was hushed, hanging on her every word, while a few others cried, "oppressive military complex!" or "dictator!" Overall, there was much less outrage than Ayan expected, and it interrupted her pace for a moment. "Triton Fleet's goal with Haven Shore is to provide a safe place for our vetted civilian population of workers, children, and elderly people, but that doesn't mean that it should not be armed, or that portions of it will not serve as a military base until we expand elsewhere. Our clash with the Carthans has taught us that Haven Shore should be able to defend itself, and the fastest way to make that a reality is to relocate some military assets to this site. Most people will maintain the same jobs here, and your lifestyle will not change much. As for governing, all Triton Fleet assets will be ultimately controlled by military officers. If you want to serve in the military arm of Triton Fleet, you are welcome to apply. If you wish to leave one of our territories, report to the nearest security officer and they will help you begin that process."

Ayan was relieved to see the last paragraph of her speech and actually found herself smiling a little at the quieted crowd. "I wanted to bring democracy and peace to Haven Shore, but it was too soon. There is a war yet to fight, and I beg you to join me. I will use all of my energy to defend you and win this war, whether it is through diplomacy or through the application of force. That is how your military will serve you, and the civilians here can help us by being patient, productive people. Nominations for council representatives will be accepted by Lacey Rosedale starting tomorrow morning. Thank you for listening, and thank you for your support in these dangerous times."

Ayan stepped aside and allowed Lacey to take her place. "I will accept nominations for twenty hours, starting tomorrow at oh-eight-hundred. Each block of one thousand Haven Shore residents will read their nominees' statements then vote. You will have two days to consider who you will vote for. The Council will convene three days later, chaired by Commander Carl Anderson or any military representative he chooses as his proxy. Partisanship is banned, laws against bribery, unlawful collusion, and personal misconduct are in place and must be understood by any council member or they will be removed from their position. We have a plan for civilian growth and leadership – please take a moment to review it so you understand your government. Thank you for your attention."

It was Ayan's last chance to speak to the solar system, and more importantly, the residents of Haven Shore, as a solitary owner. She took the central position of the dais again, seeing a sea of people who looked uncertain staring back at her. "I –" she started, and stopped as she noticed a mobile litter carrying Illoona, her latest brood, and her eldest daughter.

Lee Romita stood several metres behind them with his wife, Trina, at his side. She had short brown hair, and a rounded friendly looking face. "Haven Shore is my most beautiful dream." That was when her bottom lip quivered, and she saw beyond the speech. All at once the months of work she put in to Haven Shore, the Everin Building, and creating a community came back to her. The disappointment at being disliked by so many people, many of whom were staring at her in that room, and frustration at not making the progress she wanted were in her thoughts as well, along with the realization that she'd really be leaving. Back to space, back to living on ships, being in a military structure, and being accountable for technicians and soldiers alike. Her time as a civilian was over as well, and she didn't realize she wanted it until she felt it slipping away. Ayan cleared her throat, determined to finish with a stiff upper lip. "I want people to feel safe and welcome here, I want it to be home to a culture of peace and harmony. Those things are

338

worth fighting for, and I'll defend them. As long as there is one family making a life here with food on their table, shelter overhead, and a fulfilling place in their community, the dream is still alive."

CHAPTER 53
A LOANER

Ashley and Minh-Chu's quarters aboard the Warlord were sparse and surprisingly neat. Alice had a feeling that the tidiness was thanks to Minh-Chu's influence. He'd spent years in Freeground Infantry, something she kept meaning to ask him about. From where she lay on a slim cot, it was clear that for everything there was a place, and all things were in their place. It made the small two-person cabin seem a little bigger.

Most of the bulkhead above the double bed was painted with a display coating, and Alice stared at the twinkling image of a night sky. Ashley slept below it. She'd been the best of friends through the last couple of days, as Alice cried a river of tears, ranted about how no one would let her shuttle to the destroyer to see her father, and gave in to despair more than once. With one eye on the ship's status, Ashley supported her through it all. Alice was grateful, and a little embarrassed.

There was nothing they could do but hope that her father would be saved aboard the Triton; no one could do anything for him with the technology they had aboard the Warlord. Not even Alice could regenerate him. As she had been told time and time again, if even a few anti-framework nanobots survived, she could end up in the same state as her father, or worse.

She didn't know why she woke up in the middle of the third watch, but Alice didn't mind so much. Ashley groaned and rolled over, still deep in sleep. Alice watched her as she huffed, mumbled, "Gonna get stuck, Zoe," then settled down.

Alice snickered and started to close her eyes when her comm unit buzzed and blinked bright red. She scrambled to answer the emergency call. "What's up? I'm off shift."

"Third watch, I know," Remmy said, "But there's something crawling around on the Warlord's hull, I've linked you up with the scanners of the Sunny Shifter so you can see our readings."

"Threat identify," Alice whispered at her command and control unit. It executed one of her old pieces of software and highlighted four faint heat signatures. "They're under camouflage, it's matching the hull."

"Hey, where'd you get that program?" Remmy asked.

"It's a really old plugin for Freeground sensors I adapted to our comms. They stopped installing it before your time because people were using it instead of their own analytical tools. I'll pass it on later."

"Great, we'll have to swap code sometime," Remmy replied. "I'm going to pass this on to Warlord Command."

"Don't bother, Frost is off-duty and half my team is up right now anyway. We're due for a walk."

"A walk?"

"Yup, just what I need to clear my head, a stroll along the hull inside a nice wide wormhole," Alice said, flashing a toothy grin.

"Who ya talkin' to?" Ashley asked, half asleep.

"Just going to stretch my legs, I'll be right back," Alice told her soothingly.

"Mmm-kay," Ashley said as she lay back down.

Alice dragged her kit and her armour into the hall and got dressed hurriedly. A pair of technicians rounded the corner and immediately averted their eyes. "Oh, God, I've worn smaller bathing suits," Alice said, rolling her eyes.

"What?" Remmy asked.

"Couple night techs caught me before I got my suit on. Caught me in my undies, nothing to get excited about," Alice replied. "I'm surprised your comm doesn't have a wider focus, your profile log definitely reveals a tendency for peeking. I'm sure one of those techs could replay that glimpse for you." She knew her attempt at teasing him as revenge for getting her out of bed was clumsy, but according to his wide-eyed reaction, it was working.

"Holy hell, are you trying to get me slagged? You know who your father is, right?" Remmy said. There was a moment's pause. "I'm so sorry, I didn't mean to remind you, or get you thinking about-"

"Don't worry about it," Alice replied. "I'm lucky, there's still hope. He's still alive."

"Exactly," Remmy said, grinning a little too broadly for it not to be forced. "And he'd cave my head in if he heard a rumour that I was flirting with his daughter."

"You're flirting with Alice?" asked a shrill, shocked female voice from somewhere behind Remmy.

"No," Remmy replied, "I live strictly in Alice's friend zone, let it be known that there was never any flirting! Actually, don't say anything at all about the topic of flirting or flirtatiousness in general, mum on the presence or absence of flirting with anyone."

"Smooth," Alice remarked with a smirk as she sealed the front of her armour. She sent orders for the nearest security personnel to meet her down the hallway.

"Yeah, I run an orderly operation," Remmy replied, to which there were a few chuckles and guffaws in the background. "Seriously though, Frost has to know about this. I'm signalling him."

"I'm just about ready to go and my team is meeting me near the damaged section. It's on the same level I'm on now."

"Wait until you have his orders on it," Remmy said. "He may want to take care of this himself."

"The captain is out of commission and the first officer isn't aboard. I'm head of security," Alice said as she checked her rifle and started walking down the corridor. "I technically outrank him when it comes to incursions."

"You don't outrank an acting captain!" Remmy whispered urgently. "Oh, God, he hasn't answered yet. How do you ignore vibrations, a bright, flashing light, and an alarm that sounds like a screaming rim weasel?"

Alice met three of her team at the first intersecting corridor. They fell in step with her as she spoke to Remmy. "Well, then I definitely have to take action. I'll tell you how it turns out later."

"Wait! Take a right two doors down into that bunkroom, there's an Order Knight's heavy rifle in the net above my bunk," Remmy said.

"Oh, Remmy, you shouldn't have," Alice said with a grin.

"If you're going out there anyway, you may as well take enough firepower to give a gunship second thoughts."

Alice rushed to the hatch and looked inside. She scanned around the bunkroom reserved for Remmy's Ranger team and found the weapon. "Got it," she said as she rushed to it.

"Okay, now it has to power up, just press the-"

"Found it," Alice said as she opened a dented control cover, pressed a button, and closed it again. "I helped write the book on this gun, remember?"

"Right, forgot you're a gun nut," Remmy replied.

Alice's suit helped her balance the rifle against her shoulder as it ran through its start up diagnostic. "How'd you get this? I kept on requesting one but no one would answer me."

"It was a gift for busting the last Order bunker on Tamber," Remmy said.

"Okay, looks like everything's ready to go. Thanks loads," Alice said. She was just about to close the channel but realized something. "Oh, and Remmy?"

"Yeah?"

"You cheered me up. I had my cry and my ranting with Ash, but you got me smiling, thank you."

"You're about to go into mortal danger for which you are barely trained. Wait for Frost to respond."

"Don't spoil it," Alice said before closing the channel.

"Nice weapon," one of her officers said as she emerged from the Ranger bunkroom.

"Thanks," Alice said. "It's a loaner."

"Last time I gave a girl anything that cool I almost married her," said Havernash.

"Thankfully this is just a loaner, no crazy strings attached," Alice said.

"Marriage is not a crazy string," he replied.

"Depends on who you get tied to," Alice replied. The rest of her team was waiting beneath one of the main dorsal airlocks.

"So, what's up?" asked Havernash.

"Sensors report that there's something moving on the hull, we're going to go outside and look around," Alice replied.

"Alice, what are you doing?" Stephanie asked her over her communicator.

"Checking some sensor readings," Alice said as she entered the airlock with two of her best. "The Edxi corvette that made a close pass on us right at the end probably dropped a few people off. No way of knowing what they're doing for sure unless we get out there; the sensors are too damaged in that section to see anything."

"Wait until we're out of the wormhole," Stephanie said.

"I bet that's what they're waiting for, too," Alice said. "Besides, it's not your call. You're not aboard, and you left me in charge of counter-incursion." She placed her hand on the hull plating above her and waited for her command and control unit to start updating the state of the Warlord's damaged section.

"As first officer, it's my call," Stephanie protested.

"If you just put me on counter-incursion because you didn't think anything would happen on the Warlord and you wanted to make me feel better, then you're in for a surprise. I take this job seriously, and I'm going to make sure nothing happens to the Warlord. If Frost had any concerns about who was left in charge of internal security, then he wouldn't sleep so soundly. Remmy already sent him a notice." Alice checked the results of her more detailed scan and saw that there were vibrations and hull stress that could only indicate one thing. "Okay, my suit's picking up something from direct contact with the hull. Our uninvited passengers are starting to cut into the sections of the hull where we're sensor dead. There are already three cuts where a good kick will make a hole big enough for entry. Still think we can wait for another day?"

To Alice's surprise, Stephanie said, "You're right. They must have serious camouflage tech if we're not seeing what their tools are doing. Be careful, take as many approaches as you can."

Alice highlighted a number of working airlocks and sent her people off in pairs using her tactical system. They left right away, moving at a run. "I plan on coming out all at once, full cloaking systems on."

"Good. Watch your crossfire," Stephanie said. "I'll watch from here, not much else I can do."

"Thank you, Ma'am, I'll have them scraped off in no time."

"What do you think we'll find out there?" asked Havernash, who she had assigned as her partner for the excursion.

"Expect the worst," Alice replied. "But remember to move away from our airlock as soon as we come out. They're going to fire on what they can see, and this airlock will be it. You ready?"

"Hell yeah, let's scrape these hijackers," he replied.

Alice made sure her whole team was in position and started a countdown from three on her command and control unit. She got into position beneath the hatch, making adjustments so the tip of her loaner rifle didn't catch on the edge. She turned her shielding and cloaking systems all the way up; the system wouldn't be able to maintain that power level for more than fourteen minutes, but she hoped they wouldn't need that long.

Five airlocks popped open all at once, and Alice was through hers in a rush, leaping out and diving to one side. As predicted, the enemy concentrated fire on all but one of the hatches. Several of her people took massive shield damage, but they all managed to make it out onto the hull.

The surface of the warped hull plating was illuminated by ghostly blue and yellow light, focused by the compression barrier of the wormhole four hundred metres above. White light flashed behind them intermittently as the Sunny Shifter's thrusters fired to match the pace of the Warlord's deceleration. To her right and left, Alice could see the Warlord's thruster pylons, massive rotary thrusters, pulsing to slow the ship down. Ahead loomed the first craft to enter the wormhole – the destroyer, and she wished

344

the defensive gun turrets at the rear of that ship could help, but they didn't have the crew aboard to operate them.

Light flashed to her right, illuminating her peripheral. Her tactical system indicated that it was analysing a new type of weapon and that it was also trying to look up the race of five different types of beings walking on the damaged section of the hull. There were nine enemies altogether, and two were already firing.

Alice ducked a fraction of a second before a self-propelled weapon passed just overhead. An image of it appeared on her heads-up display as the analysis of the weapon completed. It was an explosive disc with small thrusters and beam emitters surrounding its core that projected some kind of cutter beams. "They haven't seen us yet, get into position," said Alice's second in command.

"These are Edxi," said another. The tension in her voice grated on Alice.

All of her people were firmly affixed to the hull and were moving towards their nearest targets, taking aim. Alice was surprised that the creatures didn't continue to fire on the open airlocks. Instead, they sent up several of their seeker discs and returned to work, slowly cutting circular shapes into the hull of the Warlord. Alice started closing the distance between her and the nearest Edxian, a three metre tall thing in carapace-like armour with six upper arms. The ones at the top had three main sections with long, sharp digits at the end, while the other arms were smaller, with only two sections each. It walked on four spider-like legs, unlike any Edxian Alice had known. "Take aim," Alice said, slowly unslinging her borrowed heavy rifle and kneeling only five metres away from the legs of the strange alien in front of her. Her partner did the same.

"Oh, God," breathed one of Alice's soldiers. "It's looking right at me."

"Shoot the legs!" Alice said a second too late as the Edxian facing one of the soldiers well behind her fired one of the discs, which flared violently at her squad member, slicing at his shields with super-heated beams then exploding violently when it was within a metre of him. He was flung off the hull of the Warlord towards the compression wall of the wormhole, and he managed to fire a tether line before he was destroyed crossing the energy barrier. The Edxian used the line to find its target and opened fire with a weapon that sent a barrage of exploding projectiles at Timmerman. His shields and armour only lasted seconds, and Alice's tactical system confirmed what she already knew – he was dead.

Alice fired on her own target. To her surprise, it took several concussive shots to blast her Edxian's legs to pieces and send it spiralling towards the thruster wash, where it was incinerated.

345

She whirled toward the Edxian who killed Timmerman and opened fire. The rest of her troops followed her example, opening up on all the Edxians scrambling along the hull. Her shields took several hits from the seeker discs, and she let her tracking system guide her aim towards one. It was on its way towards her when the secondary beam weapon on her rifle cut through it. She barely dodged before it struck the hull and exploded.

Her teams' excursion onto the hull had turned into a full-on shooting match. She opened fire on the next Edxian as it blasted roughly in her direction. If she hadn't already been moving, she'd be missing limbs or worse. Her rifle tore the Edxian to pieces, but not before it landed a few hits of its own, reducing her shielding down to three percent and scarring her armour with what her tactical system identified as super-heated microparticles.

Another strike caught her in the back, doing severe damage to her outer armour, but Havernash gunned her assailant down using heavy explosive rounds. She felt several ice-cold pinpricks on her skin, indicating that her armour had been breached. The inner layer of her armour repaired itself in seconds, re-sealing her from the vacuum of space. By then her rifle was trained on one of the two remaining Edxians, and she fired at what she thought was a head, a rough protrusion from the middle of its torso. "Kill him! Kill him!" shouted Nesh Samo as she fired at the Edxian, several discs closing in on her position.

"Stop firing and move! Those things can't track you if your cloaking systems get a chance to work!" Alice shouted, only too late. The discs closed in, firing white-hot beams at the soldier then exploding all around her.

Seconds later, the battle was over. Two Edxian corpses were still attached to the hull, the rest were confirmed dead and had either drifted towards the compression wall and torn apart or were somewhere ahead of the ships. The corpses would be ripped apart as they reached the forward edge of the wormhole where space was being compressed by the Warlord's systems.

She took a good look at one of the largest black-clad attackers. There were no life signs, and the main body of its armour was open to space. The shape of their armour brought back the memory of delivering stolen Edxian eggs to Zarrix. She could recall his corpulent form, scarred exoskeletal bone and leathery flesh, joints that didn't seem to bend the right way, and long, weapon-like appendages. The armour these creatures wore hid much of that detail, but they were still almost three metres tall, hunched down, with similar limbs.

Alice recalled recorded images of the other Edxians that were on the hull and lined them up at the top of her heads-up display. Some of them had two long arms, others had multiples of varying lengths, and with those multiple arms came a multitude of unfamiliar tools and weapons. They used some kind of thin black material to create three bubbles against the hull, shielding them from intense external scans while they did their work. There was a lot of new information to process, and they didn't have time.

"Okay, we have to do a detailed scan of the hull from the outside so Finn can have a clear picture of the damage," Alice said. "Then we get these corpses inside."

"Inside? Are you kidding?"

"Yes, inside. Their tech is inert, they're dead, and we have a lot to learn. These things took more than one shot from our weapons on their highest setting and killed two of us. We need to be ready for war with them."

"What the hell are you talking about? We're not at war with the Edxians, these guys must be some kind of Order supporters. No one's reporting any other Edxi attacks."

Alice touched the dead Edxian towering over her. The black outer armour was highly flexible, but her sensors read that it was almost as dense as her own armour. There were new, unknown materials at work. "The captain just told everyone what's really going on aboard that destroyer. We're only fighting the Order because they're in the way of the real war. There's an invasion coming, maybe it's already started. We'll be seeing more of these."

CHAPTER 54
THE LOATHING OF BEASTS

The mines of Coba were endless. It was easy to see why the rebels in the Pionero System would dig into the caves. Clark Patterson didn't enjoy his Beast persona often, but when he was surrounded by brainwashed Order of Eden soldiers, he enjoyed how they made every effort to avoid his gaze and stay out of his way. They were all around him as he moved through the large cavern. He could feel the gravel crunch underfoot, but the sound was drowned out by the noise of firing rifles. He left the Order Knights behind, and brought one of their heavy rifles for himself instead.

The soldiers around him in their dark green armour believed that it was a privilege to be chosen for the excursion. In truth, Clark couldn't stand any of them. He chose them because they were the least intelligent, the most easily brainwashed, and the most firm believers. To them, he was the hell-spawned master on a mission to punish those who would resist the authority of the Order. They fought well and Clark understood how useful they could be, but he couldn't stand a mindless zealot.

The ground vibrated for a moment as the heavily armoured shuttles behind them finished landing around his vanguard ship. There were another eight hundred well-equipped, trained soldiers in those ships, and they would finish clearing the tunnels or die. He wouldn't be sending another wave, not to these caves.

The large central chamber had makeshift tents crammed with cots, a kitchen made from parts of a crashed ship's galley and scavenged things from across the nearly uninhabitable surface. The cavern's top was somewhere far up in the darkness above, the broad shafts made for working transports were their only convenient way out. Clark hoped the Order Knights he'd left to defend the openings would succeed in keeping the rebels from collapsing the entrance. Tunnels led outward from there in all directions. Capturing or killing every group of rebels would take weeks –

perhaps months – without using powerful explosives. It was an option, no one would blame him, and absolutely no one would question him if he cratered a large percentage of Planet Coba, but he wasn't interested in resorting to the same murderous tactics as the governors he just replaced. Besides, there were so many different types of precious dense metals in the ground at their feet, destroying that section of the mine would come at a high cost.

A group of rebels revealed themselves momentarily, firing bursts at the soldiers deploying behind them from one of the upper cave entrances. Several detonations from repurposed explosive charges erupted amongst the troops. "They've made some kind of rocket bombs out of the charges left behind by the miners!" shouted one of the sergeants.

Clark fired his rifle towards the small cave opening, super heating the stone and driving the rebels back. "Use seeker rounds," *you idiots,* he thought, but refrained from adding. This wouldn't go well; Clark had the distinct feeling that he was wasting his time. "The rebels still think they have a chance. Some of them are close enough to the central caverns that we have a chance to catch them. The rest are escaping further into the caves. Break up into squads, send sensor repeaters so you can scan as much of the cave network as possible, and figure out how many of them there are. Chase after the closest. Now, go."

His communicator indicated that the message he was waiting for had arrived, and Clark Patterson mentally activated the hatch to his personal drop ship and walked towards it, pushing his way through the crowd of soldiers moving around him. He couldn't help but curse himself for handling the minutia himself. He wanted a distraction, and though taking direct command of a platoon seemed like a good idea at first, he found himself becoming more irritated by the second.

He needed something to do while he waited to hear the fate of the Fallen Star, however. The signal from Shozo had come through; she'd somehow managed to make a workable deal for her people.

Clark gave his heavy rifle to an awaiting service bot as he stepped onto the platform that would lift him into the passenger section of the shuttle. "You are ordered to pursue and capture rebels if possible," he told the lieutenant in charge of the cave skirmish through his communicator. "Kill them only if you are left with no other choice."

"What do we do with the prisoners?" asked the lieutenant in a surprisingly appealing female voice.

"Put them in stasis and load them onto the next transport to Upello. They'll find plenty to fight there," Clark replied, knowing that Upello was the next to be used as an Edxian brood world. In less than a month, it would be swarming with their hatched young, mindless hunters who would be hungry for the better part of three decades.

"Understood, Sir."

"One more thing, Lieutenant Turney. You will not receive any further reinforcements for this operation. If you lose over eighty percent of your forces, you are to retreat. I will not allow this operation to become a protracted engagement." He closed the channel and stepped into his private chamber as the lift platform sealed to the centre of the deck. His personal communications and command system sent information to the circular chamber so it could display everything he wanted to pay attention to. The chamber filled to his chest with water as his ship began rising up out of the cavern.

He looked around the room at all the holographic projections. It was as though all aspects of the Eden War were around him, even more so since he was closer to the Iron Head Nebula, closer to many hidden hypertransmitter nodes. A new transmission addressed to all Order Of Eden personnel appeared. It was marked by Eve as mandatory viewing. He looked at the details and discovered that it was recorded while she was on her way to the Sogarian System on an extended recruiting mission. It was central to the opposite side of the Iron Head Nebula, had over six billion people – many of whom were starving – and it was the perfect place for her to feed her saviour complex. That was the notification his comm sent him, not news from the Fallen Star.

Clark checked on the status of his tall, spike-shaped landing craft and saw that his pilots were guiding it back to the Overlord as expected, then he activated Eve's speech. The chamber's walls disappeared behind a holographic projection of an amphitheatre decorated with wood, gold, and crystal chandeliers in the twenty-first century Earth fashion. He knew this was a place she'd had built aboard the Liberator, her own command carrier. The ship had finished crossing the Iron Head Nebula and was in its deceleration cycle. The large domed windows overhead shed a ghostly blue light on the two thousand attendees.

Dressed in a long gown that flared out at the bottom and the top, she gracefully walked to the centre of the stage. The mix of light and dark greens on her dress reflected against her face and the skin exposed by the slit down the front of her outfit, giving her a strange colouring. All the jitters she suffered from when she first started appearing publicly were gone, as evidenced by her easy smile and how her gaze swept from the front rows to the back and across the audience.

350

"It is known that the fate of the Order of Eden is set, to join together and evolve past the rest of humanity. It is also known that it takes individual sacrifice and service to elevate to the exalted ranks and receive the gift of immortality. So many of you are on your way; I am so proud of the growth I've seen since terrorists killed our Child Prophet."

Clark couldn't help but scoff at that lie. Five months before, Eve and he agreed that it was time for the Child Prophet to be retired, and they leaked fake footage of him being killed in a bombing during a small rally. They treated it like a tragedy and allowed the Order of Eden to mourn with Eve appearing often to console them. After a week, they turned his death into a rallying cry for more Order of Eden followers to abandon the pacifist path and join the military. Enlistment surged past capacity, and there was a waiting list of volunteers ever since.

Eve went on, as she often did. "That was such a barrier to overcome, and we are stronger than ever. That is why I know that we will overcome this new threat I'm here to tell you about now. It is so small compared to the loss of our Prophet, but it represents a disease that plagues the rest of humanity, a disease that we will cure. I'm afraid one of the Order's oldest enemies has come to threaten us once again. The terrorist Jacob Valent has led a band of pirates against a small training ship and revealed his true nature. I warn you that what you are about to see is quite graphic, but we must be exposed to this so we know how to defeat it. The stage was overwhelmed with the image of a starship bridge. Jacob Valent was pictured holding a weapon to a young crewman's head telling him, "We're going to play a game, it's called Chinese Whispers."

The way the holographic image of the bridge lined up with the stage set the scene out like an old fashioned play, but Clark suspected no playwright would ever pen such a rage-fuelled gore show. He flinched when the young crewman almost finished counting down from ten and Jake fired his weapon. Clark couldn't help but be shocked as Jake made sport of killing crewmembers. After killing one of the crew, Jake retracted his headgear, and in the light of what Clark was seeing, how unhinged Valent seemed, he couldn't help but think it may be time for him to die. Something had driven the hero Clark Patterson once worshipped out of Jacob Valent.

By the time Jacob got the codes out of the young ship captain, Clark was thoroughly disappointed by Valent, but more importantly, he didn't understand why Eve was showing the terrorist recording to her audience, and why she didn't change what Jake said when he stated, "I'll fight my way through every captain and soldier in the fleet to get to the real war and they won't even leave a stain on my memory."

That was so potentially damning that Clark was utterly outraged. It made it seem like Jacob Valent barely regarded the Order of Eden as an obstacle, and revealed that he was fully aware that the Edxi were at the centre of the Order's involvement. That statement may not mean much to the average soldier, but the higher ranks, the few thousand who knew everything about the balance they were trying to maintain in the galaxy, could panic. Most of them were former businessmen, or from wealthy families granted governorship in trade for resources.

The playback ended with the young ship captain giving up her command codes, leaving Eve's audience with the worst mental image she could offer – that of weakness and surrender. The image dissipated and Eve stood alone on the stage. "This is one terrible man who thinks that he is powerful because he overtook a small ship on a training mission. While we should mourn for the people we have lost, we should also have faith that this villain is the perfect target for us to show the rest of the galaxy that senseless terrorism won't diminish our message or our mission. We are blessed by fate, and that will not be taken from us. This is only a test, and we will overcome it. You go with my love, my trust, and my faith."

The lights dimmed as Eve retreated from the stage. "What? What does she think she's doing?" Clark cried aloud. "You're helping him! This is exactly what he wants!" He scanned through the data stream and found the original recording of the boarding action, and was even more enraged to see that Eve hadn't used the most helpful part of the recording. Moments after taking the command codes, Jacob Valent collapsed, and the internal sensor logs from the destroyer cited a nanobot infestation as the cause. It was a trap Clark had set months before, adding a nanobot system to Order Knight framework systems so the specialist soldiers could be destroyed if they were captured or turned against their masters. It hadnt' even occurred to Clark that the nanobots in the Order Knight's armour would attack other unauthorized and unregistered framework systems if they were encountered. Jake, and possibly Alice, were infested with nanobots that would destroy all the framework technology from within their bodies, deactivating the systems and most likely killing them both.

"This is what they should see," Clark said as he mentally ordered his chamber to be drained of all fluids. He set the chamber so only he stood in light, darkness surrounding him, and he looked at the shifting colour of his carapace. The jagged shards of his outer armour were every shade of red and black as his blood pressure rose and renewed the corpulent silhouette he'd grown to hate. In this moment, he accepted it as a helpful aspect of his appearance. It was time to confirm his presence to all Order of Eden followers.

With a gesture and a thought, he commanded the holographic systems in the room to show a projection of the entire Order of Eden Fleet drifting in space behind him, and he began recording. "I am the Beast, Master of the Order of Eden War Fleet." He could feel the grinding of his facial armour as the shards moved with his speech. "You've just seen our spiritual leader, Eve, speak about the terrorist Jacob Valent. He is a misguided man from a military organization that has never made a significant mark on the galaxy. His corrupt sense of justice has already led him to a bad end. In an attempt to extend a peaceful gesture to our enemies and attract people who are suppressed by them, Eve neglected to show you the very moment when Jacob Valent fell to our superior technology. I'm showing you this now." With a thought, Clark started the playback of Jacob Valent collapsing and his friend rushing to his side. "What you have just seen is a weapon we use to counter stolen immortality systems. Jacob Valent used our technology to bolster himself, to overcome his innate weaknesses. We have turned this against him, and he is dead. His people are now in retreat, taking refuge in a place called Haven Shore, well outside of our space. They pretend that the Order of Eden does not exist because they know they are powerless against our superior might, and that a few people have as much a chance to stop us from embracing our fate as they have at stopping a tide from rising. Our destiny will be fulfilled, and every one of you is powerful enough to defeat pathetic beings like Jacob Valent." He mentally ended the transmission and ordered a communications block for Eve and her command carrier. She would only be able to reach him; as far as the rest of the galaxy was concerned, she had been gagged.

Another message appeared in his mind's eye, this one was from Shozo. "My Dominant," she began, "you were wise to direct us to Lorander. After reviewing our situation, and taking the state of the galaxy into account, we have been led to Haven Shore, where they went to great expense in creating good conditions for us to settle with people you admire – Ayan Anderson and other people from your place of birth, Freeground. I am pleased to announce that we are already beginning to mix the clean fresh water with our habitat aboard the Fallen Star, and expect to be swimming freely within a week. I will be able to send you messages in the future, but the people here tell me I must use their systems, so they can be sure we do not reveal any important information. I do not object, since you did not want us to fight in this war, and they won't be forcing us to take up arms against you, either. In my most beautiful dreams you are with us, founding a new clutch, building the glory of your House, and I hope that can become a reality soon, when you have brought peace to the galaxy."

The recorded transmission ended, and the Beast was struck still, silent. He should have armed the Fallen Star and his House, and sent them to an unexplored sector where they could search for a place that was entirely new, not directed them to Lorander. They used them as a pawn, an extra layer of protection for Tamber and Haven Shore. They tricked Shozo and now House Fallen Star was out of reach.

He could not clear his head of anger and doubt. He could barely think. "Pilot, take us back down," he commanded through the comm system.

The Beast felt his ship touch down, back in the cavern, and he commanded the platform in the middle of his private chamber to lower. "Lower the troop generation pod and activate three hundred framework soldiers," he said to the officer in the disembarking room as he was handed his Order Knight rifle. The monstrous weapon would see some use.

"Yes, Sir, your soldiers will be ready in sixteen minutes," said the armoured lieutenant. Even as he tried to stand straight, it seemed like the soldier wanted to shrink away from the Beast, and it irritated Clark to no end.

"Make sure they are all recording this engagement," he said. "The Order of Eden needs an example."

"This is not what I expected at the end of my tour of the Triton," Lacey whispered to Ayan as they sat down in the middle of the main bridge. At a glance, Ayan could see that the crew was busy managing multiple repair operations as well as normal management. She hadn't realized how much she missed the nerve centre of the great ship Triton until then, and was surprised at how comfortable the place was to her.

A look towards the ramp leading to the Flight Deck was enough of an indication to the ship that she wanted to see the large control centre beneath her feet, and the floor became fully transparent to her. Anyone else not looking towards the Flight Deck would see mostly opaque floor beneath their feet. The Flight Deck had become a fleet control centre for the small percentage of air and orbital space Triton Fleet had taken direct control of. The Haven Shore Navnet, fighter wing command, and several other space organization tasks were under way, keeping thirty officers busy, several of whom were in training. She decided to show Lacey the flight control centre later; there was barely enough room to move down there.

If it weren't for the British Alliance's help with the monitoring and control of the Rega Gain System, there would be chaos. Ayan's work in politics wasn't over. She was due to discuss the timeframe Triton Fleet would get for taking over full management of the solar system, and she hoped the British Alliance would take governance of a few worlds for two years at least. Anything to guarantee their continued presence in the system would be a positive step forward.

"I've never felt more conspicuously out of place in my life," Lacey said.

"I hear you're a logistics master," Oz said as he emerged from the officers' entrance to their right. He crossed to the centre of the bridge and sat in the middle command seat. "Good morning. Coffee is on the way, the real stuff," he said to Ayan. "Thanks to Haven Shore's pickers. Too bad you're leaving your political career there, opinion is changing in your favour since you announced that Haven Shore was going to be run by the military again."

"I think it was what you said about your dreams for the place," Lacey said. "I'll see that happen while you're up here."

"I still feel like I'm abandoning Haven Shore," Ayan said.

"You gave us the blueprint, that's what's important."

"Half of the social blueprint is a direct rip from old Freeground lifestyle, I can't take much credit," Ayan said. "The rest is either a result of our situation or Liam's input."

"Stop avoiding credit, Commodore," Oz said with a knowing smile. "You take more responsibility than you should. It's about time you let someone pat you on the back."

"He's right," Lacey said. "Carl is taking his place as governor of Haven Shore seriously. It's early yet, but it looks like he really loves it. He's happy you're up here too, we're all winners here."

Ayan didn't know what to say, and felt some relief despite the sensation of being ambushed by Oz and Lacey. "I'll just shut up and be happy then," she chuckled. "Let's finish the tour, I want to see what the Botanical Gallery looks like now, I hear there were changes."

"Make sure you take a walk along the aquatic section on your way there, the Issyrian habitat is almost finished," Oz said. "There's a new Botanical Gallery child care section too, I'm sure they'd like a visit. You can't miss it."

"Sir, we have unencrypted data coming in from the edge of the Iron Head Nebula," announced an older looking gentleman at the communications station. "It's being broadcast on all emergency and news bands, addresses the Order of Eden, Regent Galactic, and partners."

"That's strange," Oz said. He brought up the data stream and Ayan's heart jumped as the header information finished coming through and she read the origin point: The Warlord. "Obviously Jake wants everyone to see this."

"Is it just me, or does he really like grand-standing?" Lacey asked.

"He uses publicity on the networks as a tactical tool, and the British told him to terrorize everyone on the wrong side of this conflict. This could be difficult to watch," Oz warned.

The footage began to play back, starting with the image of the Warlord's guns hammering a pair of Order of Eden patrol corvettes. The warship preyed on the similarly sized, but lesser armed ships as though they were nothing more than cargo carriers. Starfighters swept by, adding their firepower to the exchange as missiles from unknown origin points swept in and exploded against the escort corvettes' hulls.

"I thought the Warlord only had a few fighters?" Lacey asked.

"They probably dropped weapons platforms using mine launchers," Oz replied. "A section of the machine shop aboard the Triton was used to put some together." They watched in silence for several moments as the exchange continued. The Warlord stopped firing as the pair of corvettes lost power. Time itself seemed suspended as the victorious ship's activity ceased for long seconds, as though it was deciding for or against mercy.

Ayan was surprised when the railguns aboard the Warlord flared back to life, ripping the hulls of the battered corvettes wide open from stem to stern. Only three escape pods made it off those ships. The last shots on each corvette struck their reactors, removing any possibility that the ships could be repaired. The Warlord disappeared, not waiting to strike their next targets.

"No prisoners?" Lacey asked. "They're not even going to recover the escape pods that made it?"

"The Warlord and her captain don't seem interested," Oz said. "Besides, I think this battle is only beginning. The stream is over an hour long."

They watched as the battle progressed and the recording followed the agile Uriel fighters, the brutal mauling the Warlord inflicted on the strange decloaked Edxian newcomers, and boarding operations led by Remmy Sands, Moira McFadden, Jacob Valent, and Stephanie Vega. Half way through the transmission, while Stephanie entered a compartment with her team and sent several guided disintegration grenades ahead, instantly killing four guards and six crewmembers from behind, Lacey stood up. "This isn't something I need to see," she said quietly. "I'll meet you in the Botanical Gallery."

"I'll see you after," Ayan replied. The broadcast from the Warlord was assembled like a Freeground visual report; there was no consideration for any viewer who hadn't seen combat or didn't know the brutality of real war. The lengths the Warlord crew went to during the fight didn't shock Ayan, but she immediately understood that the unapologetic report would force the vast majority of civilians to turn away.

Any bridge crewmember who wasn't already busy at their station watched the report for themselves, and Ayan suspected that millions of Rega Gain residents and transients were doing the same. Not even Remmy Sands and his Ranger squad told the crew of the ship they raided to surrender more than once. It was a whole new chapter in methods as far as Jacob Valent was concerned. His new command style was to offer one set of terms for surrender a single time, then kill everything in their way, and all the boarding teams shared the policy.

Remmy's team had the easiest time. Most of the crew aboard the Sunny Shifter abandoned ship in a pair of civilian shuttles before the Rangers finished forcing their way aboard. The small military staff that was left wasn't able to put up much resistance, but they tried. When Remmy's people were able to break into the forward section of the vessel, they faced eighteen zealous defenders who fought to the last man and woman. They were able to revive the first officer using the most extreme medical technology they'd brought with them, but the others were too far gone. Ayan recognized immense potential in Remmy Sands. His leadership style was absolutely straightforward, something typical of the top Ranger graduates. He told his people what to do with confidence, not bravado or aggression. His style of delegation was skill-based. He knew what each member of his team was good at, and moved them like chess pieces.

He knew to reach out beyond his team for help when it was available too, as evidenced by his contact with Alice. It surprised Ayan, but it all made sense when it resulted in Remmy breaking through security so his team could move ahead as safely and quickly as possible. Remmy Sands had the potential to become a general, but it was a little early for Ayan to tell him.

Oz focused on the boarding action of the destroyer, watching Stephanie Vega sneak and Jacob Valent rampage through the ship. The first was headed aft, the second was blasting his way to the fore. The sheer merciless quality of their tactics drove all but the most stalwart defenders back. Minh-Chu led the soldiers behind Jacob and Moira, occasionally handing more grenades and replacement shield emitters to one of the fearless leaders as they expended both in a frontal assault that showed no regard for the condition of the ship or the lives of their enemies.

At the end of Jacob Valent's rush to the bridge, Ayan heard Oz say, "No, Jake, don't do it," as Valent engaged with an Order of Eden Knight in hand-to-hand combat. Ayan and Oz watched as Jake managed to overcome his opponent. Her helmet opened and the feed jumped to Jacob Valent playing Chinese Whispers with a bridge crewmember.

Oz and Ayan were aghast when Jacob pulled the trigger the first time. After the second, Oz muttered, "What is Minh doing? He should get in there, this is something Jake is going to regret. It's not who he is."

Ayan was as shocked as Oz at first, but her longer-term reaction was more complicated. A part of her hated the waste of life she was watching, but she understood it. Just as Jake said to the captain of the destroyer, he was fighting the Order so he could get to the real war, the fight for humanity, but there was more to Ayan's thinking. The Victory Machine led her to separate herself from Jake abruptly, and as she watched Jacob Valent become something new, something made of pure, malicious anger, she realized that he would never have been able to take things so far if they were still a couple. She stared at the frozen image of Jacob Valent holding the young destroyer captain up by her braid long after the playback ended, stuck in the realization that a part of Jake's anger could come from her sudden separation from him.

"Ayan," Oz said as he stood slowly. "My ready room." He turned towards the communications team. "Triton Fleet doesn't have an official or unofficial opinion on this yet," he told them loudly enough for everyone on the bridge to hear. "Neither does any member of the Triton crew. No one comments on this until Triton Fleet Command is ready, do you understand?"

"Yes, Sir," replied an older communications officer.

Oz led Ayan off the bridge and across the narrow hallway adjacent to his ready room. It had been furnished with a wire frame sofa, three chairs, and a few pictures of the various ships Oz had served on in his career were printed on the walls. The furniture looked incomplete, just wire frame and mesh, but it was surprisingly comfortable. Ayan sat down and stood up right away.

"What's going on?" Oz asked. "I don't know how to read your reaction here, do you know something I don't?"

"Yes," Ayan said. "This had to happen. According to the Victory Machine, at least."

"You never mentioned the Victory Machine showing you a vision of Jake going off the deep end," Oz replied.

"It did tell me that putting space between him and me was important, and I know what we just saw wouldn't have happened if I were with him," Ayan said. The idea seemed less convincing aloud.

"You can't tell me that he's murdering people because of a bad breakup half a year ago," Oz said. "He's even been with someone since."

She ignored the bur at being reminded of Jake's fling with a British Alliance intelligence officer. "Think about it. The Triton is almost finished, Haven Shore is effectively operational. We'll be handing full navnet handling to them in a week. If we were together all this time, then I would have left on the Warlord with him for this trip. There would be almost no reason for me to stay near Tamber, and I'd want to be along for a big operation just like the one the Warlord finished."

Oz sat down and buried his head in his hands. "I hate that bloody machine," he muttered. "There are a lot of variables in what you're saying, but you're probably right. Doesn't matter much though, he's still broken most of the important rules of engagement."

"We need to scatter the Order of Eden's followers," Ayan said. "For a lot of them this war isn't real yet, and they typically approach every engagement with superior forces and firepower. We have to show them that, even with that, they can't expect to win every time. Jake just did."

"You agree with what he's doing?"

"The more I think of it, yes. Those bridge officers weren't there to embark on some wonderful adventure, they were going to war, to kill innocent people just like Jake said. They were wannabe murderers, and Jake stopped them. Maybe scared hundreds of thousands more."

"And inspired thousands of zealots at the same time," Oz said. "The next group of recruits will feel completely justified when they sign up for Order military service because of this. He's changed the kind of war we're going to be fighting, never mind the Edxi waiting behind the Order."

"Maybe, but this could slow down Order recruitment, push some soldiers into deserting altogether. I'd rather fight a core of a hundred dedicated zealots than ten thousand people who are just following orders," Ayan said.

"I agree, but we'll have to wait and see if that math adds up," Oz said. "At least we all know what kind of war we'll be fighting now. The British Alliance is joining in on their founders' day at the end of the week. They'll be announcing it then. Who knows what this footage will do for their recruitment."

"That's something," Ayan said.

"I prefer to put aside whatever anger he may be expressing, and examine his thinking," said a smooth, low voice through the cabin's sound system. "He proposes that he acts as an ancient doctor, cutting a cancerous mass free from healthy tissue. That is an appropriate approach to this conflict."

"Sorry, who's speaking?" Ayan asked.

"Couldn't wait until she's officially transferred to the Triton tomorrow, could you?" Oz asked, looking towards one blank wall. A live portrait of the ship appeared.

"This is an important discussion, Oz. Besides, if there's anyone I feel I don't need protection from, it's Commodore Ayan Anderson. Permit me to take this opportunity to welcome you back, Ayan. Last time you spent any significant amount of time aboard, I was asleep."

"This is the Triton's artificial intelligence?" Ayan asked.

"I'm a caretaker and operator, a living being tailor-made to live aboard the Triton for several centuries. I'm mostly aquatic, and measure fairly high on the telepathic scale, higher than the Lorander First Minister, though she does have significant reach and comprehension. Putting that aside for a moment, I look forward to meeting you in person, something we'll have to do some time after the Warlord arrives."

"It's good to meet you, too," Ayan said, regarding Oz with a raised eyebrow. She couldn't believe that he didn't let her in on the secret about the Triton. "At least now I know why Oz has seemed distracted every now and then, usually in the middle of conversation."

"I'm sorry, since he's one of my only means of conveying my opinions, I spend a lot of time communicating with him," the Triton responded.

"So you're called by the same name as the ship?" Ayan asked.

"I've had three names, to be honest," the voice overhead replied.

"Three names? You told me to call you Triton," Oz said.

"That's what you kept picturing and there was no reason to complicate things, but Ayan's mind is more well suited to layered thinking. The surface thoughts she passively shares are more compassionate and elaborate than your deeper musings. That, and she's a puzzle solver. I love those."

"So I'm simple-minded," Oz said, shaking his head.

"You have a highly motivated soldier's mind that draws on a deep well of knowledge and experience. In classic human analogy, you would be a twenty-year-old scotch with character and strength, while she is a fuzzy navel that is fresh with complex bright flavours. Both are wonderfully intoxicating, but beyond that they cannot be compared."

"Let me guess, you experienced both vicariously?" Oz asked, rolling his eyes.

"On my last tour some of the crew enjoyed their contraband a great deal, and they were surprisingly adept at sneaking it aboard. I quietly linked with them telepathically while they indulged. Only once per beverage, mind you."

Ayan was amused beyond words by the Triton's keeper, and she enjoyed taking a moment for lighter conversation, but the more important issues nagged at her. "What would you like me to call you?" she asked.

"One of my favourite handlers called me Hausgiest, and I admit I became partial to it," he replied.

The translation appeared on her command and control unit as *House Spirit*. "Then that's what I'll call you, but I'll keep your secret."

"Thank you, Ayan. I hope to meet you soon."

"You will, but what were you saying before about Jake killing officers aboard the destroyer?"

"I will elaborate on my opinion," Hausgiest replied. "His methods are morally wrong in most situations, but he did kill military personnel, making his actions defensible in this specific case. It's true that they would eventually go on to crew that ship against his allies, however distant or removed. None of those factors seem to matter to the logical thoughts I know Captain Valent had before stepping onto that bridge. While he may have seemed unhinged, his approach makes sense when you consider it tactically."

"Okay, I think I know where you're going," Oz said.

"Captain Valent is setting a standard for brutality that is so high that his allies will feel their actions in war, however barbaric, will seem tame compared to the vitriolic murders he carried out. Some of his allies will even try to best him in terms of malicious performance. The Order of Eden is facing a foe that will hesitate less in battle when going for the kill, and that is highly intimidating. Add the Warlord and their armada-of-one strategies, and you have a dreaded opponent that can appear anywhere at any time then disappear after they've taken whatever they like. May I remind you of the Triton fighter wing's motto? Deploy, dominate, disappear? It seems the Warlord beat us to it, and I can't wait to show them how the Triton executes similar strategies."

"So you support Jake's methods?" Ayan asked.

"Yes. Mathematically, his methods of intimidation stand to save human lives on both sides by aggressively concluding this war as quickly as possible. It will seem bloodier than a more careful, drawn out conflict, but on the whole, the shorter, more violent confrontation of sides will involve fewer people and force everyone on both sides to reconsider the wisdom of their cause. The Order of Eden will be reduced in number. Oz is correct in predicting that zealots will appear, and if we relent they will win, but we must not hesitate. Victories will draw recruits to either side, and we must have as many as possible as soon as we can, then celebrate them each so the entire galaxy can hear us. I know this is not the Freeground way, but the war can be won using this strategy. I urge you to consider it, and to understand that this isn't my strategy, but Captain Valent's. I'm only extrapolating his intentions from his style and the insight I gained when I read his surface thoughts and emotions weeks ago."

"Do you read everyone who comes aboard?" Ayan asked with a chuckle.

"Only a little, enough to know whether or not they can do the Triton or their fellow crewmembers serious harm. I have to protect the silverware somehow," Hausgiest replied.

"Well," Ayan sat down slowly, considering everything Hausgiest said. "You're right, this isn't how Freeground Fleet would fight this war. There would be a lot of prisoners, the Admiralty would have a hand in determining the mandate of every outgoing ship, and Jake would probably lose his command for his conduct. Freeground has never met something like the Order, though. They've never won a battle the way Jake and the Warlord crew did. Against those odds, any Freeground captain would be instructed to stand down and retreat."

"I'll support strike and fade tactics, but it's not in me to kill people who surrender to me," Oz said.

"I don't know if I could shoot someone who has surrendered to me, either. It looks like he had to work his way up to it a lot," Ayan replied. "He was so pumped up with rage and adrenaline, he didn't seem human anymore. I think – no, I know – he can't keep that up. It isn't in him. Just the same, he must know he's in a unique position with the Warlord. Nowhere in that report does it mention that his attack is sanctioned by Triton Fleet or the British Alliance. He really did present himself as a terrorist," Ayan said. "That's going to make anyone who doesn't have a real killer instinct question whether or not they join the Order."

"I believe that was his purpose, and, barring a few who will be even more steadfast because Jacob was so merciless, we're going to see a drop in Order recruitment. We will also see a rise in our own recruitment because of our association with the Warlord," Hausgiest agreed. "Speaking of that ship, the Warlord's encrypted after-action report has just finished downloading and I have bad news. Captain Jacob Valent collapsed after successfully assuming control of the destroyer. Over forty-one percent of his body has been destroyed by nanites programmed to target unregistered framework technology. His brain is intact, but stasis is failing. I'm readying a surgical bay and manufacturing organs, bone, and tissue as requested by the Warlord's ship doctor, but she warns that this will be a difficult surgery. Life changing for Captain Valent."

"Life changing?" Ayan asked.

"During the next twenty hours, all the framework technology responsible for the creation of Jacob Valent must be removed and replaced with normal human transplant material. He will be as human as you are if he survives, perhaps even more so. The Warlord and the rest of the convoy will be here in fifty-three minutes. Doctor Messana has requested that you be in the surgical bay waiting for them when they arrive."

"Why?" Ayan asked as she got to her feet.

"She suspects what I can see plainly; that you still love him, and more importantly in this situation, he loves you. It is a well known fact that the presence of loved ones can reduce pain and suffering."

Ayan was already through the door as Hausgiest started stating the well-known facts. Oz wasn't far behind.

CHAPTER 56
HOMECOMING

Watching the Warlord arrive in the Triton's main hangar didn't help Ayan's nerves. The holographic display in the medical bay was perfectly clear; it was as though she was watching from a hangar window above the scene as Agameg and a massive group of Triton crew greeted the crew of the Warlord, but it didn't match her hopes for the homecoming, and it didn't change the fact that Jacob Valent would be brought in at any moment in critical condition.

Ayan envisioned a joyous welcome for the Warlord on Haven Shore's main landing pad. The arrival of the ship and a grand reception was long overdue. There were hundreds of people, perhaps even more, who liked the Warlord and believed that its crew should be citizens of Haven Shore. The fact that the ship had been responsible for thousands of tonnes of equipment and supplies reaching Haven Shore through the Triton was an open secret, and Jacob Valent was well liked by Haven Shore residents.

That celebration would be delayed. The extensive damage the Warlord sustained in her mid dorsal section made entering an atmosphere questionable, and Doctor Messana had to get to the medical bay as quickly as possible. She had been preparing to save Jake for days, and she had more hands-on surgical experience than most doctors in the fleet.

Ayan focused in on a commotion amidst the crowd forming beside the dark hull of the Warlord and found Alice arguing with Frost. "I'll keep my vacsuit sealed the entire time," she said, "There's no way anything could get through."

"We can't let you anywhere near him until we're sure there isn't a trace of the nanobots that put him out," he said, putting his arm around her relatively small shoulders. "I'm sorry, lass. He's in good hands, and Ayan's waiting for him up there. Triton's running scans right now on everything passing through her airlocks, you know she'll catch any nanos that'll cause trouble."

"Triton's scanning now?" Alice asked.

"Aye, so you know it'll be a couple hours, at most," Frost reassured.

"Yeah," Alice said.

"Suit sealed, just in case," Frost said.

"Aye," Alice said, nodding slowly.

Ayan felt for the young woman, she'd done so well aboard the Warlord. Not being able to see her father was a terrible shadow to cast over her success. "I'll take care of him," Ayan said under her breath.

Doctor Messana emerged from the Warlord in a sealed white and red vacsuit, riding on the back of a flat bed cargo truck with three medical bots sealed in sterilization sheeting. It headed directly for a freight elevator that would carry the medical team to the floor Ayan was on, three decks above the main hangar. The celebrating crowd near the side of the ship silenced as it passed, reminded of the cost of their victory.

The most important part of her fantasy about the Warlord's homecoming on Haven Shore's dock was Jacob. She'd never consciously thought about it, but granting him citizenship and welcoming him personally was the central pillar of that dream, and without that it all felt empty.

"He's going to be all right," said one of the medical technicians as he moved a trolley with a pair of sealed containers atop it towards the operating table.

Ayan hadn't realized she'd shed a tear, and wiped the moisture away. "I know," she replied.

"I have to ask you to activate your suit's self-sterilization mode and to seal your hood, Commodore," he said as he locked the trolley in place. The surgical table was an Earth invention. It looked like a half-bubble while it wasn't in use, but when there was a patient inside, it would seal around the surgical sites on their body and use a myriad of tools to carry out the doctor's instructions. It was the best technology in the solar system as far as they knew, and from the looks of the trolleys set in a specific order around the operating theatre, they had replacements for at least half of Jake's organs and limbs. Ayan couldn't see inside the containers on the trolley, and an opaque barrier was being tested that would transmit between Ayan and everything from Jake's shoulders down, so she could only see his head when they were operating. She was more than a little thankful for that.

Lacey and Moira McFadden were settling into seating that overlooked the operating room. They waved at her from behind the transparent bulkhead, Moira offering a greeting smile, and Lacey trying her best to look cheery and failing. Oz entered and nodded at her. "It's going to be all right," he said through the communications receiver in her loose fitting vacsuit hood. "Tell him we're all here pulling for him."

"I will," Ayan replied. The transparent metal greyed so she couldn't see who was looking on, and she cleared her throat, steeling herself for whatever was to come. She wanted to be strong for Jake. There was nothing reassuring about a weepy bedside companion.

Three medical technicians stood beside different carts like bridge officers at their stations, none of them making eye contact with her or each other. The quiet made the wait even more intense, and she realized that she wasn't the only one who was nervous or worried. "You're all trained for what you'll be doing today?" Ayan asked gently.

The nearest, a young woman with cold blue eyes, looked at her and nodded. "Every one of us, Commodore."

"Then you're the right people in the right place at the right time."

"Thank you, Ma'am," said an older medical technician beside the door.

Silence settled in for another long moment before the doors opened to admit Minh-Chu and several other boarding team members from the assault on the destroyer. Between them was a gurney with a black sealed stasis bag on it. The upper half was the right shape for a man Jake's size, but the lower half was flat.

"We leave him right here until Doctor Messana gets here," Minh-Chu said as he guided the gurney to its place beside the operating table.

He crossed to Ayan and gave her a tight hug. "I'm glad you're here," he said. "Everything okay with you?"

"Yes. What should I expect when they open that bag?" Ayan asked.

"You don't look at that, all right? It got worse in transit, but he's still viable, in stasis." Minh-Chu said, holding her at arms' length. "They'll take care of his body, you take care of his soul."

"All right," Ayan said.

"Thank you for your assistance, officers," Doctor Messana said as she came through the doors with her medical droids in tow. "You got him here, thank you. Now it's time for you to get out of my operating room. You can watch from the gallery if you like."

The medical technicians pulled the sterile wrap off the medical bots quickly and made sure they were ready. "You're Ayan," Doctor Messana said as she ran her vacsuit's sterilization sequence. The room shimmered slightly as all surfaces were sterilized as well. "The captain and I had a few chats while the Warlord was port hopping around the sector. You came up more than once, almost always good things were said, but you understand I need you to be a certain way for a little while. You have to be available for him while he's awake, be positive. If he asks you to marry him, or have his babies, or to fetch the nearest moon for him, your answer will be yes and you'll mean it. No reservations, no crap from your past or his; you just love him more than anyone else and make sure he knows it. I don't care if that changes the moment we're done here, as long as you both believe it while he needs you. If you have any problems with that, you can leave without disgrace and I'll call Minh in here and he'll get by with his best friend at his side."

Ayan couldn't help but feel a little joyful as she realized that Doctor Messana was describing how she felt about Jacob Valent. Putting her guilt at leaving him and her relationship with Liam aside, she still loved him more than anyone. "It's true," she replied.

"Good. Move him, shoulders higher than legs, if you please," Doctor Messana said to the bots. While they gently transferred him to the surgical table, Ayan stared at the doctor, who had more to say. "Good, you should be here then. Before we begin, I have to make you aware of a few things. You're already avoiding looking at the bag, that's good. I won't lie, he's in terrible shape. I don't care what you've seen on the battlefield, you're going to ignore everything happening to him from the neck down while he's awake. None of it's happening as far as you're concerned. Eyes stay behind the barrier, no backing up and peeking around. If you do see something alarming, you will not react to it. If you do react to it, look at me and I'll tell him something about what's happening. Do not try to explain what you see yourself. One more thing: when the red light goes on, his wounds are exposed and your hood stays sealed. When the green lights over our heads come on, you can unseal and give him a kiss for all I care, just don't obstruct his breathing. He'll be awake for a minute, and he'll be in pain for most of that while I check his brain and nervous system function. As soon as his eyes open, you're going to talk to him like it's all wedding vows and pillow talk because you're the only pain killer he gets while we perform our tests."

Ayan couldn't help but smile a little at the doctor's straight forwardness. "Thank you, I'll do my part."

The bubble closed around the bag containing Jake and Doctor Messana immediately set to work, checking the automated surgical tools.

"What do you think, Dad? Have you gotten the scans?" Ayan asked quietly through her communicator.

"Ayan, turn on your suit's audio dampeners," he said.

Before Ayan expected it, the red lights came on overhead. An opaque holographic barrier appeared between Ayan's end at the top of the bubble and the surgical team, who seemed to overcrowd the table. She heard something that sounded like sawing and sloughing. She activated the dampener, but couldn't deactivate her fear at what was happening. "Too late."

"Look at what's happening as an engineer, Ayan," Doctor Anderson said from behind the observation gallery glass. Most of the people around him had already turned away, but he looked at her directly. "Nanobots just infiltrated his skull and are building a new one from living bone while the old, corrupt framework system is being removed. That sawing sound is a result of how fast it's happening. The Triton's surgical table is going to build fresh tissue around the new bone next, and in a few minutes you'll be looking at a brand new Jake."

Ayan took a deep breath and nodded. "Okay, that makes sense. The nanobots from the Order Knight hit his head first, so it would be worst there."

"Exactly, so everything from there on is easier if Jake's mind is intact."

"Are you sure you shouldn't be down here?" Ayan asked.

"Doctor Messana has been studying Framework technology since she signed up with the Warlord, and she's had days to put a plan together. I offered my assistance, but she already had everything well in hand. She's the best one for this."

"Okay, good," Ayan replied.

"Time to turn the dampener off, they've rebuilt Jake's head, preserving the brain. You're going to hear them removing his armour next, but you won't see anything."

"Thanks, Dad," Ayan said.

"I'll be here if you need me, but for now, just be ready to concentrate on Jake."

Ayan turned her sound dampener off and turned back towards the closed table. She could hear the creaking of metal and popping of high-powered beam emitters for several minutes. It took incredible effort for her not to scan the room with her comm unit so she could find out what was going on.

"Okay, the bag's open, his armour is retracted. Cutting necrotic material and auto suturing the sites," Doctor Messana said. "Start putting the bypass in place, please."

Ayan waited at the head of the table. She couldn't see anything through the dome of the table, and she couldn't read any of the control interfaces the staff were using.

"All right, the bypass to his head is taking over. His brain is getting oxygen now, but it's not active enough to consider him anywhere near awake," one of the medical technicians reassured her.

"Okay, our captain has a brand new face, you can expose him," Doctor Messana said. "We have four-point-three percent necrosis in his brain, so we're going to remove and rebuild those areas with our nanobots and then stimulate his brain so we can see if he made it." Everyone stepped away from the table and the green light came on.

One of the medical technicians came to Ayan's side and flashed her a smile. "Time to reveal your prince charming, Commodore." She moved the top of the bubble down to the top of Jake's neck and peeled the stasis bag material aside.

To Ayan's surprise, Jake looked fine from the neck up. Perfect is the word she would have chosen. "Go ahead and touch him, however you normally would. His head is held in place so anything you do will not affect what we're doing below the neck."

Ayan took her place at the end of the table and gingerly stroked his hair. He was warm to the touch, breathing normally. She knew it was an illusion. A machine was breathing for him, telling his muscles how to keep his tongue out of his throat, and he looked so relaxed because his brain wasn't functioning yet.

"There we go," Doctor Messana said. "The nanobots are leaving his cranium, all the bad grey matter is gone and there's some fresh stuff behind. Time to stimulate him and get some activity going so we can find out if he can come back to us."

"We have a good seal," one of the technicians announced as the green lights came on overhead. "Go ahead and deactivate your hood, the rest of his body is sealed in the surgical unit," he told Ayan.

She did as instructed and looked down at Jake's face, stroking it gently. "You said he'll be in a lot of pain."

"If we're lucky," one of the technicians said.

"Stimulating the brain," Doctor Messana said. "Like my tactless tech here said, signs of pain are good, it'll be even better if he recognizes you."

Jake's face twitched several times and his eyes squeezed shut, a tear rolling down his cheek as he groaned. It sounded strange, hollow thanks to the machine performing the duties of oxygenating his blood and breathing for him. Ayan wiped it away for him. "I'm here," she whispered.

He opened his eyes but didn't say a word as he ground his teeth.

"I need a name, soldier," Doctor Messana asked firmly.

"Jacob Valent," he replied, nearly screaming. "Everything hu-" he managed before his face flushed and he clenched his jaw.

"I'm here, Love," Ayan said, gently stroking his face. "I'm sorry for leaving, but I'm back."

"Hey! No past, remember?" Doctor Messana said. "Jake, what was the last thing you did."

"Destroyer," he shot back, "Took down the destroyer."

"Good! Now who's that woman with you?"

"Ayan," Jake said, his eyes focusing on hers completely for the first time. "Where am I?" he managed to say through clenched teeth.

"You're-" Ayan started answering, but she was interrupted by Doctor Messana.

"Where do you think you are, Jake?" she asked.

"Medical, on the Triton," he replied.

"Okay, this is going to be uncomfortable, but it'll only last a moment," Doctor Messana said. As soon as she finished warning Jake, she did something from her end of the table that made his eyes lose focus on Ayan for a moment. It looked as though he was focusing on something far past her, and his jaw fell slack.

"Doctor," Ayan warned.

"Done, time to medicate," Doctor Messana said.

Jake focused on Ayan again, the pain in his expression returning. Through wheezes and grunts he asked, "Where was I? It was like I was kicked out of my own head for a minute."

"I forced a diagnostic of your brain, you'll probably lose a couple of short term memories, but we had to make sure your brain is good for long term function. You should be feeling much better about now."

The expression on Jake's face changed in seconds, the pain draining away. "Yeah, doesn't feel like I hurt my everything. How's my brain?"

"Should be good for a couple of centuries," Doctor Messana said. "You talk to that pretty lady over there for a few minutes, I've got some work to do at this end."

"Hi there," Jake said with a cocked smile. "You know you're upside down?"

Ayan stroked his face and stared into his eyes. "Not for long," Ayan said. "Hello, Luv. I missed you."

"It's bad," he said. "You're here, sweeter than ever, so I'm probably dying or dead. Maybe I'm dead somewhere and this is about transplanting memories. You're making a new Jake in some clone body."

"You're the same you," Ayan said, "same body, same mind. No transfers. Nanobots deactivated your framework system and there was other damage, but you're fine from the neck up and some other places. They're fixing you now. I'm just here because I missed you. I wanted to tell you I'm sorry I left you, and I hope you'll forgive me."

"I'm in no position to refuse," Jake said, raising his eyebrows and chuckling. "Weird, didn't feel my chest move."

"They've got you pretty numb from the neck down," Ayan explained.

"We've got all the scans we need," one of the medical technicians said. "His head is in great shape."

"All right, you hear that, Jake? The important bits made it through. We're going to put you to sleep now and when you wake up you'll be ready for the Ranger test course."

"Want me to be there when you wake up?" Ayan asked.

"Definitely," Jake replied. "Just make sure they don't give me anything extra or leave anything out."

Ayan broke the rules by kissing him briefly and said, "I'll inspect you myself."

He had a smile on his face as he faded from consciousness.

"Okay, Ayan," Doctor Messana said. "Time for you to join your friends in the gallery, take a nap, or whatever you like until we're finished putting him back together and it's time for him to wake up."

"He's going to be all right?" Ayan realized she was still stroking his face and hesitated for a moment before backing away.

"As long as he doesn't mind being as human as any of us, he'll be better than fine. The Framework system made a real mess, so we'll be here for ten hours replacing pretty much everything, but he's out of danger. You helped us save the most important bits, the brain and the soul."

"Thank you, Doctor," Ayan said. One of the medical technicians led her toward the doorway behind her.

"Oh, and Ayan," Doctor Messana called after her.

"Yes?"

"I want an invite to the wedding when you two finally tie it up. That is if you're not the best actress I've ever seen."

"I'll make sure you get an invitation," Ayan replied.

It was real. Triton Fleet may have been headed into a war, and there was more work for her to do than she could account for, but what she felt for Jacob Valent was real, and he was alive, and that was enough.

Epilogue
The Last Two

Moira McFadden sat in the command seat at the rear of the Sunny Shifter's bridge. It was an over-padded, brand new chair with no manual controls. It would react to impulses in her brain using a low powered scanner and provide the information she wanted using holographic displays. Her words would provide other prompts. The system was good, she'd use it, but it all seemed too dainty. Manual controls would be added to the seat before the refit was done, she'd see to it.

The tour of her new ship was a quiet one, with only five people aboard and no one on the bridge. It was the way she liked it. The quiet time gave her an opportunity to truly think things through. The beast of a hauler was an excellent platform for what she had planned, and it was in surprisingly good shape.

Remmy Sands and his Ranger team had done such an incredible job at taking the ship that there were only a few signs of a skirmish in the halls. She liked the young ranger's style. He used brains and stealth, and was surprisingly decisive for someone who was so popular with his team. She reminded herself to thank him for taking the ship, her ship.

"Looks good on ye," Shamus Frost, or Shamus McFadden to her, said as he came in through the starboard door.

"Feels like it was made for lounging, not leading," Moira said as she hopped up and down in the seat a little. There was a definite overabundance of bounce in the cushion.

"That's what they feel like when they're new," Frost said with a crooked grin. "Not many of us have had the pleasure."

"You did a fine job commanding the Warlord," Moira said. "I never felt the fight outside was going to get out of hand while I was on the destroyer."

"There was a moment there, where things looked grim, but the captain's plan got us through," Frost said, "Looks like I'll be doing a lot of following his plans; he's got some recovery time and I'll be in the Warlord's command seat awhile."

"He's that bad?" Moira asked.

"Between you and me, he's got to learn to walk all over again, rebuild his coordination. Technology could help that, do some remapping, but physical therapy's the smart way."

"He seems like the type to go for the quick way when it comes to taking care of himself, I'm surprised he didn't go for remapping."

"He's got two angels on his side, Ayan and Alice. They convinced him."

"How is Alice, by the way? She lost people defending the Warlord, didn't she?" Moira asked. She liked the plucky young woman. She'd be a hell of a commander if she survived adolescence in her father's war.

"Aye, it hit her last night after Ayan told us her da would be all right," Frost said, walking around the six station bridge, looking at the pristine control stations. "She'll pull through, she's with Jake now. Tear jerker of a reunion, that was."

"So, you're going to be first officer to your girlfriend while he's out of commission?" Moira asked, smiling at the prospect.

"Co-captaining, really," Frost said. "She liked my handling of the Warlord, so I'm taking care of the ship, she's taking care of the crew."

"But there's only one captain," Moira pressed.

"Aye, that's what her rank says," Frost replied. "I'm technically the first officer. We're going back out in one week. Even got a double to stand in for the captain when we hit our next target."

"I don't even want to know who's drawn that straw," Moira said. "That is one man I would not want to try and imitate."

"Aye, he's a stand-out," Frost replied with a nod.

"With a huge target on his back. Anyone who takes him out would get a promotion and a parade. Makes me feel like I've got a great big shadow to hide in."

He looked at her from the front of the bridge. "That you have, the Warlord casts a long shadow, so does her real captain. I'm wondering, are you going to be changing the name of this ship, or are we going to be hearing tales of the dreaded Sunny Shifter in a few weeks?"

Moira laughed and nodded. "Yes, she'll be renamed. I'm breaking out the green, black, and orange paint so I can put our flag on her hull, too."

"And that flag will be painted beside…" Frost asked, eager to hear what she'd be calling her ship.

"Well, they're adding four thousand tonnes of armour, not including external plating, which will be another nine thousand tonnes, and I'm

374

requesting a bunch of triple stage railgun turrets. The commodore is helping with the designs, she says the thrust output of this ship is so high, being a heavy hauler made to pull three cargo trains and tug a ship like the destroyer at the same time, that it'll still be fast even with more armour."

"So, that's led you to which name?" Frost asked, an eyebrow raised. "Union Reprisal? Irish Temper? Gael Gale?"

"Union Reprisal, that's not bad," Moira commented before continuing, "She'll have five mine launchers, room for as many fighters as the Warlord, and nine particle beams. Commodore Anderson even promised that I'd have an improved version of the Warlord's cloaking systems installed. So, I was thinking..." Moira enjoyed testing Frost's patience. "With all that, what would the best name be for such a ship?"

"Dangerous Heavy Thing?" Frost offered, only a little exasperated so far.

"It would have to be a famous name, because this ship is going to fly along side another well known ship. More importantly, this ship's officers will be from the Irish Union, whom the Order seem to think they've conquered, and there was little chance of us surviving, so what would suit that?"

"If you're not going to tell me, I'll just leave," Frost said, pointing towards the door.

"Morrigan, I'm calling her the Morrigan," Moira said with a grin.

"I knew it!"

"Liar," Moira laughed.

"I should have," Frost replied. "The name suits the ship, or what she'll be in two weeks, and it suits you." He sat down at the first officer's station and it came to life, showing the position of the ship. The Sunny Shifter was hard docked to the new fabrication and repair facility, a sprawling latticework that could service several smaller ships the size of the Sunny Shifter or the Warlord while building a new one and performing work on a vessel the size of the Triton. Watching the facility unfold for two hours from the relatively small box the Lorander ship brought with them was something Frost would never forget. It was as though someone packed a puzzle within a puzzle, and all they had to do was build the station that would reside in the centre of the articulated metal web. "Don't know if the captain will ever trust me again, but I know what I'd like to call my ship if I ever captain one in this great fleet."

"What's that?"

"Union Song," Frost whispered only loud enough for her to hear. She'd forgotten that he was a superstitious man. That he would believe an aspiration declared too loudly could be denied by fate.

"Beautiful name," Moira said. "I'm sure you'll have a ship, there will be a few extra to go around by the end of the year. The fleet will need captains."

"You're probably right, but if I get a command it'll probably come from Commander McPatrick," Frost said, "never turned against him."

"You're going to have to tell me that story, the time you left Valent," Moira said.

"Some other time, but for now let's just say I didn't feel like I'd found my place until all this fighting started. Seems like I was made for war times, and there are days I wish I were made for the opposite. I see people building down there on Haven Shore and think, 'God would it be good to settle in to a place there and just take time with Steph.' Maybe I'd have a few boring days, but it would be so good." She watched him think for a moment before he went on. "Not for me though, maybe someday, but I doubt it. I love building a machine and sending it into a fight too much. It feels like the whole Triton Fleet is doing just that, putting it all together from scraps of metal and a bunch of bolts then running full-on into the fray. God help me, I love it. Signals are coming in from ships telling us they want to sign up since the report on our last mission went public, and I can't wait to see a flotilla of ships ready to rush in."

"I've got no head for peace time right now," Moira said. "We're alike. I don't have to tell you how I'm feeling, and I know it's taken a lot of us to a bad end. There's something I've learned about war, though," Moira said, standing and walking to the engineering station beside Frost. The bridge was too sparse for her liking; there was room for twice as many stations, something she'd have to keep in mind as she was working on converting the heavy hauler into a combat vessel. "There's almost no upside to war for soldiers like us, but there is something. You go to war, you lose friends, you lose family, but if you survive, you'll come back with friendships that last the rest of your life. It's no fair compensation, but it's something."

"It's something," Frost replied.

www.ingramcontent.com/pod-product-compliance
Lightning Source LLC
Chambersburg PA
CBHW072340020726
47506CB00004B/942